# ROGUE

### GINA DAMICO

Houghton Mifflin Harcourt
Boston New York

*For Gamma and Papa*

www.hmhbooks.com

Text set in Garamond Premier Pro

*Library of Congress Cataloging-in-Publication Data is on file.*

Manufactured in the United States of America
DOC 10 9 8 7 6 5 4 3 2 1
4500426491

# ACKNOWLEDGMENTS

This may sound weird, but I must first and foremost give thanks to the following things: bread, boredom, and crossword puzzles. This is because the idea for *Croak* first popped into my head while I was working at a bread store, bored out of my mind, and doing a crossword puzzle. This is the definitive, winning formula for book ideas, folks. Write it down.

And what a strange, wonderful, carbo-loaded journey it's been since then! It's hard to believe this series is over, and even harder to say goodbye to the characters that have been renting a room in my noggin for all these years. I know, I know — someone prep the straitjacket — but in my mind they're all Velveteen Rabbits: when you love them, they become real. I'll miss them.

What's that? I'm supposed to be thanking people who aren't works of fiction?

Fine. As always, huge thanks to my agent, Tina Wexler, the dollop of ice cream to my deep-fried Oreo, who has truly made me a better writer, and who, if she ever left her job as an agent — which she must NEVER EVER DO — I think could make a real career out of being one of those cops who talks troubled people down from very tall precipices.

Thank you to my editor, Julie Tibbott, for believing in these little stories of mine, and for paying me awesome compliments like "I admire your willingness to kill off your characters," which is really just a polite way of saying, "I think you might actually be a serial killer, and I'm fine with it."

These books would be nothing but doorstops without the tireless efforts of everyone at Houghton Mifflin Harcourt, including my publicist Jenny Groves — who, when I tell her I want to plan borderline insane things like a two-week road trip book tour, somehow approves of such madness — and Carol Chu, Betsy Groban, Julia Richardson, and Maxine Bartow.

Thanks also to Stephanie Thwaites and Catherine Saunders at Curtis Brown UK, who think that my stories have enough potential to cause international incidents, and Liz Farrell and Katie O'Connor at ICM, and Audible, for allowing me to assault my readers' ears as well as their eyes.

Thank you to Kelley Travers, photographer extraordinaire, whom I have unforgivably forgotten to thank until now, which is why she gets her very own paragraph.

To the Apocalypsies and all the other authors I've had the fortune to meet in the past year or so: you are some amazing people. Maybe a little too amazing, actually. Knock it off.

Teachers and librarians: You are the glue that holds this world together. You hear me? YOU ARE GLUE. Whenever I get to meet one of you, I'm bowled over by your enthusiasm and love for spreading the magic of reading to students. You make my cold, shriveled heart grow three sizes every time, and I so appreciate and respect what you do.

To all the bloggers and booksellers that have spread the Croaky love: Thank you so much for embracing these books, in all their offbeat glory. You, in all *your* offbeat glory, rock.

Thank you to my family and friends, many of whom probably never would have picked up a YA series about grim reapers on their own, but who genuinely seem to enjoy it now that it's been foisted upon them. I'm very grateful for your love and support, and I promise next time to not write something so dark and morbid. (Note: I will not keep this promise.)

To Alphonse Damico, Mary Damico, and Laurie Mezzalingua: You are missed. I hope you're knocking elbows with some very cool people in the afterlife.

To all the creatures living in my house: Will, thanks for staying married to me even though the vows did not read "in sickness and in health, for richer or for poorer, through first drafts and revisions, to the brink of insanity and back"; Fezzik, you're distracting, and you've now eaten roughly 85 percent of my possessions but you're still a very cute dog; Lenny and Carl, sorry we got a dog; and to the squirrel that took up residence in our walls and basement during the writing of this book, WTF GET OUT.

No thanks to leaf blowers, and the neighbors who use them constantly. It's called a rake, people.

Finally, thank you times a billion to you, the readers and fans. I can't tell you how much it means to me to hear back from all sorts of people — guys and gals, teens and not-so-teens, humans and cyborgs — and learn that these stories and characters have resonated with so many of you. It's nice to know that if these places I go to inside my head were real, there'd be a whole bunch of friends there to hang out and drink Yoricks with me. I love you all.

Which is why I feel so bad about spring-loading these pages with blow darts. Duck and enjoy!

# PROLOGUE

Grotton wondered, for a brief moment, if there were a special circle of hell reserved for someone like him — or if Dante would have to cobble together an entirely new one.

"Please," the farmer at his feet moaned. "Please."

Other than delivering a small kick to shut the man up, Grotton ignored him and went back to his task. He had to keep his wits about him, or this would never work.

The heavy smoke had darkened the thatched roof of the farmer's hut, but some small bits of light had begun to edge back in. Grotton picked up his scythe — a heavy stone made from lead, forged by his own two hands. The best blacksmith in the village, they'd called him, back before the rumors started.

He smiled at the irony, how the only people who were able to confirm that the rumors were true never lived long enough to tell anyone.

Case in point: the cowering, dirty wretch on the ground, worlds away from the puffed-up, righteous man he'd been up until a few moments before, as if someone had pricked him and let all the air out. Every few moments his gaze would dart to the two still lumps beside him, but he'd quickly squeeze his eyes shut and let out another whimper.

"I was only protecting our village," he moaned. "With a demon in our midst — "

"I'm not a demon." Grotton knew better than to engage in

conversation with the brute, but the words came regardless. "I hurt no one."

The farmer looked up at him, a swath of greasy hair falling over his eyes. "A *demon*," he insisted. "Stalking through the night, taking the souls of —"

"Of people who are already dead."

Dead and cold and filling with mold, his students liked to say. There'd certainly been no shortage of test subjects for them — the Great Plague had made sure of that. They'd called themselves reapers, which Grotton had found amusing at first — and, as their experiments continued with increased success, oddly appropriate. He was glad his students had not been identified; perhaps they'd be able to rejoin him after he fled the village.

After he'd taken care of this one loose end.

"You hurt no one?" the farmer growled. Perhaps he knew what awaited him; but then again, even Grotton did not know. They were breaking fresh ground today, the two of them — the scientist and his lab rat. "How can you say that?"

"You mistake my words," said Grotton. "I hurt no one — until *today*."

To illustrate this, he administered another kick, this time to one of the little lumps lying next to the man. That did it — whatever small amounts of bravado the man had conjured now melted away. He dissolved into sobs, putting his thick hands over his eyes to block the view of the blood seeping out of his children's skulls in thin rivulets, draining to the sunken center of the floor.

"Please," he said again. "Mercy."

"Mercy?" Grotton almost laughed. "Like the kind you showed my family?" He knelt down to look the man in the eye and spoke calmly and evenly. "Setting fire to a man's home, roasting his wife and children alive — that sort of mercy?"

"I thought you were with them . . . We needed to be rid of you, all of you, demons — "

Grotton slapped him across the face. The man went quiet.

Grotton stood back up and wiped his red-stained hands on a towel. "I already *have* shown you mercy."

The man made a noise of disbelief. "How?"

"Your children," Grotton explained in a measured voice, "are merely dead." He walked over to another heap on the ground, this one charred and black. "Your wife did not fare as well; she is Damned, her soul in unbearable pain as we speak."

The farmer cried out, no doubt replaying in his mind the way Grotton's hands had squeezed her skin and set her on fire, black smoke bursting out of her body and filling the room.

"Yet neither of those fates," Grotton finished, "are as odious as yours will be."

By now the man could barely speak. "I — I — "

"You set the fire," Grotton said, his voice growing thick, the taste of revenge on his tongue. "You made your choice."

"No, please — "

The scythe in Grotton's hand was already black, but now an even denser shadow seemed to burst out of it, surrounding his hand — as if it were glowing, but with darkness instead of light. He raised it above his head, allowed himself one last look at the man's terrified eyes, brought the blade down into his chest —

And the room went dark.

|||||||

"So all that really happened? What you did to the farmer, all those years ago?"

Grotton nodded. "More or less."

A pause. "Think you can do it one more time?"

"If you brought what I asked for."

His guest emptied the requested items onto the table. They clinked and bounced, producing a sound like wind chimes. "Here."

Grotton leaned forward, his face aglow in the light of the burning candle. "Then I believe we have a deal."

Driggs's hair was still wet.

That's the odd thought that popped into Lex's head as they ran. She and Driggs and Uncle Mort were fleeing a mob of angry villagers — in the middle of the night, through a thick forest, and in a blizzard, no less — so it wasn't as if there weren't other things to focus on.

Yet she couldn't take her eyes off his hair, which had been that way since he'd died of hypothermia a few hours before. Shouldn't it have dried a little by now? They'd stopped in Grotton's relatively warm cabin long enough for at least some of it to have evaporated. But he still looked soaked, making his dark brown hair spikier and more chaotic than it usually was.

*Appropriate,* Lex thought bitterly. Drowned hair, drowned life. Just when she thought she'd stumbled upon some evidence that proved Driggs *hadn't* just been turned into a ghost — those fleeting moments when he went solid, his fingers physically brushing up against hers as they ran — here was this hair thing, slapping her in the face.

Determined, Lex reached out for Driggs's hand but grabbed only air — not because her aim was off, but because air was what his hand was made of at the moment. She slowed her sprinting pace to a jog and tried to look straight into his eyes, but the way his head was fading in and out of existence made it somewhat difficult to figure out where his eyes actually were.

But she soon caught them — the blue one first, then the brown one. He forced a grin onto his face. "Working on it," he said, panting as he ran.

Lex swallowed and tried to look at the situation with a glass-half-full mentality. Except when your boyfriend has been turned into some type of weird part-ghost, part-human hybrid and it's all your fault, the power of positive thinking becomes a bit of a challenge. "It's really not that bad," she lied through her teeth, contorting her face into something that resembled human happiness. She would be strong. She would *not* lose it, no matter how many creepy clown smiles she had to make. "It's not."

"I know," he lied right back. Just then, he popped into tangibility, shoving his hand into Lex's and letting out a breath. "There. Easy."

"Easy?"

"If the definition of easy has been changed to 'extraordinarily strenuous,' then yes." He gave her another one of those awful grins. "Easy."

And Lex's heart broke all over again, into a million pieces, probably tearing up all her other organs in the process.

"Hurry up, you two," Uncle Mort shouted from up ahead. "There'll be plenty of time later for agonizing assessments of our cruel, cruel fate. That is, if we survive." He turned back to glare at them as he ran. "Which, judging by your glacial pace, seems like something that I'm the only one trying to do."

The spectral white figure floating just behind Uncle Mort held up a single bony finger. "Actually, if we're to be precise, I cannot technically *survive* if I am already — "

"Dead?" Uncle Mort finished for him, shooting Grotton a rude sneer before surging on ahead. "Yes, we know."

The centuries-old ghost gave him a thorny smile. "Just pointing it out."

Lex and Driggs doubled their pace, winding through the dark
trees that made up the woods surrounding Croak. Still, the mob
of bloodthirsty townspeople wasn't that far behind — Lex could
hear their shouts echoing through the snow-laden trees into the
cloudy night sky.

"Keep going," Uncle Mort yelled. "We're almost out of
the —"

He stopped running so abruptly that Lex slammed into his
back. Driggs's hand was wrenched out of hers, and he instantly
went transparent again, floating right past them. Grotton,
meanwhile, chuckled to himself and drifted above everyone's
heads, crossing one leg over another as if patiently waiting for a
train.

Lex began to rub her nose from where it had smooshed
against her uncle, but she stopped as soon as she saw why he had
halted. "Oh, shitballs," she whispered.

Apparently only half of the townspeople had been pursuing
them from behind. The other half had split off some time before,
circled around, and were now coming at them from the other
side, weapons drawn and at the ready. Norwood, the mutinous
mayor, was at the front. His face was slick with sweat and loath-
ing — unsurprising, given the fact that Lex had Damned his wife
an hour prior. Standing beside him was Trumbull — the butcher
who at one time had employed Zara but was now Norwood's
head goon — and Riley, she of the giant sunglasses and über-
bitchery.

Uncle Mort bristled. "Shitballs is right."

"Can we Crash yet?" Lex asked. Instantly scything out of

there would be the best option, but she wasn't sure it would work. "Are we out of range?"

"No more Crashing," Uncle Mort said. "Norwood being granted the ability to Damn has most likely caused a huge wave of new destruction in the Afterlife. Add that to all the other Damning that's been going on lately, and the Afterlife is probably hanging on by a thread. We can't risk damaging it further by Crashing."

Lex cringed. The Norwood thing had been her fault, too. She'd tried to Damn him, but had succeeded only in transferring some of her Damning power to him. And any time a Grim did something unnatural like that, a little bit more of the Afterlife eroded away.

And any time *that* happened, her dead twin sister, Cordy, and all the other souls in the Afterlife got one step closer to disappearing altogether.

"So . . . what's the plan, then?" Driggs asked, the opaqueness of his body coming and going in waves now, possibly in time with his heartbeat.

"Um —" Uncle Mort winced. "Hide."

Lex's jaw dropped as Uncle Mort ducked behind a tree. *"Hide?"* she sputtered in disbelief, falling over her own feet as she tried to conceal herself. "That's the best you can come up with?"

He gave her a look. "You got a rocket launcher in that bag of yours? No? Then hide it is. Grotton, get *down!*" he shouted at the ghost, who was now floating higher and seemed to be glowing more brightly.

Grotton lowered himself to the ground. "I was merely trying to provide a bit of light for your attempts at" — he let out a quiet snicker — "concealment."

Uncle Mort, suppressing the urge to reach up and smack the everdeathing snot out of their new companion, gritted his teeth. "Next time set off some fireworks, it'll be more subtle."

A bang pounded through the air. Lex jumped, a fresh batch of goose bumps breaking out across her skin as she considered the possibilities of what could have made that noise. Seconds later it rang out again, followed by a series of slightly quieter staccato bursts of sound, like a machine gun. Then, oddly, a dry, wheezing noise, as if the machine gun were having an asthma attack.

Lex squinted across the dark field and finally saw it — a tall puff of smoke slowly coming toward them. The worried line of Uncle Mort's mouth crinkled into a smirk. "That crafty old bag."

"Crafty old what now?" Lex watched the slow-moving cloud, which was now weaving back and forth in wide, erratic curves. "What is that? A car?"

"No," said Uncle Mort, standing up. "That, my friend, is far too fine a contraption to be called a mere *car*."

"What then, a truck? A tank?"

"Is it — " Driggs stopped himself, looking embarrassed.

Lex looked at him. "Were you going to say Batmobile?"

"I was maybe going to say Batmobile. What of it?"

The townspeople didn't seem to know what to make of the phenomenon either. They scrambled to get out of its way as it plowed toward them, some of them diving into the snow. Yet as the smoke picked up speed, something arose out of the murkiness — a glint of metal, a reflective glass surface — all the pieces eventually coming together to form something that was decidedly not even close to a Batmobile: a giant black hearse.

Uncle Mort grinned. "The Stiff."

The death car roared on, still sending townspeople left and

right. It soon chugged to a stop where Uncle Mort had been standing not two seconds before, just as he'd shoved Lex and Driggs into a bush to avoid getting hit.

The driver's side window rolled down. "Sorry," Pandora said. "Been a while since I drove the thing. The gearshift sticks."

"Yeah, must be the gearshift," said Uncle Mort, brushing himself off. "Certainly not your pristine driving skills or the fact that you haven't been licensed in decades."

"Is that sass? Are you sassing me?"

"I would never."

"Dora!" Lex burst out in amazement. "I thought you were in hiding! How did you find out what's going on?"

"I haven't the foggiest *idea* what's going on!" the old coot shot back. "I saw the whole town riling themselves up like it was the second coming of Elvis, and figured that if trouble was afoot, then you three were probably smack-dab in the middle of it. So I grabbed the car, headed straight for the yelling, and lo and behold, here you are." She smiled a toothless grin, quite pleased with herself. "Now get in before the unruly mob dents my paint job."

Driggs headed for the back-seat door and assumed the stance of a personal chauffeur. "Well, darling," he told Lex in a fancy voice, "here we are, dripping wet and scared and running for our lives, and yet the tricked-out ride I reserved has arrived right on schedule. Now, if we can only make it in time for the crowning of prom king and queen — "

Lex almost laughed, until the hand he was using to open the door disappeared, causing her to smack her head against the glass.

Driggs's face went red, even in its paler-than-usual state.

"Dammit. Sorry." He turned away from Lex, but not before she caught a glimpse of his throat moving up and down as if he were trying not to cry.

She tried to grab his face between her hands, but that particular part of him wasn't quite tangible. "Hey," she barked instead, insistently positioning her eyes in front of his, no matter how he tried to squirm away. "I'm fine. And you're *going* to be fine. This — all this — " She waved her hand around within his transparent torso. "It changes nothing. I still love you and cherish you and all that goopy shit that I will further expand upon when we're not about to get disemboweled by a gang of pitchfork-wielding maniacs. Got that?"

He blinked back at her, resolve slowly returning to his eyes. "Okay," he said, but in such a little-boy-lost voice that Lex's heart, now held together by the thinnest of threads, tore itself apart yet again. Surely there couldn't be much of it left.

Uncle Mort, who was watching all of this with a haunted expression that matched Lex's — as opposed to Grotton, who was pretending to file his nails — shook all emotion from his face and pushed both Lex and Driggs through the door.

The car smelled like a crime scene. There was a driver's seat and a passenger's seat, just as in a normal car, but the back end of the vehicle's frame stretched out into a creepy open area with no seats to speak of. In their place, pelts of some sort of animal were draped across the floor, and the spaces in between were covered in what looked like approximately thirteen decades of gunk.

"Oh, stunning," Lex said, gagging as she eased into the space that was normally meant to be occupied by a coffin.

"Don't you start up, missy," Pandora scolded her. "I haven't driven this jalopy in twenty-some-odd years! It's bulletproof, you know — keep it only for emergencies, hidden back behind the Crypt — ”

Driggs nudged Lex. “Just be thankful there’s not a body in here.”

“ — and you should count yourselves lucky there’s no body in here! If you want to ride in style, call yourself a limo, because I ain’t — hey! Quit straddling my gearshift!”

Grotton, gamely continuing his campaign of unhelpfulness, was now settling comfortably in the space between Pandora and Uncle Mort. “I highly recommend you refrain from spitting on me,” he said, giving her a distasteful look. “Hag.”

“Ooh! Let’s use the secret weapon,” Uncle Mort said, rubbing his hands together, his eyes lit up like those of a child’s on Christmas morning. “Just to scare them.”

Pandora grinned. “I was hoping you’d say that.”

Thrusting her hand through the obstacle that was Grotton, she put the car back into gear, executed a perfect three-point turn, and gunned it straight for the crowd of townspeople. Lex watched her push a red button atop the dashboard.

The field was bathed in light as a great plume of fire shot out of the front of the car. The townspeople scattered.

“Whoa!” Driggs yelled.

“What the . . .” Lex trailed off.

Uncle Mort turned around in his seat and smiled at her. “Told you, kiddo.”

Lex recalled her first ride into Croak, when she’d gotten her inital glimpse of the village from atop Uncle Mort’s motorcycle. This was back before she’d learned that she was a Grim, one of the few people on earth entrusted with the task of retrieving dead people’s souls and transporting them to the Afterlife. Before she'd delved face-first into the town of Croak and befriended its citizens, then later endangered Croak and majorly pissed off its citizens by being able to Damn people, sending their souls to eternal torment instead of the serene, lovely Afterlife. Before she'd shared this talent with her former friend Zara, who then used it to terrorize the Grimsphere and Damn innocent people.

Before she'd become the royal screwup she was today.

And of course, before she'd learned for the first time what a psychopath her uncle was. She smirked back at him. "Ah yes. The flamethrower always shoots forward."

"Bingo." He tapped the red button a couple more times for good measure, creating a path of melted snow for them to drive through. Lex looked out the back window. Unhurt, the townspeople slowly got to their feet, muttering at one another. Some shook their fists at the departing car. Driggs, meanwhile, was still watching the flames with glee, the word "Batmobile" begging to escape from his lips. "Don't even say it," Lex warned.

He gave her a wry look. "Hey. I wasn't far off."

The car rumbled along across the field, bouncing as Dora hit divots and tree roots and probably a whole zoo's worth of woodland creatures. "So!" she shouted, seemingly in fine spirits. "Let's catch up! Starting with the invisible boy back there. What in tarnation happened to you, Driggsy?"

Driggs ran a hand through his cold, wet hair, inadvertently spraying Lex with small droplets. "Well — "

"Speak up, boy! And make it snappy!"

"Snappy, okay. Well, Zara kidnapped me and left me on the top of a cliff to die. And then I *did* die. But not really. Actually — "

"Oh, criminy," Dora said, throwing her arms off the wheel for a second, causing everyone to grope for something to hold on to. "Like pulling teeth with this one. Lex, gimme the quick version. How'd you get sprung from the clink?"

The last thing Lex wanted to do was rehash this, but if she didn't, Dora would yell even louder, and no one wanted that. "Zara let me out."

"Why?"

"So that she could force me into doing a shift with her. Sofi helped."

"That little lying sneak," Pandora growled. "Never did trust her. Too many hair colors." She made a loud spitting noise. "So a shift, eh? And the target was—"

"Driggs."

"Why?"

"So she could threaten to Damn him if I didn't give her the Wrong Book."

"But you didn't give it to her, judging by the presence of Sir Snottington over here."

Grotton bristled, and Lex nodded. "Right."

"And instead of Damning Driggs, she ghosted him?"

"Well, no. Before she could do anything she'd planned, I sort of—"

"What?"

"Um, strangled her."

Pandora turned around in her seat, making the car swerve sharply to the right. "You what?" she squawked, her voice rising above her passengers' screeches of panic. "Zara's dead?"

Lex's knuckles were white against the door handle. "Yeah. But she was Culling Driggs's soul at the time, so—"

"So he was ghosted?"

"Half ghosted," Driggs threw in. "Or something. Grotton said he knows, but — "

Pandora blew a raspberry. "I doubt Grotton knows his ugly face from a splotch of roadkill."

"Wait a sec," Lex said, raising an eyebrow at the familiar way Pandora spoke about Grotton. "You knew about him too?" When Pandora dropped into an uncharacteristic silence, Lex threw up her arms. "Was I the only one in the dark about the fact that the evilest Grim of all time, thought to be dead for several centuries, was in fact alive and well and having a grand old time stalking me across the country?"

Uncle Mort turned around in his seat to look at Lex and Driggs. "Dora and I and only a couple other Grims knew about him. He's . . . part of the plan."

"Yeah, about that." Lex looked warily at Grotton, who was smiling back at her in a devilish manner. "You said the only way to fix things was to destroy the one who started it all in the first place. And that I'm the one who has to dispatch him, for some reason. What *is* that reason?"

"Because you're the only one who can," Grotton said. "Doesn't that make you feel special?"

Lex ignored him. "But that can't be true," she said to Uncle Mort. "I tried Damning Zara and it didn't work. It had zero effect on her. So why would I be able to kill Grotton?"

"It's a bit more complicated than killing. Or Damning," Uncle Mort told her. Then, doing that infuriating thing that he always did so well, he neglected to finish his thought and instead turned back to Dora. "Just pull up in front."

Pandora nodded. "Gotcha."

Uncle Mort was already unbuckling his seat belt. Lex had assumed that they were headed for the outskirts of town, but she'd gotten so disoriented in the escape that she only just began to realize where Dora was parking.

"I don't mean to nitpick," Lex said, looking at the metallic gadgets sticking out of the windows of a house that would have fit in a lot better on a moon colony than in the heart of the Adirondacks, "but don't you think that the first place Norwood will look for you might be . . . oh, I don't know . . . your *house?*"

"Good point, Lex," Uncle Mort said with a roll of his eyes as Pandora jolted the Stiff to a stop. "Don't know where we'd be without that brilliant strategic mind of yours."

"I'm just saying. After all that running and escaping and flame-broiling our fellow citizens, we're going to just hole up in here and wait? I want to smite the bad guys!"

"Oh, there'll be smiting, don't you worry about that. Out of the car." He picked up the Wrong Book and strolled toward the front door as though he'd simply run out to pick up a carton of eggs, not been dashing about on the lam for several months. "You too, Prince of Darkness," he called back, waving the Wrong Book.

Grotton clucked his ephemeral tongue. "So we've resorted to childish name-calling. How — "

"Childish?" Lex deadpanned.

He gave her a rude look, then reluctantly disappeared through the windshield. What Uncle Mort had said back at the cabin must have been true: Grotton was bound to the Wrong Book and had to go wherever it went.

Lex looked at Driggs, who shrugged. "Maybe there are some pizzas left in the freezer," he said.

Lex, who hadn't eaten a substantial meal in weeks, clutched her gurgling stomach and scrambled out of the car after him.

Pandora turned the car around so that its grill was facing out-
ward, readied her finger over the red button should any townspeople try to overtake the house, and waited with a wily grin on
her face.

"Hurry up, or I won't hesitate to get my roast on," she told
them. "You know how much I love a good barbecue."

They rushed into the house, but Uncle Mort had already disappeared downstairs. Lex scowled. He'd dragged them all the
way over here only to make them wait while he ran down to do
some work in his top-secret, no-trespassers-allowed basement?

Maybe they had time to eat after all.

Driggs's ravenous teenage-boy brain had already reached this
conclusion, and it had even propelled him into solid mode, as he
was rummaging around the cabinets and pulling out every item
he could get his hands on. He tossed half of the food to Lex, and
the other half didn't make it any farther than his own mouth.
Dorito bags exploded into a fine orange mist, cookies were emptied out on the table, and all other food packages were destroyed
on impact, their contents immediately consumed in as messily a
manner as possible.

"Animals." Grotton floated into the doorway from the basement and watched them with disgust. "Swine."

"You're just jealous because you can't eat," Lex said around the
approximately seventeen cheese balls in her mouth.

Grotton picked up a cheese ball and threw it at her face.

That certainly got their attention. They both stared at him
open-mouthed, a perfect orange circle now situated on Lex's
cheek.

*Ghosts can't become solid,* Lex thought. *Ghosts can't throw
cheese balls!*

And then: *That might be the weirdest sentence I've ever thought.*

"Oh, I can eat," Grotton said. "I just choose not to sully my innards with the manufactured slop of this day and age."

"Hang on," said Driggs, holding a glob of peanut butter in his bare hand. "I thought you were a ghost."

"Afraid not. I'm a Hybrid, same as you." His smile widened. "Though I don't go solid very much anymore. Too risky. But that" — he pointed at Lex's orange cheek with a snicker — "was worth it."

Lex scowled back at him. "Risky?"

He raised his eyebrows. "Why, someone might try to stab me. Or Damn me. Or *strangle* me."

Lex looked away, disquieted, even though she knew that he was pushing her buttons on purpose.

Driggs, meanwhile, seemed to have gotten some of that peanut butter stuck in his throat. "So this is it, huh?" he said quietly. "Back and forth between solid and transparent, for the rest of my — " He swallowed. "Forever?"

Grotton studied him. "If memory serves me, the transitions will be erratic at first; then, after a day or so, you may be able to control them. But before long the solidifications will be fewer and farther between, and then . . ."

When he trailed off, Driggs nodded curtly. "Mostly ghost. Got it."

Lex saw the melancholy passing over his face and reached out to him, but he waved her away, still intent on Grotton. "You said I'm a Damning Effect Reverser, too, whatever that means. And that you know why I can unDamn."

"Oh, my boy," Grotton said with a grin, "you can do so much more than that." With that, he disappeared into the basement.

Driggs scoffed. "That was helpful."

"Seriously," said Lex. "The guy's a first-rate douchecrate."

"Agreed. Shall we move on to the fridge?"

They were well on their way to eating a full spray can of whipped cream between them — one spurt for Lex, two spurts for Driggs, shake well, repeat — when Uncle Mort appeared at the basement doorway and, given the fact that neither of them had ever been allowed to set a single toe on the basement staircase, said the most surprising thing he could have uttered:

"Downstairs, kids."

Out came the whipped cream. In a perfect spit-take, too — through both mouths and all four nostrils.

Uncle Mort grinned. "If we're going to smite the bad guys, we're going to need a few toys first."

## 2

"Oh, so *this* is what's down here," Driggs said as he and Lex descended into the basement. "Only everything in the known universe."

It also seemed to be a testing ground for the limits of how much weight a bunch of two-by-eight wooden shelves could support, as all four walls of the basement were lined with them, floor to ceiling. Each held an impossible amount of weird, foreign-looking things that Uncle Mort had cobbled together, none of which Lex could identify and all of which she'd label with the highly scientific term of "doohickeys."

It made her think of her room back home. Not for the first time, she was reminded that she truly was her uncle's niece.

Uncle Mort rested his bag on the large table in the middle of the room and glanced at a laptop, which displayed a green night-vision video feed of what looked like some long white poles. At the corner of the table sat a stack of papers with a big rock holding them down — made of a material, Lex noted, that she was pretty sure didn't exist anywhere on the periodic table. Uncle Mort set the rock aside and started to sift through the papers, staring at them intently.

"Should we point out that there's nothing on them?" Lex whispered to Driggs.

"And spoil the fun of watching an honest-to-God crazy person do what he does best?"

"It's written in Elixir ink," Grotton said behind them. When Lex looked at him with the sort of expression that such a statement might elicit, he pursed his lips. "Invisible to everyone but the person who wrote it. Amateurs."

But Driggs wasn't listening. "Lex, look at this thing." He pulled her over to a purple screen that resembled a radar display, with an arm sweeping out from a point in the center, and a few triangular blips scattered around a crude map of the United States. Some of the triangles were brighter than others.

"Chicago." Lex pointed to one, then scanned all the rest. "Seattle, Boston, New York City — wait." She tapped a button, hoping that the image would zoom in, and it did. "Not just New York City — Queens! That's my neighborhood!"

Driggs frowned. "Bang and Pip came from Chicago. And I think Ferbus once said he used to live near Seattle."

Lex's eyes widened. "You think this is how Uncle Mort tracks down potential Grims?" she whispered.

"Why, yes it is!" Uncle Mort boomed in a game-show-host voice. "Grotton, tell them what they've won!"

Grotton narrowed his eyes. "Don't drag me into this."

"This is how you track down rookies?" Lex asked Uncle Mort, incredulous.

"Yep." Uncle Mort had broken away from the table, moved on to the shelves, and was now grabbing things left and right. "As soon as kids turn delinquent, they start to emit a sort of signal through the ether. The stronger the signal, the more potential they have as a Grim. All I have to do is pick out the brightest."

Driggs frowned. "Why aren't I on here?"

"You weren't the brightest. Heads up!"

He tossed something at Driggs. It looked like a little football.

It was shaped like a little football. It was, for all intents and purposes, a little football — except that it was made of gold. Driggs's eyes went wide at the prospect of dropping a priceless invention to the floor and thereby blowing up the universe or doing something equally undesirable, but he managed to catch it with only the smallest of fumbles.

"Woo!" he hooted in celebration, hoisting it above his head. "Sports!"

"I wouldn't do that," Uncle Mort said, stuffing a large compass into his pocket. "Unless you want to kick-start a new bubonic plague. If you want to kick-start a new bubonic plague, then by all means, continue with the excessive celebration."

Lex just stared at him. "You tossed a potentially plague-starting device at someone who is, at best, intermittently tangible?"

"You need to lighten up a little bit, Lex," Uncle Mort replied. "If you can't have fun at the end of the damn world, when can you?"

Lex and Driggs exchanged glances. "I hope you're kidding."

"So do I. Hand me that map, would you?"

Lex limply passed him a rolled-up world map. She was beyond trying to understand what was going on. She'd just go where she was pointed. She'd do whatever she was instructed to do. She'd stop asking questions.

"What are we doing?" burst out of her mouth milliseconds later. "What about the other Juniors? What is the plan, exactly?" She looked to Driggs for backup, but he had placed the plague-ridden football on the floor and was staring at it warily. "Why are we down here?"

"To stock up on weapons." Uncle Mort crossed to the far wall. "We need lots of 'em. Driggs, pick that up, it's not going to kill you — " Driggs gave him a look. "Okay, it won't *further* kill you. Take a couple of these, too." He handed Lex and Driggs a few thin vials of Amnesia each.

"What are these for?"

"Weapons. Aren't you paying attention?" He walked to yet another wall and began to load up on items that were, at long last, recognizable as instruments of death.

"Guns?" she asked, surprised for some reason. "Not, like, Amnesia blow darts?"

"Oh, which reminds me." He took something else off the shelf.

"What's that?"

"Amnesia blow darts."

Lex shook her head. "But why guns, if we have all of this other cool stuff?"

"Because despite our best efforts to use Amnesia as much as we can instead of lethal force, we'll probably need to kill some people, and guns kill people." He moved on to the next wall and began rifling through more gadgets. "Or people kill people. I forget how the hippies say it. Now, this one's for you, Lex. I'm going to need you to guard this with every meager iota of attention span you have left. Okay? I'm trusting you with this. Don't lose it."

Lex got all her hopes up — even though she'd gotten to know Uncle Mort pretty well by now and should have known better than to get even a small percentage of her hopes up. And sure enough, the item he gave her caused the smile to evaporate right off her face.

"Don't lose it," he repeated.

Her eye twitched. "What *is* it?"

"What does it look like?"

"An oversize hole punch."

"Exactly."

"What?" she boomed as he went back to his papers. "You get guns, and Driggs gets the deadly Heisman, and all I get is an *office supply?*"

"Yes. Don't lose it."

It took every ounce of Lex's strength to not kick the bubonic football into his face. Noticing this, Driggs swooped in and wrapped her in a calming, solid embrace. "Relax, spaz," he said.

"But he —"

"— wouldn't give you a bazooka. Oh, the unbearable trials and tribulations of the living."

Lex deflated. Nothing put things in perspective like remembering that your boyfriend had been killed not a few hours earlier and was now stuck in some hellish existence halfway between life and death.

"Sorry," she said, giving his arms a squeeze, happy that she could even do that.

"That's okay. Human problems are hard. Hangnails and tricky toothpaste tubes and getting shat on by birds and the like."

"Mondays suck too," she mumbled into his chest.

"Oh, Mondays are the *worst.*"

They hugged for a moment more, then parted — at which point Driggs's body immediately faded. "Hmm," he said.

"What?" Lex asked.

"The same thing happened when we were holding hands earlier. The second you let go, I faded."

"You think your solidness has something to do with my

touch?" She reached out for his skin, but her hand passed through. "No, that can't be it."

"Maybe you can't make me solid," he said. "Only keep me solid once I do it myself. Which . . ."

Would be happening less and less. This unsaid bit led to a pained exchange of glances — the most pained they'd exchanged yet, by far — followed by a series of nervous scratching of necks and the inability to say anything that would ever make this any less excruciating.

But at the end of it all, she put her hand in his — through his — and smiled up at him. He smiled back. They pretended this was normal, because they had to. Otherwise they'd just start screaming.

"Almost done," Uncle Mort said. He crossed back to his laptop, minimized the night-vision window, and started to compose an email.

"What are you doing?" Lex asked.

"Just leaving a parting gift with Kilda, if she's still alive to receive it," he told her. "A little educational film for her to play for the townspeople in secret. To help sway them back to our side."

"Back to our side?" Lex could hardly say it without laughing. "The townspeople hate us. They voted you out as mayor, they wanted me dead even *before* I Damned Corpp and Heloise, and — " She scowled. She was really starting to hate being able to tick off the names of the people she'd killed. "What could possibly sway them back to our side?"

Uncle Mort brought up the night-vision video again. "This."

Lex squinted at the thick white lines. They seemed familiar yet alien, like a big, picked-clean skeleton.

"I always knew Norwood's big fat mouth would do him in," Uncle Mort said. "I just didn't know he'd make it so easy for me."

Staring at the bright lines, Lex suddenly understood. "The Ghost Gum tree!" When Uncle Mort had ramped up security right after Zara attacked Driggs, he'd put in more security cameras. If he'd put one in the tree — "It would have recorded the whole thing. Me Damning Heloise, Zara giving him my Lifeglass — "

"And Norwood bragging that he blew up the fountain."

Lex should have been able to anticipate her uncle's guerrilla genius, but it still surprised her, every time. Kloo hadn't been the only one to die in that explosion — a bunch of Seniors were killed, and many others had been injured. It had enraged the townspeople, whipped them into such a furor that they'd overthrown Uncle Mort and replaced him with Norwood, never knowing that Norwood was the one responsible for the explosion in the first place.

Uncle Mort was right. This they couldn't forgive.

"If, deep down, Croakers are as loyal as I think they are," he said, "then perhaps by the time we get back, they'll be a little more open to our position. And willing to fight *for* us, not against us."

This was good news. Which, of course, meant that bad news was not far behind.

"So then — wait," Lex said to Uncle Mort. "We're escaping to Necropolis, right? What do we need so many weapons for?"

Uncle Mort paused in his work to look up at her. "Do you know of a better way to invade a city?"

"What?" Lex looked to Driggs for help, but he appeared just as startled as she did. "We're *invading?*"

"Well, yeah. Necropolis is built like a fortress. Can't just waltz in there and expect to be greeted like it's a family reunion and we're the eagerly awaited branch of really attractive cousins."

Lex was shell-shocked. "I thought — " She didn't know why, but up until now she'd believed that Necropolis was the one place they could go where they'd be safe. She thought it'd be full of all the other Grimsphere rebels, people who supported the Juniors and believed in Lex's innocence. She thought it would be a sanctuary, not a deathtrap that was even more dangerous than Croak.

"*No one* there is on our side?" said Lex. "Not even the Juniors? Aren't they being persecuted just as much as we are?"

"Yes, but that doesn't mean they'll be willing to stick their necks out for a band of notorious criminals."

"So let me get this straight," Lex said slowly. "We're leaving pitchfork-waving townspeople behind to march headlong into a heavily armed military? Why are we going to a city that wants to see us dead?"

"To be fair, Lex," he said matter-of-factly, "*every* city in the Grimsphere wants to see us dead. So it's not like we have much choice in the matter."

Lex felt sick. That whipped cream bonanza had been a huge mistake.

Uncle Mort's face softened. "We're going because what I said back in the cabin is true, Lex. All the human involvement and corruption in the affairs of death has triggered a destructive chain reaction in the Afterlife. Any time a Grim does something that we're not *supposed* to be able to do — Damn or Crash, anything outside the realm of reasonable involvement in people's deaths — another hole gets poked in the Afterlife. These transgressions against the natural order — violations, they're called — are what's causing the vortexes, the memory deletions, and whatever else is bound to pop up the more we interfere. If we don't stop the damage soon, then *poof* — no more Afterlife for the currently dead, the soon-to-be dead, or the centuries-from-now dead."

"Okay," said Driggs. "So how do we stop the damage?"

"We permanently seal off the Afterlife from the rest of the world."

Lex all but stopped breathing. *"What?"* she shouted. "How?"

Uncle Mort paused, then sighed.

"By destroying the portals."

## 3

For a moment, there was silence. "Destroy the portals?" Lex repeated in a whisper. Sealing off the Afterlife would mean never seeing her sister again, not until Lex herself died. "Completely?"

"Yes," Uncle Mort replied. "And the tunnels we use to deposit the souls, too. Once those openings are sealed, the damage will stop. The portals are in and of themselves violations of the highest order — I mean, they're giant honking holes between this world and the next, and ones that Grims are free to go in and out of as they please. They're certainly not helping matters."

"I — " Lex was too stunned to form a sentence. "Huh?"

"Of course, the act of sealing the portals is yet *another* violation," he continued, "and will most likely cause even *more* damage within the Afterlife, but you know what they say: Sometimes you've got to break a few eggs to preserve the everlasting life of mankind."

"I don't understand," said Lex. "Without the tunnels, how will Grims get the vessels to the Afterlife? Won't all the souls just get trapped here on earth?"

"Not if I can help it," he said. "Backup plans are in place, don't you worry about that."

Lex scoffed at the answer that wasn't really an answer, leaving Driggs to jump in. "Why Necropolis first?" he asked. "Why not Croak?"

"Because the portal in Necropolis is one of the biggest in the world — if the Afterlife can withstand the kickback from its destruction, then it's likely it can handle the rest of the portals being closed too. Unfortunately, Necropolis is armed to the teeth, its citizens are incredibly well trained, and the city itself has about a billion and one ways to make us all dead. The only way for us to do what we need to do is go rogue, so to answer your original question: Yes. Weapons."

Lex shook her head in disbelief. "What kind of a weapon is powerful enough to destroy a friggin' portal?" she said to Driggs.

"Oh, there's only one thing on earth that's capable of that," Uncle Mort said with a cryptic smirk, stuffing the last of the many mystery items into his bag — any one of which could be the thing that would sever Cordy from Lex's life forever.

Lex shivered.

Two sharp noises blared from outside, followed by one long, dying goose–like honk. If Pandora wasn't physically sitting atop the car horn, she was at least giving it everything her bony elbow had.

"That's our cue," said Uncle Mort, zipping up his bag.

"Wait, wait," Lex said. Everything felt as if it were unraveling — although, really, it had unraveled already. Now the unraveled bits were unraveling even further, until there would be nothing left but wispy threads of utter bewilderment. "I thought all we had to do — all *I* had to do — was destroy Grotton, and *that* would fix everything."

"It will — but we have to seal the portals first. The Afterlife needs to be stabilized." His eyes were serious now, his voice steady. "This has all been in the works for years, Lex."

"But you said I was the one who started the war."

"Let me put it this way: I built the bomb. You lit the fuse." He shouldered his bag and headed for the door. "Now it's time to blow shit up."

||||||

"What in blazes were you doing in there?" Dora said as they all piled back into the Stiff. "Poppin' peas?"

"Oh, just gathering together an arsenal that could rival that of a small country," said Driggs, settling back into the Designated Coffin Area.

Bitter, Lex held up her weapon. "See? I got a hole punch."

"Careful with that!" Uncle Mort scolded, pushing it down to the floor of the car. "Lex, please. There is a time and a place."

"What, like a regional sales meeting?"

After a couple more spurts of fire to keep the townspeople away, Pandora pulled onto the road and headed toward the center of town. Lex tried not to look at the Field, but she found that to be impossible. The melted snow around the Ghost Gum was a grisly reminder of the events that had transpired there. Whatever remained of the body had been removed, but that's where she'd Damned Heloise. And now her soul was who knew where, blindly suffering in unending agony.

*She deserved it,* a small part of Lex thought.

But did she? Really?

They passed the Bank as well, cold and unfriendly in the reflected light of the snow, not at all the cheery place it was in the daytime. All the buildings were dark, the citizens either holed up in hiding or part of the mob. Other than the ruins of the bombed fountain, the streets of Croak were empty — so empty that the passengers of the Stiff just stared out the windows in silence, probably remembering all the happier days they'd spent there. Lex certainly was. She touched the window as they passed the Morgue, wondering if she'd ever get to taste Pandora's tasty onion rings again.

Pandora was evidently wondering the same thing. She cleared her throat, then swished Grotton's ghostly form out of the way and looked at Uncle Mort. "Where to, boss?" she asked, her voice more gravelly than usual.

Uncle Mort narrowed his eyes and made a badass face, one that didn't fit at all with the words that came out of his mouth next.

"The Happy Spruce Inn."

||||||

Uncle Mort wouldn't say another word about the next phase of the plan until they collected the rest of their party, an event that Lex was simultaneously really anticipating and really dreading.

On the one hand, she'd get to see her friends again. She could stock up on some of Elysia's soul-restoring hugs and maybe feel a little less horrid about all that unpleasant business of starting a war.

On the other, nastier hand, unless Ferbus had drunk himself into oblivion since the last time she saw him, he'd notice that his best friend had been turned into some sort of ghostish creature. And he'd blame Lex with the fury of a thousand orange-haired dragons.

And he'd be correct in doing so.

Which meant there was a very good chance that Lex would be receiving a kick to the face or a knee to the gut, or he might just

go balls-out and rip out her circulatory system. It would be interesting to see what approach he would take, but not so interesting
that Lex was looking forward to finding out.

The car ride was mostly silent, with the exception of the occasional snicker or gasp from Driggs, who seemed to be having a
ball testing out the new benefits of having an intransigent body.
"Ghost perk!" he said. "Look what I made."

Lex had been staring out the window, lost in thought, but
when she looked at him, all she got was a face full of snowball.

"That's just great," she said, wiping it off as he demonstrated
how he'd stuck his hand through the roof to gather up the snow
sitting atop the car.

"And check this out." He put his hand through the front seat
and jabbed Uncle Mort in the back.

"Ow!" Uncle Mort turned around with an annoyed look.
"Must you use your newfound powers solely for irritation purposes?"

"Would you rather me wallow in the sad fact that my soul will
outlive all of yours and I'll get to watch all of you die yet never be
allowed into the Afterlife myself?"

Lex did a cursory search of the car for a bag to vomit in. Uncle
Mort went similarly pale. "We don't know that for sure."

"Well, until we do, I'm going to try to focus on the positive of
this here unbearably terrible thing that has happened to me. That
okay with everyone?"

The rest of them nodded, mute.

"Thank you." He went to remove his hand from the seatback,
but he had returned to solid mode and it wasn't coming out.
"Hmm." He pulled a little harder, but it wasn't budging. "Well.
This is an interesting development."

||||||

After about twenty more minutes, the sun began to rise. Lex stared blearily out the car window at the lightening sky. Was it morning already? She hadn't even known what time it was when Zara broke her out of the prison in the Bank's basement.

*Was that only a few hours ago?* Lex thought. So much had changed. Zara dead, Driggs half dead, Norwood Damned, Grotton alive (sort of), war started. Her world had been put into a food processor and set on purée, and all before the sun came up.

She cracked her knuckles and looked at her hands, marveling at the things they could do. They could Damn a person with a single touch. Just last night they'd wrapped around Zara's neck and squeezed the life right out of her.

A shot of bile rose up Lex's throat, stinging her insides as it went. She'd killed Zara. Really killed her, and it had taken *effort*. It wasn't like Killing or Damning, both of which required only a quick grace of the finger against the skin. Murdering Zara — because that's what it was, murder — had taken a full, agonizing minute. Lex could have stopped at any time. Every second that ticked by was another chance to let Zara live. But she hadn't stopped.

She had kept on squeezing.

Lex folded her hands away and told herself not to obsess over it. Zara used to be her friend, true, but then she'd lost her damn mind. She'd slaughtered a whole bunch of people. And now she was dead. These things happen.

*But you've slaughtered a whole bunch of people too,* Lex's nagging conscience reminded her.

She swallowed and glanced up as Pandora turned off the main road toward the hotel where her friends were staying.

*And eventually, everyone's going to find out.*

A jaunty wooden sign greeted them a few yards down the gravelly road. THE HAPPY SPRUCE INN, it said. Cartoon trees with googly eyes and idiotically smiling faces grinned down at the Stiff as it pulled into the driveway of a large, boxy building with all the charm of a haunted mental institution.

"What a lovely setting," Driggs said. "For *murder.*"

"Okay, Lex," Uncle Mort said as Pandora put the car into park some distance away from the front door. "You're going in. Now —"

"Wait, *I'm* going in? Why not you?"

"Because I'm deriving far too much enjoyment from the Stiff's leaky fumes. Now just go in, tell the person at the front desk your Uncle Mort sent you, and find the rest of the Juniors. It shouldn't be hard. You seem to have a knack for attracting large groups of angry people."

She cringed. "You think they'll be angry?"

"No time like the present to find out. Now go."

"By myself? What about —" She looked at her other choices. Pandora was picking her teeth in the rearview mirror. Grotton was Grotton. And Driggs's hand was still stuck.

"Sorry," he said to her, giving his wrist another futile tug. "The old arm-in-the-seat dilemma."

Lex haughtily unbuckled her seat belt and got out of the car. "You are the worst band of fugitives *ever,*" she said, slamming the door.

The cold, stark lobby was just as disturbing as the sign out front. Kilda could do wonders with this place, with her lavish rugs and beloved potpourri bowls.

If Kilda was still alive. Lex had no idea.

She made her way to the front desk to find a corpulent, angry-looking woman simmering in a thick cloud of cigarette smoke and wearing, in an ironic twist, a shirt commemorating last summer's Lung Cancer Fun Run.

"Help you?" the woman barked, hacking up a wet cough.

"Um —" Lex vaguely gestured down the hallway where she thought the rooms might be. "I'm looking for my friends." They were probably the only ones staying there, by the looks of the place. "My uncle —"

"Eh?" The woman leaned closer.

"My uncle sent me," Lex said, pronouncing every syllable.

She snorted. "Who's your uncle?"

Lex gritted her teeth. Even though this war had barely begun, she had already grown quite impatient with it. "Mort."

The woman froze. The cigarette fell out of her mouth but caught at the last second, so that it dangled from the very tip of her lip. "Mort, you say?" she said, the cigarette dancing as she spoke.

"That is what I said."

The woman's eyes darted off to the left. Lex tried to follow what she was looking at, but then she started hacking up another lung. "Mort?" she choked between coughs.

"Yeah, I —"

"Mort?" she was shouting. "You were sent by *Mort?*"

Lex was just about to face plant the woman's head into the ashtray when it dawned on her: she'd heard Lex perfectly fine.

She was yelling to get someone's attention. Someone who'd been waiting specifically for Lex.

And it was at that moment that she heard something that sounded a hell of a lot like the cocking of a gun.

"Ah, crapspackle," Lex said.

She backed away from the desk and toward the hallway just as Norwood emerged from the back office and fired off two wide shots.

*Whoa!* Lex screamed inside her head. *How'd he get here so fast?*

But she answered herself immediately: he Crashed. When she'd transferred to him her ability to Damn, the ability to Crash had gone right along with it, a package deal.

"I'm just the gift that keeps on giving, aren't I?" she muttered.

Lex ran down the hallway and started banging on all the doors, but none opened. A stairwell door lay at the end of the hall, so she grabbed for the handle and quickly glanced back. Norwood was on top of her —

Until someone burst out of one of the rooms and tackled him in a flash of metal and bleached-blond hair.

"Lazlo!" she shouted.

"Go!" He'd knocked the gun down the hallway, but Norwood was now reaching to get a grip on his skin, trying to Damn him. "Get the others and go!"

This was the second time Lazlo had saved her ass and the collective asses of her friends, and as much as she wanted to stick around and pelt him with thank-yous, she did as he asked. At the top of the stairs, she nearly cracked skulls with Ferbus, Elysia, Pip, and Bang, all waiting for her with bags in hand, ready to flee.

"Lex!" Elysia exclaimed, going in for the Hug.

"No time," said Ferbus, dragging them both down the hall in the opposite direction. "Mort waiting for us?"

"Yeah," Lex answered breathlessly.

"What happened back in Croak?" asked Pip. "What's going on? Is everyone okay?"

"Everyone's . . . fine." Lex glanced at Ferbus's anxious face, then looked away. He'd kill her soon; no need to bring up the Driggs fiasco prematurely. "How did you know I was here?"

Elysia gave her a grin as they ran. "Lazlo and Wicket have been sort of like our bodyguards, staying here with us for the past few days. When Mort left last night to try to break you and Driggs out, he said he'd be back soon, hopefully with you two in tow. Actually, I believe his exact words were, 'Pack your bags and be ready to go as soon as you hear gunshots.'"

Lex set her jaw. "The cool detachment with which my uncle treats my life continues to astound me."

Bang let out a laugh — though it was silent, as always. "It worked, didn't it?" she signed.

They kept running to the other end of the hallway, where an exit door led to another set of stairs. "Into the car," Lex told them as they pounded down the steps. "The big scary black one." She spotted a barely visible Grotton sitting on the roof — presumably because Uncle Mort had banished him up there so as not to upset the Juniors right off the bat. And it worked; they didn't even notice him as they piled in through the back doors.

"Hurry up!" Dora yelled. She threw the car into gear and gunned it out of there, nearly taking out the demonic tree sign as they drove away. The Juniors sat facing one another in the Clearly-There-Should-Be-A-Coffin-Here Area, backs against the side windows of the car and legs all jumbled together in the middle.

All eyes flew to the back window to watch Lazlo emerge from the building and run to a car hidden in a patch of trees. "He made it!" Elysia said, straining to see. "And Wicket's driving—they both made it!"

The two cars sped off—the Stiff in front, Wicket and Lazlo following—leaving a flustered Norwood in their wake. He let out a feral, defeated yell, then drew his scythe through the air and Crashed off to destinations unknown.

Elysia took a quick head count once she'd recovered her bearings. "Oh, thank God, you're all okay! Dora, Mort, Driggs—"

"*Ha!*" Driggs shouted, finally yanking his arm out of the seat by turning himself transparent at the worst possible moment. "Take *that*, evil . . . car . . . seat . . ."

Everyone was staring at him. Lex's stomach roiled so forcefully she thought it might erupt right there in front of everyone, a volcano splattering half-digested whipped cream all over the windows.

Elysia, Pip, and Bang all looked as if they were seeing a ghost, which, to be fair, they were. And Ferbus—

Ferbus was swallowing over and over, as if he were trying to work a chicken bone down his throat. Lex could see his hands shaking, his lips twitching as he stared at the transcendent being that used to be his very-much-alive best friend. "What happened?"

Driggs seemed as if he didn't know whether to burst into tears because of the way they were all looking at him, or console them because they needed the comfort more than he did. He chose the latter. "I'm okay," he said in a pointedly calm voice. "More or less. I'm just a little . . . deader than I used to be. Zara—" He looked at Lex. "You want to field this one?"

Lex shook her head. She didn't trust herself to open her mouth because: whipped cream volcano.

So Driggs launched into the grisly tale of everything that had happened the night before, starting with Zara kidnapping him and leaving him at the top of Greycliff to die, through the part with Lex strangling her and how he'd been half-ghosted, and ending with what little Grotton had told him about the Hybrid situation, all to a chorus of small sobs and gasps. Lex couldn't tell who was making what noise, since her eyes were shut tight the entire time.

"I don't know for sure if it's permanent, anyway," he finished, grasping for something optimistic to say. "So for the moment, I'm just not going to worry about it too much. If there's a way to fix it, we'll figure it out. And if not . . ."

"We'll fix it," said Uncle Mort, as if Driggs were merely a flat tire to be patched. "Luckily, to distract us from such unpleasant-ness, we've got plenty of other things to worry about at the mo-ment. Like what our next steps are."

"Necropolis, right?" asked Pip. "Wicket said it's built like a fortress! And they have snipers! And their *snipers* have snipers, and — "

Elysia jumped in with more questions, as did Bang, her hands flying as she signed. But Ferbus said nothing. Staring straight ahead, he opened his mouth just a crack and spoke quietly to Lex.

"Is this your fault?" he asked, referring to Driggs.

Lex wanted to deny it. She didn't want it to be true. She'd rather have blamed Zara, Norwood, anyone other than herself, because to be the one responsible for such a thing was more than she thought she could bear.

But she'd be lying.

"Yes," she answered.

Ferbus nodded his head slightly, still staring ahead, and said nothing. Which in many ways was even worse than getting punched or bitched out. Lex saw something pass through his eyes, and though she couldn't quite tell what it was, it disturbed her more than any of the other Ferbus-reaction scenarios she'd been conjuring in her mind. At least those had ended in blood, and blood she knew how to handle.

So as Uncle Mort started to outline his unthinkable portal-destroying plan for the rest of the Juniors, she stared out the window and decided to engage in the healthy task of beating herself up over it for a little while. She wished she were sitting next to Driggs, but then the thought of his misty hand brushing up against her skin made her shudder, and then *that* thought made her feel like crying.

How could she have let this happen? How could he ever forgive her? She wanted to kick her *own* head off.

*Maybe he's not a ghost at all,* she thought, once again ignoring the overwhelming evidence to the contrary. But even she had to admit she was in denial. She'd seen with her own eyes that part of his soul had flown off into the night air, escaped into the universe rather than the Afterlife, which was precisely how ghosts were made. Plus, Grotton had said it himself — they were both Hybrids. And although Lex certainly didn't trust most of the things that came out of Grotton's stupid old British mouth, she was inclined to believe this one. He and Driggs looked the same; their weird, half-tangible bodies behaved the same way. If only there were a way to tell for sure —

With a jolt, she realized that there was. "Sparks!"

Uncle Mort paused midsentence to look at her. "I'm kind of

explaining our plans here, Lex. Just because you've heard them already doesn't mean you can rudely launch into a conversation with yourself."

"I know. Just open your bag for a sec. I want to see what Driggs's Spark looks like now."

Uncle Mort paused. "That's . . . actually a good idea," he said, lifting his bag from its spot near his feet. He unzipped it, then tilted it toward the Juniors so that everyone could see.

Seven Sparks were inside — one for each of the Juniors, plus Uncle Mort. The smooth glass balls made tinkly noises as they clinked against one another, their whizzing, sparkly embers lighting up the bag like a disco ball, indicating that the people they represented were alive.

Except for one. Uncle Mort picked it out of the bag and held it up. Some of the flecks inside were still dancing around —

And some had come to a dead stop. Suspended in midair, immobile.

"Well, there's your answer," Uncle Mort said. "Half and half."

Lex tried not to be devastated all over again. She reached into her own bag and pulled out Cordy's Spark, steadily glowing like a light bulb. "But Driggs's isn't glowing, like Cordy's is," she said. "So maybe he's not dead!"

"That just means he hasn't gotten to the Afterlife," Uncle Mort continued through clenched teeth, irritated with Lex for making him state all of this appalling stuff out loud in front of Driggs. "Not even the dead half of him. Look, moving sparks mean alive. Stationary sparks mean ghost. This one has both, so — "

"So I'm a Hybrid," said Driggs. "Which we've already established and beaten deader than a dead horse at a dead-horse-beating festival." He gestured to Uncle Mort. "Carry on with the plan."

Lex sank back against the side of the Stiff as Uncle Mort resumed his speech. She couldn't lie to herself any longer. Driggs was a ghost, which meant he'd never be able to cross over into the Afterlife. They'd be together for the rest of their lives, which would be nice, but when she grew old and died, he'd be left on earth forever, stuck. She'd never see him again, and he'd be sentenced to a never-ending, miserable existence. How could she ever live with that?

She couldn't. *So fix him,* she told herself. *It's as simple as that.* Except she didn't have the slightest clue how.

" — up to the vault," Uncle Mort was saying, "destroy the portal, then split. Next, we inform the other mayors — "

"Wait, mayors plural?" Ferbus said. "Like LeRoy and — who else?"

Uncle Mort sucked in a gust of air, as if unable to believe the scope of this himself. "All of them. The other Grimsphere mayors around the world. What we do to the portal in Necropolis — if we can really manage to pull it off — is to be duplicated in Grimsphere cities everywhere, once it's proven to work."

The Juniors were staring at him, their mouths agape. "I told you, this has been in the works for a long time now," Uncle Mort said, fiddling with his scythe. "Years of planning, calculations. This is everything I've been working for."

"You got every single Grimsphere mayor in the world onboard for this?" Ferbus asked.

"A good percentage of them. And in the cities where the mayors are resistant — the ones who sympathize more with Norwood's side, with maintaining the status quo — other rebels have stepped up, volunteered to destroy the portals in secret."

"Won't be a secret once they're destroyed," Driggs said.

Ferbus interrupted. "If this is such a big deal of a plan, wouldn't it be easier and faster for us to Crash to Necropolis?"

"Crashing is just another kind of violation, and violations are what's damaging the Afterlife," Uncle Mort replied. "It's messed up enough as it is right now. I don't want to push it any more than we absolutely have to. Plus, Dora can't Crash, and we can't very well leave her behind."

"Why not?" said Ferbus. "I mean, no offense, but the old gray mare ain't what she used to be."

"Bullcrap!" Dora shouted. "The old gray mare is exactly what she used to be! And more!"

The mention of Crashing sparked something in Lex's head. "Hang on. If Norwood can Crash now, why did he just stand there when we drove away? Why didn't he Crash directly into our car?"

"Norwood's primary objective," said Uncle Mort, "is to beat us to Necropolis. Guaranteed. The president leans much closer to his side than to ours, I'm afraid, and he's going to exploit that as best he can. He knows what we're up to — "

"He knows we're trying to destroy the portals?"

"Maybe not that specifically, but he knows we're up to something nefarious. He'll want to stop us, and you can bet he'll convince the president of it too. By the time we get to Necropolis, it's likely the whole city will be on the lookout, ready to stop us at any cost. Especially Lex."

Lex flinched. Elysia — who apparently didn't give a fig that Lex now had a record of strangling her peers — noticed her discomfort and gave her arm a loving squeeze. Lex let out a long breath toward the ceiling, half expecting the coursing air to be filled with gnats and locusts. She was evil, after all. And she sure didn't deserve friends like this. They should all be as mad at her as Ferbus was, especially Driggs. She didn't deserve sympathetic squeezes. She didn't even deserve to be in the same solar system as these people.

She should be punished. She should be in the Hole.

Her nerves jolted at the thought. The Hole was the worst imaginable kind of punishment for Grims — a deep, dark pit in the middle of Necropolis. It deprived them of the bliss of the Afterlife for as long as possible, keeping them alive but under horrific conditions. Lex and the Juniors had been sentenced to it but had managed to escape before anyone could drag them there.

She doubted they'd be that lucky again.

"So we'll drive as far as we can," Uncle Mort said, finishing up his talk, "and then hide out for the night. I know a place that should be able to hold all nine of us."

"Nine?" Pip asked after getting an elbow to the ribs from Bang, who'd quickly re-counted heads. "We're only eight."

Uncle Mort glanced at Pandora, then back at the Juniors. "Okay, kids. Brace yourselves. And try not to yell *too* much."

Elysia's hand tensed on Lex's arm. "I hate when he says that," she whispered.

Uncle Mort gave them a sympathetic smile. "Remember that old chestnut about the wickedest Grim of all time?"

He pounded on the roof. Grotton's head popped down through the ceiling, a snaky grin stretching from ear to ear.

The screams were so loud, Dora nearly drove into a tree.

## 4

The stuffed buffalo head on the wall stared straight ahead, its dead eyes unconcerned with the plight of the odd crew that had just pulled in off the highway.

"You really think stopping here is a good idea?" Lex asked her uncle, eyeing the buffalo. A strange decoration for a small-town deli, to be sure, but then again Lex wasn't really up to date on the interior design trends of small-town upstate New York.

"Of course," Uncle Mort said, counting out a stack of bills and placing them on the counter. "Don't you think a cross-country run-for-our-lives road trip just screams 'time for a picnic'?"

"I would not have thought that, no."

"Well, that's because you're a total noob."

The girl reappeared behind the counter with two bagfuls of wrapped sandwiches. "That'll be sixty-seven dollars and two cents," she said, smiling sweetly at Uncle Mort.

"Thanks," he said, giving her a wink as he handed her the bills. "Keep the change, hon."

She giggled. Lex rolled her eyes.

"Smooth move, Clooney," Lex said as they exited the deli. "Do we need to pencil in some time for a sexy rendezvous? I think there's a motel down the street that rents rooms by the hour."

"Pop quiz, hotshot: Let's say someone shows up in this town and starts asking questions about a hooligan band of teenagers

accompanied by two ghosts, an ancient woman, and a devastatingly attractive chaperone. Which one do you think that girl will
be more likely to remember?"

Lex grumbled. "The chaperone."

"You seem to have forgotten a couple of key adjectives there."

"Oh, I didn't forget."

"Believe me, that girl won't dream of ratting us out. Especially
now that I've bestowed upon her the Wink of Trust."

Lex snorted. "The Wink of Trust?"

"Has gotten me out of more trouble than you can imagine. I
suggest you try it some time. Add it to your already overflowing
arsenal of charm."

As they crossed the street, a car pulled up alongside them. The
driver's side window rolled down to reveal a grinning Wicket.
"Hey, guys," she said. "You okay? Lex, how you holding up?"

Lex shrugged. "As well as can be expected."

Wicket twisted her mouth in sympathy. "Well, don't worry.
I've got your backs. Anyone try to mess with my Juniors, I'll
rocket grenade them straight into the next century."

Lex stooped down to look at the passenger's side, but surpris-
ingly, it was empty. "Where's Lazlo?"

Wicket shot a quick glance at Uncle Mort. "Working security
detail. Elsewhere."

Lex was about to ask what in the dickens that was supposed to
mean, but then Uncle Mort nodded at Wicket in a secretive
manner, which translated roughly as *Screw you and your curiosi-
ties, Lex. We're telling you* NOTHING.

So she swallowed her irritation and moved on to matters that
they might actually discuss with her. "How did you two get out
of Croak in the first place?" she asked Wicket. "Norwood had it

on total lockdown. And when Lazlo helped the Juniors escape into the tunnel — I thought he was dead!"

Wicket smirked. "Big difference between dead and playing dead."

Lex thought of his trampled body on the ground as the scene had erupted into bedlam. "Well, he fooled me."

"He fooled everyone."

"Then Wicket did the rest," Uncle Mort said, nudging her. "Tell her what you did."

Wicket gave Lex a shy smile. "I stole Norwood's car."

Lex stood back to look at the rusted gray thing. "No way!"

"Yes way. In all the confusion after the trial, I was able to slip out unnoticed. Ran to Norwood's house, hot-wired his car, then drove this baby right back into the chaos. Everyone was so surprised, they didn't even notice when Lazlo rose from the dead to hop in."

"Punching Norwood in the nads on the way, I hear," Uncle Mort added with no small amount of glee.

"As a longtime Bank employee," Wicket continued, "I already knew where the tunnel under the Bank porch came out. So we just headed up to the top of Greycliff, picked up Mort and the Juniors, and headed for the hotel."

"Wow," said Lex. "Well, thank you."

"Happy to help," Wicket said. "Kick a ton of capital city ass and we'll call it even."

Uncle Mort leaned into the window and spoke quietly. "You know our route, right? In case we get separated?"

"Roger, chief," she said with a wink — possibly a Wink of Trust. "Over and out."

Uncle Mort and Lex walked back to the Stiff, which was

parked in a small lot near the center of town. Lex let out a sigh of relief when she saw that Driggs was fully solid, so he could actually eat the food they'd just bought. Ferbus had tried to feed him a couple of Oreos earlier, but they'd just fallen through Driggs's mouth to the seat of the car.

If there were such a thing as an atomic bomb of uncomfortableness, that had been the moment of impact. Driggs looked around the car, unable to make eye contact with anyone, then said, "Okay, for the thirty-seventh time, I understand that you all feel really bad for me. And that you feel the need to be careful not to say anything that's going to make me lose it. But acting like I have Ebola is, in fact, the *fastest possible way* to make me lose it. So if we can all at least pretend that nothing has changed, that I'm still fully living and functional and the same old moron I was before, that would be great. Mmkay?"

The others finally agreed, Pip launching into a whole tangent on the coolness of being able to go through walls. Even Ferbus, who, after a couple hours of driving and growing a fraction of a percentage more comfortable with his best friend's condition, had cracked a smile, though it was probably more for Driggs's benefit than his own.

Or it might have had something to do with the bottled Yoricks from DeMyse that he'd smuggled in his bag and decided to crack open at lunchtime. "There he is!" Ferbus drunkenly shouted as Uncle Mort and Lex returned to the car with the food, sloshing his Yorick all over Driggs. "Captain Sandwich and the Condiment Kid!" He snickered. "Heh. Condom mint."

Uncle Mort distributed the lunches, and they tore in. Then, just as they would have done if they were back at the Morgue in Croak, they immediately started throwing food at one another.

"Hey!" Ferbus yelled as Driggs walloped him with his wrapper. "No fair, I wasn't ready!"

Driggs grinned. "Ghost perk: you can't get mad at me, I'm too dejected and pathetic."

"But you got pickle juice in my ear!" Ferbus turned to Elysia with a saucy smirk. "Wanna lick it out?"

Elysia made a horrified face. "Oh my hell. Are you serious?" She surveyed the group. "Is he serious?"

"Course I'm serious," Ferbus said, leaning in. "It's sexy. It's a sexy thing."

"I actually don't think it is."

"Come on, it's in all the romancey movies. Isn't there a whole pickle-juice ear-licking scene in *Love Actually*?"

"No, there is not! You've never even seen it!"

"I get the gist. It's love. Actually." And before Elysia could stop him, Ferbus planted a big one on her cheek.

"Ew! Oh God, you smell like pickles. This is *so* not the way that Hugh Grant does things! *So! Not!*"

Ferbus cackled and went back to throwing things at Driggs.

Lex poked Elysia. "The relationship is going well, it seems."

Elysia's face erupted with worry. "Oh, Lex, I'm so sorry. It just sort of . . . happened. We were in that hotel for so many days, just waiting around to hear word from Croak, waiting for Mort to figure out a way to rescue you guys. And Wicket and Lazlo not letting us leave, we just went a little stir-crazy and — omigod, I must seem like such a bad friend, and all while you were still stuck in that awful jail and poor Driggs and — "

"Lys," Lex said, taking her by the shoulders before she could launch into a full-blown monsoon of tears. "It's fine. I think we've all learned a thing or two about taking happiness where you can get it. Plus . . . you know. It's about time."

"About time? What do you mean?"

"I mean you two have been itching to get into each other's pants since the dawn of earth."

Elysia looked shocked for a moment, then sighed. "I don't know what I'm thinking," she said, staring back and forth between her mostly uneaten sandwich and Ferbus. "He's gross. He's mean. He's ugly. He's a lousy drunk, he's the biggest nerd on the planet, he looks like a leprechaun, his hair is the color of Cheetos — "

"And you luuurve him."

Elysia scowled and crossed her arms. "And I lurve him."

A giggle escaped Lex's lips, though she tried very hard to keep it in. But even Driggs was smiling, and he was worse off than any of them. They were still allowed to laugh, it seemed. Especially when Yoricks were involved.

Lex tapped Driggs on the shoulder. "Since we're in the business of treating you the same and all," she said, keeping her voice light, "you won't mind if I point out that you've got a glob of mayonnaise in your hair?"

"Not only do I not mind, but I'm also going to leave it there. As a reminder."

"Of?"

"My indomitable spirit in the face of misfortune."

Lex rolled her eyes, but couldn't hide her grin. "Here," she said, plopping down the surprise she'd bought. "More Oreos."

He lit up. "Thanks!"

"You're welcome."

He shoved five into his face at once. "Ghost perk: I can eat as much as I want and not gain a pound."

"You always eat as much as you want. And you never gain a pound."

"This is also true."

"I wonder how it'll work with . . . you know . . . the other end," Lex said.

Driggs swallowed, then looked thoughtful. "I'll keep you posted."

"Wait one flippin' minute," Ferbus slurred. "There isn't any trout in these sandwiches!"

Everyone stopped chewing to stare at him.

"Um. Should there be?" Uncle Mort asked.

"Read the sign!"

Uncle Mort followed his gaze. " 'Welcome to Roscoe, New York,' " he read off the town sign. " 'Trout Town, USA.' "

"And no trout! What a waste!"

Uncle Mort raised an eyebrow. "I'm sorry this foodie tour isn't up to your lofty standards, Ferbus. I'll be sure to refund the price of your ticket."

Ferbus shook his head. "Sometimes I wonder why we even came to Trout Town, USA at *ALL*," he moaned, swinging his arms out and accidentally smashing his bottle of Yorick on the ceiling.

"*Aggh!*" Pandora yelled as the drink rained down everywhere. "For the love of Mamie Eisenhower, it's getting into the furs!"

Elysia turned the shade of a stop sign. "We'll never be able to go out in public," she whispered to Lex, her voice furious as she watched Ferbus attempt to mop up the mess. "No restaurants, no movie theaters. Just thirty-one varieties of Hamburger Helper, one per night, month after month" — her voice went up with each word — "for the rest of my *life!*"

"Get a towel!" Pandora was still shouting. "In the back there!"

Pip yanked a towel off a pile of something and tossed it to Driggs, who used it to soak up the liquid. "Exactly what kind of animal did these furs come from, Dora?"

She narrowed her eyes. "The slow kind."

"Hey, Mort?" Pip was looking at something he'd found underneath the towel. He held up an old copy of *The Obituary,* the Grimsphere's newspaper. "Is this you?"

Uncle Mort turned around and looked. A glimmer of recognition passed through his eyes; at the same time, his shoulders deflated. "Twenty years to clean those things out, Dora. Couldn't find a spare minute?"

"I'm a busy woman."

Pip was studying it more closely. "It *is* Mort! And look who else!" Bang, looking over his shoulder, signed an excited pair of jazz hands.

Lex knew what that meant. "LeRoy too? Let me see that."

They passed her the paper. Splashed across the front page were the words TANK-BOMBING JUNIORS ARRESTED. The article beneath it had mostly crumbled away except for a large black-and-white photo of four people: a younger but still fabulous version of LeRoy; Uncle Mort at the same age, with blood on his face; a Native American girl with dual pigtail braids; and one other Junior whose face was covered by his or her hands.

Lex looked at her uncle in disbelief. "You bombed a *tank?*"

"No."

"Then — what, you bombed something *with* a tank? Where did you get a tank?"

He rolled his eyes. "There was no bomb. They got that all wrong."

"But — " She took a closer look at the photo, at the slash across his cheek. "Your scar."

Something was going on in Uncle Mort's eyes — sadness, maybe regret, or a hint of anger. Pandora whacked him with a bony arm. "Tell 'em, kid. They'll probably find out sooner or later."

Uncle Mort cracked his knuckles, then, staring out the window, cracked them again. "I was a Junior once, too," he said so quietly that everyone leaned forward to hear him better. "And much like you, Lex, I somehow got it into my head that I was pretty much right about everything, all the time."

"And the times have changed how?" Lex said.

"Well, back then I only *thought* I was right." He turned and grinned at her. "Now I *am* right."

"Ah."

"There were four of us Juniors, and we were just as close as all of you are now. We were the dream team, if ever there was one. LeRoy..." He smiled, remembering. "LeRoy was brilliant. Smooth talker, knew how to get strange things from strange places, and downright scary when he needed to be." He pointed to the girl with braids. "That's Skyla. A genius mind for planning. She's the one who fully engineered our attack, detailed our positions and timing right down to the second."

"So there *was* an attack," Lex pressed.

"Yes, but we had our reasons. It was this feeling we'd all been getting ever since we first arrived in the Grimsphere — an inkling that something about the Afterlife was off. So we did a little digging, did some calculations. And in the end, the evidence was staring us in the face: the Afterlife was eroding, and it would disappear forever if we didn't stop, or at least cut down on, human involvement in the area of death."

"Which is what we're trying to do right now," Driggs said. "Stop the violations."

"Right. But back then, we were ahead of our time. We tried to tell the mayor, but he wouldn't listen to us, thought we were just a bunch of stupid kids. Next we tried to go over his head and tell the president, but again, we were blown off. Everyone thought we were just conspiracy theorists, out to cause trouble because we were bored or couldn't hold our Yoricks."

A spark lit up in his eyes. "But we knew we were right. We *knew* it. So, desperate to get the attention of those in power, we decided to do something a little . . . drastic."

After a moment of silence, Pip couldn't help himself. "What?" he asked. "What did you do?"

Uncle Mort managed an expression that was sheepish and proud at the same time. "We smashed the jellyfish tank. Knocked Croak offline for a week."

Every one of the Juniors gasped. "You *what?*" Elysia cried.

"How did you not get exiled for that?" Lex asked, incredulous. "They'd probably throw *me* in the Hole just for jaywalking, yet you and LeRoy become *mayors?* How does that happen?"

At this, Uncle Mort looked pained. Turning his gaze to the floor, he started rubbing his scar, from his eye to his ear.

"We got creative," he said.

Before he could expand on that, though, his Cuff crackled. He held it up to his ear, frowning. "Hello?"

A muffled voice came back.

"Who is this?" he demanded, his face getting hard.

"G'day, Croakers!" Broomie's voice sang, clear and bouncy. "On the road again?"

"Broomie!" the Juniors shouted, thrilled to hear from their friend from DeMyse.

"Ask about Riqo!" Pip told Uncle Mort. Along with Broomie, Riqo had teamed up with them in DeMyse, then distracted Zara so that they could escape. Last time they had seen him, his blood was seeping into the hotel carpet as they Crashed out of DeMyse.

But Uncle Mort didn't seem to hear Pip. Agitated, he cupped his hand over the Cuff. "Cuffs can hardly be considered secure lines, Broomie. What are you doing?"

"I know, sorry about that, mate. But I figured this was too important not to pass on, no matter the risk: You've got some allies."

Smiles broke out around the car. "How's that?" Uncle Mort said.

"Kilda showed your video around, and —"

"Kilda's alive?" Lex exclaimed.

"Alive and chatty as ever. She told me that a small group of Croakers decided to up and follow you, just in case you ran into trouble. Sort of like extra backup for Wicket. So if you see anyone on your tail, *don't* just fire off a few rounds for the hell of it. Check to see if they're friendly first."

"Okay," said Uncle Mort. "Got it."

"Mort!" Pip insisted. "Ask about Riqo!"

"How's LeRoy?" Uncle Mort said into the Cuff.

"Don't worry, he hasn't changed his mind," Broomie answered. "He's solid, trust me. Plus, he knows I'll personally neuter him if he bails."

"Sounds terrifying. Thanks for the heads-up, Broomie."

"No worries! Good luck!"

Uncle Mort hung up, prompting a loud sigh from Pip. Lex, however, was frowning. "What is it that LeRoy might change his mind about?"

"Oh, his wallpaper patterns, I'm sure."

Lex rolled her eyes but didn't press further. Her record of successfully getting information out of Uncle Mort when he didn't want to volunteer it was abysmal.

"Mort," Driggs said, thinking, "if you've known for years that interacting with the portals was bad for the Grimsphere, why didn't you ban Grims from going in there and socializing with the souls? And why did you give us the ability to Crash?"

"Crashing was a necessary evil. Norwood was closing in on us, and I didn't see any other way to provide an escape for all of you. As for the portals, I couldn't let on that I still had a problem with them once I became mayor. Didn't want to tip anyone off, so it had to be business as usual."

"So you've known all along that mingling with souls and Crashing were both harming the Afterlife?" Lex said. "And you never told anyone?"

Uncle Mort glared at her. "You try juggling the governance of a town *and* the preservation of the Afterlife *and* the safety of a bunch of kids entrusted to your care," he said. "Pretty hard to pull all those off at the same time without a bit of deception."

"Hear, hear," Grotton piped up, having swooped in just in time to catch the end of their conversation. He looked pointedly at Lex. "We all need our secrets, don't we, love?"

Lex flinched, feeling cold all over.

*He knows,* she realized.

Grotton knew about all those Damnings she'd done in secret.

Of course he knew. He'd been following her ever since she got to Croak.

Her eyes stayed glued to his, those colorless, lifeless orbs hanging lazily in the stuffy car air. It took every bit of self-control to keep from visibly reacting, tipping off the Juniors that something was wrong. "Yeah," she said through a dry mouth. "We do."

Luckily, no one seemed to read anything into their frosty exchange. "Get out of here," said Driggs, shooing Grotton away as if he were a bothersome housefly. "Go read your precious Wrong Book."

"Oh, no need to read it," Grotton said with a malicious grin. "I wrote the thing, after all. I know it down to the last letter."

Lex didn't dare look away. She was holding the gaze of the man who had been responsible for training Zara, who in turn had killed Cordy. She knew she was going to kill him, for good this time. And yet something was passing between them — almost an understanding. They'd both Damned a whole mess of people. The only difference was that Grotton's Damning was legendary, whereas Lex's was still a secret.

Carefully, as if the slightest motion might cause Grotton to launch into a proclamation right there in front of everyone, she turned away, looked out the window, and swallowed as the snow-covered trees flew by.

|||||||

Some time later, Lex woke up and swept her gaze around the car. All the Juniors were conked out, even Driggs, his head flopped down on her shoulder. Carefully, she shifted him to Ferbus's shoulder instead, not wanting to rouse him awake — or worse, to his ghostly form.

As she moved, her foot hit something on the floor.

She reached for the bulky object. The Wrong Book's gold letters glistened in the light of the setting sun. She snuck a glance at Pandora, who was squinting intently at the road and not paying a lick of attention to her passengers. Uncle Mort was going over some papers he'd taken from the basement — Lex caught a glimpse of something that looked like a schematic of a tall, tapering building, like a lighthouse. She didn't know what that could possibly be for, but Uncle Mort often didn't make a lot of sense.

Yet he'd been pretty clear about not using the Wrong Book for their own needs, saying that it was far too evil and unpredictable. But how bad could it be?

She opened the cover of the book. There was no title page, no introduction.

She flipped to the next page. Nothing there either.

The rest of the pages fanned through her fingers, each one blank. Her hands began to get clammy and stick to the paper as panic set in.

They'd risked everything for this? An empty book?

"There's a trick to it," a voice whispered in her ear.

Lex jumped in her seat, then held still to make sure she hadn't woken anyone else. Bang's eyes fluttered open but closed just as quickly.

Lex turned her head to find Grotton's beside hers; he'd stuck it down from atop the roof to read over her shoulder.

"Don't *do* that," she hissed.

"Sincerest apologizes, love, but that's what ghosts do, I'm afraid." He grinned. "We spook."

Lex tried to make her voice as even as possible. "What is this?" she asked, jabbing her finger onto one of the empty pages. "A joke?"

"Elixir ink," he said. "Can only be read or revealed — "

"By the person who wrote it," Lex said with a groan, remembering what Uncle Mort had said back in the basement. "So it's useless to everyone but your dickish self?"

"Yes," he said. "Unless I'm feeling particularly charitable."

"Are you feeling particularly charitable right now?"

"Not so much after that rude comment, but — " He beamed maliciously. "Perhaps a sneak peek."

He passed his translucent hand over the page. As he did, the words became visible wherever he touched, as if he were a human magnifying glass. Lex was able to read a heading that said **The Projection** before he yanked his hand away, turning the page blank once again.

"What was that?" she asked.

"The projection process. How to briefly and temporarily project my visage away from the Wrong Book when an occasion calls for it — to drop off a note, for instance, or pop in to say hello to a new friend."

Lex knew what he was getting at. The clues he'd left for her to find at the library, the times he'd shown up in a white tuxedo to stare at her from afar —

And, of course, when he'd appeared to Zara, to train her.

"You bastard," she spat. Bang was definitely awake now and staring at her with big eyes, but Lex couldn't stop herself. "Zara never would have stolen my Damning power, never killed my sister, never fully turned into a monster without you goading her on and telling her precisely what to do. This is all your fault."

Grotton turned thoughtful. "The way I saw it, there were two options: fix the Afterlife, or put it out of its misery by hastening its destruction. I merely chose the latter. Zara turned out to be quite the violation factory, if I do say so myself."

Lex's pulse was still raging, but she kept her cool. She needed Grotton. She hated that she needed him, but as long as she still got him in the end, that was all that mattered. "I cannot wait to kill you."

"*Try* to kill me," he corrected her. "And I'm looking forward to it as well. Should be quite a laugh."

"I don't understand," Lex said, ignoring that last bit. "Why *not* fix the Afterlife?"

He shrugged. "Petty jealousy, I suppose."

Lex remembered something her uncle had said back in the cabin in Croak — Grotton thought that if *he* couldn't have an afterlife, then no one should. Her hands clenched. "Again, really can't wait for the killing."

"Oh, but you're not going to merely 'kill' me." He smiled again. "What you will do — I'm sorry, *attempt* to do — is much, much worse than killing."

Lex's breath caught. "Damning?"

He smiled harder. "*Worse.*"

When all she could do was stare, he gave her a mischievous wink. "Flip ahead seven pages."

Lex did so. His hand danced across the page for a brief moment, allowing her to glimpse the title: **THE RESET**.

"A clean slate," he told her. "For any souls who were altered in some way — ghosted, trapped, Damned." He raised his eyebrow.

"Restores them to their original condition and sends them straight to the Afterlife."

Lex inhaled so hard, her lungs nearly popped.

*All those people I Damned. And Driggs would get to go to the Afterlife after all! Or maybe* — the thought briefly flitted through her mind, not wanting to stick and get her hopes up — *maybe since he's half and half, he'll become human again!*

"This would fix everything!" Lex said, forgetting all about volume control. "This is what we need to do!"

The rest of the Juniors jolted awake at the sharp outburst.

"Yelling?" Ferbus asked, squinting in the orange sunlight. "Yelling is what we need to do?"

Lex pointed at the Wrong Book — though without Grotton's hand in front of it, all it displayed was a blank page. "There's a way to restore all souls to the Afterlife — *all* of them. Trapped, Damned — " She turned to Driggs. "Even ghosted!"

He frowned, then smiled, then frowned again, as if he were unable to decide whether it was worth it to believe her.

But his spazzy face only made Lex more antsy. "So how do we do it?" She tried to shove the book back under Grotton's floating form so she could read more, but Grotton jerked away, snickering.

"How do *you* do it," Uncle Mort spoke up. "And it's not time yet."

Lex was so flabbergasted that Uncle Mort had entered the conversation — and, even more baffling, that he knew what they were talking about — that all she could do for a moment was sputter out a series of demented questions. "Me? Do what? When? Why isn't it?"

Uncle Mort shot a look at the Wrong Book, then spoke slowly and deliberately. "When you destroy Grotton, a reset will be triggered. That much is true. All souls, however damaged, will be restored and sent directly to the Afterlife. But before you try to chop his head off—"

Lex was well on her way to trying to chop his head off. She grabbed her scythe with one hand and tried to grab Grotton's floating form with the other—but he wasn't solid, and he certainly didn't look as if he planned on becoming so anytime soon.

"You'll have to do better than that, love," he said.

"He's right, Lex," Uncle Mort said. "Simply killing him won't work. Damning won't either."

Lex thought for a second. "I know!" She dug around in her pocket, pulled out her plastic skull-and-crossbones lighter, and held it to the pages of the Wrong Book. "You're attached at the hip to this thing, right? So if it goes, you go."

"No, don't!" Uncle Mort shouted. Lex stopped. Grotton looked disappointed. "His soul is bound to the book," Uncle Mort explained, "but it's not a *part* of it. You destroy the book, it's only going to break the bond and set him free, and then you won't be able to keep him around long enough to reset anything."

With an irritated sigh Lex lowered the book and the lighter. "Okay, fine," she said. "Then how am I supposed to do it?"

Grotton flashed a taunting smile around the car as he floated upward. "You're the Last," he said, leaving through the roof. "You figure it out."

Everyone stared up at the ceiling for a few moments, then back at one another. But Lex was looking only at her uncle. "Really? Fresh out of ideas on the whole Grotton-destroying front?"

Uncle Mort was visibly frustrated. He looked at the Wrong Book. "Last time I got a look at that book — twenty years ago, when LeRoy and I first trapped Grotton in that cabin — we only got a glimpse of the reset page before Grotton realized what we were trying to do. So I know that it *can* be done, and only by an extremely powerful Grim — that's you, Lex — but I don't know how." He looked around at the other Juniors and dropped his voice to a whisper. "Which is where you guys come in. Grotton's onto my tricks, but he doesn't know the rest of you very well. You need to figure out a way to get him to reveal the rest of that page."

Bang's eyes lit up, her hand automatically snatching the Wrong Book out of Lex's. She pulled it into her lap and began paging through it. She signed something to Pip, who eagerly nodded and looked up at the top of the car, where Grotton lurked, unaware of their plans.

"We have a little bit of time," Uncle Mort continued. "I want to make sure the Afterlife is all sealed off and safe before we start sending damaged souls back into it, since a reset will cause more kickback than the effect of all the portals sealing, combined. Once they're all closed up, though, we have to at least attempt this."

"But what if it's dangerous?" said Driggs, shooting Lex a look. "For Lex, I mean?"

"Who cares?" she shot back. "I'll do whatever it takes. I said I'd fix you, and I will."

"We'll reassess once we figure out what it entails," said Uncle Mort. "All I know is this: Sealing the portals will stop the damage and prevent anything else from happening to the Afterlife. But resetting will reverse the damage completely — something that

I'm sure Kloo and anyone else who lost their memory would certainly appreciate."

Lex thought of Cordy. She hadn't seen her since DeMyse, a month ago. What if she'd lost her memory since then? What if she didn't remember Lex anymore?

"I'll do it," Lex said. "I promise."

Yet she couldn't get Grotton's smiling face out of her head. He'd willingly shown her the reset page, as if he were trying to help —

But he'd "helped" Zara, too.

And look how many people she'd killed.

||||||

A few hours later they pulled into a gas station and Pandora got out to fill up the tank. Bang was still flipping through the blank pages of the Wrong Book, nudging Pip with ideas.

Uncle Mort and Lex headed into the store to load up on more snacks — but when they got to the door, Uncle Mort swerved her away from it, leading her instead around the side of the building.

She frowned. "Um, the Doritos are this way . . ."

"The Doritos can wait."

"*Excuse* me?"

Her dread increased when she realized where he was shoving her. "Oh no. No no no."

He dug around in his pocket for quarters and stuffed a couple into the pay phone slot. "It's been months — they must be worried out of their minds."

"Yeah, but — "

"But what?"

Lex pinched her lips together, unable to come up with a reasonable excuse.

He moved in a little closer. "You think Norwood won't be able to find them if he needs to, Lex?"

With that, a cold sweat broke out against her skin. Zara had used Lex's parents for leverage; why *wouldn't* Norwood do the same thing?

She grabbed the receiver.

"They're not going to buy the usual excuses that nothing's wrong," she said as she dialed. "They'll know I'm lying."

Uncle Mort shrugged. "Then don't lie."

The tone sounded three times before her mother's voice came through on the other line. "Hello?" she said, though it came out as more of a sigh.

Lex swallowed. "Mom? It's me."

Silence, then: "*Lex!* Where have you *been?*"

Her father picked up on another phone. "Lex? Are you okay?"

"I'm fine," she said. "I'm — "

She shut her eyes to think. She had to protect them somehow. And there was no way to do that without just coming out with it.

"I'm in a little bit of trouble," she said. "I mean, I'm safe — I'm with Uncle Mort, but — "

"Put him on!" her father demanded.

She looked at Uncle Mort. He shook his head, and she couldn't blame him. Better to contain the blast radius of outrage. "He's . . . not here right now. Listen — "

"No, *you* listen!" her mother shouted. "You go *months* without calling — and then you think you can just give us a ring and tell us what to do? Jesus, we thought you were dead!"

"Calm down, Gail," her father interrupted.

"I will *not* calm down! What were we supposed to think, Lex? Especially after what happened to your sister — of *course* we're going to assume the worst!"

"Where are you?" her dad asked. "We'll come pick you up. I'll run Mort over with my car if I have to."

"No, Dad — " Lex grabbed the phone with her other hand to steady it. "I'm not coming home. There are some things I have to do. They're kind of important."

"What could possibly be more important than your own safety?"

*Saving the goddamn Afterlife!* she wanted to shout. *Saving your dead daughter's soul!*

Instead, she tried to take a calming breath. "Listen to me. There is a slight chance that you guys might be in danger. Go — "

"Us?" her mom shrieked.

*YES! Last time Zara almost slit your throat, remember?* But of course, they didn't remember. Uncle Mort had Amnesia'd them. "Go somewhere else, get out of the house, okay? How about Aunt Veronica's?"

Her father let out an impatient grunt. Lex could picture him pulling at his goatee. "We're not going to pick up and move to Oregon just because you say so, Lex."

"Although — " her mom interrupted. "There have been some strange people about." Something rustled, as if she were pulling back a window curtain. "That guy over there with all the piercings — I've never seen him before."

Lex looked at Uncle Mort. "Lazlo," he mouthed.

*Security detail. Elsewhere.* Lex made a clawing motion at his face for not telling her sooner. Even though she felt a small stab of relief, Lazlo was only one person, and she'd seen what Norwood could do —

"Exactly," Lex said into the phone. "You need to get out."

"If we really are in danger," her father said, "why don't we call the police?"

"No!" Lex said. She couldn't imagine the heights to which non-Grimsphere law enforcement would complicate things. "No, the police won't help. Don't get them involved. Just leave, okay? How about the neighbors — go stay with them!"

"Lex, enough," her father said in the voice that always meant that, well, he'd had enough. "We're not going anywhere. We'll lock the doors and not open up for strangers, but that's about as much as I'm willing to indulge in this nonsense."

Lex gritted her teeth. It wouldn't matter if they locked the doors. Norwood could Crash right into their friggin' living room. "That won't *help* —"

"Besides, if the son of a bitch who killed Cordy shows up on my doorstep, you can be damned sure I'm not just going to run away."

Lex sighed. She wasn't going to win this, she could tell. "Fine. Just be careful, okay? Be aware of your surroundings, don't go anywhere alone," she rattled off, using the same safety speech her mother had delivered a thousand times.

"I'm hanging up," her father said. "Tell Mort to call me when he's done running his cult and corrupting my daughter."

The line clicked off.

"Mom?" Lex asked after a moment. Her mother hadn't said anything in a while. "Are you still there?"

"Yes."

"Well . . . say something."

Another pause.

"There's nothing to say, Lex. We can't protect you if you don't want to be protected. We can't bring you home if you don't want to be found." She let out a shaky breath. "And clearly, you don't."

Lex was squeezing and unsqueezing the receiver so hard, her knuckles were turning all kinds of colors. "I have to do this, Mom. I know that you and Dad are worried, but trust me — it's really, *really* important. Worth risking my life for, even. I know you can't understand that, but . . ."

She waited for a response, but the other end had gone silent once again. Lex couldn't tell if her mom was thinking about what she said, or crying, or what.

Finally, she spoke. And when she did, she sounded so small and weak that Lex couldn't do anything but hang up without responding.

"Come home, Lex. Please?"

## 5

Pandora brought the Stiff to a stop around ten o'clock. The Juniors' heads bobbed up, still half asleep.

"Where are we?" Pip asked.

"Nowhere," said Uncle Mort. "Specifically, the middle of."

It certainly seemed like nowhere. The Stiff's headlights illuminated a wall of trees, the woods thick and heavy with snow. They were in a small clearing peppered with black mounds of rock. Except for a small lighted candle next to the biggest mound, the area was pitch-dark.

"Grab your stuff," Uncle Mort told them. "And flashlights on."

They piled out of the car, swinging the beams of light around, throwing creepy shadows onto the tree trunks. The big rock with the candle next to it was white, it turned out. And box-shaped.

"Is that a . . . tomb?" Elysia said.

It was. The lights darted to the other mounds, now recognizable as headstones. Most of the engraved names were too worn away to read, but Lex was able to make out a few of them: TAYLOR, SHAW, and the far too appropriate DEDD.

"And now you've brought us to a cemetery," she said. She'd gone from extreme anguish over her parents' phone call to extreme sadness and was now just tired and past caring, which meant her sarcasm factory was operating at full steam. "The party rockin' good times never stop rolling with you, Uncle Mort."

He wisely ignored her. "This place is called Grave," he told them. "It's a burial ground for any Grims who wish to be laid to rest here. Besides Croak, DeMyse, and Necropolis, this is the only other Grimsphere locale in the country. But there's no city attached — just the graveyard. Oh, and this."

He picked up the little candle next to the large white tomb and held it next to the name carved on its face, BUNKER. After a moment the door slowly began to open, making a cringeworthy noise of stone grating against stone.

"In we go," Uncle Mort said, disappearing into the doorway.

Elysia's fingernails never left Lex's arm. "I saw this in a movie once," she said, her voice still high as they walked into the tomb. "This is the part where our intestines come out."

Lex watched with vague alarm as Grotton wandered off — he seemed to be very excited by all the ambient death — but she relaxed when she remembered that he was bound to the Wrong Book, which was tucked firmly under Bang's arm. He couldn't go far.

They stepped down a narrow set of stairs until they reached a closed door. The flashlight beams danced around the space, but there was nothing to see other than Uncle Mort fumbling for something. "Just a sec," Lex heard him say. "Should be right around — here."

With a loud click the door swung open. Uncle Mort stepped in and flicked on the lights.

Lex frowned. Lights? In a tomb?

"Oh," she said as they all walked into a kitchen lined with metal shelves full of canned goods. "A bunker. An actual bunker."

"Nothing gets by you, kiddo," Uncle Mort said, dropping his stuff on the wooden kitchen table. "Only a few Grims know about this place, and Wicket is right behind us to keep watch, so it should be the safest place for the rest of you to stay while Lex and I go on to Necropolis."

All the air seemed to leave the room at once. *"What?"* Elysia cried.

Uncle Mort's brow furrowed, as if he were trying to choose his words very carefully. "I cannot overstate how dangerous Necropolis is going to be. Remember: We narrowly escaped a life sentence to the Hole. We are in open rebellion against the government. Lex Damned the mayor's wife. Most citizens of the Grimsphere think we are ruthless criminals, and they won't hesitate to nab us on sight — and with all nine of us running around the city, we'd make that all too easy for them. I can't in good conscience ask you to hurl yourselves into a deathfest like that." He took a vial of Amnesia out of his pocket. "Which brings me to this."

Lex didn't think his expression could become any graver, but it did. "You won't remember anything," he told them quietly. "Not me, or Lex, or any parts of your life as a Grim. But you'll be alive, which is more than I can promise if you continue on to Necropolis."

He placed the vial in the center of the table. The Juniors wordlessly stared at it, then at each other. No one moved.

Until Elysia stood, picked it up, and removed the stopper.

Ferbus grabbed the edge of his hoodie, pulling her back. "Lys!"

But without blinking an eye, she emptied the Amnesia onto the concrete floor, tossed the vial over her shoulder, and sat back down with a perky grin. "Oops!" she said. "It leaked."

Uncle Mort looked around the circle at the rest of the Juniors, all of whom wore the same look of defiance. He gave them a bleak smile. "Okay then," he said, nodding. "Although I wish you'd asked before destroying what would have been a very useful few drops of Amnesia, Elysia. We are heading into a deathfest, after all."

When she looked stricken with guilt, Uncle Mort smiled. "Just kidding. I have extra." He opened his bag. It was overflowing with identical vials.

"We're just past the halfway point to Necropolis, so we should arrive by the end of the day tomorrow." He pointed at the darkened doorways shooting off from the kitchen, then started to head back up the stairs. "Three rooms, one bunk bed each."

At the word "bed," Lex and Driggs exchanged glances of the lascivious variety.

"Get a good night's sleep," Uncle Mort went on, "because once we get to Necropolis . . ."

"We might have to stay awake and fight for our lives or slay an ogre or something," finished Ferbus as Uncle Mort left. "Yeah, we know the drill."

Pip hurried into one of the rooms and flicked on the light. "I call top!" he said, hurling his bag to the upper bed and scaling the ladder before anyone could protest.

"As usual," Bang signed. She took an empty mason jar from the shelf, sniffed at it, then brought it into the room along with all of her other stuff — including the Wrong Book — and closed the door.

Ferbus gave Elysia a smarmy smile. "Top or bottom, honeybunch?"

"Ew." She stomped into the room, dumped her stuff onto the bed, and sat on the mattress with her arms crossed.

Ferbus winked at Driggs. "Bottom it is, then." He dove into the room and slammed the door. Fighting commenced shortly thereafter.

Not that Lex or Driggs were around to hear it. As soon as that door clicked shut, they ran into the last room without even bothering to flick on the light switch. Laughing, Lex climbed to the top bunk, and Driggs followed her so quickly she had to wonder if he had floated up in his ghost form.

*Nope — solid,* Lex thought as he landed on top of her. *Definitely solid.*

"Sure you're okay with this?" he asked. "I mean, the call to your parents — "

"Believe me," she said, holding on to his arm as tightly as she could to make sure he stayed solid, "I'm thankful for the release. I mean distraction. I mean . . . whatever it is that I'm supposed to mean. You sure we're not going to get in trouble?"

"Mort left us alone to claim rooms. What did he think would happen? Besides, the others did it first."

"The others are not his niece, whose life he has solemnly sworn to make a living hell."

"No offense, Lex, but you seem to be doing a pretty good job of that yourself."

"Touché."

"*Merci.*"

That French exchange led to a very different kind of French exchange, one that went on for several minutes and resulted in much slobber coating each other's faces, as they both kept trying to insert all the unsaid things they'd been wanting to say to each other — since now, evidently, was the perfect time to do so.

"I lovf you," Lex said, her tongue halfway out of her mouth.

"I uve you koo," Driggs replied, his teeth otherwise occupied.

"I don't even care that you're a freak now. Doesn't change a thing."

"And I don't even care that it's partially your fault." Horniness had given them both the gift of bluntness, it seemed. "Got that? Please don't sweat it anymore. We're cool."

"Really?"

"Yeah. Does this bra open from the front or the back?"

"Back. And you're sure nothing hurts at all? I mean, your hair's still soaking wet. Think it'll be that way forever?"

Off flew his shirt, which landed on an outstretched arm of the ceiling fan. "Beats me. God, is there a padlock on this thing?"

"It's not rocket science, Driggs. It's a bra."

"It's a Rubik's cube of diabolical proportions, is what it — ha! Suck it, evil underwear!" Triumphant, he flung the unfastened conundrum across the room, where it gracefully sailed to a resting place atop the head of —

"*There's* that pesky light switch!" Uncle Mort blared as he swept into the room, bathing the half-naked forms of Lex and Driggs in a harsh, unforgiving light.

The ceiling fan turned on as well, as if happy to be invited to the party.

Mortified, Lex and Driggs fumbled with the blankets to cover themselves, but they succeeded only in poking each other in the eye. "Please, carry on," Uncle Mort said, calmly placing his bag on the lower mattress as the futile attempts at modesty continued above. "I believe you were discussing my niece's undergarments." He held up the bra in question, which Lex snatched out of his hand from beneath the covers, allowing a bevy of swear words to escape.

Driggs's shirt continued to twirl on the ceiling fan above, a festive little carousel amid the carnival of embarrassment.

"Good thing you're sharing a bed," Uncle Mort shouted up to them over more whispered grunts of "That's *my* shirt, idiot," and "Oh, God, panties. These are PANTIES." "With the Juniors in the other two rooms and Pandora keeping watch in the car, there was almost no space left for me."

Driggs's tousled head popped out, panting as he adjusted something beneath the blanket. "Uh, *we* could take the car, and Dora could stay in here with you." A drop of sweat fell from his brow onto Uncle Mort's shoe, which they both looked down at, then back at each other. "Just a suggestion."

"Nah, Dora's a snorer," Uncle Mort replied as Driggs dove back under the covers. "Trust me, we want as many walls between that epiglottis and us as humanly possible. Plus, I thought it might be fun for all three of us to bunk together. Party rockin' good times, huh, Lex?" he said, banging on the bedpost.

She gave him a look that could have easily set him aflame where he stood. "I will *end* you," she growled through clenched teeth.

"Welp!" he said cheerfully, crossing back to the light switch as the scrambling above grew ever more desperate. "I'm bushed. What do you kids say we hit the hay?" He switched off the light and with one last yank, Driggs tumbled clear off the bed and plummeted to the floor.

As if on cue, the shirt fluttered down from the ceiling fan, draping itself over Driggs's moaning, crumpled form.

Lex pulled the last of her clothes back on and looked over the edge. "Driggs? You okay?"

A weak thumbs-up emerged.

"Oh, I'm sure it's nothing a good night's sleep can't fix. Sweet dreams, kids!" Uncle Mort heartily slapped Driggs's back, then jumped into the bed, eliciting a high-pitched groan from the rusted metal. "Uh-oh! Sounds like we've got a squeaky one!"

Lex could only grip the blankets in horror.

||||||

Poor Lexington Bartleby had been through a lot in the last year. She'd buried her own sister, strangled her former nemesis, and started an international war of epic proportions.

But staying absolutely still in a twin bed next to her boyfriend and above her uncle was one of the hardest things she'd ever done.

Once, Driggs inched his hand toward her leg, but the resulting coughing fit from the bed below put a quick stop to that.

"How does he *do* that?" Lex hissed.

Driggs could only groan-sigh in reply.

But while he managed to drift off to sleep after an hour or so, Lex wasn't as lucky. She tossed. She turned. She shut her eyes and ordered herself to fall asleep, thus ensuring that she would never be able to do so. Eventually she sat up, climbed down the ladder, and made her way to the kitchen. After snapping on the light, she sank into the chair at the table and sat there for a minute, thinking.

Her escapades with Driggs, doomed as they were, had still taken her mind off the myriad of problems they were facing. She was glad for the rest stop, but staying in one place for so long was making her uneasy. Norwood knew they were heading to Necropolis. He could easily guess the routes they might take. Who was to say he couldn't just barge into the bunker right then and there, Damning them all where they slept?

Lex looked at the front door.

Nothing happened.

She sighed and rubbed her eyes. If Uncle Mort thought it was safe to stop, he was probably right. He usually was. He'd even been right about calling her parents to warn them, although that hadn't gone quite as well as she'd hoped . . .

With a sharp breath, Lex looked around the kitchen, wanting to focus on anything other than that little nugget of misery. The floor was a dirty concrete, and the shelves held a variety of provisions, the type of doomsday scenario stuff that kept forever — dried beans, canned soup, and Twinkies. More disconcerting was the counter, atop of which sat a pile of rusty knives. At least Lex thought it was rust. It could have been the other thing.

Now even more agitated, Lex got up from the chair and ducked back into the bedroom to grab her bag; there had to be something in there to distract her. She plopped it on the table and began to rifle through it, taking care to ignore her Lifeglass — the hourglass-shaped device that stored her memories — as it eagerly tried to replay that night on the cliff, displaying Lex's wet, freezing hands wrapped around Zara's wet, freezing neck.

"Great idea, Lex," she sarcastically muttered to herself. "This is helping already."

Uncle Mort still had all their Sparks in his bag, so Lex couldn't look at her own, but she always had Cordy's on hand. She held up the smooth glass sphere, squinting at the bright light radiating from its center. After a moment she put it back, wrapping it safely within the plush tentacles of Captain Wiggles, Cordy's old stuffed octopus.

Then her hand brushed against something hard. Frowning, she pulled it out to reveal the big hole punch.

She rolled her eyes. Uncle Mort may as well have armed her with a rubber chicken.

With nothing left to entertain her, she absent-mindedly turned over the device in her hands, then grabbed both its arms and squeezed, just for the hell of it. But as soon as her hands met, an invisible force caused her to fly back in her chair and topple to the floor.

Slowly, she put one hand on the table and pulled herself up. Hovering above its surface was a perfect gray circle.

Lex inched closer. It was no more than a foot in diameter, and flat — as if a dinner plate had gotten sick of being confined to the table and decided to suspend itself in midair instead. After circling it completely, she sat back down and peered into it as though she were looking through a porthole on a ship, though she could see nothing except more of the same grayness. The second she looked away, however, her peripheral vision sensed movement within.

When she squinted harder, she could tell she was right. The grayness inside the circle was moving, ebbing like clouds right before a thunderstorm.

A daft idea popped into her mind, even though it didn't quite make sense. Cautious yet curious, she bit her lip and brought her hand up to the circle, hoping that her theory was right and that she'd be able to reach inside.

But before she could do anything, a grinning face popped into view.

Startled, Lex flew back in her chair again and screamed.

"Hey, snotwad," said Cordy.

## 6

Lex clapped her hand over her mouth, but it was too late. Stirrings within the other bedrooms meant she'd already woken everyone up.

Cordy's head looked around the kitchen. "Nice setup you've got here," she said. "Top-secret safe houses really have come a long way."

"What the hell?" Lex was able to reach into the circle, but when she tried to touch Cordy's face, her hands were repelled as if they were magnetized, just as in the Afterlife.

"And are those *bunk* beds?" Cordy carried on, straining to see into Lex's bedroom. "What's the thread count on those bad boys?"

"Cordy, focus," Lex said, unable to believe how Cordy's murky surroundings were so starkly different from the normal fluffy whiteness. "Is that really the Afterlife? It's so dark and —"

"Stormy? Yeah, I know."

Their conversation was cut short by everyone else barging into the kitchen, bleary-eyed and confused.

Pip rubbed his eyes and pointed. "Lex, look! It's your sister!"

"Yes, thank you, Pip," she said through gritted teeth. She turned to Uncle Mort, whose stern face left little room for doubt that he was incredibly pissed about this whole situation.

"I didn't — I wasn't — " She turned to face the floating circle, then back to her uncle, then repeated that cycle a couple of times, really hammering home the fact that she'd turned into a lunatic.

Cordy wasn't helping. "Hey, Uncle Mort!" She gave him a sprightly wave. "And hey, loverboy," she said in a sultry voice, winking at Driggs. "You bunking with Lex? Have the sexy parties begun? She's a big fan of piñatas and jello pits — "

Lex quickly stood in front of Cordy to block her, resulting in a muffled series of protests. "You know what? I'm not going to bother with excuses," she said to Uncle Mort. "I don't know what I just did, but I'm a hundred percent sure I wasn't supposed to do it, so let's just skip over the scolding for now, and you tell me what's going on and we'll all go from there." His stern face didn't go away. "Sound coolsies?"

Cordy was shouting something about a grave injustice, but Lex stayed put. Ferbus rammed his hands over his ears. "Floating head is loud," he complained. "Make stop."

Uncle Mort, who hadn't ceased frowning since he came into the room, snatched the hole punch up from the floor where Lex had dropped it and placed it on the table. "I thought I explicitly instructed you not to use this."

"I don't even know what this *is*," said Lex.

"I told you. It's a hole punch."

Lex just stared.

"It punches holes," he added.

More staring.

Uncle Mort pinched his nose between his fingers. "Between the real world and the Afterlife. It opens up a temporary portal.

Through the Looking Glass, Alice. Do I need to paint you a picture?"

Elysia's jaw dropped. "That's the Afterlife?" she said, trying to see around Lex.

Lex stepped away from the portal to reveal a frowning Cordy. "Uncool, Lex," she said. "I didn't schlep all the way over here just to stare at your backside. Which is looking great, by the way. Have you been working out?"

"If running in sheer terror for my life counts, then yes."

"It's done marvels for your glutes."

"Enough with the glutes!" Ferbus shouted. "Mort, just tell us what to do with Floaty Head so we can all go back to sleep!"

Uncle Mort scratched his hair, transforming his already messy bed head into a thing of true chaos. "The perforator was *supposed* to be used only in the event of an emergency," he said with a disapproving glare at Lex. "In case we needed to contact the dead for some reason, or send a warning. But now that you've gone and used it, let's just call it a wash and get out of it what information we can. Sound coolsies?" he ended in a mocking tone, staring at Lex.

She looked away. "Sorry. I didn't know."

"It's a wonder you haven't blown yourself up yet," Uncle Mort said under his breath, crossing to the miniature portal. "Cordy! How are things holding up in there?"

"Not great, as you can see." She bit her lip, a mirror image of the way Lex always did. "It's like all those little cracks that have been showing up around here suddenly started to widen and get worse, and at a much faster rate, and now — " She gestured at the brewing tempest, her expression worried. "It's bad. A lot worse than it was when you were in DeMyse."

"That'll be because of Norwood gaining the ability to Damn," Uncle Mort said. "It's just one violation too many. The Afterlife can't handle it."

Lex reddened but said nothing.

"Yeah, that's what we thought," Cordy said. "Kilda snuck up to the vault and filled us in about what happened — you guys Crashing across the country, being in jail, getting convicted, and then . . . all the stuff that happened after." Lex wanted to thank her for not rehashing the whole Zara-Driggs-Norwood-Heloise debacle in front of everyone, but it seemed Cordy already knew how sensitive she was about it. Twin perk. "Sorry you had to go through all that," was all she said, looking at Lex.

Lex swallowed. "Thanks."

"Anyway," Cordy continued, "a whole bunch more vortexes popped up, and a few more people are losing their memory. Elvis forgot the lyrics to some of his songs. Abraham Lincoln can't quite remember who it is he emancipated. Tom Edison keeps wandering around and mumbling something about losing his precious, precious current."

"And the blurring!" a voice in the Afterlife distance rang out. "Don't forget to tell them about the blurring!"

"Oh yeah," said Cordy with a grim look. "That fun new problem."

"Hi, everyone." Kloo appeared, businesslike as usual and not the slightest bit surprised to have stumbled upon a mini portal full of her former colleagues. "In addition to the vortexes, parts of the Afterlife are now blurring, like they're being . . . I don't know, erased. Like someone is smearing it all away with a giant paper towel."

"Have any souls disappeared?" Uncle Mort asked.

"Not as far as we know."

"Not *yet,* anyway," said Cordy, a hint of fear flickering through her eyes.

"Then we've still got time," said Uncle Mort. He gave the two dead girls a reassuring smile. "We're working on it. Until then, sit tight."

"Sure." Cordy smirked. "We're not going anywhere."

Ferbus clapped his hands and rubbed them together. "Great! Well, I feel worlds better. Back to bed with us."

One by one, the Juniors shuffled back into their rooms, Elysia giving Lex a quick squeeze before she left. Driggs exchanged a series of looks with Lex, asking if she was okay? Yes, she was. Did she want to chat with Cordy alone for a while? Yes, she did. Okay, love you. Love you too.

Uncle Mort picked up the perforator, propped it over his shoulder, and headed for his room. "I'll just be holding on to this from now on."

"Wait," said Lex, gesturing at the portal. "What about this? Don't we have to — I don't know, close it?"

"It should close on its own in a few minutes. Like I said, it's only temporary."

"Then why did you make such a big deal about it?" she asked. "I thought I'd done, like, a shitload more damage to the Afterlife."

He turned around to look at her and spoke very slowly, as if she were a preschooler who'd just drawn all over the walls with a crayon. "The perforator is designed to inflict the least amount of damage possible to the Afterlife — still some, but since it's only open for a few moments, it's a relatively scant amount. However, there are only a number of these in the world — one per Grim town, to be precise."

"One per town . . . temporary, with just a tiny violation . . ." Lex let out a slow breath at the realization. "You're going to use perforators to replace the tunnels."

"Correct," he said. "Every Grim team in town will unload their vessels at the same time — once per day, in under half an hour. That's the best we can do." He looked at the device in his hands. "This one is intended for Necropolis, and if you'd damaged it, there would be no way to replace it. I thought I could trust you to keep it safe, but it looks like once again I was deluding myself into thinking you were capable of listening to me. That's why I made such a big deal."

Lex blinked. "Oh."

He turned and went back into the bedroom. Lex watched him, unnerved.

"Awkward," Cordy said, breaking the silence.

Lex turned back to the portal. Kloo had left, but Cordy was still there, and woefully confused. "Why do the tunnels need replacing?" she asked Lex. "What the hell were you two talking about?"

"Uncle Mort has this psychotic plan to fix the Afterlife," Lex told her. "It involves — " Her throat went dry. "It involves sealing the portals and the tunnels. Forever."

Cordy's smile faltered. "What? How?"

"No clue. All I know is that we have to seal the one in Necropolis first. And after they're all closed, we won't — " Lex realized how selfish she was about to sound, given the fact that the existence of the Afterlife was on the line, but she said it anyway. "We won't be able to see each other anymore."

"What?" cried Cordy. "That *sucks!*"

"I know."

After a moment, though, Cordy turned thoughtful. "But I guess . . . it would be no more difficult than what regular people go through, right? Like Mom and Dad having to wait until they die to see me again? Really, you and I are lucky to even have what we've had."

Lex glared at her. "I guess." She hated how optimistic Cordy had gotten ever since she died, never letting Lex just stew in her misery. It was very irritating.

"I mean, if it saves the Afterlife, isn't that a small price to pay?" Cordy went on. "Besides, when you finally do get here — and it *will* be decades from now, or I'll be very upset with you — we'll all be waiting. Like I said, I'm not going anywhere. And then we'll have the rest of eternity for you to tell me all about the amazing life you've led. And I can force you onto all of the roller coasters I've built. It'll be a hootenanny and a half."

Lex nodded slowly. "That's true."

Except that Driggs might not be waiting for her. Driggs might never get to the Afterlife at all if Lex didn't successfully trigger the reset.

It wasn't fair. Driggs being cheated out of an Afterlife like that, when there were plenty of awful people who got it automatically but didn't remotely deserve it. People like —

"Zara!" The word rushed out of her mouth the moment she thought it. She tried to look around Cordy's head into the distance of the Afterlife. "Where is she? Is she in there?"

A pained expression came over Cordy's face. "Yeah, she's in the Void, somewhere. We saw her come in when you — when she died," she said, expertly sidestepping the reminder of Lex's adventures in strangling. "But she blew through so fast, no one got a chance to approach her."

"Figures."

"Honestly, though, Lex? I don't think we'll ever see her again."

Lex grimaced. She didn't think so either.

But it was then that something sneezed on Cordy, and there was no way they could keep up a serious discussion about Zara after that. "Lum*py!*" Cordy groaned, wiping off her face. "I told you to knock that off!"

The answer she received could only be the strident cry of a disgruntled camel. Cordy fumbled with her adopted pet for a moment, but judging by her flailings, she was losing the battle. "I think he's in heat," she explained to Lex as Lumpy licked her eyeball. "He's become very . . . affectionate."

Lex pointed into the distance. "Doesn't that make your boyfriend jealous?"

King Tut, the legendary Pharaoh, was wandering aimlessly through the rolling clouds of the Afterlife, calling out for Cordy before becoming distracted by his shiny gold necklace. He paused, used it as a mirror to pick something out of his teeth, then gave it a winning smile and started to carry on a compliment-laden conversation with his reflection.

Lex raised an eyebrow. "So. How *is* the Tut?"

Cordy's eyes lit up. "Oh, you know. Stunning. Dreamy. Dynamite in the sack."

Lex's jaw dropped. "You've — "

"Well, no." Cordy said, abashed. Lumpy abruptly wandered off, as if offended by all this talk of his rival. Cordy gave her face another good wipe and continued. "So far, we've just cuddled. Some business about the gods looking down on us with unflinching scorn or something. But I remain cautiously optimistic." She waved at him. "Hey, sweets!"

Tut sauntered over to Cordy until his golden, chiseled face filled the portal. He peered out at Lex. "What demonry is this?"

"Good to see you, Tutty," Lex said. "Looking sharp."

He frowned. "I always look sharp."

"I know. Just confirming."

"The peasant looks more peasantlike than usual," Tut said to Cordy, as if Lex weren't sitting right there. "Gaunt. Malnourished."

"I was in jail for a while," said Lex. "Best crash diet there is."

"But look at her glutes!" Cordy added.

Lex stood to display her butt. Tut gave her a once-over and managed a bored nod. "The glutes are satisfactory."

"I mean, not as satisfactory as yours, obviously," Cordy said, slapping him on the ass.

Lex held her hand up to block the view. "Well, I don't need to see this."

A twitchy nose popped up underneath her hand, near the rim of the portal. "They're like this *all* the *time*. I can't bear it any longer. I can't and I shan't!"

"Edgar!" Lex's face melted into a grin as she lowered her hand. "Oh, man. I've missed you."

Edgar Allan Poe smoothed out his frock coat. "Yes. Well. Your absence has been noted as well. I'm left to fend for myself with these simpering nincompoops."

"Hey, Poe," said Tut. "Your mustache is showing!" He smiled a jockish grin and gave Cordy a high-five.

"I *know* my mustache is — that's not even a *joke* — " Edgar's lip quivered. "You see what I mean? It seems the presidents have taught him the ever-popular sport of Torture the Poet. Oh, yes. Taught. Him. Well."

Lex snickered, but her body stiffened as she thought about all that was on the line here. If they didn't succeed in preserving the Afterlife, what would happen to these guys? They'd just cease to exist?

Tut was now flicking something at Poe, who fussily swatted at his head. "Stop that at once. Quoth!" The stately black raven alighted on his shoulder, picked something out of his hair, and dropped it into Poe's outstretched hand.

Tut let out a hearty laugh. "Dung beetle!"

Edgar turned a gothic shade of red. "Oh, that is quite mature. *Quite!*" He stalked away, repeatedly muttering "Quite!" to Quoth, or himself, or perhaps a voice in his head. One could never be too sure with the soul of Edgar Allan Poe.

Tut let out a hearty chortle, prompting Cordy to smack him. "Give the guy a break, Tut," she said. "You know he gets nose-bleeds."

*"That was just a phase!"* Poe huffed in the distance.

Lex laughed out loud, then threw a worried glance back at the bedrooms. When no one emerged to yell at her, she turned to the portal —

But it had disappeared.

"Lex, wake up!"

Lex did as she was told. She lifted her head and rubbed her face, feeling the notches in her skin where the wooden kitchen table had imprinted itself.

Pip and Bang were staring at her like two frightened lemurs. "We heard something."

Lex listened. After a second, she heard a shuffling noise above her head.

Her limbs tingled. "Crap," she whispered. "Do you think someone followed us here? We're in the middle of — "

"Nowhere," signed Bang. "Yes, all Grimsphere locations are in the middle of nowhere. And yet people keep finding them, so I think that by now, discovery is a valid concern!"

Lex jumped out of the hard chair and ran into the adjoining bedroom. "Uncle Mort," she said, shaking him gently. "There are noises outside."

He swooped out of the bed fully dressed and ready for action, as if he'd known that she'd inevitably barge in to announce trouble. Which, given their recent history, was an entirely reasonable assumption to make. "For how long?" he asked her, heading for the kitchen.

"I don't know. Pip and Bang just woke me up."

More scratching noises came from above, and Uncle Mort's face went pale. "Yeah. Someone's here."

"Call Pandora — or Wicket! She's standing guard outside, isn't she?"

"Yes, but since she didn't alert us, we have to assume she's already been compromised."

The commotion had woken Ferbus and Elysia, who emerged from their rooms once again. "What now?" Ferbus whined.

"Shhh," Pip said, pointing up. "We think someone's here."

Lex's eyes lit up as an idea steamrolled into her head. "Driggs!" She ran into the bedroom, climbed up the ladder, and shook him awake. He was solid — which, for once, was not a good thing. "Driggs, wake up."

"Gah."

"There's someone here!"

"Bwa?"

"I have an idea. You can fly up there and tell us what's happening and who's out there."

Driggs stared, then continued his streak of uttering nonword words. "Heh?"

"If you're part" — she still didn't like saying the word "ghost" — "part corporeally challenged, then you should be able to fly at will, right? Or float? Bob? Something?"

"I can try." Driggs screwed up his face in concentration, but only managed to create the opposite desired effect — his body became denser.

"You!" Lex shouted at Grotton, who seemed to have materialized for the sole purpose of watching Driggs's failed attempts. "Help him!"

"I'm along for the ride to help you save the world, or some such nonsense," Grotton said testily. "I wasn't hired for pilot training."

Lex and Driggs grunted in the exact same pitch and tone. "Try relaxing," she told Driggs. "Stop thinking about making yourself transparent. Just let your mind go."

He started to fade.

"Faster!" Lex said. "Relax harder!"

"Relax harder? Never become a yoga instructor, Lex."

"Come on!"

Taking a deep breath, Driggs shut his eyes and went limp.

Three seconds later, his transparent form shot into the air, yelling *"Holy f — !"* as he dissolved into the ceiling.

Lex went back to the kitchen to wait with the others, but she didn't have to wait long; Driggs reappeared only moments later. He looked stricken, and his voice was thick as he choked out the last two words any of them wanted to hear.

"We're surrounded."

## 7

"It's Norwood," Driggs said. "And about twenty others. They're scattered all over the place. No guns, as far as I could tell, but plenty of scythes."

"Dammit," said Uncle Mort. "They probably tracked our location through the Cuffs when Broomie called. I *told* her . . ."

"I didn't see Wicket anywhere," Driggs continued. "Pandora was about to start the car and run everyone over, but I told her to wait until we figure out a plan." He looked at Uncle Mort. "So what's the plan?"

Uncle Mort was pacing. "We don't have one."

"What?" Lex jumped in front of him. "You have a plan for everything. All the time. What do you mean we don't have one?"

"I mean that all the weapons are in the car. This was supposed to be a safe house, no one knew we were coming here, and Wicket was supposed to have our backs."

"What about Crashing?" Pip said. "We can land right in the car and go!"

"*No more Crashing,*" Uncle Mort said. "It hurts the Grimsphere. How many times do I have to tell you that?"

"So what do we do? There's gotta be something!"

He shrugged. "There's always your standard method of storming the door and hoping for the best."

Lex grunted as she gripped her scythe. "I can't *believe* we're storming the door and hoping for the best."

"Relax, spaz," said Driggs. "We'll make it. What do they have that we don't?"

"Numbers. Strength. Years of experience."

"Yes, but *we've* got the incorrigible spirit of youth."

Lex rolled her eyes.

"Ready?" Uncle Mort asked them. "Up the stairs, then run for the car as hard as you can. Don't engage, just run. Got it?"

They nodded.

"Go."

Uncle Mort's method worked — but only for a moment. The second Lex burst out into open air, she realized how doomed they really were.

Even in the scant predawn light she could see that Grave was swarming with Norwood's men — Trumbull, Riley, the works. They'd clearly been planning on the Juniors Crashing out, and they were spread out all over the graveyard rather than in front of the bunker door — but they quickly recovered and launched an attack. Lex struggled not to panic. It was too dark for anyone to see what they were swinging their scythes at; they'd never hit their marks. Right?

Pandora flashed the high beams of the Stiff, and Lex could see Pip and Bang lithely darting around and over the headstones to the safety of the car. For the first and only time in her life, Lex regretted never joining the track team; knowing how to clear hurdles would have come in extremely handy at a time like this. Or knowing how to throw a scythe like a knife. Or how to fly, as Driggs was currently doing, shouting instructions at the fleeing Juniors.

But Lex did have one very important skill in her arsenal, one she'd been honing to perfection for years, and that was punching. So the first Senior to approach her got a fist right to the jaw, followed by another to the eye, and a grand-finale knee to the junk. As he sank to the ground, another quickly arrived to take his place, but Lex didn't miss a beat, slamming him into unconsciousness as well.

She was about to attack a third when a strange sight caught her eye — that of a single person standing off to the side, not involved in the pandemonium in any way. Whoever it was was handcuffed and wore a dark hood like a person about to be executed.

Lex took a step toward the figure, but before she could get any farther, another Senior pounced on her back, followed by another. Her hands started to grow hot; the unquenchable urge to Damn was right at her fingertips, waiting for her to blow. And the more she fought, the more she wanted to do it, just let fly with her powers. She'd Damn every one of these Seniors if it meant keeping her friends safe.

Yet she'd sworn to herself that she'd stop. That she wouldn't cause any more damage to the Grimsphere. That Damning was wrong, period, no matter how she tried to justify it.

But the heat kept intensifying.

To try to cool off, she paused to take stock of the situation. Pip and Bang had made it safely to the car. Elysia had just knocked someone over the head with a scythe and was on her way as well. Uncle Mort was arguing with someone as they wrestled on the ground.

But Ferbus was the one Lex couldn't stop watching. The very first day she met the kid, he'd bragged about how Uncle Mort had trained him as the Vault Post to fight tooth and nail anyone who tried to break into the Afterlife. And she'd never believed him.

She believed him now. Ferbus was a blur, fists and legs everywhere. He jumped, kicked, and hit in perfect rhythm, as if he'd choreographed the whole fight ahead of time. A pile of defeated Seniors lay around him, and more kept coming, but Ferbus took it all in stride, his face calm and stern as he dispatched them one by one.

Still, it was becoming increasingly obvious that there were just too many of them. Someone else had jumped onto the Uncle Mort pile, and he was struggling underneath to free himself. Dora, Pip, Bang, and Elysia were holding down the car as the Seniors tried, with no success, to break the bulletproof windows, but surely the Juniors couldn't last forever. And one look at Driggs's panicked face, as he had an eagle's-eye view of everything, confirmed Lex's worst fears.

They were losing.

At that moment a series of shouts rang out from the trees. Dora flashed the lights of the Stiff, illuminating the newcomers: Wicket sprinting out of the forest, fiercely shouting war cries at the top of her lungs and leading a band of people straight into the battle.

In the confusion, Uncle Mort managed to extricate himself from the tangle of Seniors and dropped in next to Lex. "Kilda's recruits," he said, grinning.

Lex realized that she was looking at Croakers: at least two dozen citizens who'd decided that Norwood was the real enemy, not Lex.

"Wow," she whispered, watching them fight.

"They'll take it from here," Uncle Mort said. The Seniors had recovered from the surprise and were now beginning a fresh attack. "Just get to the car." He pulled at her hoodie and headed for the flashing headlights, whistling at Ferbus to do the same.

But as Lex watched Riley wrap one of the rebels in a headlock, her hands got even hotter, her scythe blazing in her hand. It felt wrong for her and her friends to simply escape like this, letting Wicket and all those other Grims on their side fight for them. It wasn't fair. She couldn't ask these people to put their lives on the line for her while she got to scamper away to safety. That was exactly what had happened with Riqo and Broomie in DeMyse.

Not here. She wasn't going to make the same mistake again.

She wriggled out of Uncle Mort's grip and ran straight for the center of the fighting. "Get off of her!" she shouted at the man attacking Wicket, grabbing him, Damning him before she could stop herself. A plume of darkness erupted from the man's body as he fell to the ground in flames — and from there, it was just too easy to Damn another, one of the Seniors who'd piled on top of Uncle Mort.

"Lex, stop!" she heard Driggs shout from somewhere above her. Uncle Mort was yelling too, but she kept going, looking for her next victim, itching to feel someone else's skin burning beneath her fingers.

"I'd listen to them if I were you."

It felt as if someone had put the battle on pause. The noise died down, everyone stopping to watch Lex turn around. Someone in the Stiff even cracked a window.

Norwood stood before her. Wicket also faced her, on her knees at his feet. His hand gripped her neck, her face defiant but flickered with fear.

"You're not the only one who can Damn, if you'll recall," he said, his eyes still blazing with that crazed fervor. "I know you've had a lot more practice than I have — What was the final count? Dozens? — but I'm sure I can make up for lost time." He grinned. "So let's make this a fair fight, shall we?"

A whooshing noise sounded, followed by a brutal scream. As soon as the darkness cleared, Wicket plunged face-first to the ground, her body flaming.

No one moved, not even Uncle Mort. Everyone was staring, waiting to see what Lex would do next. Even Norwood watched her, a hint of wariness passing through his otherwise smug face.

And yet Lex felt a curious calm settle over her as she stared at the charred lump. The heat left her hands and was replaced by an odd, cool sensation. Her fingers tingled, as if they'd fallen asleep.

She'd never felt rage this strong before. It seeped into her bones, turning her whole body to ice, the complete opposite of the feral fury of Damning. As if all the events of the past few months had culminated in this one moment of pure, perfect ire.

She kept very still.

"Lex," Driggs whispered above her, drifting a few feet above her head. "Your hand."

Her eyes flicked down to her scythe. Both the weapon and her fingers were outlined in a strange dark shadow that was getting darker, like a roiling tornado.

She didn't even know what was going to happen as she raised her arm, but something compelled her. She had to plunge the scythe into Norwood's chest, she *had* to —

And then she was in the air.

Someone had hit her with a flying tackle, colliding so hard

that she soared across the graveyard, landing with a hard thump into the side of the Stiff.

Dazed, she looked at her hand. It held her scythe, and nothing more. The shadow had disappeared.

She looked up into Grotton's pointy face, barely able to grasp the fact that he'd become solid, picked her up, and flown her out of the way. "Close call," he said, his eyes inscrutable.

Lex held on to his arm for dear life. She was so out of breath she was panting. "What just happened?"

She didn't get an answer, as the car door opened and one of the Juniors quickly pulled her — and, since she still hadn't let go of him, Grotton — into the back. Uncle Mort was in the front seat, yelling something — yelling at Driggs — "Leave her!"

Driggs was hovering over Wicket's body, trying desperately to become solid.

*So that he can unDamn her,* Lex realized.

But he wasn't doing it fast enough. "Come on!" Uncle Mort yelled again, and with a furious grunt Driggs tore himself away and flew to the car.

Lex struggled to look out the window as Pandora sped off down the dirt road, leaving the rest of the Seniors to finish killing one another. In the light of the rising sun she managed to catch one last glimpse of Norwood, who gave the departing Stiff a friendly wave and Crashed away, still unaware that he was harming the Afterlife by doing so. Either that, or he didn't care.

For a minute, no one spoke. They'd all made it back to the car, a little roughed up but none seriously hurt. Ferbus and Lex both had bloody knuckles, Uncle Mort suffered a cut across his forehead, and Elysia was crying.

"Calm down, Lys," Uncle Mort said.

"Calm down? He Damned Wicket!" she whimpered. "He didn't just kill her, he *Damned* her."

"Lex Damned people too," Ferbus said.

"Yeah, but — those guys weren't — "

"What, people just like us?" he shot back. "You think they deserve eternal torment any more than Wicket, just because of the side they happen to be on?"

"Ferb," Uncle Mort said in a tired voice, "let's save the ethics debate for another time. It's a long drive to Necropolis."

Lex appreciated her uncle's stepping in — especially to stop the sort of lecture that he'd usually be the one to deliver — but Ferbus wasn't finished. "Seriously, way to Hulk out back there, Lex. That'll definitely be branded into our nightmares forever, all those bodies bursting into flame like popcorn. And what the hell was that at the end, with your hand?"

"I don't know," Lex said.

"You don't know?"

"No." She stared at the scythe in her hand. Her voice got quieter. "I have no idea."

"Let *go* of me," Grotton hissed.

Lex looked at her other hand, surprised to find Grotton at the end of it; she hadn't even realized she was still clutching his wrist. She looked from her rigid fingers up to his face. He was uncharacteristically frustrated, upset.

*He stays solid when I touch him,* she realized. *Just like Driggs.*

She squeezed him tighter. "What happened back there?" she snarled. Everyone was listening now. "What was that stuff around my hand? And why did you tackle me?" Grotton squirmed like a snake, trying to jerk away, but his wrist was thin and Lex was pissed. "Tell me!"

Grotton narrowed his eyes. "I'm not telling you anything."

His stubbornness was what tipped her off. "It's the thing that triggers the reset, isn't it? What I'll have to do to destroy you?"

Grotton's eyes widened just for a second. Enough for Lex to know that she'd hit pay dirt.

She dug her nails into his papery skin. "Very well! There is a fate worse than death, it's true," he said. "A fate worse than the Hole. Even worse than Damning."

Out of the corner of her eye Lex noticed that Bang was signing something to her: "Keep holding on to him." Then she nudged Pip, who nodded and took his scythe out of his pocket.

Grotton donned an oily smile. "Pity you won't know what it is until it blows up in your face," he told Lex, taunting her. "That's what happens with everything you do, isn't it, love?"

"Now!" Bang mouthed. She gave a healthy shove to Pip, who then grabbed Grotton's hand and, with a quick flick of the scythe, sliced off his thumb. Bang held out the mason jar she'd taken from the bunker, and the severed appendage landed neatly inside, its solidness dissolving into mist before it could produce a single drop of blood.

Everyone sat, stunned — Grotton most of all. Lex even let go, allowing his body to turn to fog once again as he stared at the spot where his finger had been. Then, gradually, a smile came back to his lips. He leaned close to Bang's face, his yellowed teeth only inches from her nose.

"Well played, girl," he sneered. "Happy reading."

With that, he floated back up to the roof. The Juniors stared at the ceiling, not daring to breathe, praying that he wouldn't go solid again and Damn them all in the space of the next second.

But he didn't. And Bang, it seemed, wasn't even concerned. Strangely overjoyed at the grisly trophy she'd taken for herself, her head was already back in the Wrong Book. She held the jar with care, grinning as the words on the page popped to life underneath its cloudy contents.

"It worked!" Pip said.

Uncle Mort seemed to be having trouble finding his voice. "To put it mildly," he croaked.

"You guys are *amazing!*" Elysia said, her mouth agape. "You're like superheroes! Or super villains! Something super!"

"Shh," Pip said as Bang read. "She found the reset page again." Bang drew the jar over the page with one hand and signed to Pip with her other hand, which he then translated. " — the harshest punishment in the known Grimsphere. To trigger a reset, a soul must be sent to the Dark."

Uncle Mort and Pandora both inhaled sharply.

"What's the Dark?" Ferbus asked. "I've never heard of that before."

Bang kept signing, her face getting paler as she read. "The Dark," Pip said, his voice dropping as he went, "is a realm of pure nothingness. A total vacuum. The absence of life; the opposite of the Afterlife. Souls that are sent to the Dark cease to exist, as if they'd never been born at all. They do not reunite with their loved ones. They do not get to spend the rest of eternity in peace. They're simply . . ." He swallowed. "Gone."

The car had fallen so silent, each pebble that crunched under the Stiff's tires could be heard.

"Forever?" Elysia asked.

Bang nodded, then resumed reading. "Forever," Pip continued, never taking his eyes off her. "Annihilation — the act of
sending a soul to the Dark — is a fate that should be reserved
only for the most evil of souls. For the utterly unforgivable."

Lex was shivering even harder now. "That's what happened
back there, with the shadow around my hand? I almost Annihilated Norwood?"

Bang held up a finger as she read some more, then nodded
again. "Sounds like it, with the shadow and everything," Pip
translated. "Because — it says that only a Grim with great power
can Annihilate a soul. A Grim whose soul has already started to
decay."

"In other words," Uncle Mort spoke up, "a Grim who can
Damn."

Lex blinked. "Me."

She stared at the pelts on the floor for a moment, then glanced
up at Uncle Mort. "So that's what I have to do, then," she said. "In
order to trigger a reset, I have to Annihilate someone. Grotton."

Uncle Mort nodded slowly. "Looks that way."

Lex glanced at Driggs, sure that he'd be aghast — but he was
looking out the window, seemingly not even listening.

The rest of the Juniors, on the other hand, were floored.
"That's — " Elysia let out a long puff of air. "That's unbelievable. I
mean, Damning is bad, but at least it leaves you with your soul,
even though it's in pain. But erasing a soul completely?" She
gulped. "Horrifying."

"Beyond horrifying," Ferbus agreed.

"Well, if anyone deserves it, it's Grotton," said Pandora.

Lex shuddered. She wasn't sure *anyone* deserved that.

The car went quiet again. Pandora turned on the radio, but all she could find was static. No one said anything for a while, until —

"He said dozens."

Lex turned to Driggs, not even sure that he'd spoken. But quite sure that he was frowning. "What?"

"Norwood said you've Damned dozens of people. But by my count there was only Corpp and Heloise — then Norwood, unsuccessfully — and then those few Seniors back there. At most, that's half a dozen. So why would he say something like that?"

The Juniors were all staring at her, waiting for her to explain it away, to come up with a perfectly reasonable explanation. And part of Lex's brain did instinctively start to formulate lies: Norwood had lost his mind, Norwood didn't know what he was saying, Norwood must have hit his head and forgotten how to count —

But she told that part to shut up. She'd avoided this for too long as it was. Her friends deserved the truth.

"Um," she started slowly, "over the past few months, when Zara was Damning all those criminals — "

She took a deep breath and closed her eyes. She couldn't look at them — especially not Driggs, who was always hardest on her for taking vengeful matters into her own hands.

"Well . . . it wasn't just her. *I* Damned some of them too. In secret. So whenever I told you I was just Damning inanimate objects or dirt or whatever, in order to discharge all that power building up inside of me — I was lying. I was actually Damning people."

Lex opened her eyes, but at the last second chickened out and looked down before she could see anyone's reaction. No one spoke, though, so she kept going.

"But I swear, I only ever Damned criminals. I never touched a single innocent, not like Zara did, going around zapping people for fun. I couldn't help it. The urge to Damn was a force I couldn't contain — I mean, you saw how it was back there. It's just too strong, and I couldn't — " She felt herself slipping, losing her conviction, starting to ramble. "But I thought carefully about who deserved it, you know? I know that doesn't make it any better, but . . . if I *had* to be Damning people, I thought it would at least be better to eliminate the really bad ones . . ."

She trailed off. They all seemed like logical arguments in her head, but out loud they just sounded deranged. "But I know I messed up," she finished, "and I'm sorry I lied to you."

The silence was too much to bear. Lex looked up.

The Juniors were gaping at her, their eyes huge. All except Driggs, who was still staring out the window, at anything but Lex.

Lex's insides fluttered at this, but she decided to first deal with those who could bear to look her in the eye. "Guys? Say something. Please."

After a moment Elysia spoke. "That's awful."

"Yes," Lex said. "Awful. I know."

Elysia's eyes were getting wet again. "Why didn't you tell us?"

"How could I?" Lex asked. "We Juniors were under enough scrutiny as it was, and the less you knew, the better, and also, um, it's *awful*." She slumped, defeated. "But I couldn't help it," she finished in a small voice.

Lex was sure they'd reached the point where everyone would begin reaching for their scythes to slaughter the fiendish hellion, but to her surprise, that didn't happen. Even more to her surprise was what happened next — Elysia wrapped her in a hug, followed quickly by Pip and Bang.

"What's happening?" Lex asked, her voice muffled by their suffocating love.

"Don't talk. You'll ruin the moment," Elysia said. "Maybe before we'd seen it with our own eyes we'd be appalled, but after what happened back there in Grave, I think it's pretty clear that this is something beyond your control. So we're still your friends, and we still love you. Now please don't make me say anything mushier, because my face already looks like a half-eaten omelet and I really don't need to make things worse right now. Okay?"

Lex's heart was soaring. Why hadn't she told them right from the start? Of course they'd have her back — they always had her back.

Her relief, however, was short-lived.

"Pull over."

Driggs was still looking out the window, but Lex could see that his face was strained. In fact, he was pulsing back and forth between solid and not, just as he had when he'd first changed. "Dora, stop," he said. "I need to get out."

Pandora looked at Uncle Mort, who nodded. She steered the car into a ditch, and before it came to a stop Driggs was out the door, slamming it as he left.

Lex watched him stalk toward the wall of trees that lined the highway and disappear into them. Several minutes passed, but he didn't come out.

Ferbus, who had neither said anything after Lex's confession nor joined in with the group hug, eyed her. "Well?" he said. "You want to go get him, Killer, or should I?"

Lex wanted to smack that judgmental look right off his face, but she opted to grab the door handle instead. "I'll go."

The woods were thick. She picked her way down the path that Driggs's intermittent footsteps had created in the snow until she began to make out a clearing in the trees, then a shoreline. She looked out across a frozen expanse of water —

Where Driggs was standing atop the ice in the middle of the lake.

Lex screeched, then stopped, thinking that maybe ice could be broken by loud noises, like snow in an avalanche. And she couldn't tell if he was solid at the moment — he certainly had been when he slammed the door, but with the fog coming off the lake, she couldn't tell anymore. "Driggs!" she yell-whispered, sliding onto the ice but staying close to the shore. "Come back! It might break!"

"So what?" he yelled back in an oddly detached tone. "I already died of hypothermia two nights ago, right? It was such a rush, maybe I should do it again!"

"Driggs!" Lex's voice got more desperate the more she focused on his face. She'd never seen him like this. He looked furious, tortured, and hopeless at the same time, all wrapped up with a neat little ribbon of insanity. "Come here," she said. "Let's talk."

Abruptly, Driggs started sprinting toward her. His feet slipped along on the ice — *Which means he's solid*, Lex thought with a lurch. Was it possible for a person to die twice?

She grabbed his hoodie when he got close. "What are you — "

"Did you feel anything?" he asked. His frenzied eyes were scanning her face, his blue eye looking lighter in the bright white reflections all around them.

Lex drew back. "What do you mean?"

"When you Damned those people," he said evenly, "did you feel anything?"

"I — I felt the burning — I mean, the Damning power — "

He gave her a disappointed look, then headed for the shore. "That's not what I mean."

"What *do* you mean?" Lex followed him onto the muddied grass. "Driggs. Look at me."

When he did, she wished he hadn't. He looked destroyed, so different from the lighthearted boy she normally knew. "Did you feel — " he started. "I don't know. Like part of your soul had died? Like your crimes were beyond forgiveness? Like you were doing something so utterly, inconceivably wrong that you weren't fully human anymore?"

Lex swallowed. In the beginning, she had, but the more her conviction grew — the more she convinced herself that she was doing the right thing — that twinge of remorse had started to fade. But it had to be in there still, somewhere — she was sure of it. "Kind of," she said. "Yes."

The faintest hint of relief passed over his face. "Good." He started walking back toward the car, but not before adding, "Otherwise I don't know how you could live with yourself."

For the first time, as Lex watched him walk away and fade back into his ghostish form, she got the feeling that they weren't just talking about her own crimes anymore.

⦚⦚⦚

The next twelve hours in the Stiff were decidedly less than pleasant. After several heated rounds of the License Plate Game, Pip decided to invent the Flick Ferbus in the Ear Game, which soon became the Ferbus Yells So Loud He Bursts Eardrums Game. Elysia yelled at him for yelling at Pip, causing Pandora to yell at everyone. "Shut the hell up or I'll wrap this car right around a tree, and don't you think for a *second* that I won't!"

"But he's flicking me!" said Ferbus.

Uncle Mort turned around in his seat. "Are we in preschool, Ferb? Is he breathing on you, too?"

"Actually, he is. And he *still* won't give me credit for spotting the Alaska plate first."

"Because you didn't spot the Alaska plate first," said Pip.

*"PIP, I SWEAR ON ALL THAT IS HOLY I WILL POP YOUR EYEBALLS OUT OF YOUR HEAD AND EAT THEM WITH A SIDE OF YOUR LEFT—"*

"Enough!" Uncle Mort yelled.

But Lex could deal with the chaos. What she couldn't deal with was the silent treatment Driggs was giving her. This had never happened before. He'd never been so mad that he couldn't speak. Hell, she couldn't remember the last time he'd been mad at *all*.

In fact, he'd decided to switch places with Grotton and ride on top of the roof. Grotton now sat among them in the cabin of the car, stroking the place where his thumb used to be and grinning at the Juniors in a most unsettling manner.

Elysia was trying not to let it get to her, but after avoiding his gaze for minutes at time, then looking back to find that he was only staring at her harder, she snapped. "What?" she hissed at him. "What are you doing?"

He cocked his head to the side. "Estimating how high the blood would rise if it were drained out of all of you." He held his hand up, level with the bottom of the window. "It'd come up to about here, I suspect."

Elysia looked at him as if he'd said . . . exactly what he'd just said. "Driggs!" she said in a fervent whisper, pounding on the roof. "Please come back!"

Her pleas were met with silence.

Elysia cupped a hand next to her face to block the view of the leering Grotton. "What's wrong with Driggs?" she asked Lex.

"I don't know," Lex said. "He flipped out over my whole Damning thing."

"Psff, yeah, what's his problem?" Ferbus said sarcastically. "Getting upset over the discovery that his girlfriend is a mass murderer? What an asshole." He gave her a Look.

She ignored him and turned back to Elysia. "It just seems so unlike him, you know? I mean, he's always gotten a little pissed when I've wanted to . . . bend the rules a little. But in the end he's always been on my side."

Elysia smiled and grabbed Lex's hand. "He'll come around. Besides — "

"Ugh, the children are emoting again," Grotton said. "No wonder the boy wants to be left in peace." He coyly raised an eyebrow at Lex and took a long, deep breath. "Though I do so love the stench of fear. It's rather . . . intoxicating."

Either Driggs couldn't hear what Grotton was saying or he didn't care, because he didn't budge from his spot on the roof. Lex nodded a thanks at Elysia, pulled her hood up over her face, and turned to the window, while Grotton just kept on staring, running the tip of his tongue over his lips.

|||||||

Some time after they crossed into Kansas, Pandora got off the highway.

"How close are we?" asked Pip as he and the rest of the Juniors woke up. It was around noon.

"Pretty close," said Uncle Mort, craning his head to look at the sparse surroundings — nothing but endless fields under an endless sky. "Another few minutes."

Lex frowned. Croak was in the middle of the Adirondack mountains, hidden from view. DeMyse was in the middle of a desert, miles away from anyone and disguised as a mirage. How could Necropolis be in the middle of a sea of cornfields, all out in the open like that?

The rest of the Juniors must have been thinking the same thing, because the questions started to bubble over. "Are we going to an airport?" Ferbus asked as Dora turned onto an even narrower road. "Are we taking a private jet to a secret remote location or something?"

"Absolutely, Mr. Bond," Uncle Mort said. "A hoverbike will be waiting for each of you as well." When Ferbus started to look even more hopeful, Uncle Mort rolled his eyes. "No airport. No hoverbikes."

"So . . . is it underground?" Elysia asked. "A whole Grimsphere city secretly thriving right beneath these farms?"

"No."

"Then what?"

"Then that."

He pointed to a small park up ahead that contained nothing more than a few picnic benches, a little chapel, and a boxy stone marker with an aluminum pole sticking straight up out of it. The American flag at the top hung limply in the breezeless air. Seeing as how there was nothing but grass and corn in every other direction, the whole thing seemed a bit out of place.

"Park over there, Dora," Uncle Mort said as she pulled onto the grass. "Find a nice place for the Stiff to . . . you know."

"Rest in peace," she said mournfully.

Lex and the Juniors exchanged worried glances. They weren't coming back to the car?

Once Dora found a suitable spot, they piled out. Driggs floated off the roof, his still-wet hair looking as if it had been eaten by a vacuum cleaner.

"Hey," Lex said.

He glanced at her, then looked away.

"Awesome," Lex said to herself as they started walking. "Good talk."

Uncle Mort led them to the stone marker. "'The Geographic Center of the United States,'" Pip read off a metal plaque. "Really?"

Uncle Mort pulled out his compass and scanned the horizon. "The Grimsphere capital needed to be in a centralized location. Doesn't get more centralized than this."

"Um, Uncle Mort?"

"Yes, Lex?"

"This is not the Grimsphere capital. This is a crappy tourist attraction, one that doesn't seem to have attracted even a single tourist."

"Yet again, Lex, I humbly bow to your powers of observation." Spotting something in the distance, he started walking away from the marker, still looking at the compass and counting his steps as he went. Shrugging, the Juniors followed.

After a moment he stopped and grinned. "There. Look straight ahead."

The Juniors looked straight ahead. The Juniors saw nothing.

"It takes a few seconds," he said. "You know, like one of those Magic Eye things. You have to let your eyes adjust and find it on their own."

Lex stared at the area he was pointing at. All she saw were the spiky green ends of cornstalks; the giant blue sky.

And a solid wall of glass.

Gasping, Lex finally saw it. She saw the whole thing; the glass had reflected the blue of the sky so well that the structure had been completely camouflaged. Even its edges were softened, shrouded in some kind of mist, causing it to blend in seamlessly with the Kansan sky. But there it was, right in front of them.

A massive, *massive* tower.

The circular base of the building was huge — probably the size of a city block. But it was also mind-blowingly tall, narrowing as it reached the top and forming a gigantic cone-shaped spire with an apex so high it was lost in the clouds.

If the earth were a unicorn, they'd just found its horn.

"Nicknamed the Emerald City," Uncle Mort told them, and as soon as he said it, Lex noticed that the glass did have a bit of a green tint.

"And in Kansas, too," Grotton snorted. "Grims think they're so terribly clever, don't they?"

The Juniors took a few careful steps forward, still staring in disbelief. They waved at the structure, trying to make the glass register their reflections, but all it displayed was more grass, more sky — as if the Croakers were invisible. Or vampires.

"This is . . . impossible," Ferbus said.

"Tip of the impossibility iceberg, my friend." Uncle Mort

waved them closer, stopping at some invisible boundary. "Now line up and stay still until I tell you to walk forward, all at the same time. You may hold hands if you like."

"What's going to happen when we walk forward?" Lex asked.

"We'll be in Necropolis." He grinned at her, counted to make sure everyone was there, then added, "And then we'll get arrested. Go!"

## 8

"We'll *what?*" the Juniors yelled. Not that they expected an answer. Uncle Mort strode forward and they followed regardless, because that's just how things worked with Uncle Mort.

But three steps in, they were no longer capable of coherent thought. Before Lex could get one syllable out of her mouth, a door opened in the cone — which was very odd, seeing a hole materialize out of the illusion of solid earth and sky — and vomited forth a veritable SWAT team of masked, black-uniformed guards, all running at the intruders and pointing some very serious-looking weapons in their faces.

"YOU'RE UNDER ARREST!" a slight guard blared at them from behind the mask. The voice sounded amplified and staticky, as if it were coming through a megaphone.

Lex was practically soiling herself in terror, but Ferbus managed to eke out a zinger. "Didn't quite catch that, what?"

"ON THE GROUND!" Megaphone yelled, even louder than before. "HANDS BEHIND YOUR BACK!"

As they got on their knees, Lex looked up at Uncle Mort and gave him the dirtiest look she could muster. "What?" he said innocently. "I *did* warn you."

Everyone was handcuffed. Except, Lex noticed, Grotton and Driggs, who had conveniently escaped by way of disappearing — or turning so transparent that no one could see them in all the confusion. Her jaw tightened, but she did her best not to show any emotion, not wanting to suggest to the guards that they'd missed a couple of their intruders.

*Please be okay,* she thought.

They were taken through the main entrance. Inside, the foyer was so expansive that despite being rushed through by the guards, Lex had time to look around and get a feel for the place..The ceiling soared above their heads, several stories high, and light streamed in through the massive window-walls — which, impossibly, seemed to be made of one single pane of glass. Several flat-screen televisions were suspended throughout the room as well, all displaying the same woman.

"Good afternoon, Necropolitans! President Knell here with some wonderful news!" she said in a friendly drawl, a huge red smile plastered on her face. Her eyes were beady but shrewd, her nose so sharp it looked as though it had been cut with a laser. Lex couldn't place her twangy accent — maybe Texan, maybe Midwestern, maybe old-timey gold prospector. She wore a set of green pearls around her neck and a smart suit jacket, its gray color perfectly matching that of her short, stylish hair. "The fugitives from Croak have been apprehended and are now in custody. So rest easy, Necropolis," she said with an even bigger grin and a singsong voice. "We've taken them a-*li*-ive!"

"Well," Lex said, "that's not creepy at all."

At opposite ends of the circular room were two escalators spiraling up the sides of the building like the twists of a soft-serve ice-cream cone: up on the left, down on the right. Grims briskly hopped on and off the moving steps, stopping only to stare at the commotion in the middle of the foyer.

And commotion was indeed what they were making. The Juniors clacked noisily across what was enough dark green marble to tile every bathroom in America. Ferbus was yelling as hard as he could into the ear of the megaphoned guard, while Bang's teeth were tightly clamped around the arm of another.

Lex just went along quietly, looking down at the large symbol in the middle of the floor — a sort of Grimsphere crest featuring two crossed scythes. She'd resisted plenty of arrests by now in her criminal career, and she'd learned one lesson: It was rarely worth the effort.

Uncle Mort had reached the same conclusion, striding silently alongside the colossal ogreish guard who had pinned his arms behind his back. He even seemed to have a spring in his step. At the front desk, between the two escalators, he greeted the flustered receptionist with a smile. "Hey, Marlene!" he said, graciously bestowing upon her the Wink of Trust as he was yanked away. "Long time, no exchange of pleasantries!"

Fed up, the guard holding Uncle Mort socked him in the face with a fist the size of a boulder. That shut him up.

Or maybe it was the sudden appearance of Norwood, who sauntered out of the elevator and approached the group, his smile so wide it had to hurt. "Welcome to Necropolis, Croakers!" he said, arms open, eyes still crazed and darting.

"Crap," Lex hissed to Uncle Mort. "We're too late — he's already here! He's gotten to the president already!"

Uncle Mort said nothing, blinking blood out of his eyes and trying to get a better look at Norwood. Lex clenched her fists. How could Uncle Mort do this to them, walk them straight into a trap?

"The president," Norwood continued, "is none too pleased with what you've been up to. I'm sure she'd like nothing more than to sentence you herself, but she's somewhat on the busy side these days — with Croak and DeMyse currently offline, Necropolis is handling the deathload for the entire country. So she has authorized me to deal with you as I see fit."

He turned to Megaphone and said with great relish, "Throw them in the Hole."

Lex's pulse quickened. That was why the president was so happy to take them alive. So she could hurl them into the Hole — probably on live television, for all of Necropolis to see.

"YES, SIR," Megaphone answered, but Norwood was heading straight for Bang, a strange new glint in his eye.

"I'll just be taking this." He yanked the Wrong Book out from under her arm. For a brief moment Grotton's grayish face appeared next to the book, flashing a triumphant sneer at Lex.

"No!" she whispered. Uncle Mort swore under his breath as well. How was she supposed to Annihilate Grotton now, with Norwood stealing him away?

Norwood turned on his heel, his eyes never leaving the gold letters on the cover of the book. He walked past the front desk to a bank of elevators sitting behind it, glass cylinders that soared up through the open air of the foyer. He boarded one and quickly disappeared up the narrow glass tube into a hole in the ceiling.

Behind the elevators was a door. The Croakers were led through it, down a long corridor. The guards took them into an empty room with a linoleum floor and white, sterile-looking panels for walls. The kind that could easily be hosed down should anything red and sticky splatter onto them.

"CIRCLE THEM UP," Megaphone instructed, closing the door and locking it with an audible *click*. The guards, holding the Juniors from behind by their handcuffs, roughly shoved them into place so that they were all facing one another. Lex tried to exchange glances with her friends but stopped once she got to Elysia. She just looked too scared.

Megaphone took a stance in the middle of the circle and turned around slowly, looking each of the prisoners in the eye.

Lex's knees started to shake. This was really weird. Previously as a detainee she'd experienced taunting, questioning, and always a bit of roughing up. But never this calm, detached staring. What the hell was going on? Why weren't they following Norwood's orders?

The answer came as Megaphone unholstered a gun and aimed it straight at Uncle Mort's face.

Lex didn't remember yelling, but the screams bouncing around the stark walls of the room suggested that she and the other Juniors had all cried out when the guard pulled the trigger. Yet Uncle Mort stood right where he had a second before, unharmed.

The big guard who'd been holding his handcuffs, however, was flat on the ground.

After a bit of a delayed response, the other guards sprang into action, but Megaphone was too quick for them; six more shots rang out in succession, each one aimed at the guards' noses with exquisite precision. In less than five seconds, all seven guards lay crumpled on the floor.

But not one of them was bleeding. Lex frowned, as did the rest of the Juniors. Their gazes jumped from the guards to Megaphone to Uncle Mort . . .

Who just so happened to be grinning like an idiot.

"What," he said to Megaphone, staring excitedly at the gun, "is *that* thing?"

"MY OWN INVENTION," the voice blared back. "OH, SORRY, HANG ON — " The mask came off and was hurled to the floor. "Oh, God, that is an *obscene* amount of face sweat. Obscene."

Lex blinked seventeen times. The woman looked just as she did in the old photo in *The Obituary,* when she'd been a Junior with Uncle Mort and LeRoy. It didn't even seem as though she had aged much — she still wore her hair in those long black braids, though a few strands had escaped and were now meandering wildly across her head — and her eyes were bright and friendly. Though she was missing a single front tooth, her playful expression plus a mess of freckles made her seem as if she were seven years old and the loose tooth had simply wiggled out of her gums during recess.

"Hi, Croakers! I'm Skyla." She gave them a deep bow, then pulled out a key and started to unlock each of their handcuffs. "Mayor of Necropolis, head of security, and, as of this very moment," she said with a glance at her fallen comrades, wincing and grinning at the same time, "fellow fugitive."

"Returning to my previous question," said Uncle Mort, yanking the gun out of Skyla's hand with a daring and — was it flirty? — expression, "what is this?"

"Amnesia gun," she said in a cocky, teasing tone. "What, never come up with such a thing in Mort's Bargain Basement of Gadgets?"

Uncle Mort scowled as he inspected the barrel. "Never could

get it to work without causing permanent disfigurement," he muttered.

"Hey!" a disembodied voice shouted. Driggs appeared out of nowhere, posed in a ridiculous, ready-to-fight stance that in no way would have been able to fend off a squad of highly trained guards. "Let them go!"

To their credit, not one of the Juniors laughed — though it was difficult not to. "We've got this, Driggs," Uncle Mort said, easing him down. "But thanks for your initiative."

Driggs looked sheepish for a moment, then turned to Ferbus. Not Lex. Apparently the silent treatment was still in full effect. "What's going on?" he asked him.

Ferbus was staring at Skyla, baffled. "Dude, I have no idea."

"Me neither," Lex said, now so out of the loop she couldn't remember how it felt to be *in* a loop. Any loop at all. "Someone explain this!"

Annoyed at having to cut his weapon inspection short, Uncle Mort handed the gun back to Skyla and faced Lex. "Remember how I told you about the band of hooligans I was a part of when I was a Junior? Meet Hooligan Number Three."

Lex turned to Skyla, grimacing as she rubbed her wrists. "Is this how you treat all your old friends, with a welcome party of weapons?"

"Nah, Mort's special."

Lex chose to ignore the smirky look Skyla gave him.

"And don't worry, the guns aren't lethal — they're stun guns, designed to incapacitate you so they can throw you in the Hole. Still hurt like a bitch, though."

"But why did you arrest us?"

Skyla put her hand on Lex's arm. "Because if there is any chance of succeeding at this ridiculously dangerous, exceedingly harebrained, impossibly impossible scheme your uncle has dreamed up, we're going to need everyone in this city to believe that I am doing everything in my mayoral power to stop you from assassinating the president."

"Assassinating the *what?*" Ferbus yelped. "We never agreed to that!"

Uncle Mort rolled his eyes. "Of course not. But that's what everyone will *think* we're trying to do."

"When in actuality," Lex said, catching on, "we're here to destroy the portal."

"Actually, destroying the portal is my job," Skyla said. "Problem is, it's all the way up in President Knell's office, which is locked up so tight that no one — not even me, her head of security — is allowed to enter. Though she seems to have made an exception for Norwood." She snorted.

"Norwood can Damn now," Uncle Mort explained. "There's a good chance he threatened her."

"Maybe. But I wouldn't be surprised if she didn't need much convincing."

Lex nodded in agreement. The president hadn't stopped Norwood from taking over as mayor of Croak or from sentencing all the Juniors to the Hole. Clearly, the woman was not a fan of Lex and Company. "And now he has the Wrong Book," she added sourly, "which we *have* to get back." Otherwise she couldn't Annihilate Grotton and there would be no resetting for any souls, Driggs or otherwise.

"Exactly," Skyla said. "So you've got a plethora of reasons to claw your way up to the top of Necropolis, which gives me a plethora of reasons to chase you. It's the perfect excuse for me to gain access — the president will think I'm trying to protect her, when in fact you guys will just be paving the road so that I can get into her office. But we'll have to be convincing; otherwise she'll catch on. Which brings us to the hard part." She cocked her gun. "You're going to have to outsmart me."

The Juniors looked from Skyla to Uncle Mort, then back to Skyla. "Huh?" said Ferbus.

"I can give you a few hints," she said, "but if we want this to look real, it has to *be* real. Most of it, at least. Otherwise we won't fool anyone — not Knell, not Norwood, and definitely not the people of Necropolis. They'll be glued to their televisions, following the hunt like it's a high-speed car chase."

She yanked a flattened roll of papers out of the pant leg of her uniform, crouched down, and rolled them out across the floor, prompting a snicker from Uncle Mort. "Ah, the return of Schematic Skyla. I've missed her so."

"Shut up, Warty Mort."

The two of them exchanged a series of familiar expressions so fast that Lex felt as if she were watching a sexually charged tennis match. It wasn't that she never expected her uncle to have a social life outside of Croak, it was just that . . .

Well, okay, she didn't expect it at all.

"Necropolis is made up of three sectors, thirty-three stories each, for a total of ninety-nine," Skyla explained, pointing at the blueprint of Necropolis. With its triangular shape and the way the three sectors were marked off, it looked like a piece of candy corn. "The bottom third, Local, is home to all Grim-related operations for the city of Necropolis — our hub, our Field, our Lair, public relations offices, and so on. The middle section, Residential, is where all citizens of Necropolis live. In addition to their apartments, it's got a whole district of Grimsphere-famous themed restaurants, plus bars, museums, libraries, bowling alleys, arcades — "

"Remember the pool table?" Uncle Mort murmured.

She looked up at him with a randy expression. "Distinctly."

Lex glanced at Elysia, who made a barfy face.

"And finally, the uppermost sector, Executive, consists of offices for the national headquarters of the American Grimsphere government, including — ta-*da* — the president's office." She drew her finger all the way up to the tip of the cone, then tapped it for emphasis. "This is where you need to get. Now, under normal circumstances, you could either take the escalators, which wind up the sides of the building just like the staircase of a lighthouse; or, if you had top security clearance, you'd be able to take the express elevators that shoot up the center. There's just one little problem with those options, and it's currently breathing on my arm."

She turned to Lex, who shrank a little and shut her mouth. "Sorry."

"Even if you did have the balls to travel out in the open, every guard in Necropolis is trained to arrest you on sight," Skyla continued. "And citizens are required to report any leads immediately."

Skimming the map, Lex's gaze caught on a large block of the Residential section labeled DORMITORIES. "What about the Juniors?" she asked, daring to hope. "Are they on our side? Would they be willing to help us?"

Skyla twisted her mouth, thinking. "Juniors are a wild card. A few of them are fed up with the way the president has been breathing down their necks, but most think that once the main Junior threat is eliminated — you — the oppression will disappear. The majority of the citizens feel the same way. *So*. You'll need to get creative." With that, she stood up and pulled a new set of schematics out of her other pant leg.

Lex scowled. Get creative? The woman even talked like Uncle Mort.

"I highly suggest you use the Backways," Skyla said, spreading out the pages to reveal a similar diagram of Necropolis, but with a different floor plan. "Any of you ever been to Disney World?"

Ferbus gave her a harsh look and pointed around the circle at each Junior. "Foster kid, orphan, foster kid, disowned — "

"Okay, so no," she said. "But perhaps you've heard of the place. What you might not know about it, however, is that the streets of the Magic Kingdom are the *second* floor of the park. The first floor is actually a gigantic underground network of hallways that connect up to the park via hidden doors and secret passageways, all so that the cowboys from Frontierland can get to their saloons without swaggering through Futureland and looking like crackpot time travelers. The same idea was applied here in Necropolis, to allow for safe and efficient passage in the event of an emergency. But since better evacuation plans have evolved since the Backways were built, no one uses them anymore — or even knows about them."

"No one but architectural geeks," Uncle Mort added.

Skyla elbowed him in the groin. "Architectural geekery is what's going to save your life."

"The more you say it, the more it sounds like a cry for help."

"Long story short," she continued, seemingly accustomed to ignoring Uncle Mort's snark, "the Backways are your best-bet highway to the top. I'm not even supposed to know about them, so it won't look suspicious if I pretend to be confused about where the hell you are." She rolled up the plans, stuck them back into her pants, and put her hands on her hips like a plucky SWAT-team Peter Pan. "Though just so you're prepared, they're not a totally comprehensive network, so there will be a few places where you'll have to sneak back into the public areas of Necropolis."

"And how are we going to do that?" Elysia asked.

Skyla grinned. "Beats me. Can't wait to see what you come up with."

"All right, enough fake planning," said Uncle Mort. "I'm assuming these guys aren't going to be knocked out forever — "

"Two hours," Skyla said with pride.

"*Two* — " Uncle Mort stared at her with an expression that morphed from outrage to envy to unadulterated lust. "Brilliant. We might just have a little time left over for — "

"What?" she said, smirking as she packed up her stuff. "Eight ball in the corner pocket?"

Uncle Mort reddened and adjusted his pants.

Lex leaned in to Elysia. "I don't even know how to handle what's happening right now."

"I can take you as far as the hub," Skyla said. "But after that, you're on your own." She asked Mort to help her climb up onto his shoulders to retrieve a prepacked bag hidden inside the ceiling tiles. After throwing it over her own shoulder and climbing down, she approached the far wall of the room and popped open a door that had previously blended in with the wall panels. Within lay a darkened hallway.

She ushered them inside and closed the door behind them. "The closest entrance to the Backways is on the other side of this next room."

At the end of the hall they reached a door, where Skyla typed a code into the keypad that sat beneath the handle. Its little glowing light switched from red to green as the bolt unlocked with a deep *click*. In the faint light, Lex could see that someone had scratched ABANDON ALL HOPE on the door's surface.

"But first," Skyla said, turning the handle, "a little unpleasantness."

IIIIIII

They stepped into a dark, smoky space. A thin trough of fire snaked around the circular perimeter, creating the effect of an ancient sacrificial altar. The air was thick with the smell of excrement and burnt oil, and although, owing to the smoke, Lex couldn't see how far the fiery light extended, she could tell by the acoustics that the room was huge.

And the only reason she could tell anything about the acoustics was because of the inhuman moans echoing off the stone walls.

The Croakers inched forward in a slow-moving clump. "What is this?" Elysia asked Lex in a frightened whisper.

"I don't know," Lex said, her eyes watering as she tried to squint through the smoke. All she could make out was a pit in the floor a few feet away. When she moved to investigate, Skyla grabbed her arm.

"Careful," Skyla said. "Stay close to me. You don't want to fall in."

"Fall — " And with a sick, sinking feeling, Lex realized where they were. "Oh God. You brought us to the *Hole?*"

"Don't panic," Skyla said in an even voice as the Juniors started to do just that. "Just keep walking and try not to look in."

A voice arose from somewhere in the room, a quivering yet monotone voice that could have come from either gender. It continuously recited the words of a poem, getting faster every time, and always shouting the last three words:

> *To sit in solemn silence on a dull, dark dock*
> *In a pestilential prison with a lifelong lock*
> *Awaiting the sensation of a short, sharp shock*
> *From a cheap and chippy chopper on a*
> *BIG*
> *BLACK*
> *BLOCK!*
> *Tositinsolemnsilenceonadulldarkdock*
> *Inapestilentialprisonwithalifelonglock . . .*

Lex's body gave a violent shudder.

The farther they got from the rim of fire — the closer to the center of the room — the more the air cleared, though it was still comparable to a thin fog. Lex could now see that the floor was dotted with dozens of holes, all approximately five feet in diameter.

She couldn't help herself. She stepped up to the edge of the closest hole, poked her flashlight inside, and peered down.

Staring back up at her was a living skeleton. Half clothed in tattered rags, he held a trembling arm over his eyes to block the light. His eyes were exceedingly bulbous, popping out from his sunken, bruised skin.

"Throw it." His voice was feeble and gravelly, ruined by years of futile calls for help. "Throw it down!"

"Um — " Flustered, Lex held a hand over her nose. The stench was overwhelming. "Throw what?"

"Please!" he rasped, staring blindly into the dot of Lex's flashlight.

Skyla yanked the light from Lex's hand. The hole plunged back into darkness, but the image of the ruined man still burned bright in Lex's vision.

"Don't talk to them," Skyla ordered. "It just makes things worse."

"Throw it!" The man called as the group moved on, his voice joining the other moans wafting up from the holes. *"Throw it!"*

This seemed to rile up the rest of the prisoners. Elsewhere in the room, a high-pitched female voice started crying, then grew louder to a moan, then became tortured screaming, a feral wail that rocked every inch of the cavern. Lex covered her ears as Skyla prompted the group to pick up the pace, but her hands weren't enough to block out the noise. It bounced around inside her skull, boring into her brain, thoroughly inescapable.

The screams morphed into words in her head: *This could have been you.*

Lex closed her eyes and broke into a run, her eyes watering.

*If you get caught, this WILL be you.*

At last the howling ceased.

Lex wiped the grime off her face and opened her eyes. She and the others were standing inside a dim, musky hallway. Skyla pounded the door shut, sealing off the last of the smoke, screams, and misery.

No one spoke. Skyla walked to a metallic box and pushed up a lever. With a crackly hum, a thin band of fluorescent lights flickered to life along the ceiling of a curving green hallway. In the flat, unforgiving light, the rest of the group all looked as traumatized as Lex did. Pip held the back of his hand over his mouth, as if he were about to throw up. Uncle Mort's head was pointed at the ground as he scratched at his head. Elysia was still shaking.

Skyla readjusted her pack and strode forward, pointing her flashlight down the corridor. "Come on," she said gently. "Let's get as far away from all that as we can, shall we?"

The group lurched forward in silent agreement.

Lex trailed behind them. They had walked all of fifty feet when she halted. She leaned against a wall and sank down to the floor, her head pressed into her knees.

Driggs was the first one to notice. "Wait up," he called to Skyla at the front of the pack. Skyla glanced back, assessed Lex's condition, and looked at Driggs.

"About two hundred paces ahead, the hall branches into two paths," she told him. "We'll wait for you there."

He nodded and crouched down beside Lex as the group strode on, Elysia lingering and nervously glancing back.

Once they were gone, Driggs swallowed. "Lex —"

"That was the worst thing I've ever seen. Or heard. Or smelled." She looked up at him, her voice hoarse. "That could

have been me, you, any one of us. It's *going* to be us, if we screw
this up!"

He reached out to stroke her arm, but his hand went through
it. "It's not going to be us," he said. "Because we're going to win.
You said so yourself. You're going to fix it."

She glared at him.

"So," she said. "You're talking to me again now?"

He stood up and scratched the back of his neck, embarrassed.
"Yeah. I guess so."

"What was that all about, Driggs? Couldn't resist the urge to
jump back up into that seat of judgment again, huh?" She was
being a total snot — she could hear it in her voice, the way she
kept sniffing and scoffing — but the Hole had upset her too much
to care. "Look, it's nothing you haven't reamed me out for before — that it's not our place, that we're not the ones who are supposed to deal out justice, yet that's exactly what I was doing by
Damning those criminals and it's super wrong and unacceptable
and I deserve to rot and fester in a dank, dark hole for the rest of
my life. I don't need another lecture. I get it."

Driggs balled up his fists. "You don't get it."

"Yes, I do. What I *don't* get is why, in your mind, it's so much
worse than everything else I've done. I mean, you know I'm evil.
You've known it for a long time now. Every time I've tried to take
the law into my own hands, even way back when I first came to
Croak and wanted to go after all those criminals, you were always
the first one to yell at me. So why would one more abhorrent
thing that I've done so deeply offend and surprise you all of a sudden?"

He was agitated, she could see. He was pacing back and forth between the close walls of the hallway, like a caged animal. "Because this time you really did it. You really did go after those criminals."

"And I'd do it again!" she shot back. "They were revolting people! I was doing the world a *favor* — "

"But what gives you the right to make that decision?"

"What gives *you* the right?" she shouted up at him. "Taking this moral high ground, this rock-solid conviction, acting like you're a friggin' saint and *I'm* the monster for dispatching these people! You act like I never even gave it a second's thought, like I'm just a bloodthirsty murderer on the prowl for my next kill. How can you think that about me? You think I haven't weighed those Damnings over a billion times in my head? You have *no idea* what goes into making a decision like that, to take the life of someone who isn't supposed to die. You've never held that power in your hands. *You've* never killed anyone!"

"Yes, I have," he said quietly.

Whatever words Lex had planned on saying next died in her throat. ". . . What?"

He held her gaze with dead eyes.

"I killed my parents."

## 9

For a second Lex wasn't sure she had heard him correctly — but there it was again, reverberating down the barren hallway, amplified and clear and thundering forever in her ears.

She couldn't talk. She could barely breathe; it seemed that all her brain activity had ceased. All she could do was look at him.

Driggs was half facing away from her, but she could see that his fingers were clawed into his still-soaked hair, his eyes red and wet and blinking a hundred times a minute. He was breathing very fast. His back heaved and trembled.

For a moment they were both very still.

"Driggs," she finally whispered.

At the sound of his name, he deflated a little, curling into himself. He crumpled to the floor across from her and put his back against the other side of the corridor. They sat facing each other with their knees bent and their feet touching, forming an *M* on the floor of the hallway.

Lex put her hands flat on the cement. She needed something stable, solid. "Driggs," she said, a little louder, but with as much warmth as was possible in such a cold, empty hallway. "Look at me."

His eyes met hers. He looked scared, lost, like an abandoned puppy. "I've never told that to anyone," he said in a small voice.

Lex didn't say anything, didn't push it.

Driggs opened his mouth, then closed it again. He seemed to

be having some difficulty knowing where to start. After a moment of thought, he finally just gave her one of his usual smirks.

"The thing is," he said, "I come from a long line of colossal assholes."

Lex held his gaze. She knew that already; she'd seen his scars. But she knew nothing about the people who'd given them to him.

He breathed deeply. "My parents beat me because their parents beat them. It was a family tradition, apparently. I bet it's on our crest, a guy waving a belt, a kid screaming and running away." He laughed at that, then stopped. "I guess that's not really funny."

He bit his lip. "I don't know if they were ever decent people — I suppose they must have been at one point, to fall in love and get married, but I never saw any evidence of that. They both had shitty jobs in sales at a farm equipment supplier — not that steady employment actually mattered, since they blew every paycheck on booze." He paused. "The only shred of humanity I ever gleaned from them was the fact that, years before, they had had dreams of opening their own business — which is hilarious, really, because they were both lousy salespeople. But then I came along and ruined their lives, so that was that. That's what they always told me, anyway. Completely ruined their lives." He counted on his fingers. "Other greatest hits included: I was the biggest mistake they'd ever made, I'd never amount to anything, and I was worthless and stupid and — the household favorite — a pointless fuck."

Lex could only stare in disbelief. "How did you turn out to be such a decent human being with all those atrocious things they said?"

His mouth crinkled into a shy grin. "I didn't believe them. Like I said, they were lousy salespeople."

Lex exhaled a half laugh.

He looked down. "I remember the night so well. It was cold, right on the cusp of autumn. It felt like Halloween, even though October was still a few weeks away. There was that crispness in the air, that smell. You know what I mean?"

"Not really," said Lex. "My neighborhood always smelled like truck exhaust."

"Well, that's one perk of growing up in the sticks, I guess." When Lex looked surprised, he frowned. "You didn't know that? Upstate New York — just a couple of hours away from Croak, actually."

Lex shook her head. Somehow, she had not known where her boyfriend grew up. He just seemed so at home in Croak — as if he'd been there his whole life — that she'd never even thought to ask.

Driggs blew out a puff of air. "My dad had just begun his nightly routine of stumbling through the door with a half-empty case of beer. But one dirty look from me was all it took for him to decide that this evening's festivities would have the added bonus of a boxing match. With his fourteen-year-old son. While my mom sat on the couch and cheered him on. He only ever had one rule: I was never allowed to hit back."

He swallowed. "Except this time, I did."

He swallowed again. "I'd had it. I was just so mad, so sick of their shit, the way they treated me, the way my life was this unending mess that I couldn't escape from. So I clocked him right in the face. Broke his nose."

Lex thought back to a few months earlier, when he'd done the same thing to Ferbus. No wonder he'd looked so disgusted with himself afterward.

"Then things got really bad. He threw his bottle at the TV and broke the screen. That really pissed Mom off, but of course it was all my fault for angering him in the first place, so I'm the one she hit over the head with another bottle — "

"She *what?*"

Driggs leaned forward and parted his hair, revealing a jagged scar Lex had never noticed. "She lost it. Just kept grabbing them out of the case and throwing them at me while Dad ran upstairs to get his gun."

Now it was Lex's turn to swallow nervously. "Gun?"

Driggs looked down the hallway, then at the floor. "I feel like this is the point where I should confess that it all went by in a blur, that I don't remember anything about it. But — shit, I still do. I remember every second."

He took a deep breath. "Dad came downstairs. Mom was still throwing bottles. I was bleeding all over myself, the couch, the carpet. Dad lurched forward, gun pointed at my head — I knew it was loaded, he always kept it loaded — and started to pull the trigger. But the guy was so damn drunk his finger fumbled and he missed. He missed the *trigger.* I saw my chance, and I yanked it out of his hands — he was so far gone, it wasn't hard. I pointed it at him, and he just started laughing, laughing so hard he began to cough and had to sit down on the couch. But Mom was still hysterical, still throwing those bottles. And when another one hit me across the jaw, that was it. I turned and shot her."

He worked his tongue around his mouth for a moment, then

said, "I'd never shot a gun in my life. I couldn't even tell you what kind of gun it was. But my aim was perfect — I hit her dead between the eyes, and down she went. It took a moment for Dad to realize what happened, but once he did, he started shouting — this awful, growling shit that wasn't even words. He didn't stop until I looked up from her and aimed the gun at him."

Driggs's breathing was getting heavier. "He wasn't scared, exactly. He was more surprised, I think. Like it had never occurred to him that I might have the guts to do something like this. He opened his mouth, and I wish — I *wish* I had stopped for a second to hear what it was he had to say. I wish I knew what it was, that last thought that ran through his brain right before I blew it out the back of his head."

Lex just gawked. She couldn't believe this stuff was coming out of Driggs's mouth.

"Hit him in the same place as my mom, right between the eyes. He was dead before he hit the ground, but I walked up to him, crying and yelling — I have no idea what I was saying — and stood over him. And then I shot him again. And again. And again. And again. And then my bullets were out and I sat down on the floor next to him and cried."

He sucked in air through his teeth. "But not because I was sad, you know? Not even because I was numb, or felt no remorse." He let out the breath he'd taken. "I was crying because I was so, *so* happy they were dead. It was the happiest I'd ever felt. I was delirious." He looked straight at Lex, and this time, there was worry in his eyes. "What kind of person does that make me?"

Lex hadn't spoken in a while, so when she did, her voice cracked. "I don't know. A human person?"

He shook his head. "I sat there for a long time, just grinning and sobbing next to the corpses of my father and my mother. I had no immediate plans. The thought that maybe I should run popped into my head once or twice, but where to? We had no neighbors. We were miles away from the closest town. I had no other family, and no way to support myself. I guess I figured I'd just wait for the cops and let the juvenile corrections system raise me. At least in jail I'd get three meals a day."

A weird whimper came out of Lex. Somehow that last bit seemed to make everything even sadder.

"But then," he said, his eyes brightening slightly, "I heard a voice behind me. He'd let himself in through the front door."

"Uncle Mort?"

Driggs nodded and collapsed back against the wall, spent.

Lex searched for the right thing to say, but she could have sat there until the heat death of the universe and never come up with the right thing. So she went for the obvious.

"I'm so sorry," she said. "I can't even imagine what it's like to have parents like that."

"They weren't parents," he said in a dark voice. "Parents are people who raise you and love you and teach you how to tie your shoes. These were just two savages who happened to live in the same house as me and yell at me to keep it down when I asked if we were having dinner that night."

Lex winced, then winced harder as she thought of all the times she'd complained to Driggs about her own mom nagging to call her. How her parents were so overflowing with love and concern that it was suffocating. What kind of a person did that make *her*?

She put her feet on top of his. "You did the right thing."

He sighed. "No, I didn't. That's what I've been trying to tell you." He leaned forward. "Lex, every single day since I did what I did to them, I have regretted it."

"What?"

"I shouldn't have done it," he said, shaking his head. "No matter what they'd done to me, it wasn't my job to punish them. I should have told someone at school what was going on, gotten them arrested or something. Not killed them."

He ran a hand through his hair, spraying Lex with water droplets. He'd become solid so gradually, she hadn't even noticed. "That joy that I initially felt?" he said. "It didn't last. On the ride to Croak, this bottomless dread sank in that was so dark and excruciating I thought I was going to drop dead myself, fall right off of Mort's motorcycle. Like I said yesterday out on that lake, it felt like a part of my soul had gone bad, so full of evil that it rotted. And I've felt that way ever since, like there's a gangrenous part of me that no one can see, but I'll always know it's there."

Lex was still rationalizing, as per usual. "Okay. First of all, you were acting in self-defense. And second of all, they were monsters!"

"Self-defense? I shot my father point-blank, execution-style. That's not self-defense, Lex, and you know it." He squeezed his eyes shut, then opened them again. "I have hated myself for this. No matter what they'd done to me or how much they deserved it, taking people's lives is wrong. It *felt wrong.* And I guess I flipped out over all those people you Damned because seeing you repeat that same mistake only reminded me of how horrible my own was."

"It wasn't a mistake," she insisted, though the look on his face put doubt in her voice. "And besides, I went after people who were just like your parents — the awful people in the world who deserved to be punished."

"Lex. Think about it. You Crash in to that crime scene and see a man dead on the ground with five — *five* — bullet holes in him and a grinning boy standing over him with a gun. What would you do?"

Her breath caught.

"You'd Damn that kid in a second," he answered for her.

Lex stared at him, numb.

*Yes,* she thought. *I probably would.*

"And you wouldn't even know why he'd done what he'd done. Or that he'd been the innocent one all along until those crucial last moments. Context matters, Lex. That's why you can't be judge, jury, and executioner. Humans make mistakes, which is why humans shouldn't be allowed to make those sorts of calls in the first place. Do you get what I'm saying?"

Lex just stared at the ground, her brain all but fried.

Driggs let the silence happen. He grabbed her hands and squeezed them. They sat, quiet, the sound from the fluorescent lights echoing the tumultuous buzzing in their heads.

Lex spoke first. "No more Damning," she said quietly. "I promise. Not even in the height of — battle, I guess, or whatever this mess is that I've gotten us into. I don't want to damage the Afterlife any more than I already have, and . . . and you're right," she said, relenting. "It's not my call."

A small smile crept onto his face. "I'm right?" he said. "Did I hear that correctly? Can I get it in writing?"

She grinned back. "Don't push it." She rubbed his knuckles, the skin mottled with what she assumed were more scars. "Have you ever gone looking for them in the Afterlife?"

He visibly shuddered. "No. *Hell* no."

She squeezed his hand again without even meaning to. It was the way he looked as if he were dangling off a cliff. She had to hold on to keep him from falling.

"Why didn't you ever tell me?" she asked.

He shrugged. "I dunno. It's hard to talk about. And I felt like a hypocrite, with all the shit I gave you. Plus, I wasn't sure if you'd . . ."

Lex frowned as he trailed off. "What?"

He tensed up. "Be horrified. Never talk to me again."

Lex nearly laughed in his face. After all the things she'd done, he was worried about *her* dumping *him*?

She smooshed his cheeks between her hands. "Here's the deal, you nutball," she said. "I love you. I don't care what you did in the past, because it doesn't matter. I don't care what you'll do in the future, because that won't matter either. Lord knows you've given me the same sort of leniency. I'll always love you. And I'm — "

"Going to fix me," he said, smirking. "I know. You've mentioned it once or twice."

Lex leaned in further to kiss him. She let go of him for a second, though, to try to move closer — and when she did, he slammed right back into transparency.

"Sorry." He reddened, then gave her a rueful half smile. "This doesn't usually happen, I swear."

Lex tried to laugh, but it didn't quite make it out of her throat. "It's getting harder to stay solid when I'm not touching you, isn't it?"

His jaw tightened. "Yeah."

A voice reverberated down the hallway — possibly Ferbus,

and possibly something about making sure the lovebirds were using protection.

Driggs rolled his eyes. "Well, we should probably go put a stop to that. Plus I don't want to get eaten by rodents of unusual size, or whatever it is that guards these creepy hallways."

Lex agreed. They got to their feet and started walking.

"Thank you for telling me," she said after they'd gone a few paces.

"Thank *you* for not vomiting in disgust," he replied. "You're the only one I've ever told besides Mort."

"So he just showed up, huh? Out of nowhere?"

"As is his way. Guess he used his little radar thingy. Except — " He furrowed his eyebrows. "Except there were no little locator triangles anywhere near where I grew up."

Lex frowned. That was strange. "And he just — what? Told you to come with him?"

"Yeah. After having a debate with himself about whether or not I was too young. I guess the pro side won out, so I went."

"And your parents didn't object," Lex said, repeating what Driggs had told her when she'd asked if they had a problem with him leaving. They were a little too dead to object.

"But why *did* he take you, when you were two years younger than the normal Junior age?" she asked, something nudging around inside her brain. "Obviously you had the requisite, um, *talents* — but if you didn't show up on the locator and you were only fourteen, why did he bother to show up in the first place?"

Driggs shrugged. "I've always wondered that myself, but never asked. Never talked about it again. Never even found out who Killed and Culled them."

Lex looked at him. "You think it was Uncle Mort?"

Driggs stopped cold. He just blinked at her, the answers to so many questions finally clicking into place. "Whoa. I never thought of that."

"I bet he saw you during his shift, then came back for you later on that night."

"But why?"

"I don't know if you've noticed, but Uncle Mort's got an entire Home Depot's worth of screws loose. Who knows why he does anything he does?"

"Yeah." He started to walk again, but his eyes were still blinking, not really focusing on the hallway in front of him. "Who knows."

||||||

They needn't have worried about Ferbus teasing them when they rejoined the group. He'd already moved on to whining.

"You said the escalators and elevators were off-limits to us, right?" he asked Skyla. She had opened another door, beyond which was a metallic spiral staircase so tall they couldn't see the top. "So that means — "

"Stairs it is," Skyla said, chipper. "And the floors here are slightly taller than those in normal buildings — "

Ferbus assumed a hyperventilating position, his hands on his knees. "Oh no," Skyla said, concern splashing across her face. "Is he anemic? Clinically asthmatic?"

"No," Uncle Mort said, thwacking Ferbus on the head as he started climbing the stairs. "Just lazy."

"Clinically lazy!" Ferbus wheezed.

They went slowly, at least. Uncle Mort and Skyla were up at

the front of the pack, talking in low whispers. Occasionally a giggle would flutter down the staircase. An honest-to-God *giggle*. From Uncle *Mort*.

"This is too weird," Lex said to Driggs, suppressing another gag. "I mean, are they a thing? Have they been going out underneath our noses the whole time?"

Driggs shrugged. "I've never heard anything about her before," he said, then added in a sour voice, "but we all know how good Mort is at keeping secrets."

"They just seem so . . . close. What was all that business about the pool table?"

"I think the less we know about the pool table, the better."

"Since it's not remotely any of your business," Uncle Mort said from up ahead, "I'm inclined to agree."

Lex cringed. "How does he *do* that?"

"Skyla and I," Uncle Mort said, loud enough for the whole group to hear, "have been friends for many years. Ever since we were Juniors, as you were so cleverly able to discover. Since we're not able to meet in person very often, we're enjoying the opportunity to catch up a bit. If that's all right with you, Your Excellency."

Lex scrunched up her nose. She wanted to argue, but he was being perfectly reasonable. She hated when he did that.

But there was something niggling inside of her — not jealousy, exactly. She didn't own Uncle Mort; he was an adult, free to have himself a lady friend if he wanted to. It was just that ever since she'd come to Croak, she'd been the only real family in his life, and they'd grown quite close, and it's not that she was opposed to sharing him, but —

Okay, it was jealousy.

"How did you get away with it, anyway?" she said even louder than before as they continued up the spiral staircase. She could at least be distracting. That was maybe her best talent of all. "I mean, you guys smashed a jellyfish tank. Isn't that a felony?"

Uncle Mort and Skyla exchanged irritated yet resigned glances, as they were trapped on a spiral staircase with these kids and the only real way to dodge any questions would involve hurling themselves over the railing. Though judging by Uncle Mort's face, he was giving it some serious consideration.

"We were acquitted," he explained, "of all charges."

"What? How?"

"Because only one of us took the blame."

"The thing is," Skyla jumped in, "the mission was a failure. The president considered it an act of terrorism, not a wake-up call. As soon as we four figured out which way the foul winds were blowing, we made a decision: Three of us would apologize for our crimes, citing brainwashing or Amnesia or whatever would get us off the hook, and thus remain in the Grimsphere so that we could continue to secretly take down the system from within." She paused, and when she spoke again, her voice was thicker. "And the other would confess everything, claim that they worked alone, and get the full brunt of the punishment — which turned out to be exile and a full memory wipe of everything having to do with the Grimsphere's existence."

Lex had inched up closer to the front of the pack; she could see that Skyla was struggling not to cry.

"The one whose face was covered in the photo," Lex said, remembering. "That's the one who took the fall?"

"Her name was Abby. The brains of the whole organization." Uncle Mort's footfall on the stairs seemed to get a little heavier.

"Smashing the tank was all her idea. The rest of us were behind it, one hundred percent, but it was her baby. And when it all went bad, she decided that she had to be the one to take the fall."

Lex considered this. Getting exiled and memory wiped was harrowing, but it sure was preferable to the Hole.

But she didn't want to think about the Hole again, ever. "Okay, but that still doesn't explain how you got elected, especially with such damaged reputations."

"You know the expression 'keep your friends close and your enemies even closer'?" Uncle Mort said. "Well, the president might as well have it tattooed across her forehead. After we all graduated to the Senior level, split up across the cities, and decided to run for office, she actually *encouraged* people to vote for us, gave all three of us her full endorsement. She knew we were planning something."

Skyla grinned. "The woman isn't completely stupid."

"The problem is that the Grimsphere's opinion is split," Uncle Mort said. He was talking to Lex as an adult now; she liked when he did that. "There are some who have remained loyal to us mayors, who believe what we're saying and agree that something needs to change. But they do so quietly, without attracting the wrath of people on the other side — like Norwood and Heloise and the president, who are more concerned with preserving their way of life than salvaging the life that comes after. But we happen to think our cause is important — because, you know, it's *saving the goddamn Afterlife* and all — and so, yes, we are willing to take some drastic measures to accomplish our goal. And the president knows it."

"Hang on," said Driggs, who'd joined Lex up in the front and was trying to follow this just as intently as she was. "So the president *knows* we're trying to destroy the portal?"

"Oh, definitely," said Skyla. "She knows full well what we're trying to do. She might even have told Norwood."

"You sort of left that part out before," Driggs said.

"But what they don't know is how many allies we have around the Grimsphere, internationally. They don't know the full scope of our plan. And they don't know that in less than twenty-four hours, Knell will no longer be president."

The Juniors gaped at one another. "I thought you said we *weren't* going to kill the president!" Lex screeched.

Uncle Mort and Skyla rolled their eyes. "We're not going to kill the president," he said. "We're just going to overthrow her."

"But . . . won't a lack of leadership cause even more problems?"

"Oh, there won't be a lack," Uncle Mort said as they reached a landing. "The Grimsphere government works a little differently than the American government. We don't have vice presidents, but there's still a line of succession. If the president becomes incapacitated or is rendered unable to fulfill the duties of the office, the presidency automatically goes to the runner-up candidate in the most recent presidential election."

"And who is that?"

But he wasn't listening to her. He was looking at the door they'd stopped at, and so was Skyla.

"Here's our next stop," she said, entering the code into the keypad. The light switched from red to green. "And where we part ways."

"Oh, good," said Elysia as the Juniors filed into the hallway behind Skyla. "So *this* is where we're going to die."

Lex could tell that Uncle Mort had no intention of answering her question. But as she followed the other Juniors inside, she kept her eyes on him, especially since he had such a funny look on his face. He was avoiding her gaze, even giving Pandora a smirk as she passed him, but Lex had seen that look many times before. The one that meant he was holding in a really, really big secret.

But his being next in line for the presidency may have been his biggest one yet.

## 10

Elysia worriedly grabbed Lex as they made their way down the long green hallway. Two doors were at the end of it — one labeled HUB, the other blank. "What are we supposed to do now?" Elysia asked. "Do you think they've found the unconscious guards yet?"

Skyla laughed. "Oh, hell no. When they find the guards and realize you're loose in the building, you'll know it."

Elysia squeezed Lex's arm tighter. "Yeah. The bullet through my heart will probably be a pretty good clue."

"Here we are!" Skyla said, gesturing to a brightened wall. "Front row seats!"

As the Juniors got closer, they saw that the right-hand wall up ahead wasn't a wall at all. It was a piece of rectangular glass that stretched about nine feet wide. The Juniors ran up to look through it, then ducked down.

"There are people down there!" Lex hissed. "They saw us! They looked right at us! They — why are you not panicking?" she asked as Skyla leaned over Lex's crouched form and peered through the glass.

"It's a one-way mirror," Skyla explained. "They can't see us, but we can see them."

"Oh."

Feeling dumb, Lex stood back up and looked through the

glass at the hub below. Spread out across a space the size of a hockey arena was a sea of activity not unlike the one found on the trading floor of the New York Stock Exchange. In one section, Ether Traffic Controllers sat at their Smacks and typed, but these people were nothing like the relatively quiet and studious employees in Croak and DeMyse; every one of the Necropolitan Etceteras was shouting instructions — at each other, at Field Grims about to go out on their shifts, and at the director, or the man Lex assumed to be the director. He was leaning against the front of his desk atop a raised platform, his arms crossed as he surveyed the action below. Flat screens on the walls displayed a list of constantly updating times, like an airport departures board — probably those of the Field Grims out on their shifts. Wires from the Smacks connected to a jellyfish tank that took up a floor-to-ceiling section of the wall; the tank was at least triple the size of those in Croak and DeMyse. Combined.

Another area of the cavernous room was clearly the Field, where the Grims scythed in and out to their targets — but unlike the literal Field found in Croak, it was a maze of cubicles. Lex watched as pairs of Grims found their way into empty stalls, picked up phones to confirm their departures with the Etceteras, then swiped their scythes through the air and disappeared into the ether.

A glass room shrouded in spiderwebs had to be the Lair, and yet another space was reserved for the tunnels, of which there were several; and therefore, no single line of Grims waited to make their deposits. Each team returning from a shift simply chose one of the many available circles set into the wall, opened the little door, and sent the Vessels on their way to the Afterlife, the entrance to which was conspicuously missing.

"They go all the way to the top of the building?" Ferbus asked.

"Yep." Skyla pointed at a series of pipes snaking their way up the wall and disappearing into the ceiling, like pneumatic tubes at a drive-through bank. "The citizens of Necropolis aren't allowed anywhere *near* our vault to the Afterlife. Since it's located in the president's office, she's the only one with access to it."

"So you don't have any Afterlife Relations people?" Elysia asked, baffled at how her former job wasn't even a job here.

"We don't need them," Skyla replied. "We're all Afterlife Relations people here."

"How's that, if you don't have access to the vault?"

"Well —"

*BEEP! BEEP! BEEP!*

An earsplitting alarm sounded as the hub became filled with a red warning light. The regular lights came back on a few seconds later, but were now punctuated by blasts of emergency strobes. The people on the floor jumped in surprise, then turned their eyes toward the flat screens, where President Knell's face had appeared.

"Citizens of Necropolis," she boomed, like the Evil Pantsuit Overlord that she was, "I may have been a bit . . . hasty with my earlier announcement. The outlaw Grims from Croak have indeed breached the walls of Necropolis as previously reported, but they are not currently in custody. Repeat: They are *not* in custody." Lex could tell by the tightness of her mouth how pissed she was to have to admit that failure. "Necropolis is now on lockdown. No one comes in, no one goes out. I realize this may be an inconvenience to some of you, but trust me, this is for your own safety."

Lex snorted. "She sounds just like Norwood."

"Our best teams are on top of the situation," Knell continued, "and are sweeping the building as we speak. But we need
your eyes and ears as well; be sure to report any sightings, and
we'll keep you updated as much as we can. But sleep easy, Necropolis." Here, she actually clicked her finger like a gun. "We'll
get 'em."

"Nice touch," Skyla muttered as the screen went back to the
departure times. She turned back to the Croakers. "So this is it:
You're on your own."

"Where will you go?" asked Pip.

"I need to get back to my control room. I lost a lot of valuable
time when those nasty Croaker fugitives knocked me out." She
grinned, flashing her holey teeth. "Try and stick to the Backways.
Remember, no one knows about them, and neither do I. Wink-
wink." She winked anyway. "But when you do have to go out into
the open, make your routes as erratic as you can. I'll do my best to
play dumb, but the president has never fully trusted me, and
she'll catch on the second I show any hesitation. You *have* to stay
one step ahead of me at all times."

"While at the same time avoiding civilians because they're obligated to report us on sight," said Lex.

"Of course they are," said Skyla. "Standard protocol."

"How do you know so much about the protocol?" Lex all but
growled. She certainly wasn't making this easy for them.

"I wrote the protocol, kid." She yanked a copy of the schematics out of her bag. "Now, take one last good look at these and
memorize as much as you — "

"Wait, we can't take them with us?" Elysia said.

"And risk the guards finding them in your possession if you
get caught? Proving that you had help from me and ruining our

operation in the process? I think not." She went back to the blue-prints. "Now. In each of the three sectors the guards will start at the bottom, search to its top, then continuously sweep back down and up again. My team, on the other hand, will be exclu-sively focused on tailing you. All the way up to the top, if every-thing goes to plan. You burst into the office, I burst in after you, and then . . . it's portal-destroying time."

Uncle Mort nodded. "Right."

"So I'll see you there," she said simply, packing the schematics away. "Good luck, you guys." She exchanged one last look with Uncle Mort, then headed out the door labeled HUB.

Lex looked back at the pandemonium below. Skyla had ap-peared in the room and was walking down a set of stairs, yelling for calm.

"This better all be worth it," Lex muttered.

Of course, Uncle Mort overheard her. He always overheard her. "You don't think saving the Afterlife is worth it?"

"Of course I do," Lex said. "I just mean that I hope it works. Sealing the portals, then Annihilating Grotton — *if* we get the Wrong Book back, that is." She sighed. "It's a lot. A million things can go wrong. And let's say we do everything right — the After-life erosion is halted, we fix it entirely with the reset — but then what? Who's to say history won't repeat itself one day? I mean, I'm not Damning anymore," she affirmed, shooting a look at Driggs, "but in the future another Grim might come along who can. Isn't it possible for someone to undo everything we're doing to repair it? And then the Afterlife erosion will start all over again?"

Uncle Mort was quiet. "Well, it's not likely," he said. "But yes, it's possible."

"Well, then—" Lex grunted in frustration. "Isn't there a way for us to fix everything permanently?"

He rubbed his chin. "I've been asking myself these questions for years, Lex. But as far as I can tell, no. There's no way to fix it forever. There's no way to prevent some bad-seed Grims from coming along down the line and committing a whole heap of new violations, trashing the Afterlife all over again. All we can do is fix it as best we can and hope that future generations don't shit the bed as much as ours has."

Lex grunted again. She hated feeling so helpless. "What about the Wrong Book?" she said. "Maybe there's something in there that can help!"

"Well, I doubt it, but—" Uncle Mort looked intrigued for a moment, then shook his head. "We're out of luck on that front until we get the book back from Norwood. Unless Bang already found something useful in it and didn't tell us," he said with a laugh, turning to look at her.

Bang didn't look back. She was reading something—something that looked a lot like a handful of papers with rough edges. As if they'd been ripped out of a book.

She signed something.

"Not yet," a smiling Pip translated. "But she's working on it."

They pounded up about twenty more stories before stopping, and only then because Ferbus's lungs had collapsed. Or so he claimed.

"Please," he gasped, sprawling across the stairs. "Two minutes. So they can reinflate."

Elysia jogged up and down around him in a spritely manner. "Kind of makes you wish you got outside a little more instead of spending so many hours on the computer, huh?"

"If said exercise involved throwing your sporty ass into a lake, then yes."

"That's really more for building upper-arm strength," Driggs said. "Not so much endurance."

"You shut your ugly face, Casper," Ferbus countered, giving him a dirty look. Driggs had figured out yet another ghost perk: while the others had to lug themselves up the stairs step by agonizing step, he was able to float right up the center of the stairwell without exerting an ounce of effort.

"You going to let him talk to me like that?" Driggs said to Lex. "Defend my honor, woman."

"Defend your own honor," Lex said, wiping her forehead. It seemed that the Croakers' steady diet of junk food was doing none of them any favors.

Except, inexplicably, Pandora. "You wusses," she said, shaking a gnarled finger at them. "When I was your age, I could do a one-handed pushup with ten canned hams on my back."

"Canned hams?" Pip asked.

"There was a war going on!" she shouted, as if this explained something.

They soon came to a landing with an unmarked door. Uncle Mort peered at it, then up the stairwell. "Okay, I've got good news and I've got bad news."

"I'm going to call shenanigans on you right there," Ferbus said, panting. "That's never true. It's always bad news and worse news."

"You think it's bad news that we're almost done with stairs?"

"No more stairs?" Ferbus blinked. "That is *great* news."

"Well, that's the problem — we're not going up any more stairs because, if memory of the schematics serves me, there *are* no stairs that go from sector to sector. Probably a security feature, designed to keep intruders contained."

They all had a hearty laugh at this.

Uncle Mort scratched his head. "So I'm not sure if we should exit here or keep going up to the next one. We're just a few stories away from Residential, and that's where it'll get dicey. There aren't as many Backways in that sector, plus there are a lot more people around, all of them on the lookout for us. And with most citizens trained in basic security protocols, it'll be like running headlong into a small army." He drummed his fingers on the door, thinking. "Up, or out?"

"Come on, it can't be that hard," said Lex, impatient.

He raised an eyebrow at her. "You want to call the shots, kiddo?" he said. "Be my guest."

They all stared at her. "Um — " She looked at the door, then up at the remaining stairs, then at Driggs, who was trying not to burst out laughing at the pickle she'd just gotten herself into.

"Up," she eventually said with gusto, trying to hide that it was a total guess. "Keep going up."

"Up it is, Magellan," Uncle Mort said, patting her a little too hard on the back.

The crew gathered their stuff and resumed their climb. A dozen or so stories later, the stairwell ended in a single door with a dusty keypad. Uncle Mort frowned. "Hmm . . ."

Driggs whispered something to Pip, who leaned forward and typed in the code.

*Beep.* The light went from red to green.

"What?" Driggs said when everyone gaped at him. "I watched Skyla type it in. I'm not *totally* useless."

"She must not have changed the codes yet, to give us a little head start," Uncle Mort said with such admiration in his voice that Lex couldn't help but scowl.

*At least they can't make googly-eyes at each other now,* she thought.

And then, *Wow, I am truly an awful person.*

Uncle Mort grabbed the door handle. "Hang on," said Driggs. "We have no idea where we are. Let me peek through to get a sense of what we're dealing with."

He disappeared into the door, only to return moments later, scowling. "Yeah, we're boned. It's the public escalators."

"Oops," said Lex.

"Then we go back down to the last door," Elysia said. "It's not far."

"Actually, I think we should stay," Uncle Mort said, rummaging in his bag. "The escalators are the last place anyone would expect us to go, all out in the open like that. Driggs, you go out and watch for a break in traffic. Once it's clear, give the signal, and we'll scramble onto the escalator as quickly and as quietly as we can."

"Are you nuts?" said Lex. "People are going to recognize us!"

He withdrew his hand from his bag, something golden glinting between his fingers. "Not with this."

"The bubonic football?" Lex said. "What are we going to do, sneeze them to death?"

"Oh, if only our paltry weapons were as destructive as Lex's diabolical wit," Uncle Mort countered, deadpan.

"I'd say diabolical wit is something that runs in the family," said Pandora.

"Don't forget the superiority complexes," Ferbus added.

"And the bossiness!" Pip threw in.

Uncle Mort cleared his throat. "As fun as it might be for us to all sit here and pick apart all the delightfully whimsical foibles of the Bartleby family, we've kind of got a war to fight here, remember? Let's go do that." He pulled a tiny pin halfway out of the football and nodded at Driggs. "Okay, go."

Driggs stuck his head back out the door, waited for about twenty seconds, then barked, "All clear! Go!"

The Croakers piled through the door and onto the waiting escalator. Uncle Mort was the last one out, gathering them together into a close-knit huddle. The door shut behind them as they ascended.

"Fire in the hole," he said.

Out came the pin. The device dropped to his feet, teetering on the edge of the step he was standing on. And just as Lex was starting to think that maybe it wasn't really a storage device for one of the deadliest diseases in human history, but instead a grenade of some kind, the gold device emitted —

A bubble.

As in a dead ringer for the kind that come out of children's bubble wands, a wobbly hemisphere that surrounded all eight of them perfectly.

"Impressive, Mort," Ferbus said, reaching for the membrane. "Do you also moonlight as a children's birthday party magician, or — "

"Don't touch it!" Uncle Mort said, grabbing Ferbus's hand

and yanking it away from the surface. "No one touch it, or it'll affect us too."

"Affect us?" Lex finally caught on. "It's Amnesia?"

"Yep." He picked up the football and stuffed it back into his bag. "But unlike Amnesia smoke bombs, which dissipate and fill the space in which they're detonated, the Amnesia grenade cloaks only those within its blast radius."

"But if there's no smoke," Lex said, barely moving her mouth as she stared at a woman only a few steps down on the escalator, a woman who happened to be reading a copy of *The Obituary*, with Lex's photo on the front page, "then people can still *see* us."

"Doesn't matter. As long as we stay in the bubble, they won't remember who we are. They'll forget that our pictures have been splashed all over the news and that they're supposed to be looking for us. See? It's already slipped their minds."

The woman looked up for a second, her eyes landing squarely on Lex. She gave her a polite smile, then went back to reading all about those dangerous Juniors who were tearing up the Grimsphere and must be reported immediately.

"Well, great," said Ferbus. "So now what do we do?"

Uncle Mort shrugged. "Enjoy the view."

And once the initial terror of exposing themselves dissipated, Lex had to admit: the view was nice.

As the escalator carried them up the curved side of the building, Lex looked out across the horizon. Kansas was so flat it might as well have been the moon — except that even the moon had craters. Kansas just had corn. Corn and grass and . . . darkening clouds. Lex frowned. Weren't there a lot of tornadoes in Kansas?

She looked up at one of the mounted television sets along the escalator's path that displayed the time, temperature, and various news items of the day. She caught the weather — clear skies? — but turned away when her photo popped up yet again. Something about the "HIGHLY DANGEROUS" warning scrawled beneath it made her skin crawl.

Looking out the window again, all she could see was more flatness, but those stormy clouds were kind of cool — they drifted by so peacefully, as if they were moving with minds of their own. One of them even looked like Cordy.

Wait a minute.

One of them *was* Cordy.

Lex gasped and almost slapped her hands against the glass before remembering not to touch the membrane. "Look!" she hissed to the rest of the group. "There are souls out there!"

Uncle Mort gave her a sly smile. "Indeed there are."

"But you said the vault is all the way up on the top floor!"

"The *vault* is all the way up on the top floor. But the atrium part of the Afterlife is all around us. That's why Necropolis doesn't need Afterlife Liaisons. Every Grim in the city has that job."

"What the . . ." Lex returned to the glass and looked more closely this time. What she had mistaken for clouds — and what she had earlier mistaken for a fog surrounding the whole of Necropolis — were actually souls. Up close, they were just as solid as they were inside Croak's atrium. Some were looking inside, some were chatting among themselves, and some were conversing with the live Necropolitans who were riding the elevator, just as Cordy was trying to do.

"Numbnuts!" she was saying, her voice coming through the glass as clearly as if she were inside. "Over here!"

"Right, sorry," Lex said, shaking the cobwebs of confusion. "Cordy. Hi."

"Dude, this place is Swankytown USA," Cordy said, her big eyes running up and down the height of Necropolis. "I mean, the size, the sophistication — the luxury apartments! You wouldn't believe how many people have pools, Lex."

"Shh," Lex hissed. The lady was looking at them again. "We're trying to go unnoticed. And how are you even seeing us right now?"

"Amnesia doesn't work on dead people," Uncle Mort said. "And I already told you, our fellow escalator passengers have no idea who we are. For the time being. As long as they stay put and no one enters the bubble, we're fine, so let's make the most of this opportunity. Cordy, what can you — "

"Oof — " Cordy huffed as Tut slammed into her. She looked angry for a second, then beamed, turning to Lex. "He's like a little puppy dog, following me everywhere — agh!" she yelled as her camel bumped into her other side. "And Lumpy, of course, feistier than ever — oww!" Poe swooped in as well, kicking her in the shins. She glared at him. "And lest we forget, Mr. Sunshine himself."

"They took my best ascot!" Poe spat at Lex. "They took it and they won't give it back and now my neck is *most chilled!*"

"His neck is most chilled, Cordy," Lex said. "Give it back."

"But Tut looks so good in it! Honeybunch, pose."

Tut, wearing said ascot and not very much else, flexed his muscles. "See?" said Cordy. "It brings out the fullness in his lips! And pants."

"Cordy," said Lex. "Ew."

*"Fine."* Cordy yanked the ascot off Tut's throat and handed it

back to Poe, who held it between his fingers at an arm's length, a most distasteful look upon his face.

"Cordy," Uncle Mort interjected, "helpful things. Please."

"Sure, yeah," Cordy said, still staring at her honeybunch's biceps. "What do you want to know?"

"You can see into all the windows, right? What's going on?"

"Well, ever since that alarm went off, everyone's been going schizoid. The place is swarming with guards — all looking for you, I assume?"

They nodded.

"Well done. I think so far you've thrown them, but..." She looked up. "They're all over the place, especially the next few floors."

"Residential." Uncle Mort nodded. "That's where they'll be thickest. What about near the top, in Executive?"

Cordy shrugged. "I don't know — the windows are blocked to us for the uppermost twenty floors or so. Sorry."

"Damn, she's good." The sparkle in his eye left little doubt that he was talking about Skyla. When Lex looked offended, he crossed his arms. "Hey, if we were defending this building instead of attacking it, you'd be very impressed right now."

Cordy pointed at him and gave Lex a questioning look.

"Uncle Mort has a girlfriend," Lex explained.

"Whaa?" Cordy said.

"Don't even ask. It's beyond our powers of human comprehension."

"Gross!"

"They even have a weird pool table euphemism for the dirty stuff."

"Super gross!"

"Here's an idea, Cordy," Uncle Mort said, his irritation barely contained. "Why don't you make yourself useful and keep a look-out for us?"

Cordy pouted. "Fine." She leaned in to Lex and pointed back at her uncle. "I want to hear more about the lovefest later."

"You really don't."

Once Cordy left, Uncle Mort nodded as they passed a hidden door similar to the one through which they'd entered. "We've just spiraled one complete revolution around the building," he said. "So we've gone up about five stories, I think. Five more, and we can get out — there should be another Backways access door there, unless —"

"*Hola!*"

All eyes flew back to the glass, where Riqo was waving cheerfully. "Pipito! Everyone! You are safe!"

The Croakers weren't as enthusiastic. "You're dead?" Pip cried, his voice choked. "You're *dead!*"

Riqo waved this minor detail away. "I am fine. I did what I always wanted: to help out in some way, to matter. And here you are, alive and fighting the good fight. It was worth it."

Lex's mouth was moving, but nothing was coming out. She never knew what to say in situations like this. She wished she had a set of greeting cards at the ready, but Hallmark probably didn't make any that said *Thank you for giving up your life so that me and my friends could escape! It was SO appreciated. XOXO!*

"What happened back there?" Elysia asked him. "When we left DeMyse?"

Riqo's face lit up. "You were no longer there to see it, but once Zara stabbed me, Broomie opened up a very large can of the whoop-ass until Zara finally Crashed out to look for you. After

that, Broomie and LeRoy teamed up and have been working together around the clock, making many preparations for the destruction of the portals." He shook his head. "Sad, no? But it will
all be for the best."

Pip leaned in and whispered something to Riqo, who winked
as he floated away from the glass — presumably back toward
DeMyse. "Good luck, Croakers! Adios!"

Lex watched him fade into the horizon, then flinched as she
spotted a bright flash of light — a metallic reflection, maybe?

"What's wrong?" Driggs asked.

She shook her head. It was gone. Either that or she was losing
it. "I thought I saw —"

"Good afternoon, Necropolis." The flat screens once again
flashed President Knell's giant floating head. Her voice was still
calm and friendly, but with a notable twinge of frustration. "Just
wanted to give y'all an update on the Croakers. Still not in custody, but my field teams assure me that they're hot on the trail."

The Juniors nervously looked at Uncle Mort, who gave his
head a dismissive shake. "You don't see any guards, do you? She's
full of shit."

"However," Knell continued, "I wanted to take this opportunity to address the Croakers personally, should they happen to be
listening. In fact, I hope they are."

Uncle Mort tensed. Cordy drifted back into view, watching
the screen through the glass.

Knell knit her fingers under her chin, a string of matching
green pearls clattering around her wrist. "In particular, I'd like to
wag my tongue a bit at Lex, the ringleader of this little group of
rebels. Yes, Lex, you: the one responsible for terrorizing the
Grimsphere and the outside world alike with your senseless

Damning sprees. Oh, sure, I could go into a whole lecture spouting this and that about what a loathsome, heinous scourge on the planet you are, but you know what, Lex? I'm gonna do you one better." Abruptly, Knell's face disappeared. The screen flickered back to life a second later, this time showing a video feed of two bound figures on the floor of a darkened room. The woman was mostly in shadow, unidentifiable under that blindfold —

But Lex and Cordy could have recognized that goatee and shiny bald head anywhere.

## 11

"I have your parents, Lex," Knell continued in a voice-over, the image of the Bartlebys still on the screen. The room they were in was stark and dirty-looking—the lighting seemed vaguely familiar to Lex, but she couldn't place it. "My proposition is simple: Their freedom for yours. Turn yourself in, and I'll let them go."

Lex and Cordy looked at each other, their faces mirrored in terror.

Knell's self-satisfied grin filled the screen once again. "As for the rest of you, *do* have a glorious day!"

Lex felt sick. She grabbed the escalator's railing, the heights and motion suddenly making her dizzy. The Juniors shot her scared glances, Driggs trying to hug her but not solid enough to do so.

"They'll be okay." Uncle Mort grabbed Lex's shoulders, then glanced at Cordy, addressing them both. "She's not going to hurt them. She needs them for—"

"Leverage," Lex spat again, for the millionth time. "Yes, I know. I'm so fucking sick of that word. And how it's constantly being used to describe my loved ones."

"Hey," Driggs said, "she protected them herself by putting them on the air. She can't hurt them now, not with the city as witness, right?"

Uncle Mort nodded. "And if we needed an even better reason to storm her office, she just gave it to us."

"But what happened to Lazlo?" Elysia said. "Wasn't he guarding them?"

"We have to assume he's been" — Uncle Mort paused to reword — "compromised."

Lex was shaking her head. "I *told* them to get out of the house! God, if Knell doesn't kill them, I'll kill them myself!"

Driggs raised an eyebrow.

"Okay," she said, cringing, "that was maybe the poorest choice of words ever."

He smirked. "And you've made a *lot* of poor choices."

"Cordy," said Uncle Mort, "I need you to spread the word: Once we start to seal the portals, the Afterlife is going to feel the repercussions. Until every one of them is closed, things will probably get worse in there, so you souls are going to have to deal with the fallout. Patch up things where you can and just try to hold it together long enough for us to do our thing."

"You got it," Cordy said.

Kloo swooped in, breathless. "Now is probably a bad time to tell you this," she said, "but there are guards coming. You need to get out of here."

While the rest of the group scrambled to leave, Lex turned back to Cordy. "I'll find them, okay?"

"I know you will." Cordy gave her a pained smile. "You loathsome, heinous scourge on the planet."

Lex grinned. If Knell intended to discourage them with her threats, the woman was stupider than she looked; all Lex could think about right now was kicking some serious Necropolitan ass.

Uncle Mort was doing some calculations. "We're still a couple of floors away," he told them. "And with the speed of the escalators versus the speed of the guards, I think the guards will reach us before we reach the door."

"So we make a run for it," Lex said.

"I don't think that's — "

"Go!" she commanded, bursting out of the bubble.

Stunned, the Juniors watched her go. Then, realizing they really had no choice but to follow their unhinged colleague, they pounded up the escalator after her.

As Kloo had promised, a team of guards was waiting, all decked out in those black uniforms and aiming stun guns. Lex hoped that one of them might be Skyla, but a quick assessment of their relative sizes affirmed that she wasn't among them.

The mountain of a guard who'd arrested Uncle Mort, however, was. "FREEZE!" he shouted.

Lex could see the door now, slowly coming into view on the right. They just had to stall for a few more seconds; then they could make a break for it.

Drawing on what must have been a burst of adrenaline — because it sure as hell wasn't a burst of good judgment — Lex thrust her hand into her bag and grabbed the first thing her fingers touched. "*You* freeze!" she yelled at the guards, holding Cordy's glowing Spark high above her head.

*Perfect.* Since Sparks were Uncle Mort's own invention and had never been produced outside of Croak, the Necropolitans wouldn't know what on earth it was. "You do *not* want to be held responsible for what happens if I throw this," she growled in a voice that she hoped was as confident and threatening as it sounded in her head.

The big guard shot a glance at the guard to his right, who gave a shrug. A lengthy pause ensued. "Lower your weapon!" he eventually yelled back, though he sounded uncertain.

Lex grinned. "Oh, I don't think you want me to do *that*."

The guard shifted his stance but made no moves to come any closer. "Stay where you are," he ordered.

The door was now within reach. "No, I don't think we will," she answered.

And then, in a surprising and not altogether wise turn of events, Lex attempted to kick down the door.

Even more surprising, it actually worked.

"In!" she shouted at her crew, who wasted no time in obeying. The guards stood at bay, still unsure about what to do; this type of situation apparently wasn't covered by Skyla's standard protocol.

Lex counted heads as the Juniors hurried through the door. Just as she was about to leap in herself, she paused. They were one short.

She whirled around. The head guard had grabbed Uncle Mort and was twisting his arm behind his back. "Go!" her uncle shouted, waving her on with his free hand.

But Lex finally did what the guards had commanded. She froze.

"Keep going!" Uncle Mort insisted, his face contorted in pain as the guard pulled tighter.

Lex blinked once, then snapped out of it. Why had she even hesitated?

In perhaps the first graceful movement of Lex's life, she darted over to the guard, raised Cordy's Spark, and brought it down on his skull. It shattered. The Spark's light went out, glass shards flew everywhere, the guard's forehead was covered in blood —

And Uncle Mort wrenched out of his grasp. They'd passed the door during their struggle, so he pushed Lex down the escalator toward the exit. Lex took one last look outside the windows at her stunned sister, then wedged herself through the narrow opening and into the green corridor.

After slamming the door shut, Uncle Mort pulled a crowbar out of his bag and wedged it into the gap underneath. "That should hold them," he said.

Lex sank to the floor to take a breather, but Uncle Mort wasn't going to let that happen. "What were you thinking?" he said, shaking her shoulders. "There's not a machine on earth powerful enough to calculate the number of ways that could have gone wrong!"

"But it didn't," she said, surprising even herself with the devilish twinge in her voice. "So maybe you shouldn't be giving me any crap about it."

He held her gaze, his jaw working. She couldn't tell what was going on in that expression of his — fear and anger, surely, with a healthy dash of disappointment — but at the moment, it didn't matter. They hadn't gotten captured, they'd bought themselves some time, and they were still on their way up the tower.

"Or maybe," she said, her lips curling up, "you're just jealous because I thought of it before you did."

His face barely changed, but it was enough for Lex to tell that she'd cracked him — his eyes crinkled slightly, and he let her go with only a mildly irritated sigh. "Come on," he said, heading down the hall. "This way."

But the Juniors were too busy fawning over Lex. Driggs was practically drooling, but Elysia was the one who grabbed her elbow. "Lex. *Lex*. That was so amazing! How did you do that? I didn't know you could kick down a door. Did you know she could kick down a door?" she asked Ferbus.

"I didn't think she could *open* a door," he said.

"Ugh, you're so mean." She turned back to Lex. "But seriously! Awesome! And you did it all without Damning anyone!"

Lex blinked. "Yeah, I guess I did. I broke Cordy's Spark, though."

"Well, that doesn't matter. It's only a measurement of life force, not her life force itself. She'll be fine."

Lex tried not to think about how dark the Afterlife was getting. *I hope so.*

After darting through a few more Backways, Uncle Mort ground them to another halt. "Here," he said, looking at the wall. "This should be about right." He got down on his knees, pulled a small pickax out of his bag, and chiseled a wad of rock out of the wall and onto the floor. "Grab a breather. This might take a while."

The Juniors were understandably confused, but they didn't hesitate to take him up on his suggestion. "Hey, Shawshank," Ferbus said to him. "You know this sort of thing takes like twenty years, right?"

"It'll take longer if he has to pry the ax out of your chest first," said Driggs with a grin.

"And then clean up all that sticky leprechaun blood," Lex added.

Ferbus rolled his eyes. "My *GOD,* you two are hilarious." He turned to Elysia. "Smack me if we ever get that awful."

"But I smack you so often," she said, "how will you know that's what I'm smacking you for?"

"We shall work out a smacking code."

"So what's going on here?" Driggs asked, pointing between the two of them. "You guys finally bumping uglies now, or what?"

Elysia crossed her arms. "Not in those exact terms, no. And what do you mean 'finally'? Ninety-eight percent of the time I've known him, I've hated him."

"Well, that's just not true at all," Driggs replied.

Elysia frowned and stomped to the other side of the hallway, muttering, "Lex said the same thing."

Lex watched her go, then switched her gaze to the youngest pair of Juniors, both sitting on the floor a few yards away. Bang was still poring over the pages she'd ripped out of the Wrong Book, and Pip was across from her, staring absent-mindedly at the wall.

Lex sat down next to him. "Find anything?" she asked Bang.

"Not yet," she signed back, setting down the jar containing the essence of Grotton's thumb. "The earlier sections were written more recently, but this part is older, and it's all in — "

Lex couldn't figure that last part out. "What did she say?" she asked Pip.

Bang signed for him. "Old English," he translated in a flat tone.

"The point is," Bang signed, "it's taking forever."

"Well, keep at it."

Bang did just that, diving back into the pages. Pip resumed staring at the wall so intently that Lex had to nudge him three times to get his attention.

"Pipster," she said. "Are you okay?"

"Hmm?" He looked at her and blushed. "Yeah, I guess. I just feel so bad about Riqo. He died for *us*. He barely had anything to do with any of this, and he's the one who got killed!"

"I know. It sucks," said Lex, certainly no stranger to survivor's guilt by now. "But at least he chose it, you know? His life wasn't stolen from him like Cordy's or Corpp's, or Driggs's — " Her voice got thicker, her stomach twisting with every name she rattled off whose life had been cut short because of her.

She cleared her throat and focused. "I mean, yes. He did give up his life for us, and I can't say for certain that we are altogether that deserving. But at least he did it willingly. That's a pretty noble thing to do, right? Way nobler than anything I've ever done. I just keep running away, leaving only the occasional blunt force trauma in my wake."

Pip still seemed sad, but not as much as he had before. "It *is* a pretty good way to die, I guess. So that your friends don't have to."

"Best way there is, probably."

He looked at her again, his eyes bright. "We'd better make it worth it, then, huh?"

Lex leaned her head back against the wall and looked at the ceiling. It'd only be worth it if they could seal the portals. And trigger a reset. And it would *really* only be worth it if they could figure out a way to prevent the damage from ever happening again, yet they still had no idea how to do that.

But all she said was, "Yeah."

"Got it!" Uncle Mort tumbled a large chunk of cement to the floor and peered into the hole it had left. "Come on," he said, waving them in.

"Through there?" Ferbus said. "It's so . . . tiny."

"Afraid it'll knock off your tiara, princess?" Pandora said, shoving him out of the way. "Let me through." She got onto the ground and wriggled through the hole until the only things showing were her stockinged legs.

"Whoa!" Driggs yelled as everyone got an eyeful. "Didn't need to see that!"

"My undercarriage is a national treasure!" she shot back. "Now get your asses in here!"

One by one, they squeezed through the narrow opening. Lex was last, and it was a good thing, too; if she'd been first, she might have turned right around.

They'd crawled into someone's living room.

"Okay, this is weird," Elysia said, looking at framed photos of the strangers' lives. "Do we know these people?"

"No," said Uncle Mort. "They're Necropolitans, so you can bet they're no fans of ours."

"Think they're fans of breaking and entering?" asked Driggs.

"Doubt it," said Uncle Mort. "But if we don't win this war, they don't get an Afterlife. So maybe they'll forgive us just this once."

He began to raid the refrigerator, stuffing several containers of leftovers into his bag. While he was at it, he egged the man's photo and drew a mustache on his wife.

"Oh, calm down," he said when he caught Lex looking at him funny. "A little vandalism never hurt anyone."

A sharp intake of breath brought his rummaging to a halt. Everyone's eyes flew to Bang, but hers were still glued to the pages of the Wrong Book. Her hand, hovering an inch over the page, held the jar as she read.

"What, Bang?" Driggs asked.

She looked up, surprised to see everyone watching her. "Nothing," she signed. "I think I figured out what these pages say. But they're — it's weird."

"Weird?" Lex said. "Do tell."

They gathered around Bang and listened as Pip interpreted her flying hands. "She says that the section she managed to rip out is kind of unusual. The rest of the book was full of instructions for Grotton's various tricks, like the reset, but this part is more like a journal."

Pip's eyebrows narrowed, as if even he didn't believe what he was about to say. "It's still kind of murky, but what she's been able to get the gist of so far is a story about Grotton torturing some farmer and his family. He kills the kids, Damns the wife, then sends the farmer to the Dark — but the strange part is the way they're talking, like Grotton was doing some kind of experiments."

"Well, yeah," said Ferbus. "He's the one who invented Damning in the first place, isn't he?"

Bang frowned, looked at the pages, then signed again. "True," Pip translated, "but he's making it sound like he invented even more than that. Like — "

Bang shook her head. "I don't know," she signed to all of them. "I'll need to read more to figure it out."

Uncle Mort scrutinized her. "See that you do."

His eyes were getting that intense look again, so Lex tapped him on the shoulder. "So," she said loudly, "what's our next move?"

He blinked a couple of times. "Well, it should be slightly easier to move now that it's getting on toward nighttime. Fewer people around, less likely we'll be spotted. On the other hand, things will be much quieter, and with you elephants stomping around, there's a greater chance of someone hearing us —"

"Hang on," said Elysia. "We're not stopping for the night?"

Uncle Mort paused to stare at her. "We're a little pressed for time here, Lys."

"Yeah, but —" She looked to Ferbus for help. "It's just that we're kind of, um, exhausted."

"And hungry," Ferbus added.

"And some of us really have to pee," said Pip.

Pandora raised two fingers. "And other things."

Uncle Mort irritably ran a hand through his hair. "So what are you saying?" he asked. "You want to camp out for the night? Where do you propose we do that?"

"Well, obviously we can't stay here," said Lex.

"But we can't *leave* until we know where we're *going*—"

"For cripes' sake, enough with the drama!" Pandora said, blowing past him. "Everything is a crisis with you people. *Stairs are hard, that tunnel's too small, my sister died*— sack up already! You really want somewhere to sleep?" She flung the front door open. "Come on. I know a place."

||||||

"The National Museum of Grimsphere History?" Elysia said, reading the sign before them.

"OH no," Ferbus said. "We're not going to have to learn things, are we?"

"And risk pushing out the space in your brain devoted to basic motor skills?" Pandora said. "Heavens, no."

Back at the apartment, she had barked at them to slink out

the door and take a quick left down a deserted hallway. Lex tried to sneak a peek at what the rest of Residential looked like, but Uncle Mort was shoving her along too quickly to get a good look. All she ended up getting was an eyeful of the green carpeting that ran beneath their feet, leading them to a large wooden door.

"Well, go in," said Pandora. "It's open to the public."

"So, for once, we won't have to destroy private property," Uncle Mort said, opening the door. "Look how far we've come, gang—"

A shriveled, bony fist punched him in the face.

Since there wasn't much force behind the blow, however, it just sort of shoved him off balance for a second. Uncle Mort rubbed his cheek, as if he'd been stung by a mosquito. "Ow."

"Don't you dare come in here!" a little man in a bow tie and suspenders yelled. He stared out at them from behind a pair of humongous old-man glasses, his wispy white hairs quivering as he shouted. When the Juniors came in anyway, he got even angrier. "Don't you dare take another step!" They took another step. "Don't you dare—"

"Turlington!" Pandora blared, holding up a balled fist of her own. "You shut that pie hole of yours or I'll stuff it with a hearty slice of knuckle cobbler!"

"Knuckle cobbler?" Lex whispered to Driggs.

"Good name for a band," he replied.

The man almost fainted. "Pan—Pandora?"

"Damn straight!" She puffed out her chest and trapped him up against the wall. "Now, you're going to let these friends of mine bunk here for the evening, and you're going to be *real* nice and *real* pleasant about it, and above all, you're not even going to *think* of ratting us out. Got it?"

"Yes, yes," he said, shaking. "Whatever you need. I think I might even have some pillows and blankets left over from the last overnight camp, in the closet behind the —"

Pandora karate-chopped the side of his head.

The Juniors watched as he went down like a sack. "What'd you do that for?" Uncle Mort asked once the poor man stopped twitching.

"He would have ratted," Pandora said with confidence. "Old Turly was my partner for a brief stint back in our younger days. Thick as thieves, we were. But he's a squirrelly bastard, I know that much."

"So are you," Uncle Mort pointed out.

"That's why we were such good friends!"

Uncle Mort stared at her for a moment more, then rubbed his eyes. "Okay. Fine. Make yourselves at home, kids. Just step right on over the unconscious senior citizen."

The National Museum of Grimsphere History had none of the sleek, modern sophistication of the rest of Necropolis. Lex didn't know what she had been expecting — dinosaur skeletons would have been cool, albeit unlikely — but this place seemed more like a library in the Playboy Mansion, provided anyone in the Playboy Mansion knew how to read. A plush red carpet blanketed the floor, the main wall was made of deep mahogany panels, and the opposite wall was solid window. From the ceiling hung a chandelier that could have paid for Lex's college education, and maybe Cordy's, too.

There didn't seem to be any exhibits, which definitely threw the room's title of "museum" into question. The shape of it was odd as well — long and thin, almost more of a hallway arcing with the curvature of the building. But as Lex brushed her hand along the smooth, polished wall panels, she began to see why the museum was set up the way it was. Centered at eye level was a thick red line that extended all the way down the length of the room. Thinner black lines hash-marked the main red one every few feet or so, with the one closest to the door labeled PRESENT DAY.

"It's a timeline!" Elysia exclaimed.

"Thanks, Captain Obvious," said Ferbus.

Elysia glared at him. "Thank *you,* Captain Overused Expression."

"No, thank *you,* Captain Shut Your Facehole."

"Captains, please," said Uncle Mort. "No fighting."

A few more feet down the line, a stunning photograph of Necropolis stretched from the floor to roughly Uncle Mort's height. The caption next to it read:

> Ain't she a beaut, folks? The largest structure in the Grimsphere, Necropolis rises hundreds of feet in the air and is enveloped by a single pane of specially made, nonreflective, camouflaged glass, A marvel of size, culture, and elegance, Necropolis is universally recognized as the crowned jewel of the American Grimsphere. Not like that monstrosity of a city, DeMyse.

Bang, having taken a break from the Wrong Book at the opportunity to read something new, tapped the words. "I thought museums were supposed to be objective," she signed.

"That's Turlington for you," said Pandora. "Always shoving his opinions where they don't belong."

More interesting tidbits popped up as they walked down the timeline. Construction of the current Necropolis building had begun about fifty years ago; before that, the entire operation was housed in an office building in Wichita. Judging by the black-and-white photo, it had sat there in plain sight for the whole non-Grimsphere world to see.

"Less attention called to it that way," Pandora explained. "No one gives a badger's bunghole about a stuffy old office."

"'McGuffin Casket Company: Corporate Headquarters'?" Lex read off its sign.

"Yep! And before that, it was Deady's Formaldehyde and Embalming Liquids!"

"Subtle."

Farther down the line was the founding of DeMyse, complete with old photos of the city. Before it was invaded by kitschy hotels and sleek nightclubs, it had looked like something out of a spaghetti Western. Lex tried to picture LeRoy in a cowboy outfit, and somehow, it still suited him. As long as the chaps had rhinestones.

"Hey, it's Croak!" Pip said.

As the first Grimsphere city founded in the New World, Croak was the sturdy cornerstone upon which Grimsphere society in America was built. Today it continues to enchant visitors — Grims and non-Grims alike — with its friendly citizenry, small-town charm, and world-famous diner, the Morgue (though I have personally always found its onion rings to be far too greasy).

"That rat bastard!" Pandora shouted.

"Wait a sec," said Lex. "There were people living on this continent long before the United States was a twinkle in George Washington's eye. What about the Native Americans?"

"Oh, they were accounted for," said Uncle Mort. "The range of the jellyfish extends all over the world, remember? No souls were left behind." He pointed farther down the timeline. "For a long time, all Grimsphere operations were centered in England. It wasn't until the late Renaissance that it started branching out to other places."

Lex tried to imagine a hub in a castle. "Don't tell me they had Smacks."

"Not as we know them today. Grims' technology has evolved alongside the rest of the world's. Back then they just infused their scythes with jellyfish venom or something."

"So England handled the deaths for the entire world?" Lex persisted. "Who did it before England existed?"

Uncle Mort shrugged. "We don't know. Grimsphere records only go back this far." He pointed to the end of the timeline, labeled MID-FOURTEENTH CENTURY. "Before that, it's anyone's guess. The true origins of the Grimsphere are mostly unknown."

"There must be artifacts, though. Old scythes or ancient scrolls or — I don't know, cave paintings of the ether?"

Uncle Mort shook his head. Confused, Lex turned to Pandora, who was doing the same thing.

"Nothing?" Lex asked. "No earthly records of Grims at all?"

"Grims are good at keeping things secret," Uncle Mort said. "It's kind of our thing."

"That's pretty impressive," said Elysia.

"Yeah," said Lex, dubious. "Like, *really* impressive. To the point of being implausible."

"Hey, look." Pip pointed at the very last entry on the timeline. "Grotton got his own sign."

The notorious mass murderer known as Grotton was responsible for the unauthorized, sudden deaths of hundreds of people — including many Grims. Grotton also developed the
practice of Damning, a practice so despicable I won't even
bother to describe it.

"In a museum," Lex said dryly. "The sole purpose of which is
to describe."

Bang walked up to the Grotton description and read it over a
couple of times, frowning. After a moment she chose a spot near
the window, sank to the floor, and continued studying the pages
from the Wrong Book.

Uncle Mort let his bag fall off his shoulder. "Well, looks like
this is our home for the night," he said. "Better get some sleep.
Tomorrow's a big day."

"But we're almost there, right?" said Elysia.

Uncle Mort laughed so hard at that, Lex couldn't help but be
a little disturbed.

After distributing among themselves the food they'd taken
from the strangers' apartment, everyone spread out to different
areas of the museum to sleep. Uncle Mort wandered back toward
the main entrance, near the present-day side of the timeline. Ferbus and Elysia retreated to the DeMyse area, while Pip joined
Bang near the windows between the eighteenth and nineteenth
centuries. Pandora returned to the Croak photo and curled up
under it like a loyal old dog.

Most fell asleep quickly — except for Bang, who kept me-
thodically sweeping Grotton's finger over the Wrong Book's
pages, still preoccupied with figuring them out.

Lex watched her while picking through some cold spaghetti. "This is going to sound bonkers," she said to Driggs, "but I wish Grotton were still here."

"Do you miss his sparkling personality? His devastating good looks?"

"Oh, shut up." She chucked a piece of meatball at him. "The guy's a stone-cold dick, no question. But with the whole Dark thing, and what Bang's been reading in the Wrong Book, I just feel like there's something we're missing, or . . ." She looked at the blurb on the wall describing Grotton's treachery. "Something off about him."

"Some *thing?*" Driggs said. "Singular?"

"Okay, there is an entire Old Country Buffet of things off about him, but I just get the feeling — it's like he knows something we don't, or — ugh, I don't know."

Driggs grinned. "You're sexy when you can't form sentences."

Lex raised an eyebrow. "So, uh, speaking of stone-cold dicks —"

"Classy, Lex."

" — Any chance you can . . . hop into your body?"

The corner of Driggs's mouth tugged upward. "I can try." He squeezed his eyes shut and started to exert some effort, as if he were lifting something heavy.

Lex couldn't help but snicker. "You look constipated."

He opened one eye. "Not helping."

She laughed again, and that seemed to do it — his body popped back into being.

There was no time to waste. "Come on." Lex grabbed his hand, dragged him to the farthest end of the museum, and plopped them both down on the floor. "Hope there isn't anyone below us."

"If so, they're already asleep. I mean, *I'd* already be asleep if you weren't licking my ear. Why are you licking my ear?"

Lex retrieved her tongue. "Because I feel like something awful is going to happen tomorrow. And I'm really hoping it doesn't involve my grisly demise, or an even grislier demise for you than your last one, but—" She swallowed. "I want this night to be a happy one, because I think they're going to be in short supply from now on."

"Yeah, but—" He glanced behind them. "With four friends, one uncle, one Pandora, and a comatose museum curator within hearing range?"

"Good point." Lex nodded thoughtfully, as if they were debating tax reform. "However: this." She grabbed his hands and slapped them onto her chest.

His eyes bulged, then met hers. "Compelling rebuttal."

Lex grinned and dove back into his face while Driggs's hands reached around her back. "Ah, the over-shoulder boulder holder," he said in a sneering voice, picking at her bra. "My old nemesis."

"Okay, don't panic," Lex said. "Do it just like we practiced."

"Right. The hook faces out."

"The hook faces *in*."

"*DAMMIT.*"

While Driggs worked his fumbling magic, Lex relaxed against the glass and only slightly wondered if any souls in the Afterlife were watching the rampant debauchery unfolding within. Eh, free show. Who cared. Her heart was too busy fluttering each time he touched her bare skin, her brain and body firing off all sorts of frolicsome hormones. She dreamily let her gaze fall on the opposite wall, where a series of photographs hung.

"Did you *add* hooks?" Driggs said, his yanks getting more and more desperate.

"Yeah, because somewhere in between all of our daring escape plans, I totally busted out my sewing..." She squinted harder at the photographs and trailed off. "...machine..."

"I'm just saying," he said. "This can't be normal."

Lex's throat had gone dry. "Driggs."

"Might there be magnets involved?"

"*Stop.*"

He stopped, freaked out by her expression. "What's wrong?"

Over the past year, Lex had been surprised by a lot of things. She'd been surprised to find out what her uncle really did for a living, and that she was destined to become a Grim just like he was. She'd been surprised when Zara revealed herself to be the murderer Lex had been hunting for, she'd been surprised when Cordy died, and she'd been really surprised to learn that she was special, like Grotton, a one-of-a-kind Grim with extraordinary powers.

So many of those times she had flipped out, lost her shit right there in front of whoever was unfortunate enough to be in the same room/building/city as she was. But the expression that Driggs saw wasn't one of outrage or horror. It was blank. The only hint that something was wrong — seriously, seriously wrong — was in the details. Her nostrils flared in and out. Her bottom lip quivered slightly. And she wasn't blinking.

"Uncle Mort," she said.

"What?" Driggs tore his gaze away from her face to look at the photograph on the wall. He frowned when he recognized it as a duplicate of one of the photos in the library in Croak, one of many taken of the townspeople every year at the Luminous Twelfth celebration.

"Go get Uncle Mort," Lex said, still staring, not blinking.

"Why? What's —" Driggs got up and moved closer to the picture, trying to figure out what she was looking at, what it was that they'd never noticed before in the photos back home.

He squinted.

Moved closer.

Found Uncle Mort as a grinning Junior. To his right, Skyla and LeRoy. And to his left —

Driggs was physically shocked back into transparency. Now a hovering shade of white, he whipped back to Lex. "I'll go get him," he said, holding a hand out to her, as if she might try to run. "Stay here."

But Lex wasn't going anywhere. She stood up and took Driggs's place in front of the photograph, keeping her eyes on the same spot until she felt Uncle Mort walk up beside her. And even then she didn't stir, just went again down the line of the four Juniors: LeRoy, Skyla, Uncle Mort, and Abby. Abigail. Gail.

When she spoke, it was only a single word, her voice no more than a whisper.

"Mom."

## 12

Lex and Uncle Mort sat next to each other on the floor. They faced the windows and looked out into the darkness of the Kansas plains. Lex wanted to believe that the stars here were even brighter than the ones in Croak, but the grayness of the Afterlife made them impossible to see.

"She was a couple of years older than I was," Uncle Mort said.

He hadn't cracked any jokes. He hadn't made excuses. He'd just sat her down and started talking, no sugarcoating involved. As she listened, Lex couldn't help but feel that he'd been waiting for this moment for a long time; he sounded relieved. As if he appreciated that she hadn't flown off the handle as she usually did.

As if he owed her the truth.

"When I came to Croak as a Junior," he said, "I took to it immediately, just like you did. I made friends fast, which had never happened before — I was the weird, violent kid whom everyone hated and who got in a lot of trouble." He let out a sharp laugh. "You have no idea how similar we are, Lex."

"You bit your classmates too?"

"I set fire to my classmates. Well, technically it was a chemistry experiment gone wrong, but parents were called, suspensions were issued." He snorted. "In school, I was hated. But in Croak, I was revered."

He scratched his head. "But as much fun as I was having, I started to feel a bit uneasy. And it didn't take long for me to figure out that a few of my fellow Juniors had the same sort of . . . inclinations that I did. The sense that even though being a Grim was what we were all really good at — and really enjoyed — something about all of this was fundamentally wrong. That human beings should never have been entrusted with the weight of this responsibility in the first place, shouldn't have been allowed to touch it with a ten-mile pole. And that eventually the system would crack. Your mother agreed. And thus was born the tank-smashing plan."

He looked at Lex. "She was the kingpin, Lex. I mean, the schemes that girl could come up with . . . they were diabolical. But they would have been nothing without her drive, the desire to actually see them come to fruition. Your mother was the one who made it all happen. Your mother was the one with balls."

Lex just shook her head. "She made me keep a swear jar in the kitchen. She despised it when I got in trouble." She swallowed. "I mean, for shit's sake, she's a history teacher!"

"Well, no surprises there. She was the best Afterlife Liaisons employee Croak ever had, until Elysia," he said. "I'm not surprised she retained some of that residual love for the ex-presidents."

Lex let out a puff of air. She should have been able to figure it out. But how could she? How on earth could she have known?

"But Mom didn't come from a crappy family," Lex said. "My grandparents were perfectly lovely people."

"Having a troubled home life isn't a prerequisite for becoming a Grim," Uncle Mort said. "It's just that those particular kids are more likely to really throw themselves into the Grimsphere, since they have nothing nice to go back to. Plus — well, there's no way to say it without sounding callous, but it's true: They're less likely to be missed once they're gone."

Like Driggs. He wasn't missed at all, and probably wouldn't have been even if his parents had lived.

"But your mom was such a natural, the mayor at the time simply couldn't pass her up. Certainly came to regret that, I bet." He let out a long breath. "It smelled like paint, I remember. Under the Bank porch, where we hid right after the attack, when they were looking for us. Someone had recently repainted the wood, and those were the fumes we were breathing when your mom begged us to rat her out. Make up some excuse, do whatever we could to be absolved of our crimes, as long as the full brunt of the blame ended up on her. Because someone had to take the fall, she kept saying. Someone had to take the fall so that the rest of us could keep rebelling against the system from within, keep planning for the final strike that would finish what we started. And even though she loved the Grimsphere just as much as we did — maybe even more — she was willing to give it up, erase every memory she ever had of the place in order to save the Afterlife — her beloved presidents, all those souls."

He rubbed his eyes. "So we did it, for her. We turned ourselves in: four accused, but only one guilty. We stood up on that fountain in front of the town and loudly lied that yes, your mother forced us into it. It was all her idea. Wipe *her* memory. Exile *her*."

He sighed. "And that's what they did."

Lex recalled something he'd said at the end of last summer. "Is that why you broke your Lifeglass?" she asked. "So they'd never find out what you guys planned?"

He smiled, pleased that she remembered. "Yes."

"Still — why didn't she get the Hole?"

"They went easy on her because she was a Junior. Tried as a minor, I guess you'd say. The mayor back then wasn't nearly as harsh as Norwood, sentencing kids to the Hole left and right."

Lex fidgeted at the memory of that awful room, those wrenching screams.

"But I cared about your mother," he said. When Lex raised her eyebrow at him, he shook his head. "Not in . . . that way. Skyla and I were already christening rooftops all over town, if you know what I mean."

"I know what you mean."

"But your mother had become a sort of older sister to me. I couldn't stand to see her thrust back into civilization without a clue, without knowing where the hell she'd been for the past few years or even how to be an adult out there in the real world. So I did what I do best. I schemed."

"How?"

"Well, I had a perfectly good big brother sitting around."

Lex's jaw dropped. "What? They always told us they met when he tripped and spilled ice cream down her shirt!"

"Who do you think pushed him?"

Lex just sputtered.

"They never suspected a thing," Uncle Mort said. "My brother had an inkling that I was mixed up in something weird — as he still does — but he didn't know his soon-to-be wife had ever been a part of it. And thanks to the massive dose of Amnesia she got, neither did she."

Lex thought on this for a moment.

"So you knew what you were doing," she said quietly. "That if my parents had kids, those kids would be direct descendents of a Grim — "

"And that those kids could possibly be the most powerful Grims ever born. Yes."

"But not if you followed the Terms, which say that relations of Grims aren't allowed to become Grims. You *brought* me to Croak. You *made* me a Grim." Her breathing was getting faster. "You didn't have to do that. You could have let me just stay in my old life. This entire clusterfuck could have been avoided, and — "

"And you'd still be miserable today."

She looked up at him, anguished. "Do I look happy to you?"

"Okay, you're still miserable, but it's because you're fighting for a cause you believe in. Look around you, Lex." He gestured at the room. "You've got friends over there who are willing to die for you. You've got a boy who adores you. You've got me. And you've got a life that you were born for. So was it worth it? You'll have to make that call for yourself. But I'd say it was."

Lex said nothing.

"And what's more," he went on, "I think that if your mom knew what you'd become, she'd think the same thing. I think she'd be damned proud of you."

Something akin to tears was brewing inside Lex, but there were still too many thoughts whizzing through her head to properly disgorge them. "Still," she said in a low voice, "you used me. You knew what I might be capable of, that I would go through all the agony of Damning, the hell that my conscience has put me through, and you didn't even care. As long as you got my Damning ability in the end, to defeat Grotton."

"That was only a contingency. Sealing the portals was my

main plan. The Grotton-destruction thing is gravy, something I only dared to hope for."

"So what? It was still part of your plan, even if it was a long shot. You needed me to do your dirty work for you."

Uncle Mort grabbed her wrist and held it up in front of her face. "I don't see any handcuffs," he said. "Did I drag you here at gunpoint? Did I ever *once* force you into a single thing you've done? Every decision you've made since you came to the Grimsphere was yours, Lex. You made your own choices, and you could have left at any time. *Any* time, and I wouldn't have stopped you. But you chose to stay. It's what your mother would have done, had she the option. Every time you've caught another blow — and you've caught a lot of rotten blows — you stayed, you rebounded, you fought even harder. There is honor in that."

Lex tried to come up with an argument, but couldn't. Even though it was easier to feel like the victim, to feel as though she had been lied to and manipulated, the truth was . . .

She *had* wanted to stay. She *had* wanted to fight.

She looked back at the photograph of her mother — young, smiling, her arm draped over the shoulder of Skyla. She'd given up everything she'd loved — everything that her daughter now loved — in the hope that things would get better in the future, that her sacrifice wouldn't be in vain.

"It's funny," Uncle Mort said. "Once the tank-smashing thing failed, we realized — the old Juniors, my old crew — we realized that our time was up, that the next generation would be the ones to fix it in the end. But I never dreamed we'd get such a strong, loyal, smart group of kids. I hoped for it, sure, but never truly believed they'd live up to my expectations, let alone exceed them like you kids have done."

He took a deep breath. "I won't lie to you, Lex: It's going to get harder. And when it does, you're the one the others are going to look to. You're going to have to step up and lead. You're going to have to make the hard decisions. In short" — he put an arm around her shoulders — "you're going to have to be awesome."

She swallowed. "How do I do that?"

"I don't know." At this, he finally smiled. "But yelling has done wonders for you so far."

||||||

Lex awoke to more gray, the Afterlife outside just as gloomy as it had been the day before. She'd fallen asleep on her stomach, but out of the corner of her eye she saw something resting on her back.

She rolled over. "Oh. Hey."

A cloud full of Driggs lay atop her. "Hey, yourself."

She sat up and rubbed her eyes. "Pretending to be a blanket, are we?"

"Nah. Just wanted to be on top of you."

She cracked a grin. "I'm not complaining."

He rolled off, lay down next to her, and put his hands into hers, literally. Lex studied him. "Were you watching me sleep?" she asked.

"Yeah. Is that weird? It's weird."

"I don't know. Maybe that's what boyfriends do."

"You just looked so pretty, dreaming like that. Peaceful, happy, not wanting to kill things."

"I was probably peaceful and happy because I *was* killing things."

"Good point." He tried to squeeze her hand, though of course she couldn't feel it. "Are you okay? After everything Mort said?"

"You heard?"

"Yeah. Actually, everyone woke up in the commotion and . . . we all did," he said guiltily. "We couldn't help ourselves."

Lex shrugged. "It's okay. I would have told you all anyway."

"I know." He glanced toward the other end of the museum. "They're ready to go. They wanted to give you your space, but we've got to get moving soon."

"Okay. Tell them I'll be right there."

A few minutes later Uncle Mort raised his eyebrow as Lex walked up to the front desk, tucking a scrap of paper into her back pocket. "If I didn't know any better," he said with a sly look, "I'd say that's the expression of a person who just cut museum property out of its frame."

"Oh, calm down," she said, patting him on the cheek as she walked by. "A little vandalism never hurt anyone."

||||||

The layout of the Residential section of Necropolis called to Lex's mind a shopping mall, with apartments instead of stores: the units were situated around the perimeter of the building, with a soaring open-air space in the center. Crisscrossing footbridges spanned the distance, a few single- and double-story staircases were scattered about, and grayish light streamed in through the gigantic window wall.

As the Juniors furtively scooted along one of the wraparound hallways, Lex snuck a glance over the balcony. They'd reached the food court section of her shopping mall metaphor; Necropolis's famed restaurant district stretched below them, with several dining balconies jutting out into the open space. They were just in time for Saturday-morning brunch too, Lex guessed, judging by the multitude of orange juice flutes and jazz quartets. The district had a loud, festive atmosphere. There was even a Ferris wheel.

Way down at the bottom, many stories below, was a large patch of trees. Little pathways wound through them. "Central Park," Uncle Mort said. "They don't get to experience much nature in here, so it's the best they can do."

Joining Lex at the railing, the other Juniors gaped at the attractions, each of them no doubt wishing they had more time for sightseeing. Bang's eyes were bugging out of her glasses at one restaurant that looked like a library, and Pip's fingers were itching at the sheer heights he could be climbing.

Driggs longingly stared at one of the jazz combo's drum sets. "I miss my drums," he said, adding bitterly, "not that I could play them."

Lex tried to ignore this little pop-up reminder of The Sadness. She was thinking, studying the Ferris wheel.

"Come on," said Uncle Mort, yanking them away from the railing. "We're too exposed, and we still need to figure out how to get up to the Executive section. So unless anyone plans on sprouting wings for the next twenty floors, we need to get on that."

"Should we break into someone else's apartment?" Elysia asked. "Try to return to the Backways?"

"Screw the Backways," said Lex, stealing a glance upward and disregarding the jarred looks on everyone's faces. "I have a better idea."

Uncle Mort wanted awesome? She'd give him awesome.

She brazenly began walking down the hallway without a thought or care as to whether people might recognize them. Anxious, the Juniors followed.

"Holy titgoblins, Lex!" Ferbus hissed, nervously hurrying to her side. "What are you doing?"

"Getting us up to Executive." She could feel Uncle Mort preparing to fire away an equally rude comment, so she turned to him and issued a preemptive strike. "You said I need to step up and lead, so I'm doing it. You trust me?"

Uncle Mort hesitated, then nodded. "Lead on, kiddo."

"Thank you. Now, break up the group a little," she instructed as they walked. "Little clumps of fugitives will attract less attention than a gaggle of fugitives."

"Gaggle of fugitives is a good name for a band," Driggs said.

"See? Look how well this is working out. You got any money?"

He stuck his hands in his pockets, but as neither his hands nor his pockets were tangible, it didn't have much of an effect. "Sorry. Plum out."

"Okay. Make yourself as transparent as you can," she told him. "Uncle Mort, money?"

"You haven't filched any from unsuspecting tourists yet?" he asked, digging into his pocket and sneaking a few bills into her palm. "Have I taught you nothing at all about fiscal responsibility?"

Lex counted the money and folded it into her palm, then reached into her bag and tucked something into her other hand. "Follow me."

With her head held high, she walked up to the hostess stand she'd been eyeing. Her fairly alarmed crew gathered behind her. "Hi," she said to the hostess. "Seven, please."

"Sure!" the girl perked, not looking up from her appointment book as she grabbed a stack of menus. "That's one whole pod, then."

A peppering of gasps erupted behind Lex as the Juniors realized which kind of pod she meant: a car on Necropolis's legendary Ferris wheel café, the Circle of Life.

"This will end poorly," Uncle Mort whispered to Lex, but she shushed him.

"Would you like — " The hostess finally looked up, dropping the menus once the recognition set in. "Oh no. You're them."

Lex donned a mock-apologetic face. "Yeah. Sorry about that. The table, please?"

"No! You're very dangerous! I have to call my — "

Her eyes crossed as Lex crushed a vial of Amnesia under her nose. The girl blinked a few times, then grabbed some new menus in a daze and staggered to the Ferris wheel, which was moving just slowly enough for people to get on. The pod that the Croakers piled into looked just like a booth at any normal restaurant, except that it was enclosed in a sphere of steel and glass, and the table had an intercom with a large red button set into it.

The hostess now spoke with a flat voice and an absent stare. "How about some Yorick coffees to get you started."

"Yorick *coffee?* Hells, yes!" Lex exclaimed. This was very exciting, as Lex had had neither a Yorick nor a coffee in quite some time, and never in the same drink, an oversight she could hardly believe she had made thus far. "Yoricks all around!"

The hostess grabbed a pot and sloshed a dark brown liquid into each of their waiting cups, which were nothing like the grungy mugs at Corpp's back home. They too were shaped like skulls, but instead of consisting of a material that was uncannily similar to the bones of a human head, they were made of delicate, spotless porcelain and were so tiny that one had no choice but to lift a pinky when sipping.

"Ew," Elysia said, wrinkling her nose after she took a sip. "So bitter."

"Shhh," Lex whispered, not wanting to ruin this precious moment with her two most favorite beverages on the planet. The familiar rush of elation shot through her as soon as the Yorick hit her tongue, and she nearly made a very inappropriate moaning noise —

But out of the corner of her eye she caught a barely there Driggs floating alongside the pod, his pale face pressed to the glass, pining for his beloved Yorick. "Yeah, it's gross," she said loudly to Elysia, sticking out her tongue in disgust and hoping that Driggs bought it.

"When you're ready to order," the hostess said, still in a flat zombie voice, "just push that button and order. At the top a waitress will bring your food and refill your drinks. Now I'd love to take a moment to tell you the specials. We have a triple waffle — "

"Actually, we're good with just the drinks," Lex said, pulling the door shut. "Thanks!"

The girl shrugged as the pod continued its ascent. "Aw, man," Ferbus said, pouting. "Triple waffle something."

Elysia was looking at Lex in awe. "Unreal. No one will expect us to have been able to board undetected, so no one will look for us in here. *And* we can get off at the top!"

"Lex!" Pip cried. "You're a genius!"

Lex smiled at Uncle Mort. "I'm a genius."

He rolled his eyes. Why did he look so annoyed? He'd specifically *requested* awesomeness. "Those Amnesia vials only last for fifteen minutes," he said, "so if she's struck by the urge to check up on her guests, we're somewhat hosed. Plus, there's still the small matter of evading the staff once we get up there, and where we run off to after that."

"Actually, we'll be one floor away from Executive," Lex answered. When Uncle Mort looked displeased, she grinned. "You're not the only one who can memorize schematics."

Now he looked even more displeased.

Lex ignored him. She was elated to have some time to themselves, all for the purposes of plotting and scheming. Driggs poked his head in to listen as she grabbed a pen from her bag and drew a crude sketch of Necropolis on her place mat. "This is where we'll get off. The border between Residential and Executive is right there."

The intercom in the table crackled to life. Thinking a waiter was about to recite the specials, Lex reached over to switch it off — but a familiar voice came through instead. And it was obvious to everyone in the car that it was speaking through clenched, angry teeth. "*Are — you — on — the — Ferris — wheel?*"

"Hey, Skyla!" Lex felt positively giddy, riding high on both the success of her plan and the delectable Yoricks. "We *are* on the Ferris wheel. It's really nice. Relaxing. Cozy."

They could hear a loud, measured breath. "I *trust* that no one saw you?"

"No one who'll remember."

"Is Mort even there?"

"Yeah, I'm here," he said. "I sort of gave Lex a little pep talk about leadership. She seems to have really taken it to heart."

Skyla made a grunting noise. "Well, tell her to be extra careful. I'm still in charge, but my second-in-command has gotten a promotion."

"Let me guess," Uncle Mort said. "The big guy we keep hitting over the head."

"You got it. Norwood seems to have convinced Knell that two teams are better than one, so he recruited Boulder to head up a second squadron. Except that that *I'm* supposed to be Boulder's commander, not Norwood, so there's a little spot of mutiny for you."

"On top of our own mutiny, currently in progress?" Uncle Mort said. "How rude of him."

"Do any of you remember how Executive is configured?"

"I do!" Uncle Mort said in a teacher's pet voice, raising his hand. When it became evident that he was the only one, he gave Lex a smug grin.

"Oh, come on," she shot at him. "Like any of us expected to survive long enough to see the top floor."

"Give us a refresher, Skyla," Elysia said.

"In Executive, the main elevator shaft still shoots straight up the center of the building, but whereas Local and Residential are made up of normal, layered floors, the Executive sector consists of two distinct halves that twist up around each other, like the red and white stripes of a barber pole. One of those stripes contains the Executive headquarters — just your standard office, with cubicles and water coolers and everything — but the other half is a . . . special case."

"She's being modest," Uncle Mort said. "It actually houses the singular reason Necropolis produces the most skilled Grims in the world — "

"Yorick coffee?" Lex asked.

He looked at her, then rubbed his temples. "No."

Skyla jumped back in. "It's a series of simulated situations that are designed to mimic the sort of extreme environments Grims might encounter on their shifts."

"Kind of like basic training," Uncle Mort added.

"My team and Boulder's team are each controlling a different half of Executive," Skyla said. "And I'm sorry to say that both options are less than ideal. On my side — the government office side — there are cameras not just on every floor, but in every room. And if Boulder and Norwood have their way, I'm sure the training modules will be charged up full blast. Not much I can do to stop that without looking suspicious."

"So we're screwed either way," said Lex. "Gotcha. Is there anything we can do to maximize our chances?"

"Just get to the express elevators in the center. Once you do, the president will freak out and give me clearance to follow you up to her office. Then, I'll — you know. Get this thing over with." She sniffed. "Gotta go. Good luck."

The intercom went silent. The Juniors nervously gulped the rest of their drinks, but Lex had already finished hers. She turned to Uncle Mort. "So . . . how *is* she going to get this thing over with? You said there's only one thing on earth that can seal a portal. What is it? Duct tape?"

Uncle Mort snickered.

"Come on," she pressed. "I know it's something in your bag of tricks, so tell me. You said no more secrets, right?"

He nodded. "No more secrets."

"Then what is it?"

"I can't tell you."

Lex wished she hadn't chugged her Yorick. It would have looked so nice dripping down the front of Uncle Mort's hoodie.

"Trust me," he said, ducking away from her hurled cup. "It's better that you don't know. It's dangerous enough with just the mayors in the loop."

A rustle of papers sounded. Bang looked up at them, then back at the pages of the Wrong Book for the umpteenth time.

"Fine, Skyla will superglue the portal shut, or whatever," said Ferbus. "But what are *we* supposed to do once we get up to the president's office? Sit back and enjoy the view? Again?"

"No. You'll be providing distraction," said Uncle Mort. "Warding off the guards and the president while Skyla does her thing, because they're not going to like it."

"Punch the president," Driggs said. "Got it."

"*Don't* punch the —" Uncle Mort started, then thought about it. "All right, if worse comes to worst, you have my permission to punch the president."

Ferbus and Driggs bumped fists through the glass.

"Wait," Lex said. "How are we supposed to 'distract' them?"

"Guns should do the trick," Uncle Mort said.

"Real guns? Not Amnesia guns? But —"

"*What?*" Pip's face had gone white at whatever it was Bang had just signed to him. He looked at his gaping companions, then back at Bang. "You'd better tell them."

"It was what you said back at the museum, Mort," she signed. "That the true origin of the Grimsphere is unknown because no one left any artifacts or records. But based on what I've been reading, that doesn't seem right. I don't think the true history of Grims faded into obscurity just because they were really good at keeping secrets."

The others exchanged glances. "What do you mean?" said Ferbus. "You think all the Grims who existed before Grotton simply disappeared? Or were killed?"

"No," she signed. "I don't think there were any Grims before Grotton at *all*."

## 13

"Okay, nobody panic," said Uncle Mort. "But Bang appears to have lost her mind."

"Hear her out!" Pip said. "Or I guess hear me out. Through her. Go ahead, Bang."

She started signing so fast, even Pip struggled to keep up with translating. "So like I said, Grotton did a lot of experiments, was sort of a mad scientist. But his day job was as a blacksmith. He bragged that he made the sharpest blades in all of merry old England. One day he took out the sharpest one he'd ever made and swooped it around through the air, and — I know this sounds psycho, but he makes it seem as though he *discovered* the ether."

Ferbus shook his head. "So the guy inadvertently created a scythe? That doesn't mean he was the first one to do it. Maybe he just joined up with the current Grims after he discovered what he was."

"That's what I thought," Bang continued, "but then he goes on to describe swirling through the ether, freezing time, landing at a target..." She paused for a moment to flip over a page. "Everything is here: Killing and Culling, crude versions of vessels, using jellyfish. It even sounds like he opened up the portals himself, constructing these big circular blades or something... I can't get the full picture, since his notes are so dense and hard to get through. But they're painstaking, and — " She picked through the pages. "I mean, his excitement is *palpable*. He honestly makes it seem like he was discovering all of this for the very first time, like no one had ever done it before. Like he *invented* the Grimsphere."

Uncle Mort was rubbing his eyes. "You're right, Bang," he said. "It does sound psycho."

She didn't seem to hear him. "Look, he even trained others — he called them his students. And they called themselves reapers. They operated a lot like a Grimsphere society does today — with more primitive methods, but the idea is the same." She held up the papers. "I don't have the rest, obviously, but you can sort of tell where it's heading — Grotton starts to get it in his head that he can play God, so he does. Experiments with Crashing, Damning, Annihilating . . ."

The Juniors looked to Uncle Mort, but he was shaking his head. "This is all well and good and would make one hell of an HBO miniseries," he said, "but there's just one problem: There were a lot of people who lived and died before Grotton came along. And we know they got to the Afterlife somehow — King Tut is proof enough of that. How do you propose they got there?"

"Ask Dora," Ferbus said. "She was probably around at the time."

"Go suck an egg!" she shot back.

"Maybe they arrived naturally," said Lex, thinking. "Without human assistance."

Uncle Mort had the frustrated look of a person trying to reason with a herd of cats. "Okay. Let's just assume, for one incredibly ludicrous minute, that all this is true. That before Grotton 'invented the Grimsphere,' people just died and automatically went to the Afterlife. Then Grotton arrives and, what, overhauls the entire system? Single-handedly?"

"Why not?" said Driggs. "He single-handedly destroyed the Afterlife, pretty much."

"That doesn't make any sense."

Lex was frenetically trying to organize her thoughts. "Wait, maybe it does," she jumped in. "Think about it. What if people died and went to the Afterlife all by themselves for, like, millennia, but then Grotton tears such a big hole in the fabric of existence that it *breaks* the system. It no longer works the way it's supposed to, can't function on its own." She tried to think of a suitable metaphor. "Like — like — "

"Like when you touch a baby bird," said Ferbus, "and then the mother bird rejects it and you have to raise it yourself?"

Elysia put her head in her hands.

"Uh, sure," said Lex. "So the humans intervene, do what they can to keep it going while they figure out how to fix what they broke. But they can't. The more they tinker with it, the more responsibility they have to take on to ensure that the process of death is running smoothly, on and on, until it depends on Grims entirely!"

Uncle Mort scratched his scar, thinking.

"But what does any of this have to do with anything?" Ferbus said. "So Grotton broke the world, and now it's our job to maintain it. We raised the frickin' bird ourselves, and it's big and strong and has, I don't know, really majestic feathers. What's the big deal?"

"The big deal," Bang signed, "is that our options aren't as limited as we thought."

"Exactly!" said Driggs, his eyes animated. "Because if all this is true, it means we *can* permanently fix the Afterlife!"

Lex looked back and forth between the two of them. "How's that?"

"What harms the Afterlife?" Driggs said. "Human intervention. Even if we seal the portals and reset the Afterlife, Grims still interact with the business of death every day — and like you said, there is always the possibility that someone will commit more violations. Damning or ghosting, or even something as simple as attacking a nontarget, like Lex always tried to do."

"Thanks for that," she said.

"So it seems to me," he continued, "that the only way to ensure that nothing will ever again harm the Afterlife is to get rid of that interaction altogether. If Bang really has read these pages right, and if Lex's theory turns out to be true, then it's possible for souls to get to the Afterlife the same way they had for thousands of years before Grotton interfered: naturally, without us Grims acting as middlemen. If you remove Grims from the equation, the Grimsphere ceases to exist, and then there's no way for anyone to harm the Afterlife anymore."

Uncle Mort stared at him. He might as well have said that all they needed to do was suck the oceans dry using only crazy straws. "Let me get this straight," he said. "You are proposing that we — and correct me if I'm wrong — somehow dismantle the Grimsphere?"

"Yeah!" said Driggs, his transparent face flushed with excitement. "Although I have no idea how to do it. And it would pretty much destroy our careers and society and everything we hold dear. That would suck."

But something had resonated with Uncle Mort, because he was making his diabolical-scheming face and running his finger

up and down his scar. "It *would* suck. But if that's what it takes for
the Afterlife to last forever . . ." He shook his head. "That's all assuming that any of this is true, which we can't confirm until we
get Grotton and the Wrong Book back. And even when we do, I
certainly am not aware of any ways to — I don't know, *unGrim*
the Grimsphere."

"Well, we might want to hold that thought anyway," Elysia
said, "because we're almost at the top."

It was as if she'd blared it through a bullhorn, the way it startled everyone out of their brainstorming. They'd been so wrapped
up in hypotheticals, they forgot they were in the middle of a
manhunt.

"Okay, hang a left when you get out," Lex said, pointing
through the window of the pod. "Those potted trees look like
decent hiding places. Duck behind them until all of us are out,
then we can break into the apartment on the other side of the
hallway."

As soon as the pod reached the apex of the wheel, a waiter
opened the door and wiggled a Yorick coffeepot at them. "Top
you folks off?" he asked with a goofy smile, one that dissolved as
soon as he caught a good look at their faces.

But Lex was ready with another vial. She pinched it into the
guy's nose, tucked the wad of cash into his pocket, and patted
him on the back as they took off. "No, thanks," she told the
waiter. "All pepped up."

"And ready to punch the president!" Driggs added.

Uncle Mort sighed. "You don't have to *announce* it."

There weren't many other people around the Ferris wheel
exit — just a handful of restaurant employees, most of whom
were too busy making triple waffle somethings to notice what

had happened to their poor coworker. Uncle Mort made a bee-line for the trees, and the rest of the group followed him. Lex stayed right on his heels as he rounded the corner, approached the trees —

And staggered back, almost falling to the floor. *"Run!"* he shouted.

Potted trees, as it turned out, didn't just make good hiding places for fugitives. They did a pretty decent job of concealing a dozen armed guards, too.

|||||||

For some odd reason, Lex focused on the carpet. It was so plush and thick that it perfectly preserved the slashes, divots, and swirls that her friends' shoes left behind as they ran. The marks spread out before her, green marks crosshatching like grass in a wind-blown, peaceful field.

But there was nothing peaceful about their current strategy, which involved darting through the halls like panicked rabbits. All previous attempts at secrecy and stealth had gone right out the massive green window as soon as the guards started to chase them. The Juniors were screaming, Uncle Mort was shouting in-structions, and Lex's heart was pounding so loud she was sure that people strolling through the park dozens of stories below could hear it.

"Left!" Uncle Mort was turning around every couple of sec-onds to shoot Amnesia blow darts at the guards, but as yet he hadn't been able to penetrate any of their thick black uniforms. "Left again!"

Lex blindly followed his instructions — or at least, her legs did. The rest of her was scrambling, trying to think of a better plan that wouldn't end with everyone she cared about getting cornered and thrown into the living hell of the Hole. *Think, think—*

"No!" she shouted in a moment of clarity, the schematics of the building reappearing in her mind's eye. She raised her voice so that even Ferbus could hear her, all the way up in the front. "To the right!"

It would be a long shot, but it could work.

She pumped her legs—regretting, yet again, that solid ball of spaghetti she'd consumed the night before—and overtook Ferbus at the head of the pack. "This way!"

It was only a few doors away now. The guards were falling behind. They were going to make it.

Lex fell upon the door and pounded it with everything she had. The others slammed into it as well, making such a ruckus that those within couldn't possibly ignore them.

And they didn't. There was a peephole next to Lex's nose, and although she couldn't see through it on her end, she could tell by the shadow under the door that someone inside was looking out. "What do you want?" a muffled voice demanded.

"Let us in!" she yelled. "Please! Hurry!"

The door opened.

Lex dropped to the floor, nearly trampled by her friends as they rushed in behind her. She looked up and counted the running bodies—four, five, six—

"That's it," Uncle Mort said, shutting the door. A second later, Driggs came whooshing in.

Lex looked up. The Juniors' dorm had appeared large in the schematics, but in person, it was even bigger. The common room

was decked out with a wide-screen television, all sorts of elec-
tronics, and really expensive-looking modern furniture. It looked
nothing at all like the dingy digs of the Crypt back in Croak.
This place was a palace.

But the furniture wasn't what was staring them down, waiting
for them to speak. Arms crossed and eyes hard, the thirty or so
Necropolitan Juniors resembled a miniature army; given the fact
that some of them might be future guards, this wasn't surprising.

"Say something," Pandora said, prodding Lex. "This was your
cockamamie plan in the first place."

"Um, thanks for letting us in," Lex said, hoping to take the
more diplomatic approach for once. Her old standby, punching,
seemed ill-advised at this juncture. "We really appreciate it."

Their faces didn't move, so Lex had no idea what they were
thinking. They had opened the door, which on the surface
seemed like a good sign, but it could just as easily mean that they
were planning to trap them and turn them in. "There are very few
people we can trust in this city," Lex went on, "and I thought that
if anyone would be on our side, it might be you guys."

The Necropolitan Juniors kept staring. One of them cracked
his knuckles.

Just then the large television on the wall sprang to life. "Good
morning, Necropolis!" Knell's homey face blared once again. "I
trust that y'all are relaxing and soaking in this fine Saturday
morning. Be sure to stop by Buckshot's Shooting Gallery this
weekend — buy five rounds, get one free!" She laughed, then
pursed her lips. "I do have one prickly bit of news, unfortunately.
It seems that despite my best and exceedingly generous efforts,
the fugitives from Croak have not turned themselves in. I highly,
highly encourage any individuals who have seen them, heard

from them, or are currently harboring them in their very living quarters, to surrender these dangerous felons immediately. Should any Necropolitans be caught disobeying these orders, their punishment will be swift and severe."

All smiles again. "Have a wonderful weekend! And if you happen to be dining at Sunset's for brunch, do save a shrimp cocktail for me!"

The screen clicked back to the Saturday-morning cartoons it had been playing before the interruption.

"You heard the woman," one of the Necropolitans said. "End of the line." He wore square-rimmed glasses, the eyes behind them beady and mean, making him look like a particularly nasty species of eel. He was obviously one of the oldest, because when he barked at a couple of smaller Juniors — probably rookies — they instantly obeyed. "Search them."

"But she's lying about us," Lex said, her tone growing stronger as the rookies' hands poked through her hoodie. "We're trying to *help*. Look, you know what's at stake here. You know how the government feels about Juniors — they think we're all as dangerous and explosive as Zara, that we're trying to incite a rebellion — "

"You *are* inciting a rebellion," another Junior countered, a girl with accusing, pointy eyebrows. "Aren't you?"

"Well, kind of," Lex said, a hint of desperation creeping in, "but we're trying to save the Afterlife — "

Another girl burst out laughing. "Right," she said. "Like we can trust the word of a mass murderer."

"That was *Zara,*" a boy jumped in. He, too, appeared to be one of the oldest, with darker skin and muscular arms. He sounded confident, as if he held just as much sway as Eel Boy.

Lex could have corrected him by saying that yes, actually, she *was* a mass murderer, but decided not to interrupt. It seemed rude.

"Besides," he went on, "why would they lie about this? The Afterlife is changing, we've all noticed it!" He pointed at the grayish view out the windows.

"Shut up, Toby," Pointy Girl said. "You're starting to sound like Skyla."

The rest of the Juniors looked split. Some of them were staring at Lex with the same brand of alarmed spite she'd grown accustomed to . . . but some of them weren't. Some of them looked worried.

The rookies, meanwhile, had confiscated all the Croakers' scythes, plus the guns Uncle Mort had in his bag and the Amnesia vials in his pockets. "Is this Amnesia?" Eel Boy said, holding up a vial. "Cool."

"What are we going to do with them?" Pointy Girl demanded.

"Turn them in," he replied. "Obviously."

"No," insisted Toby. "Guys, you've gotten the stares too. You've heard the Seniors talking under their breath. They don't trust *any* of us Juniors. But it's not us they're scared of—it's change! If Knell isn't willing to hear these guys out, then we at least need to help them be heard!"

Even Lex wanted to roll her eyes a bit at the corniness of his speech, but she appreciated the sentiment.

"Oh, let them go," President Knell drawled.

Everyone froze and stared at the television. The president's face had appeared once again, but this time she seemed to be addressing the room directly. Judging by the expressions on the Necropolitan Juniors' faces, this had never happened before; they looked as though they hadn't even known it was possible.

"Let 'em go!" she repeated, baring her teeth in a snarl. "Either the guards arrest them, or they go through the ringer of Executive." Her smile got bigger. "I, for one, would like to see just how far they think they can get."

With that, the television switched off completely.

Now the Necropolitan Juniors were really confused, and none more so than Eel Boy. Sensing that he was losing control, he shouted a desperate "Knock 'em out!" and crushed the Amnesia vial under Uncle Mort's nose.

A glazed look came over Uncle Mort's face. Eel sat him down on the sofa and quickly moved to grab Ferbus, while others seized the rest of the Croakers. Though Driggs tried to become solid and stop them, he couldn't do it in time. Within twenty seconds Pointy Face had smashed Amnesia vials into each of their faces, rendering every one of the Croakers catatonic.

Except for Lex, who — having pulled the same trick herself on the hostess — had snuck out of the room the second she saw Eel Boy raise that first vial.

She ducked into the first door she came to, which turned out to be a bathroom. Slipping on the wet tiles, she crashed to the floor, then lunged to shut the door behind her.

But she was too late. A foot came poking in, followed by Pointy Girl's face. "Found you," she said with a grin, breaking the vial against Lex's lips.

Lex slumped to the floor.

Unable to move, she stared straight out the window and into the Afterlife, watching its clouds roll by, gray and ashen with a hint of silver. She briefly hoped that Cordy might find her there and send for help, but that wish quickly dissolved, as did the rest of her thoughts. The last thing she remembered was the cool green tiles against her cheek, each one emblazoned with the mighty crossed-scythe symbol, mocking her helplessness.

|||||||

A deafening noise snapped her back. Five seconds later it pounded again, so loud the room shook.

"Oh, marvelous," she heard Uncle Mort say from the common room. "A battering ram."

Lex's throat clenched. Either the guards had found them or the Necropolitan Juniors had turned them in. She didn't remember anything of the last fifteen minutes, but she knew enough to realize they had to get out of there, now.

Just then the door burst open, hitting her in the back. *"Ow —"*

"Shh," Toby said, roughly pulling her up. "Come on, before they change their minds."

"What?" Lex said, bewildered as he pushed her into a clump of her fellow Croakers. "What's going on?" she asked Elysia.

"I don't know. I don't remember anything," Elysia said. "Maybe they decided to help us escape? Did Toby really win them over?"

"He had a little help from me," Driggs said modestly. "After that weird-ass Big Brother speech from Knell, they were a little more inclined to believe us. And, uh, I'm a ghost. I was pretty persuasive, until the guards arrived."

While one of the Necropolitan rookies redistributed the Croakers' scythes and weapons, Toby led them all to a utility closet lined with shelves of cleaning products. He flung the brooms and mops out of the way, then pointed at a grate in the ceiling. "That shaft goes up to the Executive level. Once you crawl out, you'll be in a black hallway. Turn left. We've been there before — it's part of our Junior induction process — "

"Wow," said Elysia. "Ours is just a water balloon fight."

He shook his head. "No, it's not hazing. Training is an official graduation requirement."

All the Croakers went pale at the same time. Of the two ways up to the top of Necropolis, the training side was not the one they would have chosen.

"Don't tell them any more," Pointy Girl interrupted with a mean smile. "If the legendary Croak Juniors are so great, they should be able to breeze right through."

Lex did not care for her tone.

Uncle Mort, on the other hand, did not seem to care about anything other than getting out of there. He'd already scaled the shelves and was now working to remove the grate.

"Ferb, you go first," he said, grabbing his hand once the duct was open. "Unlock the grate at the other end." Ferbus nodded and pulled himself up the shaft, his feet dangling for a moment before disappearing. Uncle Mort helped the others up one by one, working a little faster with each pound on the front door.

A minute later, a cry sounded from the ducts. "What happened?" Uncle Mort yelled up into it.

"Nothing!" Dora said. "Everything's fine!"

"No, it's not!" That was Pip. "Pandora cut her leg on a piece of metal that was sticking out! She's bleeding pretty bad!"

"Forgot to mention that part," Eel Boy said with a smirk. "Sorry."

Uncle Mort glared at him, then looked back into the duct. "I'm coming up."

"I told you to stay put, you meddling ninny!" Dora's voice came back. "I'm perfectly fine!"

"She's not!" Pip said.

"You want a wrinkly elbow to the face, kid? Because a wrinkly elbow to the face is exactly what you're about to get!"

As they kept fighting, Uncle Mort gave a weary look to Lex and Elysia, the only ones left. "That woman's leg could get chopped off and she'd say she's fine." He reached for the hatch and wriggled himself in, then turned around and looked down. "Come on, I'll pull you up."

Lex grabbed his arms and was halfway up when she heard a loud slam. The guards had broken through the front door.

"Hurry up!" she yelled, trying to climb faster. "Elysia's still down there!"

"Guys, a little help!" Uncle Mort yelled to the Croakers behind him.

More shouting came from the ducts, including the sound of Ferbus trying to push to the front to help. But Driggs got there first. He appeared next to Uncle Mort and reached down, straining to become solid as he did.

For once, it worked right on cue. "Lys!" he shouted the instant he was tangible. "Grab on!"

Shaking almost too hard to move, Elysia slapped her hand into his, her eyes wild with fear. Still dangling from Uncle Mort's hand herself, Lex could only watch as Driggs scrunched up his face and started to pull — but then seemed to falter, as if he were struck by a wave of panic.

"You're fading!" Lex said, watching as a ripple of transparency swept over his body.

"I know, I — " He shook his head and concentrated harder —

Until finally some strange force burst out of him, the shock wave causing Lex's dangling body to swing and nearly slip out of Uncle Mort's grasp. For a brief second, Driggs was completely solid—

And then he disappeared.

Elysia crashed to the ground, her fear temporarily replaced by wonderment. She seemed confused, as if she were trying to remember a dream that she'd only just woken from but had already forgotten.

She looked up at Lex. "I feel weird."

As guards flooded through the dorm, however, the terror kicked back in. Some of the Necropolitan Juniors were trying to beat them back, but the guards simply stunned them, leaving a pile of incapacitated teenagers in their wake.

By the time the guards got to the closet, Elysia was hysterical. She thrashed and kicked at them, to no avail; they easily grabbed her around the waist. Her tear-streaked face was glued to Lex's, screaming, begging for help.

"No!" Lex shouted, straining to break free from Uncle Mort's ironclad grip. "I have to get her!"

But with a grunt and a final pull, Uncle Mort yanked Lex the rest of the way up into the hatch. After that, all she could do was watch, horror-stricken, as the guards dragged Elysia away.

||||||

As promised, the hallway on the other end of the duct was indeed black. It now also featured a sizable hole where Ferbus had punched it.

"We have to go back," Lex repeated for the tenth time. She

was standing over a drained-looking Driggs, who'd popped back into existence as soon as they'd all safely piled out of the shaft and into the darkened hallway. He was switching between solid and transparent in quick, jerky pulses, as if he'd totally lost control. "We have to go get her!"

Uncle Mort sat on the floor next to Dora, staring intently at the bandage he was applying to her leg. "We can't," he said, his voice thick. "You know we can't."

Lex did know. But she couldn't bear it, couldn't bear the guilt of abandoning her best friend.

*This can't be happening.*

"Do you realize what they're going to do to her?" Ferbus shouted at Uncle Mort, his face even more wrecked than when he'd first seen Driggs as a ghost. "Throw her straight into the Hole. If she's *lucky.* What if they torture her for information?"

"Keep it down, Ferb."

Ferbus looked as though he might punch a hole straight through Uncle Mort as well, but he shut his mouth and stepped over to the grate. "I'm going back for her."

"You are *not,* dammit!" Uncle Mort grabbed him and slammed him into the wall, their faces inches apart. "Because then *you'll* get caught, and someone else will have to go back to get you, until there's none of us left and we'll rot in the Hole for the rest of our lives and we won't even have a nice Afterlife to go to after that because we never lasted long enough to save it."

Pip let out a shaky breath. "But this is just like Riqo and Broomie all over again!"

"They knew the risks," Uncle Mort replied, letting go of Ferbus but still speaking directly to him. "And so did Elysia. No one forced her to come. She was here because she wanted to be."

Every word he uttered made Ferbus angrier. "Mort, I swear to God—"

"You think I like this?" Uncle Mort said. Something in his voice changed—it wasn't hard, as it had been a second earlier. A crack had formed. "You think I like having to say these things to you, to justify all the hideous shit that happens to you kids whom I would gladly—*gladly*—give up my life for in a heartbeat? You think I don't want to go back and get her just as much as you do?" He touched his scar absent-mindedly, talking just as much to himself as to Ferbus. "Someone has to be the strong one. Someone has to keep us going, keep a clear head, focus on what has to be done without emotions getting in the way. That someone happens to be me. I hate it, but I have to do it."

Ferbus didn't meet his eyes. He looked down, his gaze ultimately resting on the grate to the air duct. "I know."

Then Lex thought of something. "Her Spark!" She lunged for Uncle Mort's bag and tore it open.

Not a single one was glowing.

She collapsed with relief, weakly handing the bag back to him. "She's still alive."

This did nothing to console Driggs. "I don't know what happened," he said, his head in his hands. "I *had* her. I made one last-ditch effort to gather my strength and pull her up, and then—I don't know, it's like I blew a fuse." He turned to Ferbus. "It's my fault. I'll—I'll—"

His face lit up as an idea struck. "I'll follow her!"

"What?" Lex said.

"You guys keep going up to the top," Driggs said, now animated. "I'll go back and make sure they don't do anything to Elysia. I'll stay as transparent as I can and keep an eye on her. If they try to hurt her, I'll — you know." He shrugged. "Go solid and kick some ass."

Lex just stared at him. "Go solid and kick some ass? That's your plan?"

"I didn't say it was a good plan," he said, shame creeping up his neck. "Obviously I can't stay that way for very long anyway, but I might as well at least *try* to use this rotten superpower for good."

Lex lowered her voice, all too aware that everyone was listening to them, but needing to say it anyway. "I don't want to split up," she insisted.

"Neither do I, but come on, Lex. You know this is the right call. You're worried about her too, and she *has* stuck by you all this time, and . . ."

He didn't have to say it. Lex owed her.

She looked at Ferbus, who was staring at the two of them with his arms crossed, his eyes red. Every time she blinked, she saw Elysia's face again, desperate, scared.

"Okay," Lex told Driggs. "Go. But please, *please,* don't get yourself killed."

He smirked. "Again."

Lex rolled her eyes as he sank into the floor. "See you at the top," he said with a wave — and then he was gone.

Once Uncle Mort finished bandaging Pandora's leg, he stood up and pointed his flashlight down the hallway. "Come on, kids. Last push to the end."

As they followed him, Lex tried to focus on one goal: getting to the president's office. That was all they had to do. But her hand kept opening and closing involuntarily, as if searching for Driggs's.

Before long, they turned a corner and spotted a door. As soon as they reached it, the fluorescent lights went out.

Followed by Uncle Mort's flashlight.

They stood there in the dark, the only sound that of their heavy breathing. "What's going on?" asked Ferbus.

"The training program is starting," Uncle Mort answered. "Stand back. And be prepared for anything."

The door opened.

A wall of solid flame jumped out.

## 14

It's not that the Juniors of Croak were poorly trained. It's just that Uncle Mort came from more of a throw-the-kid-in-the-water-until-it-either-learns-to-swim-or-drowns school of thought.

Evidently, those in charge of training the Juniors in Necropolis thought otherwise. Evidently, they thought that the best way to prepare their Juniors for the sort of horrific extremes they might encounter during their shifts — fires, drowning, plane crashes — was to put them through a series of highly realistic simulations in the hopes that they would eventually learn to stay calm under all kinds of duress.

As if the Croakers weren't running low on duress as it was.

The moment they'd walked through the doorway, their scythes had vibrated in their hands like video-game controllers. The farther into the room they went, the taller the flames grew.

"Just keep going," Uncle Mort said as the crew was bathed in another wave of intense heat. "It's the same as being out on a shift. You guys have got this."

Somewhere inside Lex, beneath the terror and guilt and general shititude she felt during every waking moment of her life now, she felt a sting of annoyance toward her uncle. Especially when she unfondly recalled the first time she'd been sent to an extreme target, and how massively underprepared she'd been for what she'd encountered. And so, as she ran through the room of fire, spurts of lava spouting left and right, above and below, she was conflicted. She was not particularly *enjoying* this little sprint through the bowels of hell . . .

. . . but she couldn't deny that it would have been beneficial.

"There!" Uncle Mort shouted, pointing through the flames at a lump propped up against the wall. "That's our target!" They dodged more spurts to get to the other side of the room, only to find that said lump was a human body, its skin blistered and burned.

But Lex had seen enough burn victims to know that they didn't look quite as melty as this, and they certainly didn't exude the smell of petroleum. The body was fake.

Fake, perhaps — but still technologically advanced. "We have to touch it, all of us," Uncle Mort told them.

As soon as they did, their scythes vibrated in their hands again. "What the — " Ferbus said.

"Scythe," Uncle Mort instructed. Shrugging, they tore their scythes through the air, just as they did out on their shifts when jumping from target to target. "We just leveled up."

|||||||

They were immediately taken to the next room — a jarring sensation, considering that they were so used to being launched into the swirling ether between targets.

They looked at the plain steel walls. "What's this one?" asked Pip, staying as still as the rest of them. "I don't see anything."

"Best just to keep plowing forward, then," said Uncle Mort. He took a step —

But his foot never touched the ground.

"Ah, weightlessness," he said matter-of-factly, hovering a few feet off the floor. "Been there, done that, right?"

Lex took a step and lifted into the air, half enjoying the queasy feeling of her stomach floating around inside her body, half hating the memory of her first extreme — when she'd been forced to hang helplessly in the air thousands of feet above the ground to Kill the victims of a plane explosion.

They started to move across the room in a sort of swimming motion, relaxing as they went. This wasn't scary. Just weird.

"I don't get it," Lex said to Uncle Mort, propelling herself through the air. "Why all these elaborate simulations? And why are the targets so far away from the starting point? When we scythe in to actual targets, they're always right there in front of us. And time is frozen — and our hoodies protect us from the elements — so why use real fire, real everything?"

"Because the human mind is a tricky little bastard," Uncle Mort said. "When Grims are thrown into scary situations, their brains still tell them to panic, despite the fact that there is really no need. If the training procedures force you to concentrate on the task at hand while being bombarded with danger from every direction, you'll be all the more levelheaded when you're actually in a safe environment."

"Ah. That makes sense, I guess."

"Of course it does. I came up with it."

"With what?"

He gestured at their surroundings. "This."

"Wait, wait," said Ferbus. "You designed this?"

"Designed it, no. I don't know what kind of situations these sadistic Necropolitans have cooked up in the time since I first mentioned it. But it was my idea to establish a training program in the first place."

"Then why don't we have one in Croak?" Lex asked.

"We do." He smirked. "You're looking at him."

Grimacing, Lex followed as they floated toward the target, a body limply suspended in space. She jabbed her finger into its forehead and even took a moment to appreciate that for the first time in her career as a Grim, she was touching targets without shocks tearing through her body.

To her surprise, she missed them.

|||||||

The blast of cold air that met them next felt heavenly . . . then a bit too chilly . . . then downright excruciating.

Lex concentrated on placing her foot down without slipping on the sheet of smooth, mirrorlike ice. The incline hadn't been as noticeable in the fire or the weightless rooms, but in here it was obvious: the floor sloped upward and curved to the right, spiraling around the center of the building just as Skyla had described. They were corkscrewing their way up to the top, one vile room at a time.

"Can we — actually — get hurt — in here?" Lex asked through chattering teeth.

"Under normal training simulation conditions, no," Uncle Mort answered. "The system adjusts itself based on your performance. If you're doing badly, it goes easy on you; if you're doing well, it gets more challenging. Normally there are systems in place to prevent it from getting too dangerous, but you heard

Skyla — they're cranking it all the way up, just for us. So I can only assume that they've turned those safeguards off."

"One can't help but wonder — if Croak had implemented similar training exercises instead of its delightful learn-as-you-go approach, might we all be better prepared for this little journey of death?"

"Oh, but then we'd have nothing to argue about right now," Uncle Mort said, breath steaming out of his mouth. "And arguing keeps the blood flowing. So in a way, I've saved your lives."

"Thanks. We'll chip in for a gift card."

The icy subzero room took much longer to get through — any false step and they'd tumble down the slope to the bottom and have to start over again — but they all managed to make it to the target.

"Lex, come on," Uncle Mort said. He and the others already had their hands on the body, but Lex had recoiled at the sight of its frozen hair.

"Oh." Uncle Mort realized his error. "Sorry, kiddo."

Keeping her eyes trained on the floor, she jabbed her finger into the dummy with a wince. She missed Driggs more and more with each passing step, yet she said a silent prayer of thanks that he hadn't had to flirt with yet another bout of hypothermia.

|||||||

They landed next on a bed of sand. Lex lifted her head. "What — "

She didn't get to finish; the water swept over her so quickly it drowned the thoughts right out of her head. She found herself in a swirl of red, underwater, face-to-face with a great white shark.

She forced herself to calm down. Panicking was useless. The shark wasn't real. None of this was real, except for the water. And she knew how to swim. She'd find the target soon enough, or one of the others would.

But the fear continued to pound as she thrashed. She looked at the direction she thought was up, wondering if there would be space to breathe if she swam to the surface . . .

Or maybe there was no surface. Maybe the water went all the way to the ceiling. Maybe the authorities were trying to drown them.

At this thought, panic really did start to set in. Her lungs and her mind were both screaming, her hair drifting into her face as she whipped her head back and forth, looking for the target, looking for escape.

Driggs's face swam through her memory. What would he say in this situation?

Probably: *Relax, spaz.*

*I can't relax,* Lex told her hallucination. *I'm going to drown, and for all I know, you might be dead already, and we never got the chance to say goodbye, and—*

Someone yanked on her elbow. With a great deal of effort she squinted through the water, through the big cloud of bubbles and puffy hair, to see Bang pulling the target toward her, tapping it to her hand.

Lex landed on her stomach, rough stone scratching through her clothes. When she tried to get up, she banged her head. Light

came from a few small bulbs set into the stone, but only enough
to give her the vaguest idea of where they were: a tiny, cramped
cave.

"Well," said Ferbus in a light voice. "This is terrifying."

None of them could stand up straight. They could barely
move; in some places there was enough room to crawl, in others
all they could do was wriggle forward on their elbows.

"Target's gotta be that way," Uncle Mort said, pointing down
a narrow passage. His voice was much less calm and collected
than it had been before. In fact, he sounded downright scared.
"Hope none of you are claustrophobic."

One couldn't *help* but be claustrophobic under these harrowing circumstances, but the faster they moved, the faster they
could get out of there. They pulled themselves forward, desperately digging their fingernails into the jagged rock, scraping their
skin —

*BOOM!*

A blisteringly loud noise rattled through the cave, vibrating
the walls. Small pieces of rock clattered to the ground, and for a
moment, everything was silent.

"What was *that?*" Lex said in a throaty voice, her nasal pas-
sages still stinging from the water.

Frantic, Uncle Mort scanned the walls. His face fell as he
spotted something. "This isn't a cave." He stuck his finger into a
small, perfectly circular hole drilled into the wall. "It's a mine."

"You mean — that blast was an explosion?"

They looked at one another for a moment, then scrambled for
the exit, faster than before, their minds a blur as they groped for
the target, wherever it was —

"I see it!" Uncle Mort said from up ahead. "Just a few more feet!"

Lex hurried faster but stopped when she heard something.

A faint ticking sound.

Ferbus heard it too. He slowed down to feel around the walls, sticking his finger into another drilled hole right next to his head.

"Oh God," said Lex.

Ferbus set a grim look of determination and covered the hole with his hand. "Go around me."

"Ferb, don't —"

*BOOM!*

Lex couldn't see or hear anything after that. She just lay on her back and stared blindly at the top of the cave, her scythe limply resting in her palm.

But something was moving. Uncle Mort was shoving the target toward them, brushing it up against their fingers.

Lex's scythe vibrated. Slowly, and wondering why in the hell she should even bother, she jerked it through the air.

||||||

Her hearing was back. Her sight was back.

But Ferbus's left hand was gone.

Or mostly gone. He stared at the bloody shards at the end of his wrist, his face blank and confused. "I tried to block the hole," he said in an amused voice.

"He's in shock," Uncle Mort said to the others, snapping into crisis mode. He took off his belt, wrapped it around Ferbus's forearm just below his elbow, and pulled it tight.

Ferbus's breathing was getting heavier the more he stared at what was left of his hand, so Lex delicately hugged him around the shoulders. He flinched at her touch, then stared into her eyes, insistent. "I tried to block the hole."

"And probably saved us all," she said, swallowing. "Good job, Ferb. You win an extra life."

He puffed out a breath of air, which Lex guessed was a sort of laugh. Appropriate, really. This entire situation was downright hilarious.

"Are we done yet?" Pip asked.

Lex realized with a start that they'd been inside the new room for at least thirty seconds, yet nothing had tried to kill them. "We're not done," Uncle Mort said, looking around. "This is the last room, I think."

Indeed, the floor was no longer sloped; it had leveled out into a perfectly circular room about a hundred feet in diameter. The floor was covered in a checkered pattern, with alternating dark and light steel square panels, as if it were one big chessboard. The Croakers stood on a raised white platform against the wall, and the target lay a few feet in front of them.

A large pole in the center stretched all the way up to the ceiling, ending in a glow of buzzing fluorescent lights. "Elevator shaft," Uncle Mort said, pointing at it. "If we can get inside that, it's a straight shot up to the president's office."

"Okay," said Lex, starting to walk forward toward the target. "Then all we have to do is — "

"Wait." Uncle Mort threw his arm out in front of her. "Don't move. There's got to be more to this."

They waited for a whole minute, but nothing happened. The

fake target lay still in front of them. Nothing else in the room moved, either. The only sounds were the hum of fluorescent lights and the drops of Ferbus's blood hitting the platform.

Lex stared at the pool of dark red forming on the polished white surface, Ferbus swaying beside it, and made a decision. "No," she said. "We don't have time."

Ignoring Uncle Mort's glower of disapproval, she rushed forward and pushed her fingers into the target's cheek.

The lights went out.

Mechanical noise filled the room, the sounds of things moving—robotic things, some kind of machinery. A liquid splashing, too. The crew stayed frozen on the platform, waiting.

After ten seconds the lights came back on. Six new targets lay scattered on different squares throughout the space, but most of the other squares had disappeared, leaving gaping black holes in their wake.

"It's a multiple," Uncle Mort said, taking stock of the numerous targets. "One for each of us." He peered down into one of the holes left by the absent panels. "Elixir," he said, frowning. "Two, maybe three feet deep."

"That's not so bad!" said Pip.

"With all the cuts and scrapes we have?" All of them were bleeding from one spot or another, some more than others. "It'd go straight into our bloodstream. We'd die within seconds. It's disorienting enough as it is airborne, in large concentrations like this." He looked up. "We're not going to last very long in here."

Yet their scythes still vibrated in their hands, insisting that they try.

Each of them landed on a different square in the room, little islands in the sea of Elixir. In every case, however, their targets sat a couple of squares away, with nothing but Elixir below. They'd have to jump for them.

"Shitballs," Lex said.

Pip was the first to leap, ever eager at the chance to flex those agile muscles of his. Bang quickly hopped to her target as well, followed by Uncle Mort. Ferbus still looked stoned, but he managed to rally enough to successfully fling himself over the gap. For a second Lex worried about Pandora, but the woman pounced across the panels like a grasshopper.

Lex, of course, was the only one who tended to crash through life without a hint of balance or grace. The one she should really be worried about was herself.

She swallowed. Her target was on a square platform to her left. A six-foot-wide gulf stretched between them, the Elixir sloshing calmly below. There was no way she'd be able to jump that far, especially without a running start.

"Come on, Lex!" Uncle Mort yelled. He was standing over his target, watching her. "We're waiting on you!"

"Of course you are," she said under her breath. She moved as far back on her square as she could go, lunged forward two steps, jumped —

And collapsed onto the target.

"Yes!" she yelled, pumping her fist into the air.

But her glee was short-lived. The lights went out again with a loud *click*. More mechanical noises, more whirring and splashing. Her scythe vibrated in her hand.

"More?" Pip cried, the desperation in his voice echoing everyone's sentiments.

"Multiple means multiple," Uncle Mort said. "Just keep going."

||||||

Lex scythed and landed on a different platform, but she couldn't tell where she was in relation to where she'd just been, or even where her new target was — because the lights hadn't turned back on.

"What's going on?" she shouted into the void. Others were yelling too. "Where are the lights?"

"I don't know." Uncle Mort sounded close to Lex, relatively speaking. "Just stay calm!"

But he didn't sound calm at all. Carefully, Lex felt around the edges of her island square, but just like last time, all the panels surrounding it had disappeared. She leaned as far forward as she dared, groping around with her scythe in front of her. Again she felt nothing. She'd have to jump, but in which direction?

And then it hit her.

"Uncle Mort, the Sparks!" she shouted. "See if they give off enough light!"

She heard him digging around in his bag. Seconds later, a faint glow popped out of the darkness. He held the bag wide open — she could see the little glass orbs within.

But the weak light that their whizzing embers threw off wasn't enough. All Lex could see was the square he was standing on, and not much else — not even the target he was supposed to jump to.

Uncle Mort kept groping for a solution. "Um —" he said. "I could throw them to you . . ."

"Don't bother," Pandora said. "You can't even see us."

Her voice seemed to come from the floor. Or maybe the ceiling. Lex was becoming disoriented, the Elixir fumes working their way into her brain. They weren't going to last much longer like this.

"Guys!" Pip yelled. "I've got it!" There arose a few sharp bursts of metal clanging, Pip's voice getting higher as he spoke. "I ended up next to the elevator shaft. I can climb up and turn the lights back on!"

"How the hell do you know that's going to work?" Uncle Mort shouted back.

"I don't! But I've watched Bang mess around with wires lots of times. It's worth a shot, right? Are there any other plans on the table?"

Silence provided that answer. "Well, no. But be careful."

In addition to the clanging noises that Pip's feet made against the metal of the shaft, Lex could make out some ragged breathing elsewhere in the room, along with a rapid foot tapping.

"Bang, he'll be okay," Lex said into her general direction. "Don't worry."

The tapping got faster.

A minute later Pip shouted down to them. He sounded miles away. "I made it!" A few more seconds of silence. Lex's heart jumped as something lit up at the ceiling, then went dark again.

"Dammit, Pip," Uncle Mort yelled, "don't get yourself electrocuted!" Lex could see his face in the ambient flicker of the Sparks. He went into a fit of coughing, the Elixir getting to him too. "Get down!"

Pip's voice came back fainter than it had been before. "It's not working."

"Then climb *down*," Uncle Mort answered. "Carefully!"

Pip didn't say anything. But there were no metallic thumping sounds either, no indication that he was following Uncle Mort's instructions.

Lex was growing more and more panicked. She reached into her bag, hoping to find something that would help. *Dammit,* she thought, finding nothing. *Why the hell did I get rid of Cordy's Spark? Cordy's glowing, blindingly bright Spark?*

"Guys?" Pip was calling down.

"What?" Uncle Mort shouted back.

"Good luck."

Lex frowned. "Pip, what?"

She whipped her gaze at Uncle Mort, and even in the scant amount of Spark light she could see that he'd gone pale. "No," he said quietly, then louder. "Pip, *don't!*"

Lex didn't know what was happening. She didn't fully understand until Pip spoke one more time.

"Love you, Bang!" he yelled, a smile in his voice. "Keep going!"

Two noises followed. That of a very fast whooshing, then a loud, sickening thud.

One of the Sparks in Uncle Mort's bag burst into light, illuminating the room. Lex could see the square she was standing on, the target she was supposed to jump to, the alarmed faces —

And Pip, lying in a broken heap on one of the platforms.

The sound that came from Bang was inhuman. She crumpled to the floor, curled herself up into a ball, and rocked back and forth, wailing like a wounded animal.

Uncle Mort took an inordinate amount of time to come to his senses, even for him. "Come on," he said, his voice gravel. He held up the blazing Spark so that it lit their paths. "Get to your targets."

Somehow, they did. Somehow, they managed to land their jumps — two jumps, in Pandora's case, since someone had to touch Pip's target. Bang was the last one to go, flinging herself into space without seeming to care whether she landed. As soon as her finger graced her target, the lights came back on. The missing panels returned, forming a solid floor once again.

And the elevator door opened with a cheerful *ding*.

## 15

The whole way up, no one spoke. Uncle Mort's face was hard. Pandora looked at the ceiling; Lex looked at the floor. Bang was curled up in the corner with her head between her knees, her body quaking every few seconds with silent sobs. Ferbus's mangled hand dripped blood onto the floor, *drip, drip* . . .

*drip* . . .

*DING.*

The doors opened.

Lex, Uncle Mort, Ferbus, and Pandora walked out of the elevator, cautious, Uncle Mort jimmying a crowbar into the door to keep it open. Bang stayed where she was on the floor, not moving, still sobbing.

They stayed close to the all-glass elevator bank; there was an additional tube next to the one they'd exited, but its door was closed. They were in the center of another circular room, this one much smaller than the last — and far brighter. Its walls were one big window, sloping so tightly toward the ceiling that they formed a point. With nothing but glass above and 360 degrees around them, Lex could see across the Kansan plains for miles — through the cloudy gray Afterlife, of course.

They'd reached the very top, the apex of Necropolis.

And yet the place felt oddly familiar. Aside from the windows-as-walls, the room bore a striking resemblance to the Oval

Office. A couple of sofas faced each other, a coffee table between them, and a large desk sat at the far end of the room. Unlike the desk in the Oval Office, however, this one was made not from wood, but from cut, polished stone, like a graveyard monument. Behind it sat an empty executive chair, and behind that, set directly into the glass, was a gigantic steel vault door.

"Dammit!" Knell shouted from behind them. The Croakers whipped around to find the woman stomping toward them, no longer the calm, poised leader they'd seen on television. Norwood was at her side, furious but wary. "What are you doing here?"

Uncle Mort put on an expression of mock confusion. "I thought you asked us to turn ourselves in," he said. "Or was that a different president-turned-kidnapper?"

While Uncle Mort worked his classic irritation tactics, Lex scanned the room. She looked from the vault all the way up to the glass tip, then around the room once more . . . then realized with a crushing dread —

There were no dark places, no hidden closets. The room was far too bright and open.

Her parents weren't there.

And as soon as she realized this, she remembered why their holding room had looked so familiar. The concrete walls, the dirty floor — it had to be the jail back in Croak, under the Bank. She'd been so convinced that President Knell had captured them, she hadn't even considered that they might be somewhere else, that Norwood could have done her dirty work for her. But Lex had spent days staring at that floor back when she was imprisoned. That's where they were. There was no doubt in her mind.

Knell sidled over to her desk and pushed a hidden button. "It doesn't matter," she said, jutting out her chin. "I just gave my guards uppermost security clearance. They'll be here any moment."

*Yes!* Lex thought. *Skyla!*

"Fabulous," said Uncle Mort, taking a seat on the sofa and throwing his legs up on the coffee table. They'd done exactly what they'd set out to do — clear a path for Skyla. "We'll wait."

Neither Knell nor Norwood knew what to do with this. They stood together behind the desk and watched the Croakers, waiting for the guards to arrive.

"I don't know what you think you're doing," Norwood said to them. "I told the president everything I know. How Lex and Zara worked together, Damning, terrorizing innocent people in cold blood all over the country. How you and your Juniors have repeatedly evaded capture and thwarted every opportunity to pay for your crimes. And as for why you're here in Necropolis, well" — he produced the Wrong Book — "your old buddy Grotton filled in the rest."

Right on cue, Grotton took form to Norwood's right. It was so bright in the office, he'd been invisible up until then.

"Sorry, team," Grotton told the Croakers. "Your secrets were too juicy. I couldn't resist spilling."

Lex had to restrain herself from lunging forward, but whether it was to grab the Wrong Book or smack him, she wasn't sure.

"You really think you can destroy the portal?" Norwood continued in a mocking tone. "Wait, wait, not just the one — all of them?"

"I *know* I can destroy the portal," Uncle Mort corrected him.

Norwood snorted. "Well, I hope you can do it from the Hole, because that's where you're going to be in about five minutes."

Uncle Mort decided to ignore him. "Knell, this is *going* to happen," he said, addressing her instead. "With or without your permission. We don't want to hurt you, but we will if we have to. I don't blame you for not heeding my previous warnings; I know that my actions in the past have not earned me your trust. But things are bad." He stood up and took a step toward her. "They're at their breaking point. If we don't do something to stop this erosion, the Afterlife will disappear."

"Bullshit," Norwood spat, getting angrier. "The Afterlife is fine. You're just using all this doomsday crap as an excuse!"

*He's losing it,* Lex thought, staring at his reddening hands.

"Tell her, Lex — tell her how many people you've Damned! How you're a threat to this world and everyone in it!" Norwood was yelling so hard, flecks of spit were flying out of his mouth.

But she couldn't take her eyes off his hands. "Uncle Mort — "

"How you Damned my wife! My men!" He inhaled deeply. "The president!"

Lex blinked. "What?"

"What?" said Knell.

It happened so fast, and he was standing so close to her, no one could have stopped him. The moment Norwood's finger touched the president's arm, she burst into flame.

When the darkness cleared and Knell was nothing more than a crispy mass on the floor, no one moved. No one spoke until Uncle Mort let out a groan, sounding more exasperated than anything. "Oh, Woody," he said, rubbing his eyes. "You stupid son of a bitch."

Norwood grinned. "Not as stupid as the band of criminals who so blatantly stormed the president's office and Damned her in cold blood. And without your loyal contingent of townspeople here to defend you, it's your word against mine." He pulled a gun out from his waistband and aimed it at them, his eyes even more demented than they'd been at the battle in Grave. "Who do you think they'll believe?"

A million things were running through Lex's mind. And yet somewhere amid the fog of what just happened, one thought above all came to the surface. She glanced at Uncle Mort, who was looking at Pandora and seemed to be thinking the same thing. According to Grimsphere law, if Knell was dead . . .

Then Uncle Mort was now president of the Grimsphere. Right?

"You sniveling snollygoster!" Pandora shouted at Norwood, stomping up to the desk. "What the hell is the matter with you? Did a team of rats gnaw out the contents of your head and refill it with their own droppings? Because YOU, sir, are the biggest shit-for-brains I've *EVER* — "

Exhaling impatiently, Norwood shot her in the chest.

The Juniors screamed as she fell to the floor, but Uncle Mort stood his ground, his face growing paler by the second.

Norwood took aim at Uncle Mort next, his face exuding a confidence that everything was going exactly according to plan. Well, his plan, at least. Obviously not Knell's. "Now, it occurs to me — and Mort, I'm sure you'll agree — that the good people of the Grimsphere will be looking for some strong leadership now, in the wake of this tragic upheaval. Of course, I haven't served as many years as you have, but I *do* have some experience with taking troubled and corrupt governments under my wing. So who better to serve them than — "

With another happy ding, the second elevator opened. But to the Croakers' dismay, Skyla wasn't in it. Stepping out instead was a handful of masked guards led by Boulder, who was clutching —

"Elysia!" Lex shouted. Elysia looked scared and small, but otherwise unharmed. She took one glance at Ferbus's injury and started to cry out, but Boulder held her tightly, one massive hand on her shoulder and the other over her mouth. Driggs swooped in behind her, stifling a yell when he spotted Dora's lifeless body.

Norwood slapped on a look of horror and immediately lowered his gun. "They Damned the president!" he shouted in mock fear, rushing out from behind the desk to the guards. "Arrest them!"

The guards were stunned into inaction for a moment, but they soon unholstered their weapons and trained them on the Croakers. Uncle Mort and company swiveled around to face them, backs to the desk. Both sides were now in neat little lines; if everyone hadn't wanted to kill one another, they could have started a nice game of red rover.

Norwood pretended to cower behind the big guard, but his jeers kept coming. "You're outnumbered, Mort. You're outranked. You're done. Cooperate, and we'll go easy on you. I mean, you'll all get life in the Hole — like you were supposed to in the *first* place — but if you go quietly, we won't have to get violent."

Lex looked from Ferbus's dripping wrist to Dora's still body on the floor. "Yeah," she growled under her breath. "Can't have that, can we?"

"Hands on your head," Boulder ordered the Croakers. "Now!"

Uncle Mort started to raise his arms, but at the last second he gave Lex and Ferbus a shove. "Behind the desk!" he shouted. They flung themselves over the top of the president's huge stone desk and took shelter under it, queasily shoving Knell's scorched body out of the way to make room.

Lex peeked out over the top. Elysia had just elbowed Boulder in the groin, wriggled out of his arms, and was running toward the desk to join them. Boulder grunted and shouted for his team to spread out and shoot — which they did, with real guns instead of stun guns this time. Panicked, Uncle Mort pulled out his own gun and started shooting back.

But Lex was the only one to notice the empty elevator door close.

Ignoring that for now, she ducked back down behind the desk and gave Elysia a quick hug. "Are you okay?"

Elysia let out a cry when she saw Pandora, then turned to Ferbus. "I'm fine. What happened to him?" He was sitting against the back of the desk with his head drooping, eyes closed. "Ferbus! Wake up!"

Ferbus groaned and opened one eye. "Hey, beautiful," he slurred, holding up his mangled hand. "Gimme five." He let out a gurgled laugh. "No, really, gimme. I need the fingers."

"He lost a lot of blood," Lex explained. "I think he's getting loopy."

Driggs popped in next to her, his face white. "Oh shit, Ferb." Then, even more horror dawning, he looked around the room, spotting Bang alone in the elevator. "Where's Pip?" he asked Lex.

She shook her head. Driggs's face fell, and Elysia burst into a fresh batch of tears.

Uncle Mort nudged Lex. With a friggin' gun. "Here. Point that way, pull the trigger."

Lex flinched. She tried not to look at Pandora, whom Driggs had moved on to, hovering over her in shock. "I can't shoot anyone!"

Even in the midst of a shootout, Uncle Mort found the time to roll his eyes. "Lex, in your short but sinful life you've lied, cheated, stolen, Damned scads of people, and started a war. Now is not the time to develop a conscience."

Lex swallowed. Heart in her throat, she peeked her head up, held the gun out in front of her, and started shooting.

"To the left," Driggs whispered in her ear. He'd materialized right next to her and was watching the room. "Right. No — left. You're a terrible shot, Lex."

"Sorry. Forgot to make time for target practice."

*Ding.*

Lex held her breath. The guards kept shooting; no one else seemed to have heard it or to notice as one more guard emerged from the elevator.

It wasn't until that guard yanked a scythe out of her pocket and grabbed Norwood around the neck that she caught their attention.

"Hold your fire!" Skyla shouted, holding the blade to Norwood's throat. Taken completely by surprise, he dropped both his gun and his scythe.

"Shoot, and I'll kill him," she said.

The room went silent. Guns were aimed, but none were fired.

"Drop your weapon," the big guard told her.

Skyla let out a short laugh. "Come on, Boulder," she said. "You know as well as I do that you could fill me to the brim with bullets and I'd still have time to slit his throat on the way down."

Boulder gripped his weapon, but didn't answer.

"Lex, your Lifeglass," Uncle Mort whispered in her ear, urgent. "Give it to me."

Confused, Lex pulled it out and handed it to him. Images started to flash through the glass as he shook it, trying to look for something.

"What's the matter with you?" Norwood was yelling at Boulder, gasping for air. "Shoot her!"

"Do it, and we're both dead," Skyla warned.

The guards looked highly uncomfortable with this situation, Boulder in particular. Until today Skyla had been their superior, their mayor. He obviously trusted her in some capacity or had a history with her, but the president had given Norwood a fair amount of authority since he arrived. Plus he was still the mayor of Croak — Boulder was obligated to protect him. "Hold your fire," he instructed the other guards, his mind churning.

"You idiot!" Norwood was trying to tear Skyla's arm away from his neck, but the woman was stronger than she looked. It barely seemed to take any effort to restrain him. "*SHOOT HER!*" His face was getting redder and redder. His hands opened and closed.

Lex tensed. She knew that look.

She knew that feeling.

"Hurry up!" she told Uncle Mort, who was still peering into the Lifeglass. "He's going to Damn her too!"

The Lifeglass flickered once more, and Uncle Mort smiled.

"I'm gonna go ahead and call a time-out," he announced,

standing up from behind the desk, "while we go to the instant replay."

He held up the Lifeglass, and there it was, plain for all to see: President Knell being Damned — by Norwood.

The guards shifted their aim as Skyla dropped Norwood to the floor. He looked stunned; even he realized how much he had just doomed himself.

Mayor or not, he'd assassinated the president.

He looked up at the sloped ceiling as if hoping to receive further instructions from on high, but found only a pair of guards closing in on him. "I — I just came here to transport a prisoner, and — the president asked me to stay on as an advisor," he rambled. "I had nothing to do with this, I swear! They're tricking you!"

But just as they were about to grab him, his expression went hard again. "I'll Damn you too!" He stood up and held his hands out in front of him. The guards froze.

"Why aren't they shooting?" Lex said to Uncle Mort. "He can't Damn them from a distance; he has to touch them!"

"Yeah, but *they* don't know that," Uncle Mort said.

Lex opened her mouth to enlighten them, but Uncle Mort hissed "No!" and pulled her closer to him. "He's doing a marvelous job of distracting them." Skyla appeared over the top of the desk and dropped down beside them. "Now we can seal the portal."

"With what?" Lex asked. She eyed Uncle Mort's bag, dying to find out what was the one thing in the world that could destroy a portal.

But instead of going for his bag, Uncle Mort reached over the top of the desk and grabbed the computer keyboard. "Here," he said, giving it to Skyla. "Do your thing."

Handing off her scythe to Elysia, Skyla took the keyboard from him and started to type. Lex noticed that her hands were shaking. Uncle Mort noticed too, because he put his hand on her knee.

Skyla hit enter, then looked at the vault door. When nothing happened, she frowned. "That was the code!"

"Shhh," Uncle Mort said. He took her face in his hands and spoke in a calm voice. "Try it again."

Skyla took a deep breath and slowly retyped. This time when she hit enter, the vault door swung out into the open sky.

Lex grinned. The tricked-out windows of the office may have blocked the souls, but a door was still a door. She looked back at Uncle Mort. He was still trying to calm Skyla down, so Lex stepped inside the Afterlife — just for a minute, for one last look.

Unlike in Croak, there were no wrestling presidents to greet her. In fact, the space was deserted, which wasn't surprising; with the entire structure of Necropolis acting as its atrium, there was no need for souls to hang around the main entrance.

"Hey, douchenozzle."

"Gah!" The Afterlife wasn't as deserted as Lex thought. "Stop doing that!"

Cordy peered into the office. "Are we winning?"

"I think we're currently at a standoff," Lex whispered. "What are you doing here?" She spotted Kloo approaching in the distance, followed by Tut. What was this, a party in her honor?

And then it hit her. The portals were closing. Forever.

They were coming to say goodbye.

Lex gripped the bottom of her hoodie. She needed something to hold on to. "No," she whispered to Cordy. "I'm not ready yet. When we go back to Croak to deal with the vault there, I'll meet up with you then!"

Cordy shook her head. "You heard Uncle Mort. Once this portal-closing party gets started, we're all going to be running around like undead chickens with our undead heads cut off, trying to keep the Afterlife together."

"But—"

"Lex," Cordy said in a firm voice. "Do what you have to do. Stop whining, find Mom and Dad, and fix up this increasingly crappy craphole of an Afterlife. You feel me, bro?"

"No, *bro,* I don't—"

"Hi, Lex!" Kloo jumped in. "They're closing up the Afterlife, huh?"

Lex bit back the rest of her argument with Cordy. "Yeah. Looks that way."

"Hope it works."

"Me too." Lex paused. Kloo was one of the souls who'd suffered from memory loss, and they'd always been cautious about upsetting her. But if this really was the last time Lex would ever see her . . .

"Hey, Kloo? His name was Ayjay."

Cordy shot her a displeased look, but Lex was defiant. Kloo, meanwhile, frowned. "Ayjay?" She thought about it harder, and Lex kept watching her face until the tiniest hint of something sparked in her eye. Kloo shook her head, and it was gone—

But hopefully it would be enough.

Tut arrived seconds later, buffing his fingernails, along with Lumpy and Poe. "I will miss the peasants, I suppose," Tut said with a melodramatic sigh, patting Lumpy's hump. "Though I will not miss their infernal interruptions." He looked pointedly at Lex.

"I can't believe you're abandoning me to these numbskulls," Poe moaned, nervously picking at Quoth's feathers. "The other day Thomas Edison stole my shoe and turned it into a battery! I can't take it anymore!"

"You'll be okay, Ed," Lex said. "And remember, someday I'll come back."

"See that you do."

Lex twisted her hoodie harder, trying not to cry at the thought of parting from her beloved Edgar Allan. "Oh, scarecrow," she said. "I think I'll miss you most of all."

"And I, you." He took off his hat, sank into a deep bow, and turned up the corners of his mouth into what might have been the closest thing he'd ever gotten to a smile. "You are the least detestable person I have ever met."

Lex squeezed her hoodie even tighter, her throat burning.

"No!" Skyla shouted from the office, snapping Lex back to the moment. Through the crack of the vault she could see that Skyla and Uncle Mort were arguing about something. "This is *my* city!"

"But this whole thing was my idea," he countered. "I should be the first, to make sure it actually works —"

"Hey." Lex turned back around. Cordy was looking at her, smiling sadly. "Let's just do this," she said. "Before we're out of time."

A rock formed in Lex's gut.

Cordy scrunched up her mouth. "Do I really have to say all the mushy stuff? That I love you and I know you're going to win and you're my favorite person out of everyone in the world, both living and dead?"

"No," said Lex, her voice hoarse. "You don't have to. I don't have to either, do I?"

Cordy grinned. "Nah. I always know what you're thinking anyway."

"Twin perk," they said at the same time.

Lex rubbed her eyes. She wanted to scream and cry and run all at the same time. This was *too hard*.

But she put on a brave face and looked for one last time at her dear departed sister. "Well," she said, hoping to sound light, "see you in fifty years."

Cordy smirked back. "You're a tough kid, Lex. I'd give it a hundred."

That did it. Tears, sobs, and a glob of snot all rocketed out of her face at the same time. She blew her nose into her hoodie, not even caring about how gross that was. It was waterproof; it would survive.

Without turning back — if she did, she'd never leave — Lex tore out of the vault. Skyla was still yelling at Uncle Mort and was near tears as well. "I'm the mayor!" she yelled, smacking him on the shoulder. "Don't you *dare* take this away from me, Mort."

He gave her a look that held a million unsaid things, but a gunshot snapped him out of it. The guards had finally realized that Norwood was bluffing, and they were firing away.

Uncle Mort nodded at Skyla, giving in. "Okay," he said, digging into his bag.

Lex stared intently at his hands, but she still couldn't see what he handed her.

Skyla smiled and took it from him. "Thanks."

"I'll see you soon. Good luck."

"You too."

Uncle Mort turned away from her and started to gather up the Juniors. "What was that?" Lex asked him. "What did you give her?"

"We've got to get out of here," he said gruffly. "This room is about to become a very dangerous place for living people to be."

"Why?"

"Because a portal is going to be put out of commission forever, and I don't think it's going to go quietly, do you?"

Lex glanced back at Skyla. She was looking up and down the height of the vault door. "Is she going to be okay?"

"Yeah, she'll be fine. Once the portal's closed —"

"*No!*" Norwood shouted, overhearing them. He was ducking behind a chair, hiding from the hail of gunfire. At this point there wasn't anything he could do without getting pumped full of lead, and he knew it. He'd lost. "You need to stop this. You have no idea what you're doing — you're going to destroy the Grimsphere!"

Uncle Mort shrugged. "Maybe."

Norwood narrowed his eyes. "Well, if you think I'm going to let you do the same thing to Croak, you're out of your minds. I'll be waiting for you." He waved the Wrong Book at them and tucked it under his arm. "Oh, and one more thing, Lex: Consider your parents Damned."

With that, he jumped out from behind the sofa. Quickly

snatching up his scythe from where it had fallen on the floor, he whipped it through the air and Crashed away.

The shooting stopped for a brief moment while the guards tried to figure out what had just happened, where the culprit had disappeared to, and what, exactly, they should do next. "Find him!" Boulder shouted at them. "Norwood's our new priority. Search the building!"

They hesitated, looking at the desk. "But what about — "

"I'll take care of these guys. Go!"

Lex was staring at the spot where Norwood had been standing, but Uncle Mort grabbed her by the hoodie and gave it a good yank. "Elevator, all of you. Run!"

He bolted for the elevator, leaving the Juniors with no choice but to follow him. They all piled into the glass tube, Bang not even flinching as they crowded in around her. She probably hadn't registered a thing that just happened. Skyla looked fairly out of it, too, Lex noticed when she looked back at her. She was watching the Juniors flee, as if waiting for them to leave.

Ferbus was the last one to stagger in. Uncle Mort removed the crowbar and pushed the down button, but not fast enough; Boulder reached a hand the size of a dinner plate through the glass doors, opening them up again. "Where do you think you're going?"

"Dammit, let us go!" Uncle Mort yelled. "You think we'd do something like this if it weren't important, Boulder? You know we're right!"

Boulder worked his jaw. "I don't know that for sure."

"Well, you're about to find out in two seconds."

Just then a small, withered hand appeared from behind and

settled on Boulder's shoulder. "Let go, kid," Pandora said, fixing her vulturelike stare on him.

"DORA!" the overjoyed Juniors yelled.

She winked at them, then addressed Boulder again. "Come on. Hop to it, Tiny."

Perhaps it was the fact that she'd just risen from the dead, or maybe her shriveled little claw was preposterously strong, but for whatever reason, Pandora's words seemed to suddenly carry an inordinate amount of weight. The look on Boulder's face was one of such intense concentration, Lex thought she could hear gears turning. "Yes, ma'am," he said, removing his hand from the door.

And then Elysia yelled something even more surprising. "Boulder, come with us!"

"Whoa, what?" Lex said.

Elysia grabbed his hand and pulled him into the elevator. "I promise we're right," she told him. "You'll see."

Lex gave Elysia her very best what-the-hell look. Elysia shrugged. "He and I sort of . . . chatted. While I was in custody."

"Elysia, chatting?" Ferbus said into the glass. "Get outta town."

The door closed, and the elevator started to descend. Skyla had opened the vault door wide and was staring into it, her hands balled into fists. Lex tried to wave at the souls inside — at Kloo, who'd looked distracted ever since Lex's cryptic name-dropping; at Tut, who was trying to give Edgar a wedgie; at Edgar, who was futilely trying to escape said wedgie; at Cordy, grinning and waving back as if she were on a parade float —

But someone else had appeared in the Afterlife — and the closer she got, the more recognizable she became. Especially with the light glinting off her silver hair.

"Zara!" Lex shouted, pointing.

In an instant Zara caught Lex's eye and erupted in a flurry of animated gestures. She pointed at herself, then started rotating both hands, as if she were miming using a steering wheel. She was yelling, too, but Lex couldn't hear anything through the glass of the elevator.

"What?" Lex shouted.

But it was too late. The elevator sank below the floor of the office, and Zara and Skyla and the Afterlife disappeared from view.

## 16

The Croakers plummeted back to earth in a narrow tube that didn't stop for five whole minutes.

"It's in express mode," Boulder explained. "No stops."

Lex turned to Uncle Mort. "What was that all about?" she asked him. "What could be important enough for Zara to dare to show her face again?"

He shook his head, looking up. "I have no idea."

Everyone's nerves were jumpy as they descended; they were obviously waiting for something to happen, but none of them really knew what they were waiting *for*. Most of them slumped down to the floor, but Lex paced around the small space, wanting to smash the glass with her hands. Forget about Zara — Norwood had the Wrong Book. *And* her parents. What was he going to do to them?

"So we're going back to Croak, right?" she asked Uncle Mort.

"That's the plan." He turned to Pandora. "Are you all right?"

"Right as rain," she said, taking off her shirt to reveal a bunch of metal spatulas situated around her chest. She put a finger through a newly formed dent. "Though I can't say the same for the old chain mail."

Driggs snickered. "Homemade bulletproof vest, Dora?"

"I'm a very important lady!"

Elysia, meanwhile, was in full-on crisis-relief mode, one arm

around a half-conscious Ferbus, the other around the still-sob-
bing ball that was Bang.

"She's a good kid," Boulder said out of nowhere. Lex and
Driggs looked at him, eyebrows raised. "She told me what you
guys were fighting for, why you did all that bad stuff you did. And
if Skyla's part of it too —" He shrugged, creating more ripples in
his neck muscle. "I trust her. If what she's doing makes the Afterlife safer, then I'm okay with it. Otherwise, what's the point? If
we don't have anywhere nice to go after we're dead?"

Driggs let out a puff of a laugh. "Well put."

Lex was still wary. "You can vouch for this guy?"

Driggs nodded. "He's cool. A perfect gentleman, which is
more than I can say for the other guards."

Elysia shot him a look, then pulled her sleeve down over a few
conspicuous bruises on her arm. She looked at Ferbus. He hadn't
heard.

Lex inspected Driggs's knuckles, which were bloodied. "Wait
a minute. Are you saying that you did, in fact, get solid and kick
some ass?"

"They were roughing her up a little, so I returned the favor.
Luckily, we got interrupted by the call up to the office, so it didn't
get as bad as it could have." He looked at Ferbus's hand, then at
Bang. His face tightened at the reminder of Pip's absence. "And
not as bad as you guys had it."

Lex swallowed. "Yeah."

Driggs frowned, but then his eyes lit up. "Hey, wait a sec. I can
do the same thing for your parents!"

"Huh?"

"I can go back to Croak and bust them out!"

"But what if you can't . . ." She stopped, not wanting to hurt his feelings.

Too late — that miserable expression of frustration and helplessness was back on his face. "I'll do what I can," he said quietly.

Lex grabbed at his arm, even though her hand went right through. She didn't want him to leave, but she didn't want her parents to be left alone, either. She didn't know what she wanted.

"Let me do this," he said. "I can't do anything for you here, I can't — " He snorted sharply. "Just let me do it."

Lex closed her eyes. "Okay," she said. "Go. Get them out if you can."

He brought his lips to her forehead and kissed it, though she felt nothing. "I'll see you there."

Uncle Mort nodded his approval and told them, "We'll be there as soon as we can. We need to make a little" — he looked at Ferbus — "pit stop."

Driggs looked more than disturbed by that last part, but he turned to Lex, mouthed "Love you," and was gone.

They rode the rest of the way down in silence, Lex wondering the whole time how it could possibly get worse than this, but knowing with certainty that it would.

When four minutes and fifty-five seconds had elapsed, Boulder reached out and pressed a few buttons. The elevator screeched to a halt.

"What are you doing?" Lex asked.

"The citizens will be expecting us to get out at ground level.

They'll mob us," Boulder said. "This is the second floor, so we can hopefully get the jump on them. It'll give us enough time to explain what happened."

The door opened into a space that looked like a hotel corridor. Boulder exited the elevator and crossed to a large painting, which he removed from the wall to reveal a door.

Uncle Mort raised an eyebrow. "Backways?"

Boulder nodded. "Skyla isn't as slick as she thinks she is."

Elysia helped Ferbus up from the floor while Lex grabbed Bang by the elbows and pulled. She arose without a struggle, but her hair still covered her face. What little amount of skin Lex could see was wet with tears.

They walked through the door — Boulder barely fit — and pounded down one last set of stairs. "Hang on. I remember this hall," Elysia said as they walked. She pointed. "There, that's where — "

*Driggs and I had a lovely discussion about how he murdered his parents,* Lex silently filled in. She missed him already.

Then she frowned. If this was the same hallway, then that door Boulder was now opening led to . . .

"Oh, no," she said. "Not again."

The smoky, suffocating air of the Hole wafted out into the hallway, turning Lex's stomach. "We'll go fast this time," Uncle Mort promised when he saw her face. "Come on."

And so for the second time in two days they marched right back into hell on earth. Lex plugged her ears, not wanting to hear a peep out of those tormented souls, but she couldn't drown out the guy who was still going on about sitting in solemn silence on a dull, dark dock.

"I'm going to throw up," Lex said to herself, or Elysia, or

maybe no one at all. The room was even worse than before. The screaming girl they'd heard the first time was getting louder, more desperate. Lex thought about closing her eyes, but falling into the Hole was absolutely the last thing she wanted to do. So she stared at her sneakers instead, causing her to bump into Elysia.

"What are you doing?" Lex screeched, her voice veering into hysterics. "Why'd you stop?"

She could barely be heard over the screaming girl, who seemed to be very close. Extremely close.

In the Hole Elysia had paused to stare into.

"Norwood said he had other business in coming here," Elysia said. "That's what he said, that he was transporting a prisoner."

At the word "prisoner," Lex's mind flew back to the battle at Grave. There had been someone standing off to the side wearing an executioner's hood. Was that who Norwood was talking about?

Lex looked down and squinted hard as the smoke cleared.

The screaming girl — the prisoner — was Sofi.

In the space of only a few days she'd already lost a ton of weight. Her eyes were bloodshot, her hair wild and strawlike. The unbearable wails kept coming out of her cracked, chapped lips, her always perfectly manicured nails ripped and torn from clawing at the sides of the Hole.

Now Lex really did think she was going to throw up. Sofi had betrayed her and all of Croak, had helped Zara kill Driggs, and had generally been a jealous asshat ever since Lex met her . . . but she didn't deserve this. No one deserved this.

"Keep moving, girls," Boulder called from up ahead. "Come on, we're almost out!"

"There's nothing we can do," Lex whispered, pulling on Elysia's arm, yet unable to tear her eyes away.

Elysia pressed her lips together, resolute. "Yes, there is." In one swift movement she drew Skyla's scythe out of her pocket, dropped it to the floor, and, with a twitch of her foot, kicked it into the Hole.

The noise of it clattering down the stone sides faded as Elysia grabbed Lex's hand, taking off again. They rushed toward the door that Boulder was holding open for them and burst out into the brightly lit hallway.

"What did you do that for?" Lex asked her as they ran. "Uncle Mort never gave Sofi the Loophole — she can't Crash!"

"I know," Elysia said, her jaw set. "It wasn't for Crashing."

|||||||

The lobby of Necropolis was pure chaos.

Word had spread that President Knell had been killed, but the citizens seemed to be wildly confused about who had done it and whether they were still on the loose. Some had gathered at the windows, craning their necks to get a glimpse of the office, while others stood in aimless clusters, looking around for any more danger that might be lurking —

And fully unaware that the danger was marching right through the lobby. "Someone's going to recognize us," Lex said to Uncle Mort without looking at him or moving her lips.

"No, they're not," he said, staring forward, keeping the same straight face. "The guards aren't even watching."

He was right. What few guards were left in the lobby were

scattered, disorganized. They shouted for the citizens to remain calm, all the while sounding fairly panicked themselves. No one knew what had happened, as the only witnesses were now casually strolling toward the front door without a single eye looking their way.

Until the receptionist let out a shriek. "There they are!"

Uncle Mort let out a huff of defeat. "Mar-*lene*," he whined. "I thought we were *cool*."

"So much for the Wink of Trust," Lex said.

The citizens surrounded them, forming a tight circle with the Croakers at its center. "Where do you think you're going?" one man shouted.

"They're the ones!" said another woman. "The fugitives from Croak!"

"What happened up there? What did you do to her?"

"They're saying the president was killed!"

"She was," Boulder boomed above all of them. Jaws dropped. "But not by these folks. By Norwood."

The new mayor of Croak must have made quite a good name for himself in the greater Grimsphere since taking office, because the hushed whispers that spread through the crowd were laced with the sting of betrayal. "So, uh," continued Boulder, whose training clearly did not include a unit on how to make eloquent, historical speeches, "we have a new president now — "

Lex almost forgot! She turned to Uncle Mort, but he was inching closer to Pandora. "You ready?" he quietly asked her.

Dora grinned. "Have been for years."

Boulder grandly gestured to the people in the lobby. "All yours, Madam President."

Elysia and Lex gasped in perfect harmony. Even the half-un-conscious Ferbus gurgled something.

"Thanks, kid." Pandora took a big step out in front of every-one and assumed the air of a grizzled five-star general. "Now then. For years this place has stunk to high heaven," she said in a voice that was much louder than her tiny frame should have been able to produce. It filled the lobby. "Run by a bunch of knuckle-heads who couldn't recognize disaster when they saw it right in front of their faces. Or worse, chose not to. Well, all that's going to change."

Lex had been so out of it, she'd barely noticed that when Dora took her shirt off in the elevator, she continued to change her whole outfit: she was now wearing a black hoodie, cargo pants, and boots instead of whatever it was that old women wear. She looked imposing, staunch, like a drill sergeant. Scary.

"Odds are," she continued, "you're not going to like these changes. They will upheave your way of life, and they're not going to be easy to accept. You might protest against them, and that's certainly your right, but believe me, these changes are for the better. Furthermore, let it be known that my full support is behind this brave band of yahoos standing behind me, and anyone who tries to interfere with their objectives will hence-forth be prosecuted to the full extent of the Terms of Execu-tion."

She clapped her hands together. "That's all! Any questions, the door to my office is always open. Er — once I get a door. Heck, once I get an office."

At that, the crowd dissolved into frenzied murmurs, but the tone was calmer than the panic they'd been swept up in just moments before. "That oughta hold 'em," Pandora said, dusting her hands off. "You kids ready to go?"

"Not yet," said Uncle Mort, reaching into his bag. "Here." He handed her the perforator. "Just remember to brace yourself. It's got a kick to it."

Then, to the Juniors' surprise, he swept her up in a hug. Lex couldn't hear what they were saying to each other; she was still too busy trying to process what was happening. The only thing she caught, as Dora patted him on the back, was her telling him, "You'll do just fine."

She turned to the Juniors and gave them a warm smile. "Good luck, kids. And stay out of my kitchen!" she said, wagging her gnarled finger. "That deep fryer'll singe your eyebrows clean off!"

The Juniors were still too stunned to speak. They just watched as President Pandora strode off to greet her new citizens, head held high and hunch straightened out, looking taller than she ever had before.

|||||||

Though no one tried to stop them as they exited the building, Uncle Mort and his crew still ran as fast as they could, giddy to be free from that tower of nightmares.

They booked it out the door, past the geographic center monument and the abandoned Stiff, and into an adjacent field. Lex looked back at Necropolis. Through the windows she spotted guards running up and down the elevators, but they were getting hard to see; the smoggy layer around the surface was growing darker, as if every soul in the Afterlife was arriving to watch what happened next.

"We have to get to a hospital," Elysia said, straining under the weight of Ferbus. "We're losing him."

"Your FACE is losing him," Ferbus confirmed.

"No hospitals," Uncle Mort said. "They'll ask for IDs, and we don't have any. We're short on time, too."

"Then where are we going?" Lex asked.

"To our 'in case of emergency.'" He dug around in his bag, shoving aside Pip's glowing Spark with a wince. "I was hoping we wouldn't have to resort to this, but — " He pulled out a picture and showed it to them. "This is a house outside of Baltimore, Maryland. We'll have to Crash — which for the record I am *not* thrilled about, but we are officially out of options."

Lex frowned. She'd never seen that house before, nor did she know anyone who lived in Baltimore.

"Everyone got it?" Uncle Mort held it up to each of them one more time. "Bang? Come on Bang, look." She still wasn't showing her face, but she briefly swept her hair aside to look at the photo, then gave a slight nod.

He did a quick head count, his mouth sagging at the reminder of their dwindling numbers. "Okay, see you there. Ready — "

He was cut off by a sudden rumbling in the ground. They glanced back at Necropolis.

The glass was beginning to tremble. It was making a strange vibrating noise, too, as if the whole building had been pricked like a tuning fork. The cloud of souls outside shimmered, then became blurry. There was nothing the Croakers could do but watch —

As the president's office exploded.

Every inch of the glass cone's tip shattered, bursting into a billion tiny stars that glittered as they mushroomed away from the building. With the exception of the heavy stone desk, all the furniture soared off into space as well, followed by the president's singed corpse. Even the vault door flew away, hurtling into the distance like a Frisbee.

All at once the thick layer of souls surrounding the building disappeared.

"She did it!" said Elysia. "Skyla closed the portal!"

Uncle Mort didn't even seem to hear her. He tore his scythe through the air, his eyes never leaving the blunt, newly leveled surface of Necropolis.

## 17

The house was a crack den. It had to be. One whole side of it was covered with graffiti, a couple of windows were broken, and the overgrown grass reached the top of the mailbox — which was also broken.

But Lex's mind was still back in Kansas. "What *happened?*" she said to Uncle Mort as they ducked behind some hedges. "That was a really big explosion — is that what you were expecting? You think Skyla's okay?"

"Yes, that's what we were expecting. Yes, I'm sure Skyla is fine — " He counted heads again, then frowned. "Where's Elysia?"

Lex looked around. "She didn't Crash through?"

"She was right next to me," Ferbus said, struggling to remain conscious. "She scythed at the same time we did!"

"Okay, calm down." Uncle Mort raised his scythe again. "I'll go back and look for her. Don't move."

Ferbus lay down as Uncle Mort Crashed out. "As if this could have gotten any worse," he muttered.

Lex stared at the pulpy dregs at the end of his arm. How could she ever make this up to him? She could try to fix Driggs, she could apologize every day for the rest of her life, but sorrys didn't put hands back on wrists. And now, Elysia —

Was kneeling right in front of them, clinging to Uncle Mort.

Ferbus tried to grab her but was too weak, so Lex jumped in instead. "What happened?" she asked, hugging her.

"I have no idea!" Elysia's eyes were gigantic, though for some reason she was also half laughing. "I scythed along with the rest of you, but it didn't work! I couldn't Crash!"

"I had to pull her through," Uncle Mort said with a frown. "Lys, try it again."

Elysia tore her scythe through the air, but nothing happened. It didn't rip the air or expose even the smallest sliver of ether.

Uncle Mort rubbed his chin. "Strange."

"I know, right?" she exclaimed, unable to keep the smile off her face.

Ferbus gave her an odd look. "What's with you, Chuckles?"

"Nothing! Just happy everyone made it!"

Uncle Mort raised an eyebrow, then stood up from their hiding place. "Come on." He motioned for them to follow him to the front stoop, where he reached for the doorbell. "Now, don't scream, any of you. When the door opens, don't scream, don't gasp. Don't react in any way. Deal?"

"Deal."

Yet when the door opened to reveal the eye-patched man within, Lex's eyes widened. "Deal off."

"*Ayjay!*" Elysia shrieked, obliterating the rules Uncle Mort had set forth for them. "What are you — "

Uncle Mort cut her off with a nudge and elbowed his way into the house. Lex and the others followed while a confused Ayjay held the door open, his good eye darting around the room. He didn't recognize any of them. "Who are you people?"

"Are you alone?" Uncle Mort asked.

"Yeah, but — "

"Close the door."

Ayjay finally came to his senses. "No." His bulging muscles — which Lex noticed had grown even bulgier than the last time she'd seen him — flexed menacingly. "Get out or I'll call the police."

Uncle Mort snickered. "No, you won't." He helped lay Ferbus down on a couch that Lex was sure housed several colonies of insects.

"Whoa!" Ayjay finally noticed Ferbus's wounds. "Hey, I don't want any trouble, all right?"

"Ayjay — "

"How do you know my name?"

"I was your social worker," Uncle Mort said. "After your accident, when you were in the hospital. I know you don't remember me — "

"No, I don't."

" — but I remember you. And I know that you're a good kid. And you're going to help me fix this other good kid, because you're not the type to just sit around and watch while somebody else suffers. That's why you're pre-med, right?"

Lex bristled at this new piece of information. Ayjay, going to med school? But Kloo was the one who'd always wanted to be a doctor; Ayjay had dreamed of opening a gym. A quick glance around the room confirmed it, though. A pile of organic chemistry textbooks sat atop the end table along with a few dog-eared pages of notes.

Ayjay was thinking. "I don't know how to suture," he said. "I haven't even gotten into school yet."

"Look, we're not cops," said Uncle Mort. "I know what you do here. And if there's at least one thing you know how to do, it's stitch people up."

When Ayjay opened his mouth to protest, Uncle Mort moved in closer and cranked up the badass. "Don't lie to me. I know all about you. I'm not here to get you in trouble, I just want your services. Now, are you going to help, or are you going to let this kid bleed out all over your couch?"

Ayjay resisted a moment more, then exhaled hard through his nose, his nostrils flaring. "Be right back."

As soon as he pounded up the stairs, Lex exploded. "Okay, what? *What?*"

Uncle Mort sat on the couch and gently rolled up Ferbus's sleeve. "After Ayjay left Croak, he fell in with a gang of drug dealers," he said matter-of-factly. "At first he was just their muscle, but as time went on, it became obvious that he was a little more gifted than the rest. As a weightlifter, he knew a lot about the human body, plus a fair bit of Kloo's medical knowledge had rubbed off on him, so — "

"So — what, he became a mob doctor?"

"Yeah. Sort of."

"So when gang members get into their little shooting matches — "

"Turf wars," Elysia interjected. They both turned to stare at her. "What?" she said innocently. "I do watch television, you know."

"When they get shot," Lex asked her uncle, "he fixes them up?"

"Better than going to a hospital or getting caught."

Lex let out a puff of disbelief. She looked around the house, its den the very definition of filthy. A couple of pizza boxes littered the floor, and there were traces of some substance on the table that she was fairly positive she didn't want to know about. There were also piles of clothes, a couple of duffel bags, and, disturbingly, a box full of toys.

Poor Ayjay. He'd erased his memory of Croak, all to spare himself the pain of losing Kloo, and for what? This? He'd have been better off with the grief.

"At least he's trying to straighten up," Uncle Mort said, as if he'd heard Lex's thoughts. He nodded toward the textbooks. "He's smart. He'll make it out of here."

"If he doesn't get himself killed first."

Uncle Mort didn't respond to that. A moment later Ayjay reappeared with a handful of supplies. "Should we be expecting company anytime soon?" Uncle Mort asked him.

"Doubt it," Ayjay said. "This is mainly my place. They only come here when something, uh, goes wrong."

He paused in the doorway, taking in the strange company he was hosting. Three teenage girls, one possibly crying behind all that hair. An adult who knew all about him. And a kid whose hand had been halfway blown off by something much worse than fireworks.

Lex inwardly cringed. Ayjay didn't know who they were; he had no reason to help them.

But he did. He sat down beside Ferbus on the couch and lifted his maimed arm. The blood had congealed into a black mess, with small shards of bone poking out. "How did this happen?" Ayjay asked, wincing.

"Doesn't matter," Uncle Mort said. "What can you do for him?"

Ayjay furrowed his brow. "I can't fix this. I can only do damage control." He inspected the makeshift belt tourniquet. "Danger of infection, gangrene —" He looked at Uncle Mort. "It's gotta come off."

Ferbus jumped, somehow wrenching himself up to the surface of consciousness. "No," he slurred, weakly thrashing. Uncle Mort held him down. "Don't!"

Uncle Mort nodded. "Do it."

"But —" Ayjay leaned in and tried to speak in a hushed tone. "I don't have the surgical instruments for this."

Uncle Mort didn't falter. "You got a toolbox?"

Ferbus's eyes bulged.

Then he started screaming, and Elysia began to cry, and somehow Lex's synapses connected enough to realize that this would be a good time to grab Elysia by the shoulders and pull her away. "Shh, it's better this way," she heard herself say. She'd gone on autopilot; she had no earthly idea if it was better this way.

"Don't," Ferbus choked, grabbing Ayjay with his good hand and indicating his eye patch. *"You know what it's like."*

"Sorry, dude."

Ferbus could see that he was losing, so he stopped to stare at Ayjay, breathing heavily. "How'd you lose your eye?"

Ayjay's hardened face cracked just for a moment, and a well-worn confusion poured out. "I . . . don't know."

"*I* do." With his last bit of remaining strength Ferbus tightened his grip. "Stop this and I'll tell you."

Ayjay hesitated. But Uncle Mort shook his head. "He's delirious. He's lost too much blood."

The doubt remained on Ayjay's face, but only for a few seconds more. "Knock him out," he told Uncle Mort, getting up and tossing him a rattling pill bottle.

Ferbus watched with wide, petrified eyes, knowing what was about to happen, but also knowing that he was far too weak to stop it.

Ayjay pounded back up the stairs. "I'll get the saw."

|||||||

Lex stared at the empty pizza boxes.

*That's where it all started.*

She'd accidentally set a pizza box on fire back at the Crypt in Croak — Damned it, though she hadn't known at the time that that's what she was doing. She'd done it right in front of Zara, too, confirming that she possessed the powers that Zara so desperately wanted to steal. It had snowballed from there, and months later, here they were. In some drug dealer's house, waiting for her friend to wake up to a freshly amputated hand, wondering if her parents were still alive, and preparing for the battle that would finally finish what she'd started.

She glanced at the bloody gauze covering Ferbus's stump, then back at the pizza boxes.

It couldn't come fast enough.

A clang came from the bathroom, where Ayjay was cleaning his tools. Uncle Mort had run to the store to buy some more painkillers, Elysia was curled up asleep next to Ferbus, and Bang was back in her fetal position on the floor next to the couch, also conked out.

Ferbus stirred in his sleep. He opened one eye, looked at Lex, then closed it again. "You did this," he slurred before drifting back to sleep.

Lex fought a wave of nausea. She didn't blow him up herself, but it was her fault he'd even been in Necropolis to begin with.

"I'll fix it," she said, robotic.

Ayjay appeared in the doorway and flicked on a light switch, startling Lex. She hadn't even realized it had gotten dark out.

She couldn't help herself. "So what made you decide to become a doctor?"

He regarded her carefully. "I'm not sure," he said. "I don't remember liking science as a kid, but when I woke up from my accident, it was like . . . I don't know, there was this little voice telling me I had to do it. Like it was my calling or something." He shrugged. "So I listened."

*The little voice's name is Kloo,* Lex thought. *FYI.*

As if regretting that he'd opened up so much about himself, Ayjay cleared his throat and went on the defensive. "Listen, who are you guys? Really?"

"We told you —"

"You think I'm stupid?" Ayjay nodded at Uncle Mort. "He's no social worker."

Lex was a good liar, but not this good. There were too many cracks in their story. "No, he's not."

"Then what? Did you know me before my accident? Do you know what happened to me?" His eyes were troubled as he looked at Ferbus. "He said he knew."

*You were injected with Elixir and almost murdered by a homicidal maniac. That's how you lost your eye. Then said maniac went on to blow up our town. Your girlfriend was killed. You erased your own memory, which had previously held several years worth of rather good memories — of being rescued from your crappy home life, taken to Croak, trained as a Grim, making friends, and falling in love. You were happy. Once.*

"Sorry." Lex's gaze returned to the pizza box. "I don't know."

Frustrated, Ayjay ran his hand through his hair. The blond streak in his fauxhawk had long since faded. He got up from the couch, faced the wall, then turned back around. "You know, I — " His eyes went wide. "What the hell is *that?*"

Lex whipped around to find Driggs hovering behind her. "Ayjay?" His voice was astonished, as if *he* were the one looking at a ghost instead of the other way around.

Ayjay, meanwhile, was freaking the hell out. "Get it out of here!"

Driggs looked stung. "I'm not an 'it.'"

"He doesn't know who we are, remember?" Lex whispered to Driggs.

But Driggs wasn't listening. He was just staring at Ayjay's disgusted face, his own melting into a mess of humiliation. "Sorry. I'll go."

"Wait!" Lex jumped up. "What about my parents?"

"They're still in jail under the Bank. There was no way I could break them out without getting caught, but they're okay for now. Guards are under strict orders not to hurt them. Probably because Norwood plans to use them as a bargaining tool, as usual."

Lex wanted to scream with relief, but instead she frowned. Driggs was acting very weird, even for him. "What's wrong?"

"Nothing."

Ayjay was still going ballistic. "What the hell *is* that?"

"Trick of the light," Lex said irritably. "Driggs — "

"Get it out!" Ayjay yelled.

"I'm *going!*" Driggs exploded, his face so unbearably sad that Lex skipped a breath. "I'm going."

He started to fade away, but she reached out to stop him. "Come outside," she said. "Please. Let's talk, away from him."

Driggs paused but then nodded, disappearing through the wall.

"Stay here," Lex instructed Ayjay — but he'd already fled up-stairs.

She went out the back door and found herself in the most depressing backyard in existence. Rusted swing set: check. Empty sandbox: check. Old car with its wheels missing, propped up on cinder blocks, featuring several bullet holes: check, check, and check.

Driggs was hovering over one of the swings, pretending to sit on it. Lex sank into the one next to him. "Are you okay?"

"I can't live like this," he said, staring ahead, his eyes glassy. "I'm not even human."

"You are," Lex insisted. "Sort of."

"I'm not." He raised his arms, then dropped them in a hope-less shrug. "Humans can touch things. Humans can feed them-selves Oreos. Humans can *drum.*"

His voice cracked on that last word, and Lex finally caught on. He must have visited his room back in Uncle Mort's house, tried to pound away some of his frustration, and failed to even be able to do that.

So here were his miseries at last, all piling out at once: every-thing he'd been dealing with since they left Croak, all the little deaths he'd been dying every day. Lex knew they were in there somewhere, knew that he was devastated. But he'd hidden it so well.

"Humans can walk into a room without being shrieked at and scared of. Humans can kiss their fucking girlfriends." His words were angry, but his voice just sounded sad. "I can't do any of those things. I can't do *anything*."

Lex desperately wanted to say something that would make him feel better, but she couldn't come up with a thing. And even if she could, whatever it was would probably be so lame that she'd want to punch herself in the face.

"I can't live this way," he said again. "One foot in the world of the living, one foot in the world of the dead. I can't. It needs to be one or the other."

"Well, that's what the reset is for, right? When I Annihilate Grotton" — Lex's voice quivered a little on that part — "you'll either be restored to your human form, or . . ."

"Or I'll be dead. In the Afterlife, at least — but dead." He shrugged. "Grotton told me it has something to do with percentages, that it all depends on how much of my soul escaped. If it was less than half, I'll live. If it was more than half, I'll die."

Lex took a few measured breaths, digging up every ounce of strength to refrain from crying. "I'll fix it," she said for the billionth time. "I'll send him to the Dark, I swear."

"But what if it doesn't work?" He looked so worried. "I've barely been able to live this way for a week; how am I going to do it for eternity?"

"It *will* work," she said, this time with more force. "Are you seriously calling into question my ability to kill things? Me?" She grinned and switched to a demonic voice, raising her arms like claws. *"THE MOST POWERFUL GRIM IN THE WORLD?"*

Driggs stared at her. Then he laughed.

And *that* happened to be Lex's favorite sound on the planet. "Driggs?"

"Yes?"

"You can still try to make yourself solid, right?"

"Yeah. If Norwood does anything to your parents, I'll — "

"My parents can handle themselves. Dad's a big, burly guy and Mom was a former Grim, for shit's sake. If this really is your last night on earth, we're going to make it a good one." She got up from the swing, walked across the moonlit yard to the junk car, and patted its door. "Hop in."

Driggs eyed the bullet hole inches from her hand. "Hop in . . . to the Cracktastic Deathmobile?"

Lex tapped the frame impatiently. "I was thinking Hump Buggy, but sure. Whatever you want."

The smile that broke through Driggs's face lit up the yard.

He flew in through the nonexistent driver's side window while Lex ran around to the passenger side and opened the door — which came off in her hand and fell to the ground.

"Um — oh." She looked at the rusty debris that rubbed off on her fingers, then at Driggs. "I broke the door."

"Further adding to the already swanky ambiance," he said, gesturing at the ripped car seats, the torn-off side mirrors and cracked windshield.

She jumped in. "So. It's rustic."

"Cozy."

"Spiderwebby."

"Filled with rodent feces."

"Correction," Lex said, sniffing at the pile at her feet. "Highly fragrant rodent feces." She winced. "Maybe this isn't such a good idea."

"Hey." He looked serious. "Lex, I need you to know something, and I'm only going to say it once: Not even the tallest mountain of raccoon droppings could ever get in the way of my love for you."

"That might be the most romantic thing you've ever said to me."

"It's Shakespeare. One of the sonnets."

They were silent for a moment.

Lex eyed the floor. "So . . . how do we do this?"

Driggs squirmed. "I'm not sure. Let me just, um, get a body here."

He started to strain, then stopped and looked at her, slightly panicked. "And just for the record, before this whole ghost thing I could last until the cows came home. Until the cows came home, the barn door locked behind them, and milk poured forth from their swollen —"

"Manhood duly noted, chief," she said, holding up her hand. "No need to paint me a picture."

"Good. Because I've never done this before, and I'm not really sure what picture I should be painting."

"Well, neither have I, so . . ." She waved her hand. "Just keep going."

But whatever he was doing wasn't working. He closed his eyes, his voice worried. "Shit."

"Hey, I have an idea," Lex said. "Give me a sec."

He kept trying. "Idea as in 'good idea,' or idea as in 'let's take the Ferris wheel, everyone, I'm sure it'll be a carefree ride of thrills and delights and whimsy' — "

"Does this help?"

Driggs opened his eyes and, in the space of a yoctosecond, popped right into a solid body. Lex half expected to hear a wacky *boing* sound effect.

She grabbed his arm to keep him that way, while he kept on staring at her bare chest. "So," he said, swallowing, "good idea, then."

"Thank you."

He pulled her close and gave her a kiss. "And thank *you* for sparing me your devil corset."

She held it up and waved it in his face. "It's a standard bra, Driggs. From, like, Target."

"Satan employs many disguises."

"Like you're from the Land of Superior Underwear. Let's see what sort of designer boxers you've chosen to grace my presence with today." She unzipped his pants and looked. "Dude. Penguins?"

"Um, penguins are officially recognized as the most adorable bird on the planet," he said, a hint of anxiety creeping into his voice. "What's wrong with penguins?"

"Nothing — "

"And igloos. See their little igloos?"

"Yes — "

"The Santa hats are a bit much, I'll give you that, but they were a Christmas present, okay? And if I'd known that I was going to die while wearing them and be forever doomed to their Arctic quirkiness — and of hypothermia, too, how's that for irony — "

"Driggs," she interrupted, grabbing his chin and boring her eyes into his. "I thought we were on a tight time frame here."

"Right." He scratched his head. "I think that perhaps, since I'm talking way too much, there is the slightest chance that I might be a tiny bit nervous."

Lex smirked. "Relax, spaz."

"Oh, no way. You do *not* get to use that against me. I just — " He scratched his head. "I want this to be perfect."

"I'm not sure we're capable of perfect. Would you be willing to settle for cracktastic?"

Driggs thought about this, then nodded. "I would."

With that, they started making out so heavily that Lex was sure the gas tank would explode and send them both to a firebally grave. They stopped only once so that Driggs could point at the fogged windshield and say, "Remember that scene from *Titanic* — "

"Yes, Driggs. Everyone remembers that scene from *Titanic*."

"See? Classic cinema."

"Just please don't start shouting that you're the king of the world, or I swear, I will not hesitate for one second to cut off your — ow!"

"What?"

"Gearshift. Stabbing me. In the back."

"Okay, maybe if I lift you this way — "

Her elbow knocked into something. The windshield wipers sprang to life.

"Oh, this is fun," she said. "Now all we need is some whipped cream and a video camera."

Driggs laughed and squeezed her tighter. "Lex?"

"Yeah?"

"You're ridiculous. I love you."

She felt a lump rise in her throat, but she pushed it back down. Not now. She ran her hands through his still-wet hair and looked into his blue-brown eyes. "I love you too."

He ran his hand down her cheek. "And Lex?"

"Yes?"

"There's a bug in your hair."

"Even better."

She gave him another quick peck, then looked in the mirror to investigate her hair. "*Shit,*" she said, her eyes opening wide. "Don't move."

"Why, are you sticking to the leather seat? Because I am all kinds of sticking to the leather seat, in places that I didn't even *know* about —"

"No. Slightly bigger problem," she said, still frozen. "Uncle Mort: staring. Us: very naked."

"Crap." Driggs tried to wipe his face clean of saliva, though there was a sizable amount. "Think he can see us?"

"He's not a dinosaur, Driggs. His vision doesn't depend solely on movement."

"Okay, you really need to stop basing your entire knowledge of dinosaurs on what you learned in *Jurassic Park.*"

Lex shushed him again, poked her head up over the headrest, and made eye contact with her frowning uncle.

Cringing, she held her breath and waited for the yelling and separating and lifelong grounding to commence, complete with a sideshow of exposed body parts flapping whimsically in the night breeze —

But he just turned around and went back into the house.

"What . . . just happened?" Driggs asked.

"I'm not sure," Lex said. "I think we just got consent to do — "
She waved her hands. "You know. Stuff."

"Then stuff," he said, taking her back into his arms, "is what
we shall do."

So they did stuff. All night long. Awkward, sweaty, inexperi-
enced, painful, wonderful, gearshift-poking, windshield-wiper-
waving stuff.

And it couldn't have been more cracktastic.

## 18

"Rise and shine, Croakers!" Uncle Mort's Cuff shouted early the next morning. "G'day? Anyone there?"

The Juniors jolted up from the makeshift beds they'd fashioned for themselves around the living room — except for Driggs, who'd gone back to Croak to check on Lex's parents, and Ferbus, who was still sleeping, snoring, and drooling.

They huddled together around Uncle Mort. "Broomie?" he rasped into his Cuff, still half asleep.

"Yeah, I've got some bloody good news. It worked."

That woke him up. "What do you mean?"

"I mean, sealing the portal — it worked!" she exclaimed. Lex could just imagine her with a giant Yorick in hand, sloshing it around. "It just occurred to me that you had no way of knowing that, so I thought I'd check in. The plan is officially working. The Afterlife hasn't lightened up any yet, but hey, we'll take what we can get, eh?"

"How do you know that for sure?" Lex asked.

"Lest you forget, we had a portal ourselves up until a few hours ago. The souls inside were kind enough to fill us in, Pip among them."

Bang tensed up and grabbed Elysia's arm.

"Pip's okay?" Elysia asked.

"Oh, more than okay. He's with Riqo, and they're as happy as pigs in slop."

A tiny smile formed on Bang's face.

"Some girl named Sofi, too. She said to tell Elysia thanks, whatever that means."

"How's everything else going in DeMyse?" Uncle Mort asked.

They heard a slosh of liquid and a gulp. "Swimmingly!" she said, mouth half full. "Only one problem: that dillhole Norwood is still Crashing around like a drunken elephant —"

"Actually," Uncle Mort said with a bit of guilt, "that was us."

"Oh. Well, knock it off. Violations can still cause damage — and the portal destruction itself is far from a delicate procedure. The blast zones around them are hit pretty hard."

"And — your portal?"

"Yep. LeRoy took care of it. Blew the hub clean up, but we're all right."

Uncle Mort looked visibly relieved. "Good. Now we can start spreading the word —"

"Start? What do you think I've been doing all night long?"

Puzzled, Uncle Mort reached into his bag and pulled out a rolled-up sheet of paper. Lex recognized it as the world map he'd taken from his basement. But what she hadn't noticed then were the little dots spattered around in nearly every country.

"Grim towns!" Elysia said.

There they were, all over the world. Some, like Croak, were green, while Necropolis and DeMyse and many others were red. In fact, some of them were switching colors before their eyes.

"Whoa," Lex said, pointing at one that had just turned red, right in the middle of Australia. "What happened?"

"The mayor of Perish just destroyed its portal," Uncle Mort explained.

*Just like the keypad doors in Necropolis,* Lex thought, *but the other way around.* Green to red, doors to the Afterlife locking them out forever.

She surveyed the map. There weren't many green ones left. "You were right," she said to Uncle Mort. "The mayors really are sealing the portals."

"Yeah," he said, lightly running his fingers over the dots, his eyes filling with something that Lex assumed was gratitude. "They are."

"At this rate," Broomie said, "they should all be closed up within a few hours. Once they are, Mort, you take care of the last one, and bam — damage stopped. Then Lex does her thing, zaps that Grotton dickwad to kingdom come — and double bam, damage reversed!"

Lex felt like retching at the prospect, but she said nothing. "One small snag, though," Broomie said. "You'll have to get past Norwood. Sounds like he and all the other gun-toting blokes in Croak are gearing up for a showdown."

Lex swallowed. "One that will probably involve my parents."

"Most likely," Broomie said. "Pandora issued a national statement requiring all Grims to do as you ask, give you anything you need, and get the hell out of your way. She said compliance is mandatory, but Norwood doesn't give a bugger what she says. So be prepared for a bit of a tussle."

Uncle Mort nodded. "This is more than I could have hoped for. Thank you, Broomie."

"No worries, mate. Good luck." She clicked off.

Uncle Mort sat quietly for a moment, looking at the map, then stood up. "Okay, you heard the woman," he said flatly. "We leave for Croak in a few hours." He tossed the map to Elysia. "Lys, you're on map duty. Let me know when all the cities have changed to red."

"You got it!" she said, eagerly rolling it out in front of her.

"Until then, I'm going to take a walk," he said, getting up. "Won't be gone long."

Lex watched him go. He drifted out the door, his eyes vacant. Was he just tired, or was he acting weird?

Lex rubbed her eyes again, then glanced at Elysia, who was *definitely* acting weird. The girl was grinning from ear to ear, staring at that map.

"Lys, what's going on with you?" Lex asked. "You seem . . ."

She couldn't put her finger on it. Elysia was just as scared and miserable as the rest of them, Lex knew, especially after everything that had happened in Necropolis. Still, she was unmistakably bubblier than usual.

"Different, right?" Elysia put her elbow on the table and propped her chin up with her hand. "I *feel* different. I don't know — lighter, somehow. Like, you know how back when you were in school, you'd be so worried about the end of the year, with all the tests and finals and stuff, and then when they were all over and it was summer vacation, you just felt like this big weight had been lifted off of you and all you had to worry about was what time the pool opened so you could go swimming all day?"

"Uh — sure."

"That's what it feels like!" Her eyes were sparkling. *Sparkling.* "I know it doesn't make any sense with everything that's happened, especially since we're all about to die in this carnagepalooza, but it's the truth. I feel — I feel — "

"Perky."

"*So* perky!" Elysia shook her head. "I'm really, really sorry, Lex. It's awful, isn't it? I don't know what's wrong with me. It's not like I'm *happy* that any of this has happened."

"Of course not," said Lex. "Still — when did you start feeling this way?"

Elysia frowned. "I think it was after I got caught by the guards. Maybe I was relieved, you know? I mean, our main goal in Necropolis was to not get caught, so once I got caught, it was like, well, there's nothing else I can do, right? Pressure's off. Plus, Boulder was really nice to me, made me feel comfortable and not completely scared out of my gourd — "

"You said you felt weird."

"Huh?" Elysia asked, thrown.

"Driggs grabbed you and tried to pull you up into the air duct, but then he disappeared and you fell down to the floor," Lex said, slowly recalling the series of events, "and you said you felt weird."

Elysia scrunched up her nose. "Did I? That whole thing was a blur. I barely remember it."

Lex thought for a moment, then dug around in her bag and pulled out her Lifeglass. She hated looking at the thing — it stored way more bad memories than good ones — but its replay function had saved their asses once. Maybe it could again.

She put it on the table and peered into the upper bulb. Images from the past few hours started to flash through the glass, but in reverse, like a DVD skipping back through its chapters: the call from Broomie, Lex and Driggs undressing in the car . . .

Lex reddened. "You probably weren't supposed to see that."

"Come on, Lex," said Elysia. "We heard the whole thing."

Lex reddened some more.

The images kept coming. The arrival at Ayjay's house, the ex-

plosion at Necropolis, the president's office, the training modules. Then there it was: the Junior dorm.

Lex shook the Lifeglass, trying to make it play forward. She'd
never quite learned how to work it. "There," she said, pointing at
the air duct. "Driggs grabbed you, you fell back down to the
floor, and — there's that strange look on your face. What were
you thinking at that moment?"

Elysia's eyes widened. "Something happened when Driggs
touched me," she said, and Lex remembered it too. That weird
shock wave that had emanated out of him. "It was like he'd
punched me, but with — I don't know. Air? A magnetic force
field or something?" She shook her head. "I don't know. But I
meant it, I *did* feel weird. And ever since, I've had all these nutty
happy feelings."

Lex puffed some air out of her mouth. "Strange." She picked
up the Lifeglass and gave it another shake, hoping to turn it off,
but it started rewinding again. "No, *stop*," she scolded it.
"Don't — "

"Wait!" Elysia grabbed the Lifeglass out of her hands and
paused it. "It's Zara!"

It *was* Zara. And she looked just as surprised as they did.

"How?" Lex said, utterly confused. "The only time I saw Zara
was in the president's office, and this isn't . . ."

It was then that she spotted the tiles. Dark green, with little
crossed scythes in the middle of them.

"Holy shit," she said, goose bumps firing up and down her
arms. "The bathroom in the Juniors' dorm. I was staring out the
window. I saw a flash of silver right before I zonked out — it was
right after they Amnesia'd me!"

"So you wouldn't have remembered this!" Elysia added.

"Shh!" Lex hissed, even though the Lifeglass didn't have sound.

Zara, despite her many flaws, had one major thing going for her: intelligence. Even at that moment, freshly strangled and probably hating Lex more than she ever had, she had the presence of mind to remember that as well: the Lifeglass had no sound. So she thought for a moment, ducked away from the window, then came back with a piece of paper — or whatever the equivalent was inside the Afterlife. It said:

I HATE YOU, LEX.

Lex felt a stab of guilt. Zara let the piece of paper fall, but there was another behind it. And another.

BUT I LOVE IT HERE. THE AFTERLIFE IS BETTER THAN ADVERTISED. I DON'T WANT IT TO DISAPPEAR.
SO I LOOKED FOR HELP. AND WHAT I FOUND WAS CORPP.

Lex and Elysia both gasped. After Lex had accidentally Damned Corpp, he'd gone deep into the Void for good, not wanting to see the living anymore. It was just his way of dealing with death; he wanted to paint and explore the Afterlife, not get caught up in the past.

HE WASN'T HAPPY TO SEE ME, OBVIOUSLY. BUT HE TOLD ME SOMETHING THAT I THINK CAN HELP.

**WHEN YOU DAMNED CORPP, DRIGGS UNDAMNED HIM — OR SO WE ALL THOUGHT. BUT THAT'S NOT WHAT DRIGGS DID.**

Lex didn't dare breathe. Neither did Elysia; they both watched, not blinking, not wanting to miss what came next.

Not that they could have. Zara held that last paper up longer than any of the others, emphatically pointing and even mouthing the words.

**DRIGGS UNGRIMMED HIM.**

A choked noise sounded behind her. Lex whipped around to find Driggs standing there, looking at the words in the Lifeglass with just as much confusion and shock as the girls were feeling.

"What's going on?" he asked, his voice shaky.

It took Lex a second or two to find her voice. "It's Zara," she told him. Bang and Ferbus were listening too now. "She left me a message that I hadn't remembered, because the Juniors Amnesia'd us. She said . . ."

She didn't need to tell him what Zara said. By the look on his face, he'd seen everything.

Driggs shook his head. "That can't be true."

"Except —" Elysia's eyes widened. "Oh my God, that's *it!* Why I felt so weird after you touched me, why I haven't felt like myself ever since, why I couldn't scythe! You — I — " She grabbed the edges of the coffee table. "I'm not a Grim anymore!"

Driggs's eyes were darting around the floor. "But how could — I didn't mean to —"

"But you did," Grotton's voice growled.

The Juniors screamed. Grotton floated through the doorway, leering at them.

"What are you doing here?" Lex said.

"Oh, I came for the decadent atmosphere," he said, sniffing his nose at the dusty lights. "But I stay for the adolescent screeching."

Lex wanted to grab him around the throat. "*How* are you here? I thought you were shackled to the Wrong — oh," she said, remembering. "You can project yourself."

"Precisely." He glanced at Zara, frozen in the Lifeglass. "So you've figured it out, then?"

"Figured what out?" Lex asked. "If anything, we're more confused than we were before!"

"Why?" he replied. "The answer's right there in front of you."

"But what does Driggs have to do with anything?" she shot back. "You said it yourself — I'm the Last!"

His smile grew and grew, Cheshire cat–like.

"I wasn't talking to *you*, love."

All eyes in the room flew to Driggs.

"Okay," Driggs said, holding his hands out in front of him. "Let's all just hold the goddamned phone here. I *can't* be the Last." He pointed at Lex. "You're the only second-generation Grim in existence! You're the one Damning and ghosting and obliterating the Afterlife! No offense."

"None taken."

"I just — how could it be *me?*"

"Good question," said Grotton, floating to Driggs's side and whispering in his ear. "It's a pity Mort's stepped out. He's the one who brought you to the Grimsphere in the first place, isn't he?

And at such an early age, too. Strange of him to make an exception like that, hmm?"

Something cracked in Driggs's face. "He knew?"

When no one offered an answer to that, Driggs sat down on
the floor, too shaken to remain standing. "This still makes no
sense," he told the carpet. "I'm not a second-generation anything.
I'm nothing like you two," he said, gesturing at Lex and Grotton.
"I'm not exceptional in any way at all. So why me?"

"*Because* you're not exceptional!" Lex blurted. She gave him a
sympathetic look. "I mean, you are to me. But — what did Uncle
Mort say back in his basement when we were looking at that
rookie radar machine — "

"What, that I was a really rotten Grim when I first came to
Croak?" Driggs said. "Way to kick me when I'm down, Lex."

"But that's my point. Maybe you weren't supposed to ever become a Grim at all!"

He frowned, but didn't say anything.

She joined him on the floor and tried to catch his gaze. "Think
about it, Driggs. Did you turn delinquent just before you became
a Grim, like the rest of us?"

"Of course I did, you know that! Shoplifted, got into
fights — "

"But did you do all that stuff because you couldn't help it, because you were strangely compelled to do so? Or were you acting
out because of your parents?"

"I . . ." He looked even more confused. "I don't know. I was so
young."

"Exactly." She looked up at the other Juniors. "The rest of us
didn't go bad until a couple years before coming here — when we

were around fourteen. Which means that when you came to Croak, you couldn't possibly have turned yet. Uncle Mort must have picked you — "

"Before I even showed any signs of being a Grim," Driggs finished.

"So what does that mean?" Ferbus piped up, trying desperately to keep up with this conversation. "You were never supposed to be a Grim at all?"

"Maybe not." Heads swiveled to the front door, where Uncle Mort had silently appeared. "Or maybe so," he added. "Never did figure that part out."

He walked in, looking very tired as Driggs stared at him. "I was the one sent to Kill your parents," he confessed. "I still did shifts back then, before my mayoral duties became too time-consuming. I saw you there, standing over them, and I — " He shook his head. "I don't know. I saw something in you. You hadn't shown up on my radar, and you hadn't gone delinquent, but I just had a feeling that you belonged with us."

"Hey!" Elysia said. "Maybe that's why you can unGrim, Driggs! Because you're the only Grim who's secretly good, unlike the rest of us evil death folk."

"But I *can't* unGrim," Driggs said, throwing Uncle Mort a desperate look. "Can I?"

Uncle Mort sat down on the couch next to Ferbus. "I don't know," he said, scratching his scar. "The mounting evidence is hard to ignore."

"So if Driggs can unGrim," Lex slowly started, "then he can do what he did not only to Elysia and Corpp, but to the entire Grimsphere population. Remove all traces of our powers from

the world. If he gets his body back, he can essentially...
destroy the Grimsphere."

It seemed that all the air rushed out of everyone's lungs at the
same time. "Wow," said Elysia. "That's a pretty big deal."

"No. It's batshit *crazy*," Ferbus said, looking at Uncle Mort.
"Right? Tell them that's batshit."

But Uncle Mort was thinking. "It could work. If what Bang
read from the Wrong Book pages is true, if the world is capable
of going back to the way it was before Grotton came along"—
a sharp growl from Grotton confirmed this theory— "then erasing all Grim powers would certainly ensure that no one could
commit any violations ever again."

Grotton looked shaken, upset that they'd discovered his secret: that he'd created the Grimsphere, that he'd so severely dis-
rupted the natural order of things.

"So that's your plan, then?" he sneered, fading. "Norwood
will be most displeased to hear it."

He disappeared.

The Juniors were still reeling. "But—" Ferbus sputtered. "Being Grims is what we do. It's who we *are*. How can we just give it
up like that?"

Lex couldn't imagine giving it up, but it was hard to argue
with Uncle Mort's logic. "Well," he said, "I guess it comes down
to the question of what's more important—maintaining the
Grimsphere and its cushy way of life, or ensuring the safety of the
Afterlife for yourselves and for generations to come?"

Elysia shrugged. "Maybe sometimes you have to topple a secret empire that's been around for centuries in order to save one
that's been around forever."

"Some*times?*" Ferbus asked incredulously. "When exactly has this happened before?"

Uncle Mort ignored him. "This could work," he said, the wheels turning. "Of course, it's all contingent on the reset, and whether Driggs has enough human in him to become permanently solid again."

"Whoa, whoa, whoa," said Ferbus, swinging his stump. "Are we seriously considering this bonanza of insanity? Look, it's not that I don't *want* to give up my job and lifestyle and pretty much everything on this earth that I care about, but what gives us the authority to make a decision like this? How can the dissolution of a society be green-lit and carried out by a bunch of ragtag rebel teenagers and their — no offense, Mort — deranged leader? Shouldn't the rest of the population have some sort of say in this? Before we so rashly take away their entire way of life?"

"We've already been given the green light," Elysia argued. "By, if you'll recall, the *president*. All the mayors of the world, too — they wouldn't have sealed the portals if they didn't believe in the cause."

"But none of them planned for it to go this far," Ferbus argued back. "We'd be pulling the rug out from under thousands of people. Robbing them of their livelihoods. And they won't know what to do with themselves — it'll be total anarchy. Most of them never went to college or learned a trade; they'll have to start their lives all over again. It'll be just like Ayjay, multiplied across an entire society!"

"But it would be for the best," Lex said quietly. When they all stared at her, since this was the last thing anyone ever expected to come out of Lex's mouth, she shrugged. "Humans never should have been entrusted with this responsibility in the first place, as flawed and vulnerable to corruption as they are." She looked down. "As I was."

Driggs was shaking his head, unable to comprehend the scale of what they were discussing, and him the lynchpin of all of it. Finally he looked at Uncle Mort. "What do you think?"

Uncle Mort was quiet.

"I think," he eventually said, "we Grims have had one hell of a run."

## 19

"Ready, Lex?" Uncle Mort asked a couple of hours later. The second-to-last dot, on the Brazilian coast, had switched to red just a few moments before.

It was time to go back to Croak.

Uncle Mort packed up his bag while Ayjay watched from the hallway, his arms crossed. Elysia and Ferbus were already waiting in the backyard with Driggs. Bang sat on the couch, still sullen — but ever since Broomie had told her that Pip was all right, she'd allowed a little bit more of her face to peek out from behind her hair.

Lex nodded. "Yeah, I'm ready."

"Good." He reached into his bag, pulled out a vial of Amnesia, and started walking toward Ayjay. "One last order of business, and we'll be on our way."

Lex tensed. She thought she'd reached a good, sane place: she'd spent a wonderful night with Driggs, she was onboard with this nutzoid plan of theirs, and she was ready for the next step. But the moment she spotted that vial of Amnesia, something in her snapped.

*"Don't!"* She grabbed Uncle Mort's elbow, yanking him back, and marched toward Ayjay.

Bang's eyes widened.

"I lied," Lex told Ayjay. She could sense Uncle Mort fuming behind her, but she didn't care. "When you asked me if I knew you. I *did* know you. We all did. We were your friends — we lived together, worked together — you even had a girlfriend. That's how you lost your eye, protecting her. You were a part of something special, and there were people in your life who cared about you. You can't go back to that life — actually, if we do this right today, none of us can go back — but just remember all that, okay? Remember it."

Ayjay's mouth was moving, but nothing came out. Lex turned around to face Uncle Mort. He was staring at her, his expression unreadable.

After a moment he shook his head, put the vial back in his bag, and walked up to Ayjay. "Thanks for your hospitality," he said, shaking his hand. Without another word he turned around and walked out the back door.

Bang looked up at Lex, making eye contact for the first time since they'd left Necropolis.

Lex shrugged. "You wouldn't want to forget Pip, would you?"

Bang smiled.

Lex helped her off the couch and joined the others in the backyard. Uncle Mort was examining Ferbus, who, considering that he'd been forced to come to terms with a lot of major changes in the past twenty-four hours, was doing relatively well. He'd even come around on the unGrimming thing, though it was hard to tell whether he actually agreed with it or had just caved under Elysia's relentless badgering.

"Feeling okay, Ferb?" Uncle Mort asked.

"Oh, definitely. One thumb way, way up," he said with a smirk. "I gotta hand it to you, Mort, you were quite the helping hand back there. Give him a hand, folks."

"How long do you plan on keeping this up?"

"Oh, for the next decade. At least."

"Good luck with that," Uncle Mort told Elysia.

She sighed. "It's a drop in the bucket at this point."

Ferbus pretended to put both hands on his hips. "What's that supposed to mean?"

"It means that you were already a whackjob without a missing limb, and this is only going to make you weirder."

He grinned. "I should get a hook. And a parrot."

"Oh God." Elysia buried her head in Lex's shoulder. "We're going to be *those* people. He's going to buy a three-cornered hat, and then a puffy shirt, and next thing you know, he's building a mini golf course with waterfalls and anchors and swashbuckling songs blaring out of speakers that look like rocks, and *I'm* the one who's going to have to smile and work the cash register while children come from all over to take pictures with the damn pirate." She glared at Uncle Mort, though that weird bubbliness of hers was still in her eyes. "I hope you're happy."

He snorted. "Ecstatic."

||||||

They Crashed to Greycliff, Bang pulling the no-longer-Grimmed Elysia through and Driggs arriving via his ghost skills.

He stared at the spot where he'd died. "Couldn't you have picked a less emotionally scarring place, Mort?"

"Sorry about that. Arriving within the town limits would have set off alarms. And this way we can get a better idea of what we're dealing with before we storm on in."

But the advantage didn't make them feel any better, and neither did the cheerful sunshine illuminating the valley below. The snow that had fallen a few days ago had already melted, and from their spot atop the cliff they could tell that Croak was deathly quiet — and so battered, Lex barely recognized it. Hinges hung from the library doors. The Morgue's windows were broken, one of its red stools lying on the sidewalk outside. Many of the stores on Slain Lane were boarded up with plywood. Attempts had been made at rebuilding the fountain, but they were half-assed at best — the obelisk was crooked, and the fountain itself dry and mildewed. Only the Bank remained relatively the same, sunny yellow as always.

"What happened?" Elysia breathed. "Who trashed our town?"

Lex pointed. Armed men — the ones who'd stayed loyal to Norwood even after his implication in the fountain bombing had come to light — were patrolling the street in pairs, shotguns slung over their shoulders. There were no other people to be found, and no Norwood, either.

"They couldn't *all* have left," said Lex. "Everyone on our side — gone?"

"Well, some of them died at Grave," Uncle Mort reminded her. "And the rest are in hiding, I'm sure."

He backed away from the cliff's edge and gestured for them to follow. "So here's the plan. We take the tunnel down to the Bank. Driggs, Elysia, Ferbus — you fend off the goons, create a distraction. Bang, you sneak away and head over to Norwood's house to find the Wrong Book. Lex, you come with me into the Bank and fight off the guards inside so I can get up to the portal."

He paused, swallowed, then continued. "Once the portal is

sealed, Lex, you're up. Hopefully Bang will have found the Wrong Book by then. If not, that becomes the priority. Find Grotton, make him solid, and Annihilate him. Voilà — Grotton's gone forever, Damned and ghosted souls are restored, and Driggs gets his beloved body back."

"Hopefully," Driggs added. "Fifty-fifty shot."

Uncle Mort gave a weary nod. "Hopefully. And if you do, then it's unGrimming time. But a lot has to go right to get to that point, so we need to make sure we all know what we're doing. Any questions?"

Elysia and Ferbus started trading ideas on how to outmaneuver the guards once they got to Dead End, but Lex was too distracted to listen. It wouldn't be long now. All she had to do was send Grotton to the Dark, and Driggs would get his life back. He'd either be human or he'd be dead, but at least he'd be whole.

Her insides, though, were writhing. She'd Damned so many people and hurt so many others on top of that — one more shouldn't make a difference, especially someone as wicked as Grotton. If anyone deserved such a Dark fate, it was him.

But she couldn't get Driggs's voice out of her head. *No matter what they'd done to me,* he'd said about his parents, *it wasn't my job to punish them.*

She shook her head and looked at him, but he was listening intently to Uncle Mort. *You can't be judge, jury, and executioner,* he'd added. *Humans make mistakes, which is why humans shouldn't be allowed to make those sorts of calls in the first place.*

And she'd promised him that she'd stop Damning, that she wouldn't make those kinds of calls anymore. And Annihilation was *so* much worse. Could she really make an exception for this?

She shook her head. Of course she could. Annihilation was the only way to fix Driggs.

And that was a promise she intended to keep above all others.

"Lex?" Uncle Mort said. She looked up to find him staring at her, impatient. "You ready?"

She nodded and squeezed her scythe. "Yeah."

"Good." He threw his bag over his shoulder — then, as if realizing something, took it off and set it down on the ground. The only thing remaining in his hand was his scythe.

Lex blinked. *He's leaving his bag?*

But he swept them all toward the rock before she could figure out why. He took one last look at the town below, gave it a sad smile, and shoved them forward.

"See, Driggs?" he said as they squeezed into the tiny tunnel, Bang lighting their way with Pip's Spark. "Now Ferbus gets to revisit *his* own personal hell. I strive to provide equal opportunities for emotional scarring, you see."

Ferbus, trying his hardest not to imagine any mine holes drilled into the walls, cringed. "You're too kind, Mort."

▏▎▍▌▏▎

As quietly as they could, the Juniors emerged under the porch of the Bank and snuck through its little wooden door out to the streets of Croak. But it took only a second for one of Norwood's men to notice them and sound the alarm.

"Don't move!" Trumbull yelled, pointing a gun at them. Riley joined him at his side, along with a few others.

*There aren't so many of them anymore,* Lex thought, becoming hopeful. *Definitely not as many as there were before!*

"Maybe some of the morons in this town have been fooled by 'President Pandora' and her 'proclamations,'" Trumbull continued, his voice dripping with mockery, "but unfortunately for you, they're not the ones with weapons."

Lex glanced at the apartments that were visible from where she was standing. There were people peeking out from behind the blinds, watching the scene unfold as if it were a Wild West showdown.

"Hands in the air!" Trumbull shouted. "Walk toward us, slowly. If you try anything, we'll blow your heads off!"

"No, we won't," Riley hissed at him. "Norwood wants her alive!"

"So?" Trumbull said, grinning. "He didn't say anything about the rest of them."

He took aim.

Yet before he or anyone else could squeeze out a single shot, a great roar erupted from the buildings of Croak. The townspeople came pouring out from every direction — the library, the Morgue, the stores on Slain Lane — dozens of them, all wielding homemade weapons, scythes, or whatever blunt objects they were able to find around their houses.

A shovel hit Trumbull squarely between the eyes, and Riley took a scythe slash all the way up her arm. "Trumbull, shoot them!" she shouted, holding her hand over her bleeding arm.

But in their confusion Norwood's men had scattered, and only a handful had their guns out; they'd been prepared to defend against the Juniors, but they obviously and erroneously believed they'd already taken the fight out of any dissenting civilians. Small fistfights were erupting all over Dead End, cries of pain bursting down the small street as Lex and the other Juniors watched in horror.

"Why are we watching in horror?" Ferbus asked. "Let's kick some ass, shall we?"

And so, yelling and charging and waving their scythes in the air, the Juniors jumped into the fray.

Lex couldn't be sure what was happening to her friends as they fought. At one point she spotted Elysia biting Trumbull's arm, Ferbus clotheslining Riley, and Bang zipping around like a gnat, yanking people's feet out from under them. Lex fought too, though she was having a hard time keeping her hands in check; every time a Senior approached, they alternated between hot and cold, as if unsure whether she should be Damning or Annihilating.

*Neither,* she tried to tell them. *Not yet.*

Time seemed to slow down. Bodies littered the ground — an image Lex had seen repeated so many times by now, the settings and victims were all starting to blur together. The upper hand kept switching back and forth between sides — just when it seemed as if Trumbull and Riley were beginning to beat down the Croakers to the point of defeat, the townspeople roared back even stronger than before.

Lex did a quick recon. Bang had managed to slip away and was running for the outskirts of town. Elysia and Ferbus were holding their own, and Driggs was confusing the hell out of everyone. Uncle Mort had made it up the stairs of the Bank and was gesturing wildly for Lex to follow.

She pounded up the steps and followed him into the lobby. It didn't look anything like she remembered; the space that Kilda had tried so hard to keep homey and welcoming had fallen into ruin. The red velvet couches were slashed, potpourri littered the floor, Kilda's desk looked as if it had been raided —

And something behind it was whimpering.

"Kilda!" Uncle Mort said when they found her cowering underneath. "Are you all right?"

"I tried to lay low, but Norwood still made me come into work!" she said, her eyes frantic. "They pointed guns at me the whole time! They spilled my potpourri!"

"I know," said Uncle Mort. "Listen to me. Is anyone else in the building?"

"No one except for the guards! They ran upstairs!"

Of course they did — to guard the most important thing in the Bank. "What about my parents?" Lex asked. "Are they still locked up in the basement?"

Kilda shook her head. "No, Norwood took them out a few hours ago! I don't know where they went!"

Lex jumped up. She wanted nothing more than to go look for them, but Uncle Mort put a hand on her arm. "Later," he insisted. "After."

Kilda started to curl up into a smaller ball, but Uncle Mort held her shoulder. "Kilda — " He paused, searching for the right words. "Thank you for all you've done for this town."

She looked confused. "What?"

"No one ever gave you enough credit. But Croak couldn't function without you." He patted her once more and stood up to leave. "Now get out of the building. Run."

For the first time ever, Kilda was speechless.

So was Lex. *What was that all about?*

|||||||

They booked it up the stairs and burst into the office. Unsurprisingly, the guards were waiting for them, poised to fire.

But at long last Uncle Mort's Amnesia blow dart came in handy. He slipped it out of his pocket, brought it to his mouth, and sprayed Norwood's men with about a dozen darts, turning his head like an oscillating fan and hitting every one of them in the neck.

"Down the stairs," he commanded once the glazed look settled over their eyes. "And out of the building. Go."

The last one was even polite enough to close the door behind him. Lex looked at her uncle. "That was really impressive."

"Couldn't have done it without these guys." He nodded to the Lair and the multitudes of spiders within that were mere minutes away from getting blown up. "So long, little dudes," he mumbled, crossing to the keyboard on the desk, "and thanks for all the Amnesia."

Lex watched as he started typing. "How are you going to open the vault?" she asked. "Norwood's at least smart enough to change the code — "

The door swung open.

He smirked at her. "And I was at least smart enough to put in an override back when I was mayor."

The Afterlife was darker than ever; the kickback from the sealed portals had done quite a number on it. The Void glowed a little brighter in the distance, but elsewhere in the atrium swirled ominous, near-black clouds. There were no souls to be seen, not even any of the wrestling ex-presidents.

Lex focused on the office desk instead, the one Ferbus had

been sitting at when she met him for the first time. Was that really only nine months ago?

"So how do we do this?" she asked. "Another fancy grenade, or what?"

He didn't say anything, just stared at the vault.

She raised an eyebrow. "Uncle Mort?" she said, trying to snap him out of it. "What is it? The thing that closes a portal?"

He hesitated — then spoke calmly, evenly. "A living person."

She frowned. "What?"

"A living person must enter the Void," he said. "That's what destroys the portal."

Lex didn't understand. He wasn't making any sense. "But you handed Skyla something, right before — "

"Yeah," he said with a bittersweet smile. "A billiards ball. Inside joke."

"You said she was fine."

"She is fine," he said, swallowing. "Or she will be, once the Afterlife is restored."

"The After — Skyla's dead?"

Lex felt a part of herself shut down. She shook her head, grabbing Uncle Mort's hoodie as she realized what he was saying. What he was going to do.

"It's okay, Lex," he said with a wince-smirk.

Her fingernails dug through the fabric to his skin. "No," she said, her voice breaking. "*No.* Why you?"

"Captain goes down with the ship."

"But . . . there has to be another way. What about Bang? She misses Pip, she'd be happy to do it! Or hell, we can throw Kilda in there!"

"Once again, Lex, your utter disregard for human life is staggering."

"I mean it!" she shouted, hysterical. "Why does it have to be you?"

"Because it has to," he said gently. "Think of all those mayors in there who willingly gave up their own lives, all because I told them to. How can I ask them to do that without doing it myself?"

"I don't know! Just don't go. *Please.*"

"It's not up for discussion, Lex." He cracked the bones in his neck and rubbed his hands together. He looked nervous.

Lex stared at the floor, numb. That's why Broomie had called instead of LeRoy. LeRoy was dead. That's why Skyla had been so insistent that she be the one to destroy the portal in Necropolis — she wanted to be the one to sacrifice herself. Skyla was dead. All the mayors in the Grimsphere — dead.

Everyone had had a part to play. Including Lex.

And Uncle Mort had known it for a long, long time.

She felt herself getting delirious. "Did you realize from the start that I'd become a Grim?" she asked him, manic. "I mean, you gave me the hoodie way back when I was eight, you had to have . . ." She trailed off. Was there really a point in rehashing all of this? Now, of all times?

He looked at her. "No. I thought there was a good chance — and even when you were a kid, I saw some signs, the beginnings of aggressive behavior — but no, I never knew for sure. Just like I never knew for sure with Driggs. It's not an exact science."

"I don't get it," she said. "I mean, why me and not Cordy?"

He shrugged. "Luck of the DNA, I suppose."

"But you *did* plan it all out from the beginning. You fixed my mom up with my dad, knew she'd probably have kids and that eventually you'd try to use those kids to fix the Grimsphere."

"Christ, Lex, when you put it that way, I really sound like a monster." He snickered, but his smile faded. "But yes. I did all that. And I did it knowing full well that whoever that kid turned out to be, they'd have to go through hell in order for this plan to succeed. My hope was that in the end, that kid would realize it was all for the greater good. But now . . ."

He swallowed and looked at his hands.

"I love you, kiddo," he said. "Like you're my own daughter. I never wanted kids, but if I did, I'd want them to turn out exactly like you."

Lex wanted to say something, but she didn't trust her voice not to catch.

He smiled. "You can be the biggest brat in the world sometimes, but you're smart and you're strong, and you've made the best choices possible under the conditions I've put you through. I wouldn't change a thing about you. Not one thing."

He walked over to stand in front of her. "It was awful, what I did. Setting you up, using you like a pawn. Though to be completely honest, I can't even say that I regret it. It worked, after all. You became the sort of person I'd hoped — and feared — you'd be, the only one in the world with a fighting chance of saving the Afterlife." He bit his lip. "I don't regret it. But for what it's worth, I'm sorry." He held her gaze, and his voice turned to gravel. "I *am* sorry, Lex."

Lex blinked. What was she supposed to say to that? The man had brought her to Croak to further his own agenda, hoping that she'd be the weapon he needed, and in the process of reaching her full potential as that weapon, she'd be required to do terrible things, become a terrible person. Her sister had even been dragged into it, only to be killed for her troubles. How could Lex forgive him for that?

But if she hadn't come to Croak, she never would have found out who she was meant to be. She'd discovered the one thing that she'd been amazingly good at. She'd made friends for the first time in years, fallen in love, and been given a purpose in life — and a noble one at that, one that would save the souls of all those who'd come before her.

The truth was, she'd forgiven him long ago.

She wanted to tell him so, but she couldn't manage to do anything but look up at him with watering eyes and nod.

He seemed to understand. He swept her up in a hug, put his face on top of her head, and combed his fingers through her hair. They stayed that way for a long time — too long, probably, given the urgency of the situation. But they couldn't seem to let go.

"Are you scared?" she finally spoke.

"Of dying?" He swallowed. "Yes. Of course I am."

They were silent again.

"Please don't go," she whispered, squeezing him tight. By this point she wasn't even bothering to keep the tears from falling. "I need you."

"No, you don't." He pulled away from the hug to look at her. "You are more than capable of doing the rest of this on your own. Everything we've been through in the past few days, the decisions you've made — "

Lex winced, remembering all those disapproving looks he'd given her. "I know, I'm sorry — I'll do better, I promise!"

He looked at her in disbelief, then closed his eyes as he spoke.

"Lex, I've been so goddamned proud of you I couldn't even speak."

Her jaw went slack.

A large boom erupted somewhere in the Afterlife, followed by a disturbing crackling noise. "I have to go," he said to Lex, though it also seemed as though he was steeling himself. "I have to go."

He put one foot into the Afterlife. "I'm going to rush to the Void as fast as I can, so the Bank will probably blow in less than a minute. Crash out of here so you can get away in time. Then find Grotton. Got it?"

Lex nodded, barely hearing him.

He gave her one last hug. "You know, I meant what I said that day, after Cordy died," he said. "You really are a good kid."

With that, he stepped all the way into the Vault. He swallowed once, straightened his hoodie, and began to close the door. There was fear in his eyes, but also strength, plus something that Lex couldn't identify but sure as hell hoped she had inside of her, too.

"Bye, kiddo," he said with a grin. "Be good."

She held her hand up to the Vault as it closed, keeping it there long after the floor started to rumble.

## 20

If Lex hadn't Crashed out to the Ghost Gum tree and seen it with her own eyes, she never would have believed it.

The Bank — command central of Croak and portal to the Afterlife — blown into a million pieces.

The debris rained down on the Field like an asteroid shower, many pieces still smoking, though oddly not on fire. Screams arose from Dead End, and through the smoke, Lex could see people running, panicking.

She felt numb, nonexistent. All she wanted to do was sit down on the ground and sob.

But she couldn't. There was still so much left to do.

Like find her parents. Squinting through the haze, she entertained the ridiculous notion that they might just waltz out of a nearby building, safe and sound —

She turned around, and that's when she saw them. Not safe and sound, but tied up and bloodied, Norwood dragging them across the Field.

Lex had heard of tunnel vision before, but she had never experienced it until that moment. Her eyes zoomed in on her parents, everything but their terrified forms being pushed into blurred edges around her vision. "Stop!"

Norwood looked at her, then at the decimated Bank, his face twisted in a combination of hatred, determination, and abject fury. His hands were so red they were glowing; Lex could see them from where she stood.

"Why?" he spat, radiating rage. The portals were gone, the Afterlife sealed away forever. He was losing, and badly. The only bargaining chip he had left was the Wrong Book, tucked under his arm.

*Crap,* Lex thought. *How am I going to get that back from him?*

"I'd hoped to bargain for the portal with your parents' lives," he went on, "but it looks like you and your uncle beat me to it. So I'll just be Damning them. They're useless to me now. Should have done it when I fried Lazlo in the first place."

Lex took a step back toward the tree. As she did, she got the strangest sense of déjà vu — she'd been at the same place only a short time ago, when Zara had released her from her cell and taken her to this very spot. Here they were again, but during the day. A bright, sunny day.

But this time the fate of the Afterlife was at stake.

The townspeople were approaching now, and it looked as though they had won, at least for the time being. Norwood's men were being restrained, and the Juniors were all safe, though bloodied and bruised. Bang jogged up from the direction of Norwood's house and gave Lex a helpless shrug, while Lex's parents cried out and struggled against the bonds around their wrists and ankles. Lex fought against every instinct in her body that compelled her to run to them. Instead, she clenched her fists and stayed where she was.

This had to go perfectly, or it was all for nothing.

"Go ahead, Damn them," she said, trying to keep her voice calm. "I'll just bring them back!"

Norwood laughed. "Ah, yes. Grotton told me you'd say that. The reset, is it? Sounds wonderful and all, but with what your wisp of a boyfriend plans to do if he becomes human again, I think I'll pass."

"But if we have the power to end Heloise's suffering, why would you pass that up?" Lex dropped her voice. "I know you can't stand me, Norwood. I know that what I did to your wife was awful. But I can fix it. Let us do our thing, and I can send her right to the Afterlife, torture-free. Think about it." She moved in closer. "You know what's happening to her right now. Eternal torment. Pain. Misery. You really want to leave her to that? When you could have done something to help reverse it?"

Norwood looked fairly tortured himself, his eyes swimming with confusion and doubt. "What other choice do I have?"

Lex held his gaze. "Give up."

For a moment Norwood looked hopeful. Relieved, almost.

But his face quickly soured. "You goddamned kids." He spat at the ground. "You ruined everything. This is all I've ever worked for!" he said, yelling now. "The Grimsphere is my *life*. I gave up everything — any shot at a normal life, money, travel, a family — " He swallowed. "We wanted kids. But we couldn't have them here. So we slammed that door and never looked back." He looked at her. "And for what? For you brats to just waltz in and bulldoze it all as if it were *nothing* to you?" He shook his head. "No. Not gonna happen."

He held up the Wrong Book and brought his reddening hand to its pages. "I think it's time for Grotton to go see the world, don't you?"

They'd run out of time.

Lex saw the unthinkable unfold across her mind. Grotton would fly away, never to return, and she would never get the chance to Annihilate him. Driggs would be a ghost forever, wandering the earth alone until everyone he ever knew was long gone. The Afterlife would fall into decay and one day disappear completely —

"*No!*" She lunged forward with a shout — but someone swooped in front of her, blocking her path.

"Stop," Driggs whispered. "Let him do it."

"What? Why?" Lex hissed. "Grotton will get away!"

"No, he won't. Trust me." He nodded his head. "Move closer, but slowly."

Lex did, carefully edging toward Norwood and the book in his hand. As she did, she spotted Grotton's face hovering a few feet off the ground, his gradually solidifying form glimmering in the sunlight, his smile of anticipation growing wider and wider.

That's when she realized what Driggs was thinking.

The second Norwood's fingers touched the Wrong Book, it went up in flames. Grotton burst into wild laughter, so ecstatic that he turned solid.

Solid enough for Lex to grab his wrist.

Stunned, he looked down at her hand and tried to twist away, but she wasn't letting go. As long as she held on to him, he'd stay solid.

As she gazed into his eyes, she felt it again, just as she had that night in Grave — a cool, searing rage that plunged through every inch of her body. The power to Annihilate.

A shadow began to form around her scythe, enveloping her hand. She raised it —

Then stopped.

Grotton had caved in on himself. He shrank and shuddered, his eyes drowning in fear. "Please, love," he whimpered. "Don't."

Lex's scythe almost slipped from her hand. She hadn't been expecting this. Grotton was unimaginably evil — this had to be an act, right?

But his dread seemed genuine. She could feel the sweat from his arm mingling with hers. The man was truly terrified.

Just as Zara had been when Lex wrapped her hands around her throat.

Lex gripped her scythe tightly. The shadow was still there. She felt the smooth black obsidian sliding beneath her skin — hard, cold, dependable. It had stayed true to her to the very end, just as Uncle Mort had promised.

Uncle Mort.

*Be good,* he'd said. Those were his last words.

Was sentencing a man to eternal darkness good? Even if that man deserved it?

But she didn't *know* that he deserved it. She *thought* he did, but it didn't matter what she thought. As Driggs said, she couldn't be judge, jury, and executioner. It wasn't her call.

The reset had to be triggered, though, in order for Driggs to get his body back and dismantle the Grimsphere. Someone had to be Annihilated. Someone had to be sent to the Dark.

*But it doesn't have to be Grotton.*

||||||

There were no tunnels of light, no choirs of angels. Lex's life did not flash before her eyes; it thundered and convulsed, like a city under siege.

‖‖‖‖‖

*Images of her and Cordy, their dad taking them outside at night and tossing them into the air, telling them to grab the moon, then catching them in a tangle of hugs.*

‖‖‖‖‖

She let go of Grotton.

‖‖‖‖‖

*Mrs. Bartleby had a propensity for losing rings. Not only did a stuffed Thanksgiving turkey once claim her engagement ring, but when the girls were five, the kitchen sink swallowed up her favorite — a gold band set with her daughters' birthstone. She'd plunged her hand into the drain, groping blindly until she finally gave up and sank to the floor, crying and shaking, calling her husband to come home and take the plumbing apart.*

*Lex, meanwhile, had snuck up to her room and taken out a pair of scissors, a piece of paper, some crayons, and a piece of tape.*

*"Here, Mom," she said, handing her a paper replica of the ring. "Please don't cry."*

*And Lex could never figure out, as her mom swept her daughter into her arms, why that made her cry even harder.*

‖‖‖‖‖

She took two steps back.

||||||

*Lex and Cordy on their first day of middle school — Cordy with glasses and Lex with braces.*

*"They're going to call us the Doubleugly Twins," Cordy moaned.*

*"If they even thpeak to uth at all," Lex replied, still not used to all that dental hardware.*

*Cordy scowled. "As long as we stick together, we should be okay. Right?"*

*Lex didn't think so. But she squeezed her sister's hand and nodded.*

*"Yeth."*

||||||

Lex looked at Elysia, who had run up to the Ghost Gum tree along with Ferbus and Bang. She was confused, wondering why Lex was just standing there looking at her. Then, with a dawning horror, her eyes widened.

||||||

*The girls on the soccer team, looking through the classroom windows at Lex stuck inside, serving yet another detention. How they laughed and cupped their hands around their mouths, whispering mean things about her. The way it made Lex feel as though parts inside of her were dying, wilting like dead flowers.*

*Then, the polar opposite — the first time Elysia had hugged her, that radiating warmth that only a friend can provide. The way it made Lex feel as if those wilted parts were coming back to life, blooming brighter than ever.*

|||||||

Driggs understood next. The shock was so great that he turned solid and started to run toward her, to stop her.

|||||||

*The bus station, when they'd sent her off to Croak. The wetness around the rim of her mother's eyes, the way her dad couldn't quite look at her, the way both of their voices got stilted and heavy when they said goodbye.*

|||||||

Lex looked at her parents. Though they were totally unaware of what was happening, they knew their daughter was in danger. They were panicking, screaming around the gags in their mouths.

She reached into her bag. The Lifeglass slipped into her hand immediately. She glanced at it for a split second but looked away before it could show her any images.

She picked Bang out of the crowd. Bang was watching Lex intently, for once her eyes completely visible.

Lex tossed her the Lifeglass, followed by the photo of her mother as a Grim.

"Tell them," Lex said.

|||||||

*Uncle Mort, wild and fearless, picking her up on his motorcycle and driving her to Croak for the first time.*

*And the way he patted her head after Cordy had died, after Lex had transferred her Damning power to Zara and started all this.*

*"You're a good kid," he'd said. "You really are."*

|||||||

Ferbus was different. He, too, realized what was happening, right around the same time as Elysia and Driggs, and his eyes bulged as well. But when he looked at Lex, she was looking right back at him.

He would never forgive her for what she let happen to Driggs. Since the minute he'd found out, he had kept a reserve of residual hate, and it had only grown over time. So he'd be the only one strong enough.

Lex nodded at him.

He nodded back.

And threw up his arms to block Driggs and Elysia, restraining them.

|||||||

*Driggs. The drumming, the Oreos, that devastatingly adorable blue eye. The way he made her feel like she was the best person in the world, even when nothing could be further from the truth. The way he'd wormed his way into parts of her heart that were dark and raw, and made them bright. That smirky smile.*

*She couldn't let him wander the earth alone forever.*

*She couldn't.*

|||||||

Lex wrapped both of her hands around the scythe. She took one last look around — at Norwood, who was completely unaware of what she was about to do; at the townspeople, battered but victorious; at a miserable, confused Grotton; at Ferbus, Elysia, and Bang, who were crying; and at Driggs, who looked as though his soul were being shredded by shrapnel, one gash at a time.

She'd never see any of them again. Nor Uncle Mort, nor Cordy, nor her parents. But at least this way, she'd ensure that they got to see one another.

At that thought, Lex felt lighter. She'd certainly been no angel in her life; maybe she deserved this, maybe she didn't. But someone had to do it. And pride swelled within her when she realized she could be the one.

So she grinned at her friends, raised her scythe high above her head —

"*LEX!*" Driggs cried, his face consumed with misery. "What are you doing?"

*Be good.* "Fixing it," she whispered, closing her eyes.

She plunged the scythe straight into her chest —

And everything went Dark.

## 21

Driggs's hair was dry.

He kept running his hands through it as he lay flat on the ground, staring up at the black branches of the Ghost Gum tree. Like everyone else within the town limits of Croak, he'd been knocked to the ground the moment Lex had done ... what she'd done. A fierce wind had swept through the Field — some later claimed they saw the faces of Damned and ghosted souls in the breeze — along with an otherworldly moan that sounded like a contented sigh.

Driggs felt dizzy, sick, as if he were underwater. Everything was blurred. Sounds came to his ears in the form of muffled, mashed-up noise — Elysia sobbing, the townspeople shouting, Norwood yelling at them to shut up —

*Norwood.*

Driggs sat up and looked around. The Ghost Gum tree's pure white bark had turned black — starting first at the trunk, then stretching out to the ends of every branch, like a shadow passing in front of the sun and shading it permanently. Beneath it, where Lex had stood a second earlier, was nothing.

And Norwood was still yelling.

Driggs scrambled to his feet. He stalked across the Field and without a second's hesitation grabbed Norwood, looked him in the eye, and punched him in the face.

Norwood's fiery hands instantly returned to normal. The

punch had been hard, but it was the shock wave emanating from Driggs's fist that knocked Norwood back down to the ground.

"What happened?" Norwood asked, patting himself. "I feel — like I'm — "

"Not a Grim anymore," Driggs rasped. "You son of a bitch."

Norwood's screams of anguish faded into the background as Driggs turned around, took a moment to collect himself, then walked toward the townspeople. He had to do this now, or he never would. "Line up," he told them, his voice shaky. "And put your hands out."

He explained as best he could what he was doing, why the Grimsphere had to be undone. Predictably, they were hesitant. "I'm not going to hurt you," he reassured them. "But this has to be done. You want an Afterlife, you want all this to be worth it, you want Lex — " His throat caught, and he turned his back to them, unable to breathe.

After staring at the tree for a moment, at the spot where he'd last seen her, he found his voice again. "I know it's a lot to ask," he said, turning back around, "but — "

He stopped, shocked. Every single one of them had lined up in a crooked row facing him, palms out.

Dazed, Driggs walked up to Kilda, the first person in line. He was about to place his hand atop hers, but at the last minute he turned it sideways and shook it instead.

"Thank you," he told her, meeting her eyes as the shock wave blew her hair back.

He did that all the way down the line, shaking hands, un-Grimming them, and thanking them — even Trumbull and Riley, who didn't bother to make eye contact. Ferbus and Bang were the last to go, and them, he hugged.

When it was all over, he returned to Lex's parents. Elysia had untied them, sat them up, and was now petting their hands, as was her way. "Are you okay?" he asked them.

"What's going on?" Lex's mother cried, clinging to her husband. She looked at the tree, then back to the spot where her daughter had disappeared. "Where did Lex go?"

"She stabbed herself!" Mr. Bartleby was shaking uncontrollably. "What did she do that for?"

Driggs wanted to console them, but their tears broke him. A thousand swirling emotions all fought for space in his newly restored body — pride in what Lex had done, awe at her courage, gratitude for her sacrifice, guilt that she'd done it for him, anger that it had come to this — but a suffocating grief eclipsed them all. He crumpled to the ground, fighting to catch his breath, wondering how in the hell Mort would have handled this.

As if in answer, something hard in his pocket bruised up against his leg.

He pulled out the vial of Amnesia. Lex's parents didn't need this memory; there was no reason for them to live with this pain. They'd never fully understand what she'd died for anyway, or why. It would only torture them, and he was pretty sure he'd be tortured enough for the rest of his life for all of them.

He uncorked the vial and leaned in —

But a hand fell on his arm.

He turned and looked at Bang, whose eyes bore into his. She clutched Lex's Lifeglass, her mouth opening to speak.

"Don't."

# POST MORTEM

"Think you can do it one more time?"

"If you brought what I asked for."

Grotton's guest emptied the requested items onto the table. They clinked and bounced, producing a sound like wind chimes. "Here."

Grotton leaned forward, his face aglow in the light of the burning candle. "Then I believe we have a deal."

He removed his scythe from his pocket, but Driggs couldn't tear his eyes away from the table. "What do you want them for, anyway?"

"For curiosity's sake," Grotton said. "I'm a scientist too, if you'll recall."

"Fine. Whatever."

Grotton gave him an amused look. "What did it feel like?" he said, leaning in. "To spend a year traveling the world over, meeting every Grim on the planet, only to suck the powers right out of them? To watch their faces as you made their lives go up in a puff of smoke? How did it feel?"

Driggs stared at him. "Necessary."

Grotton folded his hands under his chin. "I heard a rumor," he said, "that if you'd just touched the obelisk in every Grim town — the one that all Senior Grims touch to be inducted — that would have done the trick just as easily. And yet you chose to shake every citizen's hand instead." He stared him down, then let out a harsh laugh. "Think that makes you noble?"

Driggs exhaled wearily. "No," he said. "I think it made my wrist hurt."

Grotton pursed his lips, disappointed. "But now you're back. Seeking my services."

Driggs held his gaze. "And to remind you of your promise."

"Just as well," Grotton said with a sneer. "I can't stand it here any longer. The tourists. The happiness. The — " He suppressed a gag. "The *children.*"

"Grims are a fertile bunch. Who knew?" Driggs rubbed his eyes. "Kilda says they're finally going to clear away the ruins of the Bank and erect a memorial playground in its place. For the kids."

"Sounds terrible. Lex would have hated it."

Driggs clenched his fists at the idea of Grotton assuming to know anything at all about Lex, but he let it go. "Yeah. She would have."

"At least the orange-haired one's mini golf course is doing well."

Driggs stood up. He hadn't come here to reminisce. "Come on," he said. "Let's get this over with."

Grotton kept watching him. "How can you be so sure I'll keep my word?"

Driggs sighed. "I can't. I just have to believe that there is a tiny shred of humanity left in you somewhere. Lex was able to see it. I trust her."

Grotton twisted his mouth. "Well, I still might not do it. And even if I do, I'm not sure which method I'll choose. Stabbing, drowning, asphyxiation. There are so many lovely ways to go."

"I really don't care how you do it," Driggs said. "Just do it. And soon. You're the only one left, and until you're gone — "

"There are still Grimming powers left on earth, yes, yes," Grotton said, waving him away. "I'll go, you have my word. Assuming, of course, that there is an Afterlife to go *to*. We still don't know for sure that it worked, do we?"

"Guess you'll just have to find out when you get there. Be sure to send a postcard."

Grotton smiled wickedly. "Then again, the Dark is uncharted territory. Curiosity may get the best of me. This proposed experiment of yours is a good one, I have to admit, and requires no small amount of bravery. Perhaps I can muster enough of that for myself after all."

Driggs glared at him. "Don't you dare."

They were silent for a moment.

Grotton abruptly stood. "Very well, Last," he said, a shadow forming around his hand. "I hope you find what you're looking for."

For the first time since the day Lex ceased to exist, Driggs smiled — and not the fake, reassuring smile he'd given to the hesitant citizens of the Grimsphere, nor even to the other Juniors when they often asked how he was doing, always with that aching sadness in their eyes.

A real smile. Although, really, it was more of a smirk.

"I hope so too," he said, raising his head up as Grotton brought the scythe down.

||||||

Grotton did not keep his word.

Well, he was forced to, eventually, but many, many years later than he'd promised Driggs. The reset had returned him to his human form, and so death did one day come for him, despite his best efforts to escape it. But he did uphold his end of the bargain in spirit — in all of his extra decades on earth, he never exercised his Grimming powers again, never Damned anyone for fun, never committed any violations. He lived out the rest of his life as a normal human being, and so it was *almost* as if Driggs had un-Grimmed him. Almost.

In fact, if anyone had bothered to visit his cabin in the last days of his mortal life, they might not have suspected that he had ever been a Grim at all . . . if it weren't for his collection of those strange little glass bulbs.

Cordy's, Pip's, and Uncle Mort's, glowing just as brightly as they had when Driggs emptied them out onto the table. Elysia's and Ferbus's, which had both burst into steady balls of light a few years before, within mere days of each other. Bang's, whose embers still bounced around, still set off fireworks — though they probably wouldn't for much longer.

And then there were the Sparks of Lex and Driggs — empty, dark. The same as they'd been ever since they disappeared, all those years ago.

|||||||

Except.

Except in the dead of night, when Grotton would cover all the others up. Ever the scientist, he'd blow out his candles and make the cabin as dark as he could. Only then could he see them.

Even with those old eyes, he could see them — one in the center
of each of their Sparks — specks so faint they were virtually invisible, like pinpricks —

He knew he was being foolish. He knew that where they'd
gone was nothing but emptiness, nonexistence, Annihilation. He
knew that it was absurd to believe that somewhere in the vacuum
of nothingness, their souls had found a way to exist — or, even
more absurd, found each other. As a man of science, he knew better than to entertain such notions.

And yet he did.

Because right down to his final moments, Grotton could have
sworn that something deep inside those Sparks was glowing.

And getting brighter.